ALICIA ALLEN INVESTIGATES 3

MURDER IN HAND

ALICIA ALLEN INVESTIGATES…

A CRIME TRILOGY
by
CELIA CONRAD

1. A MODEL MURDER
2. WILFUL MURDER
3. MURDER IN HAND

ALICIA ALLEN INVESTIGATES 3

MURDER IN HAND

Celia Conrad

Barcham Books

First published in Great Britain in 2012 by Barcham Books, an imprint of
Creative Communications, Suite 327, 28 Old Brompton Road, London, SW7 3SS
barchambooks@btconnect.com
creativecom@btconnect.com

ISBN 978 09546233 4 0 (0 9546233 4 7)

Designed by Andrew Dorman
www.andrewdorman.co.uk

Printed and bound in Great Britain by CPI Group (UK) Ltd, Croydon CR0 4YY

In memory of Trevor

Chapter 1

June 2008

'One of my clients told me today that somebody is trying to kill him,' I said casually, turning to Alex who was sitting cross-legged on the grass next to me, scrutinizing his *Evening Standard* for the latest Test and cricket results. It was one of those rare flaming June days and we were relaxing in Kensington Gardens soaking up the late Friday evening sunshine. Alex did not respond, but as he was so engrossed in his paper I suspected he had not heard me. I repeated myself, except this time I stressed the words and addressed him by name to attract his attention. '*Alex*, one of my clients told me today that somebody is trying to *kill* him!'

'What?' he replied, putting down his newspaper and looking up. 'You've got to be joking, Alicia.' Clearly stunned by my statement he stared at me open-mouthed for a split second before continuing to speak. 'At least, I hope for your sake you are,' he said, closely observing my expression and holding my gaze as he turned onto his side to face me. He propped himself up on one elbow.

'I wish I was. I've never been more serious. It's been preying on my mind all day.' I removed the plastic lid from the tube of *Light* Original Flavour Pringles I had brought to the park, peeled away the airtight seal and offered it to Alex. He took a handful and passed it back to me.

'I can imagine,' he said, munching on a Pringle. 'I'm finding it hard to get my head around what you've told me.' He paused for a moment and cleared his throat. 'It isn't exactly every day that a client walks into the office and tells his solicitor that someone's trying to kill him. It certainly *hasn't* happened to me!' There was a touch of irony in his voice.

'He isn't some madman who came in off the street, if that's what you think,' I replied defensively, biting on a Pringle a little too vigorously for my own good and in the process catching my lip. 'I've been acting for him for a while now.' I nursed my lip with the tip of my tongue.

'So you believe him?' He continued to eat his Pringles.

'Well, I have no reason to disbelieve him, but I really don't feel that this is some fanciful notion of his.'

'Based on the facts he gave you?'

'That, and a gut reaction.'

'Right…' Alex did not sound convinced. 'And did he give you a reason why anybody should want him dead?'

'He doesn't know why. He told me that…'

'But if he's in danger, why didn't he go straight to the police instead of coming to you?' said Alex, interrupting me before I had a chance to finish my sentence and relay to him the details of an alleged attempt on my client's life. 'It *is* after all a police matter and not something you can deal with. You *have* made your position clear, haven't you?' He gave me a knowing look. 'Your duties to your client only stretch so far. You mustn't feel obligated to him.'

'It's not that simple.'

'Why not? What's so complicated about it?' I did not respond. 'Come on, Alicia,' said Alex, rolling his eyes upwards and sounding exasperated. 'Don't tell me you've offered to help him?'

'Not in the way you think.'

'I'll take that as a "yes" then. Have you discussed this with Graham?' Alex was referring to Graham Ffoulkes, one of the Partners in the firm and my immediate boss.

'Of course, I have. He is fully apprised of all the details and understands the situation and mine.'

'I don't follow.' Alex furrowed his brow.

'Let me explain.'

'I wish you would.' I sensed the irritation in Alex's voice. 'Why do I get the strong feeling I'm not about to like what I hear?'

'My uncle recommended the client to me.'

'Your uncle?' Alex helped himself to another handful of Pringles.

'Yes. Uncle Ludovico. My mother's brother. I thought I'd told you about him?' Alex looked vague. 'He's an attorney in New York. He's a commercial lawyer, but a number of his clients are of Italian descent, and he has contacts in Italy because of his knowledge of Italian law.'

'How did your uncle end up in the US and your mother in the UK?' asked Alex, digressing slightly and in between mouthfuls of Pringles.

'My mother came over here to study and she met my father. The rest, as they say, is history. Uncle Vico always wanted to live in New York. He's lived there for over thirty years and I don't think he'd ever return to Italy.'

'Is he married?'

'He's a bachelor. Why?'

'I just wondered. I take it this client of yours is an Italian New Yorker and knows him professionally?'

'Not quite. His parents emigrated to the US and Fabio Angelino, my client, was born there – but the connection is actually through Uncle Vico's long-standing friendship with Fabio's father, Emilio, whom he met when he first moved to New York, at some society function for Italians abroad.'

'So it wasn't a professional relationship at all?'

'No, purely personal, even though Emilio was an attorney himself. Uncle Vico also happens to be my client's Godfather.'

'Which puts you in an invidious position, doesn't it?' I shrugged my shoulders. 'Doesn't your uncle know that you should never act for friends or family? It invariably ends in disaster,' said Alex with a hint of sarcasm. 'What exactly are you doing for Fabio Angelino?'

'I'm dealing with the Probate of his mother's estate.'

'How? I mean, why is he applying for Probate here when the family is from New York? Surely that would be the right forum.'

'It would be except the family relocated to the UK seventeen years ago and all the assets are based in England. I made his mother a new Will last year.'

'Oh, I see. Why did they relocate?'

'You know, Alex, for someone who is set against me involving myself with Fabio's affairs, you seem rather interested in them,' I said dryly, but with a mischievous smile, as I reached for the tube of Pringles, tipped out an exceptionally large handful and proceeded to eat my way through it.

'I'm always interested when it comes to your welfare, as you know. I admit that I'm intrigued about this client, but I'd be lying if I said I wasn't extremely concerned about your involvement in the matter, not to mention any potential dangers. I do appreciate, though, that since you're acting for him, and he's a friend of your uncle, you're inevitably wrapped up in his affairs whether *I* like it or not. And far be if for *me* to tell you what to do…'

'It hasn't stopped you before,' I quipped, swallowing my last Pringle.

'Then why mention him to me at all? You must have realized how I'd react. Why do you always have to jump down my throat? You're very frustrating sometimes.' Alex lay on his back, closed his eyes and put his hands behind his head.

'I'm sorry,' I said gently, prodding him. 'I shouldn't have said that. I take it back. I know you're simply trying to protect me.'

'Somebody has to…from yourself mostly,' he replied slowly, opening his eyes. He paused momentarily before continuing to speak. 'So why did the family relocate?' he asked with a forgiving smile as he sat up.

'Emilio's expertise was in banking law and international finance and he was offered a position with a US firm of Attorney's in London; it was an excellent opportunity and he accepted it. I don't suppose it was too much of a wrench for him as his parents had died by that stage and Evelyn, Fabio's mother, was half-English anyway with roots here.'

'Then Fabio's maternal grandparents live in England?'

'His maternal grandmother does. Evelyn's parents came to London to be with her not long after Emilio's mysterious disappearance,' I said, dropping the line and waiting for Alex's reaction. 'When her father died a few years ago, her mother decided to stay here for good and sold up everything in New York.'

'I don't follow,' he said, leaning forward and sounding perplexed.

'Well, she's English, but Fabio's maternal grandfather was American. They met in London, but after they married settled in New York where Evelyn was born and raised.'

'I meant about Emilio disappearing.' Clearly the mystery surrounding Emilio had engaged Alex's interest. I could tell from his eyes that he was totally hooked and hoping that I would feed his curiosity about the whole matter.

'I was coming to that. He vanished sixteen years ago while on a business trip to Sicily.'

'How? What happened to him?' He was looking at me very intently.

'Nobody knows. Missing, presumed dead. His body was never found.' Alex raised his eyebrows in astonishment.

'I can hardly believe what I'm hearing, Alicia. Are you suggesting that Emilio could have been murdered?'

'Yes. It was never ruled out, but without a body or any evidence there was no proof. According to Fabio the police investigation was a complete shambles.'

'What if Emilio was bumped off by the Mafia and now they're after his son?' said Alex fervently. 'That would explain why someone is trying to kill him.' I looked at Alex quizzically. 'Come on, Alicia, it's not as if Fabio is receiving death threats out of the blue, is it? Obviously there's something sinister in his family's past and it's returning to haunt him.'

'It's possible I suppose. But whatever happened to Emilio took place many years ago. Why wait so long before coming after Fabio? It doesn't make sense, unless of course he has unwittingly stumbled across something which he wasn't meant to. I don't know. My view is that if it is the Mafia and they wanted Fabio dead, he would be.'

'You really think so?' Alex sounded deflated by my lack of enthusiasm for his theory.

'Oh, yes. As for Emilio, Fabio says that with no other reasonable explanation for his father's disappearance, the investigators in Sicily conveniently concluded that it was likely he had been murdered by the Mafia, but there's no proof of it. According to Fabio – and I've also asked Uncle Vico about this – they reached that conclusion rather too quickly. The problem is that nobody was able to piece together the events immediately prior to Emilio's disappearance, and to this day there are many unanswered questions for which we'll probably never find the answers. But even if he was murdered, who's to say it was a Mafia job? It doesn't necessarily follow that every crime in Sicily is carried out by the Mob you know! Then there's the question of motive. The investigators glossed over that completely.'

Despite what Alex thought about my willingness to assist Fabio, and the awkward position in which I found myself due to the nature of his relationship with Uncle Vico, I was all too aware of the potential can of worms which could be opened if fresh enquiries were made into the disappearance of Fabio's father. Also, bearing in mind Fabio's situation, I was concerned that no action should be taken which would risk his safety. For these reasons I was perhaps slightly more circumspect about the situation than usual.

'But you'd agree that it is possible that Emilio's disappearance, and what's been happening to Fabio, have a common link?'

'I guess so.'

'You don't sound very convinced, Alicia. If it isn't the Mafia, who do you think is trying to kill Fabio?'

'I have absolutely no idea,' I replied with a sigh as I delved into the tube of Pringles and retrieved yet another large handful. 'I don't know enough about his family and his Italian background to form any sort of opinion.' I lay back on the grass and savoured my Pringles.

'You seem to know a fair amount.'

'But only what I've been told, and by people who don't have all the facts at their fingertips.'

'What about your uncle? He must be a good source of information?'

'Yes,' I replied, sitting up and facing Alex. 'Uncle Vico certainly knows a great deal more about the Angelino family than I do, but when Fabio first instructed me I asked him about Emilio. He told me that he made independent enquiries at the time but nothing came of them.'

'Maybe you should ask him again. You might be surprised at what he can dredge up from his memory when pressed on the subject. Have you spoken to him since your meeting with Fabio this morning?'

'Not yet, no. It was too early to call him and then he wasn't in the office when I tried this afternoon, mid-morning his time. I'll give him a ring either later this evening or on Sunday unless I hear from him first,' I replied, glancing at my watch. It was a few minutes past eight.

'Is Fabio OK about you discussing all this with your uncle or with me for that matter?'

'Oh, yes. He likes Uncle Vico kept in the picture and, when I mentioned your background to him, he was keen to have your input.'

'Why were you talking to him about me?' Alex looked at me quizzically.

'Your name came up in conversation. Don't worry. It was in a purely professional context.'

'That's a shame. I take it your uncle and Fabio are close?'

'Well, they've only seen each other infrequently these past seventeen years, but I have the impression that they are. Fabio speaks highly of my uncle and vice versa, and I know from what Fabio has said, that his mother regarded my uncle as Emilio's best friend. I think that's why, after Evelyn died, Fabio contacted Uncle Vico and asked him for his advice on what to do about her estate.'

'And he kindly advised Fabio to consult you! How did she die?'

'She wasn't murdered if that's what you're thinking. She suffered a massive stroke, but she'd been ailing for years. Her health deteriorated after her husband disappeared.' I had kicked off my shoes when we first sat down, so I retrieved them and slipped them back on, reached for my handbag which was on the grass next to me and stood up to leave.

'And there was me thinking that there's a conspiracy to kill his family: first his father, then his mother and now him,' said Alex flippantly and remaining seated.

'Very funny, Alex. But do you see me laughing?' I said, pointing to my mouth and grimacing.

'You haven't told me what's been happening to Fabio,' Alex replied, ignoring my remark. Still he did not move.

'That's because you interrupted me before I had a chance to,' I said in a chiding tone, but winking at him at the same time. 'Come on, I'll tell you on the way home.' I caught hold of his arm and tried to pull him up. 'I'm really thirsty. I desperately need a drink.'

'I'm not surprised after all those Pringles you've eaten,' said Alex, picking up the almost empty tube, handing them to me, grabbing his suit jacket and *Evening Standard* and rising to his feet. He flung his jacket over his shoulder.

'Speak for yourself.'

'Happily.'

'Hmm… You know, Alex,' I said as we ambled towards Queen's Gate, 'I feel really sorry for Fabio. He's had a difficult time.'

'When you start to feel sorry for your clients, Alicia, I start to worry.' Alex momentarily stopped walking as if to emphasize his point. He sounded serious; evidently he thought it was an issue.

'Why?' I glanced sideways at him.

'Because that's when they take advantage of you.'

'Take advantage of *what* exactly?'

'Your good nature.'

'You think so, do you?'

'I know so,' he said, nudging me in the side with his elbow.

'It's as well I have you to keep me in check then, isn't it?' I caught hold of his hand.

'That'll be the day! But I'm working on it. Come on, let's get that drink.'

Chapter 2

'Go on then,' said Alex, handing me my red wine, putting his glass of beer on the table and taking a seat opposite me. We had stopped off at the Anglesey Arms on Selwyn Terrace, a short walk from my flat, and were sitting at one of the wooden tables outside. Alex took a swig of his ice-cold beer; there was condensation on the outside of the glass and, as he picked it up, a droplet of water trickled down the side. 'Don't keep me in suspense. You haven't finished telling me about Fabio.'

'Apparently, it happened last weekend,' I replied, leaning across the table so Alex would not have to strain to hear me. The pub was heaving with people – which was only to be expected on a balmy Friday evening in summer – but that meant it was very noisy. There was a particularly exuberant group of youngsters at the table next to ours who seemed to be making more of a racket than everyone else in the pub put together.

'What did?'

'Fabio went on a trip to see his sister in Italy and...'

'Sister? I had the impression he was an only child,' said Alex, cutting in and setting down his beer glass. He placed one elbow on the table, rested his hand on his chin and inclined himself towards me.

'No. He has a twenty year old sister, Giulia.'

'How old is Fabio then?'

'Mid-thirties, so he's a lot older than her. He's also very protective of her.'

'That's understandable. I feel that way towards my little sister too. What does she do?'

'She's a student at *L'Università per Stranieri di Perugia*. Do you want to finish these off?' I asked, offering Alex the remaining Pringles. He shook his head.

'You eat them. Studying what?'

'I'm not sure,' I said, sipping my wine. 'Fabio mentioned that she's already completed a diploma in Italian language and culture and now she's taking one of the degree courses, but which one I couldn't tell you.'

'You were about to fill me in on Fabio's jaunt to Italy.'

'Well, I wouldn't quite call it that,' I replied, taking another sip of wine. 'Their mother's death really hit Giulia hard and Fabio has been travelling out to Italy as much as he can to keep an eye on her these past few months. He thought she would like to spend a weekend at the Amalfi coast, so he booked her on a Friday afternoon flight to Naples, met her at the airport, and they drove in his hire car to Atrani where he had rented an apartment by the beach.' I removed the lid from the tube of Pringles, and tipped out the remainder onto the table.

'Go on,' said Alex, picking up his glass.

'On the journey from the airport he noticed a blue Alfa Romeo Spider with blacked out windows following them in the distance, except he didn't read too much into it until he saw the car again the next morning on his drive into nearby Ravello. The only way up to Ravello from the apartment was via a narrow and winding hill road which is dangerously close to the edge in parts.'

'You've been to this part of Italy?' asked Alex, reaching across the table for the last few Pringles despite having indicated that he did not want them.

'I spent most summers in Italy as a child either in Tuscany or at the Amalfi coast. Although Nonna lives in the Cilento region at the southern end of the Gulf of Salerno, and further down from the Neopolitan Riviera, the Amalfi coast was my father's favourite destination. So, in answer to your question, a number of times, although I haven't been to Ravello for a while.'

'You were saying about the blue Alfa Romeo.'

'Oh yes. Fabio had been driving for barely a kilometre when he spotted the Alfa Romeo in his rear view mirror. He said that the car seemed to come from nowhere and, as he proceeded up the hill, it was threateningly close to his tail forcing him to drive faster. Whoever was driving repeatedly sounded the horn and Fabio thought he or she wanted to overtake, so he steered across the road but no attempt was made to pass him. Then the driver accelerated and rammed into the back of his hire car in what he assumes was a deliberate attempt to force him off the road. This caused him to veer towards the edge. That isn't the sort of road where you'd want to swerve or misjudge one of the turns because you'd go straight over the cliff and plunge into the waters below.'

'I presume that was the general idea, Alicia,' said Alex, clearing his throat. What happened next?'

'Somehow Fabio managed to turn the wheel in time to avoid crashing, but he vividly remembers spinning around and skidding across the road. Given the high speed at which he must have been travelling, it's a miracle he survived unscathed. Goodness knows how he succeeded in getting the car back on course without losing control of it.'

'Being Italian he's probably a natural driver,' said Alex, slightly sarcastically. I laughed. 'What car was he driving?'

'A Fiat Stilo.'

'That's a nippy little car, but no match for an Alfa Romeo, I'd have thought. Did I tell you about *my* new car?' he continued enthusiastically.

'No. Why would you? You never tell me anything.' I teased, picking up my wine glass. This was the first time he had mentioned it – to me anyway. I decided not to ask him for details about the car and wait to see if he volunteered any.

'I'm collecting it tomorrow. Fancy coming out for a drive?' He seemed keen to show it to me.

'I'd love to, but I'm going to my mother's for the weekend.' Alex looked disappointed. 'Nonna arrived today and we're having a family dinner in her honour tomorrow evening. My sister will be there too. I'm sure I told you Nonna'd be staying for a few months.'

'Why would you? You never tell me anything,' said Alex whimsically.

'Touché.'

'What time are you leaving tomorrow?'

'Around mid-morning. Why?'

'Because *I* could give you a lift. Your mother lives near Haslemere, doesn't she?'

'Yes.'

'That's easy enough to get to. It would give me an excuse to give the car a run out into the country. I won't be able to stay as I need to be back in London by the evening and…'

'That's OK. Are you sure about this?' I said, interrupting him. Alex had not yet met my mother, let alone my grandmother, and I thought he was rather brave to take on meeting both of them at the same time. At least he already knew my sister Antonia.

'I wouldn't be offering if I wasn't.'

'All right. I was hoping to be there around lunchtime. What time can you pick me up?'

'I'm collecting the car early but I've a few errands to run, so around eleven. Is that OK?'

'Perfect. I'll tell Mamma to expect you.'

'Good. I look forward to meeting her.'

'Really?' I gave him a searching look.

'Yes. Really.' He leant forward and lightly squeezed my hand. 'You were telling me how Fabio survived,' he said, reverting to our original topic of conversation. How on earth did Fabio get away?'

'He didn't have to. Lady Luck must have been smiling on him that day.'

'What do you mean?'

'As he rounded the next bend there was a coach coming in the opposite direction and he had no choice but to slow down and make way for the coach driver to pass. The driver of the Alfa Romeo was barely a few metres behind him but, instead of stopping, accelerated and shot off up the hill overtaking Fabio and narrowly missing the coach as he sped through the gap.'

'And he didn't get the number of the car or see who was in it?'

'The car had blacked out windows.'

'Oh, yes, you said.'

'As for the registration number he was concentrating so hard on staying alive that making a mental note of it was the last thing on his mind.'

'But with no registration number how can he be sure that it was the same car that followed him the day before?'

'He's sure. He's a typical Italian male. He has an eye for beautiful cars – and women.'

'That's not a privilege reserved purely for the Italian male population, Alicia!' Alex sounded disgruntled. 'Anyway, even if he's right, he can't prove it.'

'I know.'

'Does he really think somebody was out to kill him? Maybe it was a case of mistaken identity or road rage. Perhaps he cut the other driver up on the motorway down to Atrani and he or she came after him. I know that may sound far-fetched but it isn't impossible, even if improbable.'

'No. I agree. We have to consider every possible scenario. I did think that myself and said as much to him when he gave me the facts. I initially tried to make light of the whole thing, joked about the number of fast drivers in Italy, particularly near Naples, and tentatively suggested that he might have inadvertently irritated the driver of the Alfa. But I must admit I don't think it was a case of road rage. *If* Fabio is telling me the truth and his account of what happened is accurate, then I am inclined to the view that the driver of that car was out to kill him.'

'Which takes us back to the motive and my point that his father's disappearance is in someway connected to all this.' Alex seemed determined to link the two, but I remained sceptical.

'Although,' I continued, thinking out loud, 'what puzzles me is that there have been no other attempts to kill him, so possibly the incident with the Alfa was purely to warn him off but off what I don't know.' Counter to my warning theory and in support of that for attempted murder was the fact that Fabio could very easily have crashed over the cliff and died. And from Fabio's account of events that seemed to be exactly what the Alfa driver intended.

'Do you think Fabio might be lying, Alicia? After all there were no witnesses to the car chase. I know he refers to the coach driver but that driver never actually witnessed the Alfa trying to force Fabio off the road. All he saw was the Alfa overtaking him, and there is a big difference between speeding up behind another driver and overtaking him as opposed to chasing him and attempting to ram him off the road!'

'I agree, but still I find it hard to believe that he has concocted the whole story. Anyway, I assume the back of the Fiat was damaged and the police would have noted that when they inspected it.'

'If indeed they did.'

'Well, even if they didn't, the rental company would have seen it.'

'Yes...you're right.' Alex nodded his head in acknowledgment. 'He reported the incident to the police then?'

'Yes, but they weren't convinced by his story.'

'I see,' said Alex in a clipped manner, folding his arms and sitting back. There was something about the way he said it which irritated me.

'But that doesn't necessarily mean it's untrue, Alex,' I snapped.

'I was commenting, not judging, Alicia. Don't be so defensive.' He unfolded his arms and leaned forward. 'Where was Giulia at the time? I'm presuming she wasn't with Fabio since you haven't mentioned her.'

'At the beach in Atrani.'

'OK. Let's assume, for argument's sake, that the intention was to murder Fabio – don't you think whoever it was might also want Giulia dead?'

'Fabio believes not, but I feel she could be in danger as we don't know who's behind all this.'

'Exactly. Bearing in mind he says he has no idea why anybody should want him dead, it seems pretty ridiculous to me to rule out the fact that his sister is a potential victim too, especially if it has something to do with what happened to their father. If that was my sister, I'd be frantically worried about her staying out in Italy alone, especially if the police didn't take his run-in with the Alfa seriously.' Alex drained his glass and put it down very firmly on the table as if to emphasize his point.

'Yes, even though later that day he had cause to call them again.'

'But unless I misheard you, I thought you said there haven't been any other attempts on his life,' said Alex, looking rather confused.

'No. There haven't. In the afternoon he and Giulia went to Vietri because Giulia's really interested in ceramics and that's *the* place to go for them. When they returned to the apartment it had been ransacked. The police reckon that it was some sort of opportunistic burglary.'

'And they didn't feel it was connected to the incident earlier in the day?' Alex sounded surprised.

'No. They said it was coincidental. Apparently there have been a spate of break-ins to holiday apartments in the area and according to them this one had the hallmarks of the others. It did cross my mind that it could have been made to look like that.'

'True, but if a local gang is targeting tourists thinking that they might have cash and passports lying around in their apartments, it is quite possible that the same gang is responsible for the break-in. Was anything taken?'

'No, but maybe they found nothing to steal. Oh, I know it sounds ridiculous, Alex, but instinct tells me there's more to this even though the facts don't add up.'

'It does seem rather strange to say the least. Do you want another drink?' Alex pointed to my glass.

'I haven't finished this one yet,' I replied, taking a sip of wine.

'I'll just have a half then. You sure I can't get you another?' I shook my head. 'I'll only be a tick,' said Alex, getting to his feet. It seemed an age until he returned and while I waited for him I glanced around at the people sitting outside. The group of high-spirited youngsters had expanded and since they had run out of seats a few of them were standing close to our table. Alex had to elbow his way back to his seat, but a petite girl with short mid-brown hair closest to our table moved forward at the exact moment he was about to squeeze past them, causing him to bump into her knocking her glass of wine flying and over him. She was lucky his glass of beer did not slop all over her, but at least he was drenched with white wine, not red.

'I'm terribly sorry', she said in a high-pitched little voice, looking up at him shyly from behind her fringe. Alex put his beer glass down on the table and wiped his wine-stained shirt with his hand.

'It was entirely my fault,' he replied. 'I didn't see you there. Let me buy you another glass of wine.'

'Oh, don't worry. I've drunk too much already tonight anyway,' she squeaked. 'You've done me a favour. Sorry about the shirt,' she continued, looking at me sheepishly.

'Soon remedied,' I replied.

'You sure I can't buy you a drink,' he said. She shook her head. 'All right.' Then turning to me he said, 'Shall we go? I think I've lost the taste for my beer now.'

'I'm not surprised,' I replied, standing up. I picked up my handbag, handed Alex his jacket, and we made our way out into the street. 'If you take your shirt off when we get back to the flat I'll sort that stain out for you,' I said as we walked along the road.

'Now there's an offer I can't refuse!'

Chapter 3

I turned over in bed and fumbled for my watch on the bedside table. I was annoyed because it was after ten and I had wanted to be up by eight. Normally it would not have mattered in the slightest if I had overslept, but this was one Saturday morning when there was no time for a lie-in. I peered at my clock radio and noticed that I had forgotten to flick on the alarm switch, so I had nobody to blame but myself. I leaped out of bed, drew back the curtains and opened the window. There was more of a breeze than the previous morning, but it already felt very warm and anyway the forecast was for fine weather the whole weekend; perfect for a drive out into the country.

Aware that Alex was a stickler for time, I knew to expect him at eleven exactly. It would have been easier if he had stayed the night, but it was his decision to return home, not mine. I took a quick shower, ate my breakfast while dressing, grabbed my toiletry bag from the bathroom and packed a few essentials into an overnight holdall. I rushed around the flat, loaded the dishwasher, made my bed and had a general tidy-up. It was still only ten to eleven, leaving me enough time to check my e-mails and make a quick call to my friend Jo. I had not heard from Uncle Vico, but that was probably down to the time difference and I e-mailed him instead to let him know that I would be at Mamma's until Sunday evening and to telephone me there.

Since it was such a lovely morning I had opened my French windows to let in some fresh air. I picked up my cordless handset and sat out on the balcony to 'phone Jo. From that vantage point I had a direct view of the Square and the road below and would see

Alex arriving.

'Jo, it's Ally. How are you?'

'I'm not feeling very good today.' She sounded out of sorts.

'Why? What's wrong?'

'I've been off-colour for a few days. It's probably a tummy bug or something.'

'Oh, I'm sorry. You do sound a bit groggy. Have you been to the doctor?'

'No, but I'm sure I'll be fine in a day or two. It's funny you should ring because I was going to call you this morning anyway.'

'Really?'

'Yes. We haven't spoken for a few weeks and I was wondering how you are. Is everything OK?'

'Hmm... I'm fine. I should have called you but I've been working flat out these past few weeks.' Although Jo was my best friend, and I trusted her completely, and she was an ex-policewoman, I did not mention anything to her about Fabio. Alex, as a fellow solicitor, was bound by the same rules of professional conduct as myself, and I had authority to discuss the matter with him. I knew that Jo would never breach a confidence, and I would have valued her opinion, but I could tell her nothing. 'Nonna arrived yesterday. She's staying with Mamma and I'm spending the weekend with them.'

'Oh, that's nice. How's Alex?' she asked at the very moment I heard that characteristic roaring sound associated with the engine of a sports car coming from the street below.

'He's well. If I'm not mistaken that's him now,' I said, standing up, looking over the balcony and observing a silver BMW Z4 which had stopped outside the house. 'He offered to give me a lift.'

'Don't let me hold you up then. Give me a ring after the weekend and let's have a proper catch up.' Alex stepped out of the car, glanced up, saw me and waved. He was dressed casually in an open-necked pale blue cotton shirt, black cotton jeans, ecru linen jacket and wearing his trademark Persol sunglasses. I waved at him and walked inside the flat.

'I will. Get well.'

'Thanks. Bye, Ally.'

'*Ciao.* Bye.' I bolted the French windows and observed Alex settling back into the car. I double-checked to make sure I had everything I needed, picked up my keys, mobile, handbag and holdall, double-locked the front door and ran down the stairs.

'Your chauffeur awaits,' said Alex, beaming at me through the open window as I approached. He leaned across to the passenger side and opened the door for me. I bent down and looked inside.

'Hmm…very luxurious,' I said, feeling the soft leather on the seats. 'What colour do the manufacturers call this?'

'Pearl grey.'

'And the metallic paintwork?' I stood up and looked at the exterior.

'Titanium silver.'

'I like the three-spoke steering wheel with gear changes,' I said, bending down again and pointing at it. 'I *am* impressed.'

'Are you getting in or are you going to stand there all day?' Alex glanced at his watch.

'Don't be so impatient. I was merely admiring the fantastic bodywork.' I dropped my handbag onto the floor in front of the passenger seat, popped my holdall into the back and eased into my seat in as ladylike a manner possible. This was no mean feat, bearing in mind the seat was very low and I was wearing a denim knee length skirt which had a habit of riding up when I sat down.

'I think you've stolen my line.' Alex patted my knee.

'That's a bit of a cliché, Alex. You'll really have to think up something more original than that,' I teased, inclining my head towards him to kiss him, but at that very moment he turned to take his jacket off and caught the side of my right cheek with the back of his left hand.

'Alicia. I'm so sorry,' he said, and sounded it. 'Are you OK?'

'I'll survive,' I replied, rubbing my cheek. I was more stunned than hurt. 'It's nothing,' I said, removing my hand.

'Your cheekbone looks a bit pink. Do you want to go back in and put some ice on it?'

'No. Look,' I said, pulling down the sun visor and peering at it in the mirror, 'it hardly notices at all. Don't worry about it. It was an accident. It's not as if you meant to knock me. What model's this car?' I asked, putting on my seat belt and trying to change the subject.

'Z4 3.0si Sport Coupé. Are you sure you're OK?' Alex continued to peer at my right cheek.

'Perfectly, but remind me not to try and kiss you again,' I said, laughing. 'Is your shirt OK by the way?' He nodded. 'I really like the design of this car,' I continued. 'It certainly looks the part,' which it did with its long bonnet, sporty front apron, integrated spoiler and twin-tail exhaust pipe, 'but what about performance? Does it deliver? After all, you're the one always going on about appearances being deceptive.' I threw Alex a mischievous sideways glance.

'You won't be disappointed.'

'I hope not.'

'Did you manage to speak with your uncle?' asked Alex as we headed towards the A3. The traffic had been heavy along the Fulham Road and all the way into Putney, and I sensed Alex was frustrated because he was itching to put his foot down.

'No. I was going to call him after you left but was really tired and not in the mood to go over everything again. I've e-mailed him and he knows I'll be at Mamma's.'

'Does she know I'm driving you?' he said, rapidly accelerating from the traffic lights and continuing forward onto Putney Hill, taking full advantage of the clear stretch of road ahead.

'No. I thought we'd surprise her.'

'Oh, Alicia, you are the limit. You said you were going to tell her I was coming with you. You really should have. I feel very rude just turning up like this.' Alex sounded irritated with me but I decided not to heed him.

'It's more fun this way.'

'For you, perhaps, you little minx,' he said, giving me a knowing look. 'Well, provided she doesn't mind me descending on her unexpectedly.'

'Of course she won't. She'll be in her element. The more the merrier.' We were now approaching the A3 and Alex seemed to lighten up which was a relief. The fact that he knew he would able to drive at more than a snail's pace probably had something to do with it.

'Hmm… I know that your grandmother is over for most of the summer and you'll want to spend time with her, but I was wondering whether you've made any holiday plans yet.'

'To be honest I haven't really thought about it. I might wait and see how things pan out. I was intending to fly out to New York to see Uncle Vico at some point, but I'm not sure when. Mind you he'll probably come over here to see Nonna anyway.'

'You should still go to New York.'

'I'd like to. It's years since I've been there.'

'I wouldn't mind another trip there myself. Isn't that where Cesare relocated?' Cesare Castelli was a former neighbour and used to live in the apartment above mine. He had moved out a couple of years earlier and subsequently sold the flat to Paolo who was one of his Italian banking friends. Alex had never really warmed to Cesare, partly because he saw him as a rival for my affections, even though Cesare and I had never been and never would be more than friends.

'Yes. It is. I think he's very happy there.'

'How do you know?'

'He contacted me.'

'When? I wasn't aware he was still in touch with you,' he said flatly.

'Well, I wouldn't call it that exactly. He used to e-mail me regularly but I haven't heard from him for quite a while now.'

'I see.' I could hear my mobile ringing in my handbag and

reached down to answer it. I suspected that it was my mother and she was 'phoning to find out where I was and what time she could expect me. Knowing her she had already called me at the flat to check if I was on my way. Her number was saved in my contacts list and her name appeared on the display.

'*Pronto. Ciao, mamma.*'

'*Ciao, carina. Non mi hai telefonato prima di partire.*'

'*Mi dispiace.*'

'*Sei malata?*'

'*No. Sto bene. Non preoccuparti!*'

'*Quando arriverai qui?*'

'*Il più presto possibile.*'

'*Ti amo troppo.*'

'*A presto, mamma. Ciao. Ciao.*'

'So how's your mother?' asked Alex, throwing me a fleeting sideways glance.

'She's fine.' I replaced my mobile in my handbag.

'Everything all right?'

'Oh yes. She was worried because she hadn't heard from me and she thought I might be unwell. I told her I was OK, I was running late earlier and we'd be there soon.'

'I'm not surprised she worries about you.'

'What do you mean?'

'Well, don't you think she has cause considering all the things that have happened to you over the past few years?'

'She worries *too* much.'

'No comment…and another thing, did I hear you correctly when you said 'we' just now?' He threw me another sideways glance. 'I can barely understand one word of Italian, but I'm sure you didn't mention *me* anywhere in that conversation.' I shrugged my shoulders.

'What's the acceleration for this car?' I replied, ignoring Alex's remark. We were now on the A3 and Alex was taking full advantage of the clearer road to pick up some speed.

'0-62 in 5.7 seconds and 7000 revs per minute. Tell me about the rest of Fabio's family?' he asked, finally changing the subject.

'He hasn't mentioned anyone apart from his sister and grand-mother. His parents were both only children.'

'Then it's fortunate for Evelyn that her mother was able to move back here to be with her after Emilio's disappearance. She must have needed her support.'

'Yes. Financially, as well as emotionally. To put it bluntly, without Emilio's body she was unable to obtain a death certificate and to apply for Probate of his estate.'

'Which meant she couldn't inherit his money?'

'Exactly. The death certificate couldn't be issued until he had been missing for seven years. Evelyn had the option of applying to the Probate Court for Emilio to be declared dead sooner, but this would have been a laborious and expensive process. I think her parents offered to cover the legal costs but, according to my uncle, Evelyn refused to pursue it because she always hoped that Emilio would miraculously return.'

'That's so sad.'

'It is. I think what's worse is that she died never knowing what had happened to him.'

'When was Emilio's estate sorted out?'

'About seven or eight years ago, I think.'

'Did you have any hand in that?'

'No. I wasn't even qualified at the time, but the firm who dealt with his late father's affairs were Smythson, Reid & Monkton.'

'Presumably Fabio told you that?'

'No. Remember I told you I made his mother a new Will last year?' Alex nodded. 'She gave me a copy of her old Will and the name of the firm was on it.'

'Right. Did she give any reason for not reinstructing Smythson, Reid & Monkton?' I shook my head.

'I think she came to me purely through the connection with

Uncle Vico.'

'I wonder why she instructed that firm in the first place.'

'I don't know. Perhaps it was recommended to her. Don't forget Emilio worked for a US firm of Attorney's in London. One of the lawyers there could have put her on to the firm. It does have an excellent reputation for this type of work.'

'Have you dealt with them?'

'Yes, when I was a trainee at Withins & Co., on a disputed inheritance claim.'

'Well, that's another avenue of enquiry worth following up.'

'Unfortunately, Evelyn isn't here to ask about the firm, but Fabio might know about it as, unlike Giulia, he was old enough for his mother to involve him. This isn't something he and I have ever touched upon.'

'Why would you? It's only now we're discussing it that it seems relevant.' Alex paused for a moment. 'It's strange talking about Fabio and his family like this when I haven't even met him.'

'Oh, but you have.'

'What do you mean? I think I'd know if I had.' Alex looked puzzled.

'You may not have met him, but you've certainly seen him.'

'When? Where?'

'He was sitting in reception a couple of weeks ago when you came in to pick me up. Do you remember him?'

'Vaguely. I probably only looked at him fleetingly. He has very dark hair as I recall.'

'You're guessing. You don't remember him at all, do you?'

'Does he have dark hair?'

'Yes, but that could be a calculated guess on your part knowing that he's half-Italian.'

'You have a very suspicious mind, Miss Allen.'

'That's how I've survived so long.'

Chapter 4

We turned in from the road and drove along the gravelled driveway to my mother's house. I was surprised to see Antonia's red Mazda parked outside because I was not expecting her to arrive until later. There must have been a last-minute change of plan.

'What a lovely house,' said Alex as we pulled up alongside Antonia's car.

'I suppose it is,' I said, looking up at it. With its Georgian style windows, half-white stucco and half-brick walls it was rather pretty. 'My father loved it here. It's where we all grew up. He was particularly fond of his garden. I'm sure you noticed the shrub beds and borders when we came up the drive.' Alex nodded. 'They're entirely my father's own work.'

'The garden looks fantastic. But how does your mother manage to keep it so immaculate? There's quite an expanse of lawn,' he said, pointing to the area which surrounds the house.

'Well, she's a keen gardener, but she pays someone to come in and mow the lawn for her. I'll show you around later if you like.'

No sooner had we parked than my mother and Antonia appeared outside to greet us so they must have heard us arrive. There was no sign of Antonia's boyfriend, Tom, and I wondered if he was in the house with Nonna.

'*Ciao, mamma,*' I called over to her as she walked down the flagstone path leading from the house towards the driveway. I opened the car door and attempted to clamber out without my skirt riding up. Alex retrieved my holdall from behind my seat and sprinted around to my side to give me a helping hand. He then walked to the back of the car and opened the boot.

'*Ciao, mamma.*' I kissed her on both cheeks and then hugged her.

'*Ciao, carina. Sei molto magra. Devi mangiare più!*'

'*Smettila, mamma!*' I replied.

'Oh, Mamma, don't worry about Alicia,' said Antonia, putting her arm around me and squeezing me. 'She eats far too many Pringles to ever fade away completely. 'Hi, Alex,' she said, sauntering over to him. 'I didn't know you were coming. You're looking very well. I like your car. Is it new?'

'Yes,' he replied, closing the boot. I noticed he was carrying a sturdy carton containing two bottles of champagne.

'Oh, I'm sorry, Alex,' I said turning to him. 'Let me introduce you to Mamma.'

'How do you do, Mrs Allen?' he said. 'This is for you,' he said handing her the champagne. 'I thought you could drink this tonight at your family dinner.'

'*Grazie mille. Sei molto gentile. Benvenuto!*' she replied, taking the bag and bending forward to kiss him on both cheeks. '*Piacere. Piacere.* I am so very pleased to meet you. Call me Lucia.' If I was not mistaken she winked at him.

'I've heard so much about you from Alicia,' I heard Alex say.

'Really?' She caught hold of his arm and glimpsed back at me. 'It was good of you to drive Alicia here today,' she continued, glancing over at his car.

'My pleasure. I hope you don't mind me dropping in on you unexpectedly.'

'No. *È un piacere averti qui.* You are most welcome. Come on into the house and meet Nonna. I expect Alicia has told you she's staying with me for a while.' Alex and my mother walked on ahead leaving me with Antonia.

'*Stai bene, Toni?* Where's Tom?' I asked.

'He couldn't make it.'

'*Che peccato!*'

'He asked me to marry him.'

'*Che notizie fantastiche. Sono molto felice per te,*' I said enthusiastically. Only, from her miserable expression it was clear that she was not at all happy. '*Cosa c'è?* You don't want to marry him?' I asked, scanning her face.

'Yes, but Tom wants to move back to Australia and I'm not sure I want to live there. Everything would be perfect if it wasn't for that.'

'Oh, I see. I'm sorry.' I put my arm around her. '*Dimmi tu come devo fare con te!*'

'*Che fare?* Ally.'

'Only you can decide that. If you're worried about leaving 'the family' just remember that, apart from Mamma and me, most of our immediate family aren't here anyway!'

'You trying to get rid of me or something?'

'*Certo che no!*'

'Don't say anything to Mamma.'

'*No di certo!* It isn't my news to tell. Why don't you come over during the week for a sisterly night in?'

'Yes. I'd like that.'

'I'd better go and rescue Alex. I've left him at the mercy of Mamma – and Nonna! They will be cross-examining him as we speak!'

'How are things going with him anyway?' Antonia gave me a searching look.

'We're fine, just fine.'

'Alicia,' my mother called out. She was standing in the open doorway. '*Ludovico è al telefono. Ha ricevuto la tua posta elettronica. Vuoi parlare con lui adesso o dopo?*' I was keen to speak to my uncle and there was no time like the present.

'*Adesso. Entriamo comunque.*'

'*Va bene.*'

'*Tutto bene?*' asked my mother when I stepped out on to the sun terrace after finishing my call. Everyone had gathered for pre-lunch drinks or, from the looks of it, a pre-lunch Cinzano and Soda.

'*Oh sì. Abbiamo parlato del più e del meno,*' I replied, without providing any details and glancing at Alex. I would tell him about my conversation with Uncle Vico later, when nobody was around.

'*Ciao, nonna!*' I said enthusiastically, walking over to my diminutive grandmother who was sitting in one of the padded garden chairs and kissing her on both cheeks before hugging her tightly. She was looking quite well despite her crippling arthritis. Now that my mother was older, the family resemblance between them was uncanny. They both had the same hairstyle; long hair swept back into a chignon except Mamma's hair had only a few grey strands and Nonna's was almost white. Facially they were very similar; oval faces, hazel eyes, long thin noses and high cheekbones. Nonna's were quite rosy from all that Southern Italian sunshine.

'*Ciao tesorina.*'

'*Stai bene, nonna?*'

'*Sto bene, carina. Sono molto contenta di vederti.*'

'I hope they haven't been asking you too many questions, Alex,' I said, sitting down on the sunlounger next to him. He put his arm around my shoulders.

'I've been talking to your mother and Antonia mostly. Your grandmother doesn't seem to understand me,' he replied, smiling over at her.

'Nonna doesn't speak much English so we invariably have to translate for her,' Antonia chipped in. 'Alicia and I generally talk together in English with the odd Italian phrase chucked in here and there.'

'I noticed.'

'We hardly ever speak Italian with Uncle Vico either,' said Antonia. 'For some reason he almost always chats to us in English.'

'I'm going to see if I can give Mamma a hand and make myself a drink.' I stood up. 'Do you want another?' I said, addressing Alex and observing that his glass was almost empty. He nodded. 'Antonia?' She shook her head. As I went to pass Nonna she grabbed my hand and whispered something, but I could not hear what she said and bent down close to her.

'*Tuo ragazzo è molto bello. Sono tutto presa da lui! Benfatto. Molto benfatto.*' She patted me on the arm and winked at Alex. It must have been obvious to him who she was talking about.

'Now that we're alone you can tell me what information you gleaned from your uncle,' said Alex, putting down his coffee cup. We were sitting out on the sun terrace after lunch. Mamma and Nonna were both upstairs resting in true Italian siesta style and Antonia had gone out to see an old school friend. 'You must have been talking to him for at least a quarter of an hour. Was your conversation productive?'

'Yes. Apparently Fabio called Uncle Vico this morning, told him what happened in Italy and asked him for his take on recent events.'

'What did he say? Does he feel they're connected to Emilio's disappearance?'

'He agrees that it's quite possible, but like me he's not convinced that it has anything to do with the Mafia, just as he wasn't convinced that Emilio was murdered by them. Do you want to see the garden now?' I asked, standing up.

'I'd love to.' Alex raised himself to his feet. 'I still don't see how he can be so certain. From what you tell me there's no evidence to confirm Mafia involvement, but there doesn't seem to be any to disprove it either.' We ambled from the terrace along the path to the upper lawn which surrounds the house. I wanted to show Alex the lower lawn which is interspersed with mature rhododendron, laurel, variegated holly and magnolia trees and is my favourite part of the garden.

'Remember I mentioned he'd made independent enquiries when Emilio disappeared?' I said, turning back to Alex who was dawdling behind me.

'Yes.'

'Well, I thought he meant in Sicily, but today when I asked him about that he said he did make enquiries there, but not only there.

You see I had the impression, mistakenly as it turns out, that Emilio went to Sicily on a business trip, but according to his closest colleague Gregorio Pellegrino at Scarpetti, Steiglitz & Co. ...'

'The US firm of Attorneys Emilio worked for?' asked Alex, interrupting me. I nodded.

'...what he couldn't understand was why Emilio was in Sicily at all, because so far as he was aware he had no affairs to attend to there and was supposed to be in Rome.'

'Maybe there was a change of plan. It doesn't necessarily follow that because this Pellegrino character didn't know about it that there was anything sinister involved.'

'I agree, but I'm merely relaying what my uncle told me. We know Emilio flew to Sicily from Rome because of the plane records, but it's after he arrived in Catania that everything becomes blurry. My uncle's enquiries drew a blank on that front.'

'When did he first speak to Pellegrino?'

'He went to see him after Emilio disappeared and spoke to him on a couple of occasions during the course of the investigation. Apparently, Pellegrino's the one who recommended Evelyn to Smythson, Reid & Monkton to deal with the Probate side of things. Pellegrino couldn't help her himself because that's not his area of expertise.'

'So, now we know why she instructed that firm. You said you thought it might be through a work colleague.'

'Hmm... Uncle Vico says Emilio met Pellegrino while he was still working in New York, which means he'd known him for a while.'

'A trustworthy source then?'

'I couldn't say. Anyway, Pellegrino told him that the client for whom Emilio had been acting was based in Rome and Emilio was helping him raise finance for some speculative property deal. Unfortunately, the deal collapsed, the client lost a substantial sum of money and committed suicide.'

'That rules out one suspect anyway,' said Alex glibly.

'Trust you to come out with something like that. You're incorrigible!' We reached the flight of twelve York stone steps at the end of the upper lawn which lead to the lower lawn.

'I thought that's what you like about me,' he called out as I clambered down the steps.

'Part of your irresistible charm, you mean?' I said with a wry smile turning back. I reached the bottom and Alex bounded down after me.

'You were telling me about the client who committed suicide,' he said, catching hold of my waist.

'Oh yes, Pellegrino said that the family blamed Emilio for the suicide and that when Emilio disappeared suspicion fell on the client's brother who is alleged to have threatened Emilio. There was no evidence to pin on him, though, and that side of the investigation fizzled out. Mafia involvement wasn't considered at that stage. It was only later that it was conveniently concluded that the Mafia must have had a hand in Emilio's demise.'

'The family could have hired a hit man in Sicily to do him in. That seems to be a perfectly logical explanation.'

'But what we don't know is why Emilio went to Sicily in the first place.'

'He was probably lured there under false pretences.'

'But why didn't he tell his family about the trip?'

'Perhaps he was having an affair! You tell me.' Alex shrugged his shoulders. 'Do you know any more about the client who committed suicide?'

'His name was Luigi Fagiolini. Uncle Vico said he'd e-mail me the details of the case.'

'If your uncle felt so strongly about all this, why didn't he persist with his own enquiries?'

'He tried to, but he was thwarted at every turn. Besides, he was based in New York and he had neither the time nor the resources to continue with any meaningful sort of investigation.'

'No, I suppose not. When are you seeing Fabio again? What

fantastic roses,' said Alex, commenting on the row of Queen Elizabeth roses bordering the lawn.

'Monday… The roses are lovely, aren't they? You should have been here in April when the magnolia blossom was out. It was particularly beautiful this year; one big mass of pinkish-white flowers. It's a pity you can't stay for the party tonight,' I continued, changing the subject. 'Nonna really likes you. Have you seen the way she keeps winking at you?' Alex laughed. 'Mind you, I saw my mother wink at you earlier. You've certainly charmed them both.'

'Your grandmother seems lovely. It's a shame we can't understand one another very well.'

'If you spoke to her in English she would get the gist of the conversation. She understands more English than she lets on. She's just naughty and pretends not to. She can be very mischievous sometimes.'

'Hmm… It must run in the family.'

'I'm sure I don't know *what* you're talking about.'

'I think you mean *who*, Alicia?' I did not respond. 'Was she discussing me earlier?' he asked.

'Yes, but she was very complimentary.'

'What did she say *exactly*?'

'Now wouldn't you like to know that?'

Antonia drove me home on Sunday evening which gave me an opportunity to talk to her about Tom's proposal and proposed move. Although nothing was resolved, I hoped she felt better for our conversation. She dropped me off at my flat in South Kensington and, as it was only early evening, I decided to pop in to see Dorothy Hammond, my elderly neighbour who still lived in the garden flat, and give her the tiramisù Mamma had made especially for her.

'Oh, hello, dear,' she said, opening the door and ushering me into the hall. 'What on earth's that?' she asked, espying the covered dish I was holding.

'A present from Mamma,' I replied, handing it to her. She

carefully lifted off the aluminium foil and peeked inside.

'How thoughtful. I shall enjoy that.' She covered it over, walked through to the kitchen and put it in the fridge. 'Do you have time for a cup of tea? I was about to make myself one when you knocked,' she said, flicking on the switch of her electric kettle. 'It won't take a minute.'

'Always. Let me give you a hand.' I reached up to the cupboard and picked out two floral decorated china cups and saucers.

'Was that Alex's car I saw yesterday morning?' asked Dorothy nonchalantly as she carefully put a couple of heaped teaspoons of leaf tea from the caddy into her white china teapot. I knew Dorothy liked Alex and that she was curious about 'us', but she was too polite to ask me any direct questions.

'Yes. He gave me a lift to Surrey. My grandmother arrived on Friday.'

'I remember you told me she was coming to stay. It must have been wonderful to see her.' I nodded. She took a milk bottle out of the fridge and put some milk into a jug. The kettle boiled, I poured the hot water on to the tea-leaves, put the teapot, jug of milk, cups and saucers onto a tray, carried it through to the living room and placed it on the side table. I usually did this when I went to see Dorothy, which was a regular occurrence.

'You seem very tired,' I said as she settled back into her chair. She was looking rather drawn. I pulled up the tapestry cushion behind her to make her more comfortable. As was his custom Smoky, Dorothy's Persian cat, sidled up to her and then slid under her chair.

'It's partly this dreadful heat. I've hardly slept this past week. It's been so humid and hot at night. But I think I overdid it yesterday and I'm paying the price for it today.'

'Why? What did you do?' I asked, pouring the tea.

'I went to Glyndebourne.'

'I recall you saying your niece was taking you, but I didn't realize it was this weekend.' I handed Dorothy her tea.

'Yes. Mary,' her niece's daughter, 'came to collect me about half an hour after you left with Alex and brought me back this afternoon. It's been a tiring weekend but well worth it. It was a splendid performance.' I poured myself some tea and sat down on the two-seater sofa opposite Dorothy.

'What did you go and see?'

'The programme's over there on my desk,' she said, pointing to it. I placed my cup and saucer on the coaster on the side table next to me, crossed the room and picked up the brightly coloured annual guide to the festival. Dorothy had bookmarked the relevant pages.

'Rachmaninov's *The Miserly Knight*,' I said, reading out loud. 'I'm not familiar with that opera. Oh, and Puccini's *Gianni Schicchi*, the one with one of my favourite arias: *"O mio babbino caro"*.'

'Yes. It was delightful. I thoroughly enjoyed the whole evening. We had a marvellous picnic too.'

'You certainly had perfect weather for it.'

'Actually, it was a little too hot for me to sit out on the lawn, but we found a cool spot up on the veranda overlooking the gardens.'

'I'm really pleased you went. It's good that you're getting out and about.'

'I like to keep active as you know. That's why I work in my garden. How are things with you?'

'OK, thanks.'

'And what about work?'

'Fine. I'm enjoying my time at CFP & Co. I couldn't ask for a better boss than Graham.'

'Yes. I can imagine that makes all the difference. Do you have any interesting cases on at the moment?'

'Not particularly,' I replied, turning away to avoid Dorothy's all-too-knowing gaze.

'Well, you never can tell who might walk into your office.'

'Yes. Indeed you don't.' And in my experience nothing could be nearer the truth.

Chapter 5

'Do you think your father was murdered, Fabio?' I asked, putting down my pen and looking at him intently across my desk. He furrowed his brow as if he was in some way perplexed by my question, and pushed back a lock of black wavy hair which had flopped down onto his forehead.

'I do. Why are you asking me this?' he replied, his deep brown eyes scanning my face. Although he had lived in London for over seventeen years he had a distinctive New York accent – unlike Giulia, whose American accent was imperceptible; but then he had spent all his formative years in New York, whereas Giulia was only three when the family left and barely remembered her life before the move to England. They were both bilingual, but Fabio had never spoken with me in Italian.

'Because the other day you told me you have no idea why anybody should want you dead. Bearing in mind you think your father was murdered, I find it hard to believe it hasn't crossed your mind that his death is in someway linked to the events of last weekend. When I relayed the facts of your case to Alex, he was of the view that they might be.' Although I had expressed my doubts to Alex on this I was keen to hear Fabio's viewpoint.

'It's interesting that Alex should say that. It's certainly been preying on my mind a good deal, Alicia. It's not that I don't think there might be a connection, only that I can't fathom out why anyone would come after me, especially after all this time.' At that moment there was a brief tap on my office door, the door opened and Danielle, my secretary, popped her head around it.

'Sorry to disturb you,' she said, addressing us both but smiling broadly at Fabio, 'Only I wondered if you wanted a cup of tea or coffee?' I glanced over to him. He shook his head.

'No. We're all right, thanks, Danielle,' I replied, turning to her. She found some excuse to pop into my office whenever he attended for a meeting and seemed completely enamoured with him despite being nearly twenty years his senior. Admittedly, he was rather suave and sophisticated, which was definitely part of the attraction.

'Oh, OK. Well, just ring if you change your mind.' She continued to gaze at Fabio.

'We will,' I said, smiling at her. Danielle left. 'What about Angelo Fagiolini?' I said, swivelling around in my chair to face him. Angelo was the brother of Luigi, the client who had committed suicide. As promised, Uncle Vico had sent me an e-mail with details about him which I had picked up when I returned home the night before. 'I appreciate that nothing was proved but he was accused of conspiring to kill your father.'

'And you think he's seeking to avenge himself by exacting his revenge on me? I think that's highly improbable, Alicia.' I looked at him quizzically. 'Well, for a start I don't believe he actually had anything to do with my father's disappearance.'

'How can you be so sure?' I put my elbows on my desk and leaned forward.

'Because when my father went missing, Luigi's wife, Anna, contacted my mother. Unfortunately, my mother isn't here to confirm this, but she told me Anna was grateful for everything Emilio tried to do for her husband.'

'Then the family didn't blame your father for Luigi's suicide?' Now I was confused as well as intrigued.

'No. Quite the contrary, in fact. Anna said my father warned Luigi about his investments and told him not to proceed with the deal.'

'But what about the conspiracy theory? Where did the evidence for that come from?' I sank back in my chair feeling slightly bewildered.

'Independent witnesses, so I understand.'

'Who were they?'

'I don't know.' Fabio shrugged his shoulders. 'We couldn't get any information out of the authorities who investigated Angelo's alleged involvement.'

'But that's ridiculous.'

'Tell me about it.'

'Hmm… You don't suppose that somebody tried to frame Angelo, do you?' I could tell by the blank expression on Fabio's face that this was something he had never thought about.

'But why would they do that?'

'To create a smokescreen and ensure that suspicion fell on him and not the actual murderer.'

'It's possible, I suppose.'

'Yes, but certainly not impossible. Apart from acting for Luigi Fagiolini, do you have any idea what else your father was working on or who he might have been working with around that time?'

'Gregorio Pellegrino is the only colleague I actually know of by name. My mother was already acquainted with him because he worked at the same firm as my father in New York before moving to London himself. He tried to help her sort out the legal side of things.'

'Yes, my uncle told me. I think it might be beneficial to talk to your father's former colleagues, especially Gregorio Pellegrino. I would have thought that of all the people he worked with, he would be the most valuable contact.'

'I appreciate your point, but I can't see how much good it would do to speak to any of his colleagues because they would all have been interviewed at the time, and we probably won't be able to locate half of them now anyway,' he said rather half-heartedly.

'Not necessarily. You'd be surprised who we might find and what they have to tell us. I feel that it's an option worth considering.'

'But what are you hoping to find, Alicia?'

'An alternative suspect.'

'I don't understand. Do you think that my father could have been murdered by one of his colleagues?' Fabio sounded incredulous at my suggestion.

'I do. Let's look at the situation logically. A work associate would be well-placed to know about both his business affairs and whereabouts. Maybe one of them wanted your father dead, knew about the deal in Rome turning sour, took advantage of the situation and seized the opportunity to kill him or arrange for him to be murdered.'

'What about the independent witnesses who confirmed that Angelo threatened my father?'

'They could have been anybody for all we know. You said you never discovered who they were. What if they *were* colleagues?' Fabio did not look at all convinced by my wild theory.

'OK,' he said, smoothing back his hair, 'Where's your motive? Why would any of my father's colleagues want him dead?'

'Perhaps he had to be removed.'

'For stumbling across something shady, you mean?'

'That's one possibility, I suppose.' I had not actually reached the stage of considering what the various alternatives might be.

'But if you're right why would they want to threaten *me*? I'm sorry, Alicia, but your theory doesn't make sense.'

'I agree it seems far-fetched, but I don't see anyone else coming up with any suggestions,' I replied slightly defensively. I was annoyed that Fabio dismissed my thoughts on the matter out of hand and he clearly noticed my irritation.

'I'm sorry, Alicia. I didn't mean to pour cold water on your ideas and I value your input, truly I do. I realize that you're only trying to help me. It's just that...'

'It doesn't matter. I'm sorry too. I spoke out of turn. Who's the lawyer at Smythson, Reid & Monkton that Pellegrino recommended to your mother?' I asked, digressing slightly.

'Roland Kettering. I should think he's getting on for retirement now if he's still at the firm. Do you know him?'

'Not personally, no. I know of him though. He sometimes lectures at conferences on Estate Planning. Did he do a good job for your mother over the Probate of your father's estate?'

'Yes. Pretty much. It was a long drawn out process, of course, because of the circumstances. I don't need to explain that to you. You're all too familiar with how these things work.'

'I think you should also go and see him. It can't do any harm to talk to him about your father's case and maybe he still has the file archived somewhere.'

'Well, I suppose if I'm going to start digging around in the past I might as well be thorough. Would you come with me? I'd be very grateful if you did.' I had anticipated the question from the moment he walked into my office that morning, so it was not unexpected. Although I had reservations about involving myself further, bearing in mind I was the one encouraging him to take this course of action, I felt I could hardly refuse his request.

'Yes. Of course I will. I think that in the first instance the best thing is for you to fix up meetings with Pellegrino and Kettering and then to liaise with Danielle over my availability because she arranges my diary. She can always shift my appointments around to accommodate you if necessary.'

'Thanks. I really appreciate that. Your uncle said you'd help me.'

'Hmm... Did he now?' Uncle Vico had certainly dropped me in it this time. Alex was right about that.

'How's Giulia?' I asked, changing the subject.

'She's well. I spoke to her yesterday. She was spending the weekend in Orvieto with a friend from university whose family have a villa there.'

'Oh, good. How's she bearing up?'

'She's OK. She's thrown herself into a new project. I'm pleased because it really seems to be taking her mind off our mother's death.'

'What's she doing?'

'She's been trying to research our family background in Italy. You see, apart from our maternal grandmother and a few distant cousins on her side, we don't have any family. Giulia's very keen to trace our Italian roots and track down any Italian relatives, but we know very little about our paternal grandparents only that they came from somewhere near Lucca. The problem is they died when I was very young and I don't recollect them ever talking about their life before they moved to America. I wish I'd asked my father about the family when I had the chance, but as they say hindsight is a wonderful thing.'

'Yes…it certainly is.'

'Giulia thought that since she's in Italy she might as well take the opportunity to see what she can find out.'

'That's going to be quite a challenge.'

'That's what I thought. Which is why I wondered if you could help?'

'Me? In what way?' I asked slightly cautiously.

'Giulia and I may have Italian names and speak Italian but our knowledge of matters like this is rather limited. I thought that since you come from a family which has such close links to Italy and as you're a lawyer you'd have a much better idea of how the system works and could give us some guidance.'

'How to find family records you mean?' He nodded. 'Well, in Italy the set-up is different from here. As you know Italy is divided into *Regioni*, which are further divided into *Province*, and which are sub-divided into a number of *Comuni* – which I suppose we would call municipalities. The records of individuals are kept at *Comuni* level, while property records are kept traditionally in hard copy form at the *Province* level. Each *Comune* has various administrative functions including keeping a registry of births and deaths and a registry of deeds, for example.'

'So how would we go about searching for our family?'

'If it was me, I'd start looking in the *Provincia di Lucca* itself. You'd need to find out which municipality your family came from.

You can do a lot of the groundwork on the internet. There's a centralized, searchable database where you can check the ownership of Italian properties. If you have your grandparents full name, date and place of birth and an idea of the town or specific region where they lived, you can carry out a search online and obtain details that way.'

'But that's fantastic. You're very up to speed on all this search stuff. It's remarkable.'

'When you're acting for Italian clients who may have assets in Italy, or English clients who have bought a second home there, you need some knowledge of Italian property law and inheritance law even to begin to advise them. That's especially so when it comes to making a Will or dealing with the Probate of an estate. Italian inheritance law is not the same as here and a lot of people don't realize that. But I'm not an expert on this area by any means, as I don't deal with enough cases on a regular basis.'

'I'll pass on what you've told me to Giulia. Thanks very much.'

'No problem. The other thing you should consider doing, if you haven't already, is to put yourself on the AIRE list.'

'What's that?'

'The Association of Italians Residing abroad. It's an overseas version of the Vital Records Office, *L'Ufficio Anagrafe*. What's good about the system is that the Vital Records Office for each *Comune* keeps the corresponding records of those Italians who have transferred their residency to other countries. If you want to research your family history it's worth searching the AIRE files in the *Comune* from which your family comes. You never know what information you might turn up.'

'How would we go about registering our details?'

'I believe you have to go to the Italian Embassy and ask for a form *'Dati Anagrafici.'* You should be able to find the form on the Embassy website.'

'We'll definitely do that.'

'Good. I hope your research is successful. You'll have to let me know how Giulia gets on.'

'I will.'

'How are things generally?' I asked, changing the subject yet again.

'Work's fine. I've got quite a big project on at the moment which has been taking up a lot of my time. We're converting an old farmhouse in Suffolk and it's rather a challenge to get the design right, although I'm enjoying it.' Fabio was an architect by profession, but from what I could gather he had a flair for interior design as well.

'I'm pleased, but I meant with you personally? I'm concerned about you. All this recent business in Italy must be very unsettling. Don't take this the wrong way but do you *really* think that somebody is out to kill you?' I sensed he might react adversely to my question because he would think that I did not believe him, but I felt compelled to ask it nonetheless.

'You mean because they haven't succeeded yet?' he retorted. He stood up and started to pace the floor.

'No. Not at all.'

'Well, what *do* you mean?' he said testily, turning around and gesticulating at me. 'The police in Italy weren't convinced by my account of what happened with the Alfa driver, and consequently the police here weren't very constructive when I went to ask them for assistance. What must I do to prove that I'm telling the truth? Be found lying murdered in a pool of blood somewhere? Of all people, Alicia, I thought you believed me and that I could count on your support.' He sounded genuinely desperate and I felt slightly guilty for asking the question. In the circumstances pressing him for a response seemed pointless.

'You do have my support,' I replied, retaining my cool and trying to reassure him. 'I wouldn't have agreed to come with you to see Pellegrino or Kettering otherwise.'

'I'm sorry, Alicia,' he said, sitting down again, 'but I feel so angry with the police. Do you know how it feels to be dismissed like some madman? I just wanted them to believe me.'

'Listen, this may be a bit of a long shot, but my friend Will Brook's ex-CID. He primarily works as a private investigator these days, but I could give you his card if you're interested?' From the expression on his face it was evident that he was.

'Is he any good?'

'You might say I'm biased because he happens to be married to my best friend but, yes, I think he's excellent at what he does. I've worked with him on a professional basis before. Why not have a chat with him. He has so many contacts in the force. He knows his way around these things far better than I do. Maybe he can persuade someone to listen to you.' Talking about Will and Jo reminded me that I had promised to telephone Jo after the weekend. I had intended to ring her that morning, but Graham was away, I had been dealing with some of his clients and, as luck would have it, had not had time to make the call.

'OK. If you have his details, I'll look him up.' I pulled open the untidy top drawer of my desk and rummaged around for one of Will's business cards. I was sure I had a couple in there somewhere amongst the numerous paper clips, pens and other stationery items which I seemed to have accumulated.

'Here you go,' I said, retrieving one from under a pad of Post-It notes, leaning across my desk and handing it to him.

'Thanks,' he said, taking it from me. I observed him as he took out a small soft brown leather wallet from the inside pocket of his suit jacket and slipped the card inside. I caught a fleeting glimpse of the Armani label at the top of the pocket as he opened the jacket. He was always impeccably dressed, but this was the first time I had seen him wearing a suit. 'I can't tell you what a relief it is to have you on side. What would I do without you?'

'Hmm…' I forced a smile. For as much as I was drawn to his case, I knew that he was completely depending on me to help him and that expectation weighed rather too heavily on my slight shoulders.

I was extraordinarily busy for the rest of the day and did not have time to think about Fabio until Will called me late that afternoon when I was on my way to an external meeting.

'Hello,' I said, catching my breath as I answered my mobile. I noticed that the battery was almost flat even though I had only charged it the night before. Evidently there was something wrong with it and I needed a new one.

'Are you OK, Alicia?' I wondered if he was ringing me because Fabio had contacted him.

'I'm fine. Just in a bit of a rush. I've a meeting with one of Graham's clients and I ought to have been there twenty minutes ago.' I was hotfooting it down the street on my way to an appointment with some Charity Trustees and was behind schedule because my last client had arrived over an hour late. 'It's been a hectic day.' I sighed resignedly. 'And the battery on my mobile is about to die on me so I can't talk for long. How are you?'

'I'm all right thanks. Listen, I won't keep you as I realize you're in a hurry but I wanted to let you know that I had a call from Fabio Angelino this afternoon.'

'Already? I didn't think Fabio would contact you this soon. I should've rung you to give you advance warning. Sorry for dropping you in it like that. I hope you don't mind me referring him to you?'

'Not at all. There's nothing to apologise for. I'm happy to help if I can. From the few background details he's given me, it seems a rather intriguing case.'

'It is. Have you arranged a time to meet?'

'I'm on my way to see him now at his house in Chiswick.'

'That's quick work.'

'Well, I initially suggested tomorrow, but he seemed agitated so I've jigged around my engagements to accommodate him.'

'That's very good of you.'

'Oh, it's no trouble at all. You're assisting him I understand.'

'Hmm…' was my rather non-committal response.

'I'm looking forward to meeting him.'

'How's Jo? Is she feeling better?' I asked changing the subject.

'She's still quite poorly actually.'

'Oh no. Tell her I'll give her a buzz later. I've been meaning to call her all day but I haven't had a moment's peace.' I could hear my mobile beeping as the battery started to fail on me.

'OK. Hope your meeting goes well.'

'Thanks, Will. Bye.'

I had told Danielle that I would return to the office after my meeting to drop off the files, as they were cumbersome and I had no desire to lug them home with me. I thought that, since I was going back, I might as well check my e-mails and pick up any messages that had come in while I was out. Danielle would have already gone as it was after six; she never stayed beyond five-thirty if she could help it because she had a long train journey home. I knew that she would have left any memos for me on my desk.

I took the lift up to the office and, when the doors opened, I saw Peter Crawford, the Matrimonial Partner, standing waiting to take the lift down. I exchanged a few brief pleasantries with him, he disappeared into the lift and I walked through to reception. Susannah, our receptionist, was so engrossed on the 'phone that I did not stop to talk to her and proceeded down the corridor to my office. I was surprised to see the door open and as I walked inside Danielle came rushing towards me.

'Oh, Alicia. Thank goodness you're here,' she gushed.

'Why? What's the matter?' I replied, looking at her hard. 'I didn't expect to see you. Why are you still here?' I quizzed, dropping the files onto my desk. I knew instinctively that something was very wrong.

'Will Brook called as I was about to leave. He was desperate to speak to you. He said he left a couple of messages on your mobile.'

'But I only spoke to him a few hours ago. I had to switch it off during the meeting and I didn't bother to switch it back on because the battery's flat.'

'He did mention something about your mobile which is why he rang the office.' Whatever Will had rung about had to be urgent as otherwise he would have waited until I arrived home. My initial thought was that he was 'phoning because Jo was seriously ill.

'Did he leave a message?'

'Yes. I'm sorry, Alicia, but I have some dreadful news concerning Fabio Angelino.' Although I was relieved to hear that Jo had not taken a turn for the worse, I felt sick to my stomach at the thought of the fate that might have befallen Fabio.

'Tell me he's not dead, Danielle?' I said, sitting down at my desk and bracing myself for the words I expected to hear.

'It's not Fabio who's dead, Alicia.' She took a deep breath. 'It's Giulia.'

Chapter 6

'You're a very difficult woman to get hold of,' said Alex playfully, and winking at me as I opened the front door. 'I've been 'phoning you all afternoon.' It was nearly nine at night and he must have travelled straight from work as he was still wearing his suit. 'Actually, I was worried about you,' he added, stepping into the hall. 'I couldn't leave the office early this evening otherwise I'd have come over sooner. Is everything OK?' he asked concernedly, peering at me. 'You're very pale. Are you all right?'

'I'm fine. I'm glad you're here though,' I replied, putting my arms around him and hugging him.

'Hey, sweetheart,' he said softly, holding me tightly. 'What's the matter? What's happened?'

'Giulia's dead,' I replied, looking up at him.

'What?' He let go of me, stood back and simply stared at me for a moment, clearly shocked by my statement. 'When? How?'

'I don't have many details yet. It's all a bit vague. Come and sit down.' Alex slipped off his shoes, as he usually did, dropped them in the hall and followed me into the living room. 'Can I make you something to eat? You must be starving,' I said, thinking that Alex would not have eaten dinner.

'Thanks, but I'm not really hungry. I had lunch with a client today.'

'Oh, OK,' I replied, sitting down on the sofa.

'Did Fabio tell you about Giulia?' he asked, removing first his jacket, and then his silk patterned tie. 'I remember you said you were seeing him this morning.' I watched him as he carefully rolled up the tie and popped it into one of the jacket pockets, folded the jacket and placed it on the arm of the sofa.

'No. Will rang and spoke to Danielle when I was out at a meeting this afternoon.'

'Will? How's he involved? I don't understand.' Alex sat down on the sofa and inclined himself towards me.

'Because this morning I recommended to Fabio that he contact Will as I thought he might be able to put him in touch with someone in the police who could assist him. As it happens, Will arranged an appointment with Fabio this afternoon and it was while they were together that Fabio received the call about Giulia.'

'Oh, I see. How grim. Didn't you pick up any of my messages?' I saw Alex glance at my mobile which was lying on the coffee table.

'No. I switched off the handset when I went to my meeting because the battery's kaput. I need to buy a new one.'

'That explains why you didn't ring back then. Was Giulia murdered?'

'We don't know yet, but in light of recent events I can't help feeling that it's a strong probability.'

'What did Will say?'

'I only spoke to him briefly, but apparently her tutor was concerned when she didn't turn up for class and she couldn't be located. There must be more to it than that though. Fabio told me this morning that Giulia spent the weekend at Orvieto with a university friend so maybe she didn't come back from there, although Will didn't mention where her body was found or how she died. I'm not sure whether he even knows and I didn't like to press him on the 'phone. He said he'd talk to me later. He mentioned something about accompanying Fabio to Perugia, but everything's up in the air at the moment and I have no idea what their plans are.'

'Hmm… It's strange because, when we discussed this the other day, I was concerned about Giulia's safety as I wasn't convinced that only Fabio was at risk.'

'Yes. I know.'

'If Giulia was murdered, which I agree seems likely, it strikes me that maybe she was the intended victim all along and not Fabio.'

'But what about the incident with the Alfa? Fabio is adamant that whoever was driving was out to kill him.'

'It's possible the driver mistakenly believed that Giulia was in the car with Fabio. Let's suppose the murderer was prepared to go to any lengths to kill her. That might include killing her brother too, if that was the only way to do it. People like that are pretty ruthless. Remember you said Fabio had to stop to allow the coach to pass. Perhaps the Alfa driver saw that Giulia wasn't in the car with Fabio and that's the reason why he or she gave up the chase and sped off.'

'That's feasible I guess. But what if the murderer seeks both their deaths and still intends to come after Fabio? I wish I knew why though. For now the motive is completely eluding me.' I sighed.

'Oh, well. There's no point in us theorizing until we find out from Will whether or not she was murdered.'

'No. You're right. Do you want a drink?' I asked. 'There's some beer in the fridge or you could have wine if you prefer.'

'I'll have a beer.' I went to stand up. 'You stay there,' he said. 'I'll get it. Can I bring you anything?'

'There's an open tube of Salt and Vinegar Pringles in the cupboard opposite the fridge. I could do with some of those.'

'OK.' Alex gave me a knowing smile, disappeared into the kitchen and returned moments later with a Peroni beer and the Pringles. 'You should have shares in these,' he teased, putting the tube down on the coffee table in front of the sofa.

'You eat them too,' I protested.

'I know. I'm so easily tempted,' he said, sitting down again and taking a sip of his beer.

'I'm leading you into bad ways, am I?' I replied, curling up on the sofa.

'I sincerely hope so,' he said, setting his beer down on the coffee table, leaning over and kissing me on the neck.

'How about exercising some self-control?' I said, laughing and wriggling away.

'I don't have any,' he replied, looking up momentarily. 'Besides, a little of what you fancy does you good,' he said, pulling me towards him and placing his hand inside the back of my T-shirt.

'Only a little? You do surprise me.' My landline started to ring, which distracted me, and I made a move to answer it.

'Leave it. Whoever it is can wait,' said Alex, nibbling my ear lobe.

'I can't. It's probably Will.'

'OK. If you must,' said Alex reluctantly, letting go of me and standing up. I jumped off the sofa and bounded to the 'phone. Alex disappeared in the direction of the bathroom.

'Hello,' I said, answering it. It was Will. 'How are things?'

'Not good. Fabio's in a terrible state. You haven't spoken to him then?'

'No. I called him while I was still at the office and left messages on both his mobile and at home.'

'I think he said he was going to his grandmother's tonight.'

'Oh, right. When are you flying out to Perugia?'

'Tomorrow morning.'

'It's extremely good of you to go with him at such short notice and especially as you only met him this afternoon.'

'Well, the nature of my work means that I invariably have to do things without advance warning.'

'Yes, of course.'

'After what happened with the police in Ravello, I think he's desperate for some support. I'll do what I can to assist.'

'I can't think of anyone better to have on side. You're so experienced in liaising with the police on investigations such as this.'

'Only in the UK, Alicia. How I'll fare in Italy is another matter. I'm not overly familiar with the procedure there.'

'You're too modest. Anyway, I suppose you'll be receiving some assistance from the British Consulate. After all, Fabio and Giulia both have British passports through their mother.'

'Yes.'

'I thought that in matters such as this the death is reported to the Consulate who then asks the UK police to inform the next of kin in person.'

'Correct.'

'Then I don't understand. You told me that Fabio received a call. Surely the police didn't ring him?'

'It wasn't the UK police who informed him, Alicia. It was actually someone from the university, but I'm sure Giulia's death will be reported to the Consulate and the usual procedures will be set in motion.'

'Fabio will need to contact the Consulate anyway to register her death.'

'But her death will be registered in Italy.'

'Yes, although there's nothing to stop him registering it at the British Consulate and then he'll get a UK death certificate. The Consulate can also offer information about the local police which makes your task easier when it comes to the investigation out there.'

'OK.'

'Have you found out what happened to Giulia yet?'

'Whether she was murdered, you mean?'

'Yes. I was thinking along the lines of 'if' and 'how'.'

'Her body was discovered at Lake Bolsena this morning. It's believed she drowned, but how she drowned is another matter. Everything points to her having been murdered. We won't find out for certain until tomorrow.'

'Drowned, possibly murdered,' I repeated for Alex's benefit. He had returned to the living room and was sitting on the sofa sipping his beer and listening intently. 'Lake Bolsena is quite near Orvieto. I imagine the police will be interviewing the family of the friend she stayed with at the weekend,' I said, thinking out loud.

'I expect so.'

'Will, are you at home?'

'Yes. Why?'

'I wanted a quick word with Jo, that's all.'

'She wants to speak to you anyway. I'll put her on. She's in the other room. Just a second.' I listened to the sound of Will's footsteps on their wooden floor as he walked with the cordless handset. He said something to Jo and then I heard her voice on the line.

'Hi, Ally. Are you OK?' She sounded much brighter.

'I'm fine thanks. You seem much better tonight.'

'I am.'

'I'm sorry I didn't call you today.'

'By the sounds of it you've had other things to worry about. Listen, why don't you come over tomorrow evening, if you've got time that is?' she said expectantly. I glanced over at Alex. He generally went to the gym on Tuesday evenings. I had thought that Antonia might pop in for dinner but it probably suited her later in the week when Tom was working.

'I'd love to.'

'Well, if you can't make it, let me know, otherwise see you around seven. I'll hand you back to Will. He's making faces at me to give him the 'phone.'

'Oh, OK. See you tomorrow.'

'Bye, Ally.'

'Bye.'

'Hi again, Alicia,' he said. 'I'll give you a call when we get there and let you know what's happening.'

'OK. What time's your flight?'

'Mid-morning; but we won't arrive there until about four because we couldn't get a direct flight and have to fly to Milan first and then on to Perugia.'

'You were lucky that you were able to book a flight at such short notice and especially at this time of year when all the tourists are flocking to Umbria.'

'It wasn't easy. Speak to you later.'

'Yes. Keep safe. Bye now.'

'Bye.' I replaced the handset on the base unit as it needed

charging. The last thing I needed was the battery on my landline to be flat. 'Did you get the gist of that?' I asked Alex as I picked up the tube of Pringles from the coffee table and rejoined him on the sofa.

'Pretty much. You really do have the most interesting clients, don't you?'

'I wouldn't put it quite like that,' I replied, removing the plastic lid from the Pringles and offering them to Alex. He shook his head.

'I was being sarcastic. I don't suppose there's anything that can be done this end to further the investigation.' I felt that Alex was anxious to protect me from future involvement in the case even though he knew very well that it was too late for that.

'Probably not in relation to Giulia, no, but I agreed to help Fabio reinvestigate the mystery surrounding his father. I could try and make progress on that in his absence.' I helped myself to half a dozen or so Pringles, replaced the lid and put the tube back on the coffee table.

'By doing what exactly?'

'I suggested to him that his father's colleagues might be able to shed some light on his disappearance. After all they worked with him on a day-to-day basis. It did occur to me that one or more of them could be behind what happened to him.' I popped a Pringle in my mouth.

'And you said as much to Fabio?' I nodded. 'I think I can see where you're going with this line of argument. But you haven't answered my question. What do *you* intend to do?'

'I proposed to Fabio that he set up meetings with Gregorio Pellegrino and Roland Kettering to see what information he could get out of them.' I munched on another Pringle.

'I know who Gregorio Pellegrino is, but where does Roland Kettering fit in?'

'He's the Partner at Smythson, Reid & Monkton Pellegrino recommended to Evelyn,' I replied, clearing my throat.

'To sort out the Probate of Emilio's estate?'

'Yes.'

'Has Fabio met with them yet?'

'No. We only discussed it this morning.'

'So what can *you* do about it?'

'Fabio asked me if I would accompany him.'

'And you agreed?'

'It was the least I could do bearing in mind it was my idea to set up meetings with them in the first place. The thing is, he was supposed to contact them to sort that out and then come back to me, but I don't expect he had a chance to do that today and I should think that it's the farthest thing from his mind right now.'

'Hmm… I'm sure it is. Don't jump down my throat, but it did occur to me that we could be approaching the mystery surrounding Emilio's death from the wrong angle.'

'What do you mean?'

'Everyone assumes that he was murdered – but we don't have a body.'

'But that doesn't mean he wasn't. We've already discussed this.'

'Wait a minute. Let me finish,' said Alex, holding up his hand to stop me talking. Suitably admonished, I sat back. 'What I'm trying to say is that we don't actually know if he *is* dead. For all we know he might have wanted to disappear. Maybe he had to.'

'To get away from somebody or something?'

'Quite possibly. He could be out there now with a new identity.'

'But that doesn't explain why Giulia has been murdered and, if what you say is right, surely it's more important than ever that we speak to his colleagues and find out what he was involved in at or around the time he vanished?'

'But that will have to wait until Fabio's return now, won't it?' I sensed that was what Alex was hoping.

'Not necessarily. If I have Fabio's authority for them to speak with me, then I'll go and meet them alone. Don't look at me like that,' I said, noting Alex's anxious expression. 'Fabio needs all the help we can give him right now.'

'Maybe he does, but not if it requires you putting yourself at risk.

You feel sorry for him, so you want to help him. I understand it, but I don't like it.'

'I know what I'm getting in to. I have mixed feelings about my involvement, believe me, but it's something I have to do.'

'I seriously worry about you sometimes.'

'The only way we're going to find out anything is by asking questions, Alex. I thought you were intrigued by this case.'

'I am, but I've a vested interest in keeping you in one piece. That's my first priority.'

'If you're that worried about me why don't you come with me, then you can keep tabs on me.' I snapped.

'I don't want to keep tabs on you. I only want you to be safe.'

'I'm sorry. I know you care about me.'

'I don't just care about you. I love you.'

Chapter 7

'Alicia,' mouthed Danielle as she poked her head around the door of my office, 'I know you're on the 'phone, but I have Fabio Angelino on the line.'

'Could you hang on a second, Antonia,' I said, and put my hand over the mouthpiece.

'I asked him if you could ring him back but he's at the airport and I think he's pressed for time. Do you want to take it? I've put him on hold.'

'Of course. Give me a moment to get off the 'phone and you can put him through.'

'OK,' she said, shutting the door quietly. I removed my hand from the mouthpiece.

'Sorry, Antonia,' I said. 'Could I ring you later? I have to take an urgent call from a client.'

'OK. But don't forget.'

'I won't. *Ciao.* Bye.' As soon as I put down the receiver Danielle transferred the call from Fabio.

'How are you?' I asked gently.

'Numb,' he replied. 'I can't believe this is happening. Giulia had so much to live for, Alicia.' I could detect the emotion in his voice, but he was remarkably controlled. I was straining to hear him because in addition to the general noise of the departure lounge his voice was almost obliterated by a Tannoy announcement in the background.

'Is Will with you?'

'Yes. We're boarding in a few minutes. That's why I was anxious to speak with you. Thank you for your messages. I'm sorry I didn't call you last night but I was with my grandmother. As you can imagine she's absolutely distraught.'

'I'm sure.'

'Would you let your uncle know what's happened? I will ring him, but I can't face it right now.'

'Of course.'

'Could you do something else for me?'

'Yes, if I can.'

'Would you be prepared to go and see Pellegrino and Kettering by yourself?'

'If that's what you want.'

'You don't mind?'

'No. I had already decided to ask you if you'd like me to see them on your behalf. Although I doubt they'll be willing to talk to me without obtaining the go ahead from you first. Are you sure you don't want to leave the meetings until your return?'

'I have no idea how long I'm going to be here, Alicia. I feel quite strongly about finding out what happened to my father and Giulia's death doesn't change that. If anything it makes me more determined than ever to get to the bottom of it all, so I don't want any delay.'

'OK. What about fixing up the appointments?'

'Well, after I left you yesterday morning, I put in a call to both Pellegrino and Kettering's offices and spoke to their secretaries who both said they'd have to get back to me with proposed time and dates. I briefly explained the purpose of the meeting, gave them your name, who you are, and said you'd be accompanying me. I actually rang them both again this morning, said that it's unlikely I'll be able to attend, but you'll be there on my behalf, you have my authority to speak to them, and left Danielle's details so they can liaise directly with her. I appreciate I should have asked you first, but I had the feeling you'd be prepared to see them alone.'

'That's fine. Does Danielle know all this?'

'Yes. I filled her in while you were on the 'phone. I have to go. The plane's boarding. Thanks for everything, Alicia. Bye.'

'Bye.' And he was gone.

I e-mailed my uncle with the dreadful news of Giulia's death and asked him to call me as soon as he received my message. Then I had a quick word with Danielle about scheduling the appointments with Gregorio Pellegrino and Roland Kettering. She expressed her surprise at Fabio's remarkable composure. She could not believe how calm and collected he was when he spoke to her. I was impressed by his incredible strength of character, but not amazed by it, because in my experience it was not unusual for people to become stronger in the face of adversity.

I had barely finished perusing the post and was about to pick up the 'phone to return Antonia's call as promised when Graham strolled into the office.

'Thanks for attending that meeting yesterday,' he said, smiling broadly as he took a seat in the chair opposite me. 'I'm sorry you were lumbered with it at such short notice.'

'Oh, that's OK. I think it went well. They want to restructure the charity. I'll ask Danielle to type up my notes. You should have them by the end of the day.'

'Drop them on my desk when you're ready. There's no rush,' said Graham, in his usual easy-going manner. He was definitely the most reasonable and likeable Partner for whom I had ever worked. It made a change to be in a relaxed working environment and this was something I was still not quite used to even after working at CFP & Co. for some time. But that was probably because Graham, unlike some of the other Partners in my previous firms, had a formidable intellect and did not find it necessary to undermine his staff to conceal his own shortcomings and promote himself. 'Now bring me up to speed on Fabio Angelino's case.'

'The Probate of his mother's estate is progressing without any glitches, so far anyway.'

'That's good, but I meant since we spoke last Friday about the alleged attempt on his life. I was very shocked to hear about his sister's murder. It's appalling news. I understand from Danielle that you've arranged to meet a couple of his father's former colleagues to ask them questions about his disappearance?'

'Giulia drowned. I expect we'll find out if she was murdered today or tomorrow.'

'Hmm... And the meetings with the former colleagues?'

'Nothing's been fixed up yet. Only one of them's a former colleague. The other is the solicitor who dealt with the Probate of his father's estate.'

'Who's that?'

'Roland Kettering at Smythson, Reid & Monkton.'

'I wouldn't have thought you'd get much joy out of him.'

'What makes you say that? Do you know him?'

'Oh yes. He was my Principal when I was doing my articles and must be in his sixties now. Professionally he's sound, but personally I don't like him. He's a prig, has absolutely no sense of humour and takes himself far too seriously to do a job like ours. And he's insensitive. There is a possibility that he might warm to you though.'

'Why?'

'Because he's an Italophile. I recall him boring us to tears about his acquisition of property in Tuscany. He has contacts in Italy and used to go there for work, so he said.'

'That must be how he knows Gregorio Pellegrino,' I said, thinking out loud. Graham looked at me quizzically. 'He's the former colleague I'm hoping to meet and the one who recommended Fabio's mother to Kettering in the first place.'

'Oh, I see. Listen Alicia, I understand that Fabio instructed this firm through the connection with your uncle, but that was to deal with the Probate of his mother's estate; you must not feel obligated to him to take on matters which fall outside the solicitor/client relationship. I am very concerned about your involvement. I know you want to help, but certain issues are better left for the police to investigate. Do not put yourself at risk unnecessarily.' He stood up, leaned across the table and squeezed my hand before turning and ambling towards the door. 'Keep me informed. OK?' he said, pausing and looking at me hard before leaving.

Although Graham was being paternalistic I could not take offence at his comments because I knew he was well-meaning. I was fortunate to have a boss who cared about his employees' welfare, which was still a rather novel concept for me.

I managed to speak with Antonia and pencilled in dinner for Thursday evening, which was the evening that suited her best. I worked productively up until lunchtime when I went out for a walk to St James's Park, and to buy a new mobile – which of course I could not use straightaway as the battery needed charging. From mid-afternoon onwards I could not concentrate at all and repeatedly looked at the clock hoping for Uncle Vico to call and wondering when I would hear from Will. Although I knew that Fabio and he would not arrive in Perugia until later that afternoon I did not really expect him to contact me for a while at least.

I was slightly preoccupied by Alex's suggestion that Emilio might still be alive and, although I initially dismissed the theory as preposterous, with every passing moment I became increasingly uncertain that it was. A possible connection between recent events and those of sixteen years ago preyed on my mind too.

I did not intend to stay late at the office because I wanted to be with Jo by seven, but it was now after five and Uncle Vico had still not 'phoned. Since I would be home late and he would be unable to reach me on my mobile, it seemed preferable to ring him. The reason why he had not responded to my e-mail, however, was simply because he had not received it; apparently there had been a major network problem with the computer system in his office. It was typical that this should happen on a day such as this.

I relayed to him the details of my conversations with both Will and Fabio, and he was shocked to learn the news that Giulia was dead. I explained that I hoped to set up meetings with Pellegrino and Kettering as Fabio wanted to reinvestigate that side of things and had asked for my assistance.

'Do you want me to come with you?' he asked, in his strong Italian accent. Despite living in New York for most of his adult life he had never lost it and I could detect not even the hint of an American one.

'Are you intending to be in London then?'

'Yes. I thought I might surprise Nonna and fly over.'

'Oh, that's wonderful news.' I had thought that my uncle might perhaps come to England while Nonna was staying with Mamma, and in the circumstances his visit could not be timelier. 'When?'

'At the end of the week. So I'd be available to accompany you to your meetings if you would like that.'

'It would be useful, especially since you're already acquainted with Mr Pellegrino.'

'I'm also curious to check out Roland Kettering.'

'I'll try and arrange everything to coincide with your stay then. Does Mamma know about your impending trip?'

'I was about to call her when you rang.'

'I'm really excited now. I can't wait to see you.' I was looking forward to catching up with him because it had been a few years since we last saw each other.

'And I you.'

'I'll see you soon then.'

'You will.'

'Bye.'

I tried to call Alex before I left the office but there was no reply on his mobile so I left a message to remind him that I was seeing Jo. I bought a mini-bouquet of flowers for her en route. It was made up of cream, lilac and pink stocks, creamy avalanche roses, and lilac agapanthus. I arrived at her flat a few minutes after seven.

'Hi, Ally,' she said, flinging her arms around me. 'It's so good to see you.'

'You too.' I tried to hug her but it was a bit difficult with my briefcase in one hand and the flowers in the other. 'These are for you,' I said, standing back, putting down my briefcase and offering her the bouquet. 'Are you feeling better?'

'Yes, I am. Thank you,' she replied, taking the flowers from me and then smelling them. 'They have such a beautiful fragrance. Give me that,' she said as I removed my jacket. She hung it up on the coat rack at the far end of the hall. 'I'll just pop these in a vase and then we can have a proper chat,' she said, walking through to the kitchen with me in tow.

'I've made coronation chicken. Is that OK with you?'

'Perfect. Have you heard from Will?' I asked, watching her untie the bunch of flowers.

'I wondered when you were going to ask,' she replied, glancing up at me.

'Well, have you?'

'Yes, about half an hour ago. He's very sorry he missed you.' She proceeded to cut the stems of the roses. 'Don't worry. You needn't concern yourself about breaching any client confidentiality. Will explained to Fabio that I used to be a policewoman and I work with him. Actually, I think he's relieved that he has so many people on his side for once.' She was quite right, of course. It was a relief to be able to discuss the matter with her after all.

'What did Will say?'

'It's what you suspected, Ally,' she replied, opening the kitchen cupboard in the far corner and reaching up to the top shelf for a vase. It was just as well she was tall. 'The pathologist's report confirmed that Giulia was murdered.'

'Anything else?' Jo started to arrange the flowers in the vase.

'She was dead before she hit the water.'

'Then what did she die of?'

'She was asphyxiated.' She put the vase into the sink, turned on the tap and filled it with water.

'What steps can Will and Fabio take out there?'

'Well, I guess they'll start off trailing the police investigation and see what that turns up, but Fabio wants to put his feelers out and make enquiries of his own. Will said Fabio's keen to talk to Giulia's university pals. Fabio's going to take your advice and register Giulia's death at the British Consulate as well.' She lifted the vase out of the sink. 'There…aren't they magnificent? I think I'll put them in the centre of the dining room table.' She disappeared for a moment. 'What would you like to drink?' she asked as she walked back in to the kitchen. 'Wine?'

'Yes. That's fine.'

'Oh,' she said, perusing the wine rack, 'I thought we had another bottle of red. Will must have drunk it. Do you mind having white?' she asked, opening the fridge door. I shook my head. 'I have some here,' she said, pulling out a bottle of Frascati and holding it up. 'Is that OK for you? I'm sorry, I know you prefer red being a Tuscan girl.'

'I drink Roman wine too! Anyway, we're having chicken so white's perfect.' Jo handed me the bottle and took one wine glass out of the cupboard.

'Aren't you drinking? Oh, I suppose it's because you're still not feeling one hundred percent.'

'I'm OK, but I'm giving up alcohol for a few months as I'm pregnant,' she said, dropping her voice.

'Oh, Jo, you're not?'

'I am.'

'Will must be delighted that he's going to be a father?'

'He's more excited than I am. When I told him he was ecstatic.'

'When did you find out?'

'Yesterday. That's why I really wanted to see you today, to tell you. It's early days so we don't want to broadcast it yet.'

'No. Of course. Oh, I'm so pleased for you both,' I said, giving her another hug. 'It's lovely to end the day on some good news for a change.'

Chapter 8

Knowing that my uncle was coming over from New York at the weekend, I hoped to arrange the meetings with Gregorio Pellegrino and Roland Kettering after his arrival to enable him to accompany me. Danielle set about this task early on Wednesday morning and called Gregorio Pellegrino's secretary first. She was informed that his only availability for the next few weeks was at six on Thursday evening.

On tentatively requesting that the meeting be deferred to the following week, Danielle was firmly told that I was lucky he could accommodate me at all considering his busy schedule and it was either that date or nothing. Despite his secretary's unhelpful attitude, I remained open-minded and positive about the information I might ascertain from him. When Fabio rang during the course of the morning I explained the situation.

'See him tomorrow, Alicia. I see no benefit in postponing the meeting until your uncle arrives. What about Kettering? When are you seeing him?'

'Danielle's trying to fix something up as we speak. How are you?'

'I can't tell you how grateful I am to have Will with me. It would be awful to be out here alone.'

'I'm glad. What's happening with the investigation?' I asked gently.

'We're trying to piece together Giulia's last movements, but it's proving difficult.'

'What about the friend she stayed with in Orvieto?'

'We know that on Sunday evening, Laura, her friend, was feeling unwell and decided not to return to Perugia until Monday morning. Laura's father dropped Giulia at the train station in Orvieto about five and that's the last they saw of her. None of her fellow students in Perugia realized she was missing at that stage.'

'They wouldn't would they, because so far as they were aware she was with Laura in Orvieto?'

'Well, yes. On Monday morning Laura called Emma, a mutual friend of theirs, to say that she was worried about Giulia. She had sent her a couple of text messages and repeatedly called her, but had received no response which was completely out of character for Giulia. It was only at that point that either of them thought something might be wrong and of course she didn't turn up for class.' He paused momentarily and took a deep breath. 'Her body was later discovered washed up on the beach at Castiglione del Lago,' he said, slightly choking on the words. I thought he was remarkable to maintain such a grip on his emotions in the circumstances.

'But that's at Lake Trasimeno. I thought she was found at Lake Bolsena?' If she was found at Lake Trasimeno rather than Lake Bolsena then that put a different complexion on the investigation.

'No. Where did you get that from?'

'Will.'

'He's mistaken. He must have misheard me.'

'Oh, right. Then the likelihood is that she returned to Perugia, isn't it?' I asked, knowing that Lake Trasimeno was within a fairly short driving distance of the Umbrian capital.

'Yes. That's the way it looks.'

'And something the police should be able to establish relatively easily I'd have thought.'

'I hope so.'

'Have you spoken to Emma and Laura?'

'Only Emma. Laura's still in Orvieto. She wasn't well enough to return to Perugia on Monday and then, of course, the news came that Giulia was dead. I understand she's taken it very badly and hasn't really been in a fit state to help the police. Will and I are heading down there tomorrow. I'll let you know how it goes.'

'OK. Don't forget I'm seeing Pellegrino at six, so I probably won't be home until eight. Also, I'm expecting my sister for dinner tomorrow night but feel free to call any time.'

'All right. Thanks for your support.'

'Take care. Oh, Fabio,' I said, remembering that I had not told him about Uncle Vico, 'are you still there?'

'Yes.'

'I spoke to my uncle.'

'Thank you.'

'He's coming over to see Nonna, so he'll be here for a few weeks. I did think that he might be able to help us.'

'Let's talk about that later. I have to run. Bye, Alicia.'

Setting up a meeting with Roland Kettering proved to be less tortuous because his secretary was exceptionally helpful. The only problem was that he was away on holiday the next week, and it was a question of either waiting until the end of the week following his return, or seeing him at eight-thirty on Friday morning. Although Uncle Vico was keen to meet him and it would have been useful to have his company, bearing in mind Fabio was eager to avoid any delay, I opted for the Friday appointment.

Later that day I was dwelling on my forthcoming meeting with Pellegrino, and more particularly thinking about the questions I would ask him, when I realized I had not rung Antonia as promised.

'You're not calling to cancel, are you?' she asked, sounding slightly grumpy.

'No. Just to let you know I have an external meeting at six tomorrow and I should be home by the time you arrive, but don't panic if I'm not. I'll ring you when I'm leaving the meeting anyway if I'm going to be late.'

'*Va bene*. Where's your meeting?'

'At another firm of solicitors.'

'I really don't understand why you chose to do all this Wills and Probate stuff, Ally. It seems the dullest area of law imaginable.'

'You'd be surprised. There's never a dull moment in this office. Anyway, I'd better go. I need to sign my post. I'll see you tomorrow. *Ciao, carina.*'

'Ciao. Bye.'

I was signing my last letter when my direct line rang. It was Alex. 'Perfect timing,' I said.

'Why?'

'Because I'm about to finish up here and head home. How was your day?'

'Fine. Everything's going well on this deal but there are some long nights coming up. Did you have a good evening with Jo?'

'Yes. It's always lovely to see her.'

'And she's better?'

'Much.'

'I picked up your message when I left the gym. Have you sorted out your mobile yet, only I've called it a couple of times today but you've not answered?'

'I did buy a new one yesterday, but I was running late this morning and forgot to pick it up!'

'It's easily done. What's happening on the case? Have you heard from Fabio today?'

'Yes. We spoke this morning. There have been a few developments both here and in Italy.' I filled Alex in on the events of the past twenty-four hours.

'Hmm… I know you might not agree with me, Alicia,' he said, having listened patiently to all I had to tell him, 'but I feel that there simply has to be a link between all these incidents in Fabio's family.'

'I didn't, but now that Giulia's dead I'm not so sure. I think you could be right. I'm hoping to glean something from Pellegrino and Kettering when I meet them.'

'Are you sure you're OK going alone?'

'Yes. Perfectly. Don't worry.'

'Do you have anything planned for tomorrow evening, only I thought you might fancy doing something after your appointment with Pellegrino?'

'I'd love to, but Antonia's coming round for a heart-to-heart.'

'Oh, that sounds heavy.'

'Yes. You don't want to know about it believe me.'

'What about tonight then?'

'No plans. I thought I might have a quiet night in. Shall I make you dinner?'

'You're always cooking for someone or other. Let's go out and have some fun. You need a bit of a break from all this Fabio stuff. Why don't I scooter over and pick you up about seven-thirty? Have a think about what you want to do.'

'OK. I will.' Danielle opened the door and indicated that she needed to speak to me urgently. 'Sorry, Alex, but I have to go,' I said, and gestured for Danielle to stay.

'Is everything all right?' he asked, picking up my clipped tone.

'Yes. Danielle wants a word before she leaves. I'll call you back.'

'Don't worry about it. I'll see you later. *Ciao*, bella.'

'*Baci ed abbracci. Ciao.*' I put the 'phone down.

'What is it, Danielle?' She was looking agitated.

'Will rang.'

'And?'

'Oh, Alicia…'

'What is it? Tell me.'

'He's gone missing.'

'Who has?' I asked, with an increasingly sinking feeling. Although I posed the question, it was not necessary because I already knew what her response would be. 'Who has?' I repeated.

'Fabio Angelino.'

Chapter 9

The offices of Scarpetti, Steiglitz & Co. were based in the City, at
the lower end of St Paul's Churchyard. Since I had to make my way
there from my office in Belgravia I left ample time for the journey.
Fortunately, there were delays on neither the Circle nor Central lines
and I arrived at St Paul's tube station with ten minutes to spare. I
had been determined not to rush because it was another scorching
summer's day and I had no desire to arrive at my meeting more hot
or flustered than was absolutely necessary. I ambled down the hill
past Wren's great cathedral and it was a few minutes before six when
I pushed open the revolving doors of Scarpetti, Steiglitz & Co. and
stepped into an impressive air-conditioned marble entrance lobby,
which even had its own fountain display. If these premises were
anything to go by, this was a highly successful commercial law firm.

I walked purposefully towards the reception desk which was
directly opposite the entrance. There were two receptionists sitting
at either end: one with shoulder length fair hair who was bashing
away at her keyboard as if her life depended upon it, and another
with dark brown hair scraped back into a rather unbecoming pony-
tail who was on the telephone. I noticed that they were both wearing
crisp white cotton shirts and the same navy jackets which were
obviously part of their uniform. As I approached, the fair-haired
receptionist looked up at me and stopped typing.

'Can I help you?' she asked, smiling broadly, and scanning my
face. I hoped that I did not look too unkempt. It was the end of the
day after all, I had come straight from work and I was feeling weary.

Mind you, my late night out with Alex probably had something to do with that. My working day had actually been quite productive and I had also received the good news that Fabio had reappeared unscathed. After the scare the night before this was a great weight lifted off all our minds. Apparently, on the spur of the moment, and without telling Will, he decided to take a trip to Castiglione del Lago alone, to the spot where Giulia's body had been found. I do not think that any of us could castigate him for not informing us where he was going in the circumstances, even though he had half worried us to death.

'Yes. My name's Alicia Allen,' I replied, pushing my hair back off my face. 'I have an appointment with Gregorio Pellegrino at six.'

'Could you sign in, please,' she said, pointing to the visitors' book just to the right of me, and handing me a visitor's pass with a metal clip, the type that never hangs straight on your lapel. I proceeded to complete the necessary details in the book. 'If you'd like to take a seat over there,' she continued, indicating to the area with leather sofas behind me and situated to the right of the main entrance, 'I'll let Mr Pellegrino's secretary know you're here.'

'Thank you,' I replied. I had nothing to read so before I sat down I picked up a firm's brochure from the stand in the corner of the reception area. While I waited I flicked through it and scanned Gregorio Pellegrino's profile, which confirmed what I already knew: he was a commercial lawyer specializing in finance and banking law and practised in New York before moving to London, just like Emilio. Unfortunately, there was no photograph of him, so I would have to keep guessing as to his appearance for a few more moments at least.

'Miss Allen.' I looked up. The fair-haired receptionist was standing in front of me. 'Mr Pellegrino will see you now. You need to take the lift to the third floor and his secretary will meet you there. If you'd like to follow me, I'll show you where the lifts are.' I stood up and she led me to them. They were on the far side of the building, away from reception. Mr Pellegrino's secretary was indeed waiting for me, a small wiry figure with cropped shiny black hair. She did not say one word as I followed her along the corridor to his office. She knocked on the door and then opened it.

'Miss Allen for you,' she said, standing aside allowing me to pass. I was struck by the vastness of his office and the floor-to-ceiling windows which made the room exceptionally light. I observed the rather rotund man with heavy features and curly grey hair which was receding at the front, sitting behind the desk. That was glass too. He stood up from his leather executive swivel chair, rounded the desk and held out his fleshy hand, which I dutifully shook. I noticed he had short, stubby fingers. He was only of middling height, but because he was vastly corpulent he had a looming presence. I estimated that he was in his late fifties or possibly early sixties.

'Please,' he said, pointing to the leather chair in front of his desk. 'Take a seat.' He spoke with only the trace of an Italian accent and if anything I could detect a slight American one. I felt consciously awkward as he eyed me up and down. He squeezed back behind his desk and lowered himself into his chair. 'Would you like a drink?' he asked.

'Water, please.'

'Annette,' he said, addressing his secretary who was still hovering in the doorway, 'please bring us some coffee and a bottle of water. Sparkling or still?' he asked, turning to me.

'Sparkling.'

'OK,' she replied, and left the room closing the door firmly on her way out.

'I appreciate you meeting with me today,' I said, sitting forward. The chair was uncomfortable as it was rather low and sloped backwards.

'Yes, well I'm happy to accommodate you, but I must admit I'm slightly intrigued by your request,' he replied, leaning back in his chair and scanning my face. 'What is it you want to know?' Although he was perfectly charming, there was something about him that made me feel uneasy, and it was not only the way he was looking at me.

'Fabio Angelino was hoping you might be able to shed some light on what happened to his father. We appreciate that there was an investigation at the time, but I'm sure you'd agree that it didn't reach a satisfactory conclusion,' I said expectantly, hoping for a positive response. It was difficult to ascertain what his thoughts were from his inscrutable expression.

'Well, everybody did what they could,' he replied matter-of-factly. 'The conclusion that was reached was acceptable in the circumstances.' Considering that Emilio was supposed to have been a close friend, this was not the answer I had anticipated.

'Do you really think so?'

'I very much want to help you, Alicia. May I call you that?' he said, folding his hands and resting his elbows on the table. I nodded. 'And I understand that this must mean a great deal to Fabio now that his mother has died and with the tragic news of his sister's recent death, but I fail to see how I can assist.'

'How do you know about his sister?' I asked, straying from the point.

'Because Fabio called my secretary, told her she had died and that you would be coming here alone as he had to leave for Italy immediately.' He responded quite aggressively; it appeared that he was riled by my questions, which I found strange. Fabio had of course spoken to Annette, but I was not sure of the specifics of their conversation.

'Sorry, I'm not making myself clear. I meant to ask you 'what' you know about it.'

'I don't understand the question. She drowned in a tragic accident, didn't she?'

'No. Mr Pellegrino. She was murdered.'

'What!' he exclaimed; he certainly seemed genuinely shocked. 'How did she die?'

'She was asphyxiated and then dumped in the water to make it look as if she'd drowned.' I noticed Pellegrino swallowing hard.

'And you believe that her murder has something to do with Emilio's disappearance?'

'Possibly,' I replied evasively as I did not want to divulge too much information, bearing in mind the whole purpose of my visit was to find out what he knew and to evaluate him as a possible suspect. If my "colleague" theory was correct I saw no reason to rule him out just yet. The fact that he had been a friend of Emilio and then Evelyn made that less likely, but I felt that he was not being entirely candid with me. If he really wanted to assist Fabio, I would have expected him to be more forthcoming. I certainly had no intention of mentioning the alleged attempt on Fabio's life which was the reason I had become embroiled in all this in the first place. At that moment Annette returned with the coffee and mineral water. She put down the tray on Pellegrino's desk and left the room.

'May I ask how you came to be instructed by Fabio?' he said, handing me the bottle of Highland Spring and the glass. Knowing that he had recommended Evelyn instruct his friend Roland Kettering to deal with the Probate of Emilio's estate, he was probably wondering why Fabio had not instructed him to deal with that of his mother. I watched him as he ripped open a sachet of Demerara sugar, tipped the contents into his coffee and stirred it around purposefully with a teaspoon.

'Through my uncle.'

'Your uncle?' He took a sip of coffee.

'Yes. He was a personal friend of Emilio and he's also Fabio's Godfather. You've met him actually.' For a split second Pellegrino sat back and closed his eyes as if he was somehow trying to recollect who my uncle was. I unscrewed the cap of the bottle of water and poured some into the glass.

'You don't mean Ludovico Magnani, by any chance?' he said, opening his eyes and looking at me.

'Yes.' I swallowed a mouthful of water.

'So you're his niece?' I nodded. 'My, my! What a small world it is! Is he still based in New York?'

'Yes.'

'I remember him well. I think we met only once, but we spoke on the 'phone a couple of times at least. I recall he was making enquiries of his own, which is why he contacted me.'

'I know. It's actually as a result of a conversation with him that I suggested to Fabio that we set up this meeting with you.'

'I see. But if you've already spoken to your uncle then why do you need to ask *me* any more questions?' He took another sip of coffee.

'Because, with all due respect, Mr Pellegrino, we do not accept the conclusions reached by the investigators in Sicily. For Fabio to have any chance of making progress with this case, it is vital that we investigate any leads we have in the hope of finding new evidence. To this end, we would like to track down as many of the colleagues Emilio was working with at, or around the time, he disappeared and re-question them.' I swallowed a couple more mouthfuls of water.

'But that's not going to be easy after all this time. How do you propose to manage it?'

'Maybe you can help with that.'

'How?'

'By putting me in touch with Emilio's colleagues.' He did not respond, but merely sat back and finished his coffee. 'It would also be of assistance to know more about his clients.'

'Well, that I could not tell you because of client confidentiality.' His tone was patronizing.

'I'm fully aware of the rules. I'm simply curious about his client list. Did any of them hold a grudge against him? Were any of them based in Sicily?'

'Emilio acted for a number of Italian clients. We both did. I still do.' His answer was evasive, but I tried to press him nonetheless, even though he was likely to equivocate.

'As a fellow Partner in the firm and someone who worked closely with Emilio Angelino, you are a specialist in the same field of law after all, you must have known who was on his client list, what he was working on and who with.'

'Yes, of course.' He could hardly deny knowledge of Emilio's business affairs. The likelihood was that after Emilio disappeared he would most likely have taken over responsibility for his workload before delegating it out to his numerous assistants.

'Then perhaps you could answer a point which has been puzzling me.' I felt that since he was being obstructive he would probably not answer it or at best vacillate, but it was worth pursuing nevertheless. 'You told my uncle that the police in Rome arrested Luigi Fagiolini's brother, Angelo, on suspicion of conspiring to kill Emilio.' Luigi Fagiolini was the client who had committed suicide.

'Well, they did. The case was dropped because there was insufficient evidence. What's your point?' he asked, sounding irritated. I felt he was beginning to get rattled.

'The evidence for his arrest came from independent witnesses. Fabio doesn't know who they are. Do you?'

'Me? Why should I know?' he replied defensively. 'What makes you ask?'

'It occurred to me that you might have some idea who it was, that's all,' I said casually, trying to defuse the situation. 'You asked me a few minutes ago whether I thought Giulia's murder and Emilio's disappearance are linked. May I ask you what you think?'

'I couldn't say. I suppose it's possible.' Again he evaded the question.

'Your acquaintance with Emilio went back many years. I understand you worked together in New York. Do you know anything about his family background or past that could help us shed light on either of these tragic events? Maybe there is something or someone we don't know about which or who could help us.'

'So far as I'm aware Emilio was an only child and his parents were immigrants from Italy. I can't tell you any more than that.' Unfortunately, that response took me no further forward either. I observed Pellegrino looking pointedly at his watch. I decided there was no purpose in persisting with my line of questioning and rather than him dismissing me, I decided to be the one to terminate the meeting and stood up.

'Thank you so much for your time this evening. It's been enlightening,' I said sarcastically. He seemed relieved that I was leaving. 'Oh, please don't bother to get up,' I said as he made a move to do so. 'I can find my own way out. Well, thank you again.' I offered my hand to him across the table which he took, turned and walked to the door. As I opened it, I spun around to speak to him. 'Goodbye, Mr Pellegrino.' I gave him a penetrating look.

'Goodbye,' he replied, and I left.

I followed the corridor back to the lifts. I called the lift and was standing waiting for it to arrive when Annette appeared. She held out her hand to me and, although it struck me as a rather odd thing for her to do, and I did not wish to be impolite, I took it.

'Thank you for coming in today,' she said, placing her other hand over the top of mine, and at the same time pressing a piece of paper into my palm. 'You seem like a good person. I know you'll do the right thing,' she added, squeezing my hand with both of hers and looking at me very hard. She sounded calm, but I could tell she was afraid because her hands were trembling. 'Please don't contact me. I won't be able to help you.'

'I don't understand,' I replied. 'Do the right thing about what?' The lift arrived, she let go of my hand and I stepped inside.

'Well, thank you for coming in, Miss Allen,' she said, in an official manner, no doubt for the benefit of the people in the lift who would have seen us together, and then the doors closed. I was perplexed by this unexpected turn of events and desperate to look at the piece of paper, but there were three other people in the lift and so I had no other alternative than to defer reading it until I was off the premises. Finally, we reached the ground floor. I still had my visitor's pass so I hastened over to the reception desk to return it and sign out. I had put it inside my handbag for safekeeping but in my haste to unzip my handbag and retrieve the pass I dropped the piece of paper. One of the men who had been in the lift, and who was walking behind me, must have seen what happened and picked it up.

'Yours, I believe,' he said, handing it to me. 'Keep Britain Tidy and all that,' he added pompously, and strolled off. I put it carefully in my jacket pocket, handed back my pass, signed out and left the building.

On my way to St Paul's tube station I called Antonia on her mobile to advise her that I would be home in approximately forty minutes. There was no response and I left a message. Fortunately, I did not have to wait more than a minute for a Central line tube to Holborn where I changed for a southbound Piccadilly line one to South Kensington. I managed to find a seat, and took the folded piece of paper out of my pocket. It was typewritten, unsigned and read as follows:

Contact Caterina Bartoldi. She used to work at the firm with Emilio Angelino. You'll find her at Williams, Ricks & Stone. Ask her to tell you what happened to Rosetta Bartlett.

Chapter 10

Although I was stunned to receive the note, I actually felt encouraged by its contents because I now had something concrete to investigate. It meant that the trip to the offices of Scarpetti, Steiglitz & Co. had not been entirely wasted and my instincts about Emilio's colleagues being in some way connected to his disappearance might be right. The fact that Mr Pellegrino was deliberately evasive when I mentioned contacting them confirmed, in my mind at least, that he was either trying to conceal something or shield someone, and that someone could well be himself.

What I did find hard to reconcile was the difference between the caring, considerate man I had expected to meet and the hard-nosed, unsympathetic individual I found facing me across the desk. It was hard to believe that this was the same person who went out of his way to help Evelyn; but I had also observed his charming side for myself.

As for Annette, she could not be loyal to Pellegrino if she was willing to give me information, and yet, she must have worked for him for at least sixteen years if I was reading between the lines of that note correctly. It occurred to me that she might have been deliberately unfriendly to Danielle on the telephone to create the impression that she was indifferent to Fabio's plight, so that no-one would suspect her for assisting us, but why she was willing to help perplexed me. She was definitely nervous of anyone seeing her give me the note and clearly afraid of something.

If Caterina Bartoldi was working at Williams, Ricks & Stone she could be located easily. There was no guarantee she would speak with me and I had a strong feeling that she might not be willing, which gave me some concern.

I came out of South Kensington tube station and, as I crossed over to the Old Brompton Road, I heard my mobile buzzing in my pocket. My immediate thought was that it was Antonia returning my call, or more likely wanting to know how much longer it would be before I was home. The sun was shining on the screen and I could not see who was ringing.

'*Ciao, sorellina,*' I said, answering it.

'Alicia?' It was Will. I knew that he and Fabio had intended to travel down to Orvieto that day to question Laura but, with all the commotion over Fabio's disappearance the previous evening, I wondered whether they had actually made it.

'Oh! Hi, Will. I thought it was Antonia.'

'So I gather.'

'Yes, I'm expecting her for dinner. I'm running a bit late and she's probably waiting for me at home. How are you?'

'We're both fine. We're in Orvieto.'

'Have you seen Laura?'

'Yes. Fabio wants to talk to you. I'll hand you over to him.'

'OK. Take care. Oh, and Will, congratulations by the way. Jo told me about the baby.'

'Thanks. Speak to you soon. Bye, Alicia.'

'*Ciao.*'

'Hi, Alicia. How did the meeting with Pellegrino go?' asked Fabio.

'Put it this way, he wasn't at all helpful. I'll tell you about that in a minute. I want to hear your news. What did Laura say?' I asked as I turned into Onslow Square. I hovered on the pavement. I did not want to return home until I had finished this conversation.

'Not much. She insists she doesn't know anything, but she's very distraught and I'm not convinced that she's being completely honest with us.'

'Maybe she's afraid of something.'

'That's my feeling exactly. It's very frustrating though. I wish she'd talk to me. Giulia was *my* sister after all.' My heart went out to him.

'Don't give up on her. Let her know where you'll be for the next few days. With any luck she'll call you.'

'If only I shared your enthusiasm. What if she doesn't?'

'Then go and see her again.'

'I wish you were here. I think she'd open up to you, and you have a way of extracting information out of people.'

'You give me too much credit. I wasn't exactly successful with Pellegrino this evening.'

'I'm really surprised he was so unobliging. Knowing how kind he was to my mother, I would have expected him to go out of his way to accommodate us. Tell me what happened?' I filled Fabio in on my conversation with Pellegrino and then told him about Annette. 'Well, it looks like you've had a more productive day than I have,' he said. 'But this puts a completely different spin on things. When you indicated to me the other day that you thought one or several of my father's colleagues could be involved, I admit I regarded your suggestion with muted scepticism, but now I really think you're spot on.'

'Hmm... Well, let's not get too carried away quite yet. My theory is still unproven.' Although I believed we were on the right lines we had no evidence to substantiate it. I was conscious not to build up Fabio's hopes only for them to come crashing down. That would be the last thing he needed, especially in the circumstances.

'But what about the note?'

'We follow it up and see where it leads us. Have you ever heard of either of the names mentioned?'

'No. I don't recall my father ever referring to them, but then there's no reason why he should. I vaguely remember Annette, but she never worked for him. Maybe you should call her and ask her to give you more details.'

'If she was able to speak to me openly she wouldn't have given me the note in that clandestine manner. Anyway, she made it very clear that she doesn't wish to be contacted and I'd be unwilling to do anything which will put her at risk.'

'You could always go to the police.'

'And tell them what? The note in itself proves nothing. We have no evidence remember.'

'What do you think happened to Rosetta Bartlett, Alicia?'

'I expect she's dead.'

'How do you work that one out?'

'Because the note tells us to ask Caterina about her. If she's alive, why would we need to? We could speak to her directly.'

'She might have gone away.'

'True. But do you really believe that?' I for one certainly did not.

'Are you happy to pursue that side of things?'

'If you want me to.'

'I do. Let's hope Caterina will talk to you.'

'We'll soon find out. I'll try and get in touch with her after my meeting with Roland Kettering.'

'Oh, yes of course. You're seeing him in the morning, aren't you? With any luck he'll be more amenable than Pellegrino.'

'I wouldn't bet on it, but you never know.'

'I'm going to Florence tomorrow, to the British Consulate to register Giulia's death.'

'OK. Hope they're helpful. I'd better go. Antonia's waiting for me. I'll call you tomorrow. Take care now.'

'You too. Bye, Alicia.'

I walked past the railings at the front of the house and saw Dorothy waving to me from her living room window. She was beckoning for me to come in. Her front door was ajar and as I pushed it open and stepped into the hallway I could hear Dorothy pottering about in the kitchen.

'Is that you, dear?' she called out.

'Yes,' I replied, shutting the front door.

'Your sister's here. We've been waiting for you in the garden,' she said, walking into the living room. I followed Dorothy out onto the patio where Antonia was sitting under the shade of a large umbrella.

'You've been ages,' said Antonia, peering at me through her sunglasses and sounding disgruntled. Clearly she had had time to shower and change before making her way over to me because she was looking remarkably fresh. I was feeling particularly grimy after my journey home on the tube.

'I did call you. Didn't you get my voice message?'

'Oh yes. But I didn't think you'd be this long,' she said, glancing down at her watch. 'Fortunately, Dorothy rescued me and invited me in for a drink.' I noticed the jug of homemade lemonade on the table.

'You must be very thirsty,' said Dorothy, pouring me a large tumbler full and handing it to me.

'Thanks,' I replied, taking it from her and smiling. 'I am. It's so hot today.'

'Yes, it is. Have you had a difficult day?'

'An eventful one. Your flowers are holding up well in this heat, Dorothy,' I said, changing the subject and looking at Dorothy's cornucopia of trailing mauve and pink petunias and white geraniums in the centre of the garden. 'What are those pretty multi-coloured little flowers over there?' I asked, pointing to the troughs on either side of the French doors.

'Those are busy Lizzies. I like them because they come in a variety of colours but they need to be watered much more frequently than the petunias and geraniums and these days I find lifting the watering can quite difficult.' I had noticed that Dorothy was becoming increasingly frail.

'I could pop down and do that for you in the morning before I go to work,' I said. 'It would only take me five minutes.' I was conscious that she was very independent and would never ask for any assistance even though she needed it.

'That's very sweet of you, dear, but I really don't expect you to do that for me.'

'Well,' I said, finishing my glass of lemonade and putting the glass on the table, 'we'll talk about that later. I suppose I should think about making a start on dinner,' I said, turning to Antonia. 'Would you like to join us, Dorothy?' Antonia kicked my foot under the table in protest.

'Oh, no, dear. You two want time together. I shall enjoy sitting out here for a while.' Antonia looked relieved by that response and wasted no time in standing up.

'All right. Can you manage that?' I asked, observing Dorothy as she put the three empty glasses and the jug on the tray. I picked it up for her.

'Oh, thank you,' she said. I carried it through to the kitchen and she followed me out. 'Take this,' she said, handing me a Hayley Westenra CD. 'She sings *"O mio babbino caro"* on it. I thought you you'd like to borrow it.'

'That's so thoughtful, Dorothy,' I replied, taking the CD. 'I'll see you later.' I pecked her on the cheek. 'Thanks for the drink.'

'Oh, yes, thanks,' said Antonia, who was already waiting by the front door with her hand on the latch itching to leave.

'Keep an eye on the penne,' I said to Antonia. 'I'll only be five minutes.'

'Why? Where are you going?' she replied, glancing at me. She was sitting on the sofa with her feet up on the stool and flicking through the television channels with the remote controls.

'For a shower.'

'Oh, all right.'

When I returned to the room Antonia was still watching television and I doubt that she had actually moved.

'Do you want green salad with your pasta?' I asked, walking through to the kitchen, turning the gas down under the saucepan of penne and taking a jar of home-made tomato sauce and some rocket out of the fridge.

'Yes, that'd be great,' she called out. I took the lid off the jar and poured some of the sauce into another saucepan to heat it through. I washed the salad and put it in a glass bowl. 'Oh, and Alex rang while you were in the shower,' she said, appearing in the kitchen doorway.

'What did he say?' I said, taking the colander out of the bottom cupboard to the left of the sink, picking up the saucepan of penne and draining it.

'Oh, I didn't speak to him. He left a message on the answer-phone.' I reached into the store cupboard for a bottle of extra virgin olive oil and balsamic vinegar. I poured out a spoonful of the olive oil and tossed the pasta in it. 'He wanted to know how your meeting went with Pellegrino. Anyone I know?'

'No,' I replied, tipping the pasta back into the saucepan, picking up the smaller saucepan of heated tomato sauce and stirring it in to the pasta. 'Pass me those bowls would you,' I said, pointing to the ones on the work surface. She handed them to me and I served up.

'You're very tense,' she commented, picking up the bowls of pasta. 'What's going on?'

'Nothing. What makes you ask?' I said, opening the kitchen drawer and taking out the cutlery.

'Because I know you; and Alex sounded anxious.' I sprinkled the salad with olive oil and balsamic vinegar. 'You're not working on anything bad are you?' I picked up the cutlery, the salad bowl and my large pepper mill and we walked through to the living room with them.

'No. I'm just helping out a client.' We sat down at the table. 'Oh, I've forgotten the Parmesan cheese and the wine,' I said, and went to fetch the cheese and an open bottle of Chianti from the kitchen.

'Don't you want to listen to Alex's message?' asked Antonia as I returned to the living room.

'Yes, and I'll ring him later,' I replied, putting the cheese and wine on the table. I sat down again, picked up the pepper mill and twisted it a couple of times until I had enough cracked black pepper on my pasta.

'When I've gone, you mean?' I did not respond. 'Are you and Alex going to move in together?' she asked, sprinkling Parmesan cheese over her pasta.

'I thought you'd come over to talk to me about Tom,' I said, and then I noticed we had no wine glasses. 'Have you reached any sort of decision yet?' I took a couple of glasses out of my dwarf cabinet next to the dining room table, poured some wine into her glass and handed it to her.

'There's been a new development.'

'Right,' I said, filling my own glass and taking a seat. 'What's that?'

'Tom and I got engaged yesterday and we're staying in London, for now anyway.'

'Oh, that's fantastic news. I'm so happy for you.' I rushed around to her side of the table to give her a hug.

'We're shopping for engagement rings on Saturday, but you can't tell anyone until he has bought it for me.'

'It's not for me to say anything. Aren't you coming to see Uncle Vico at the weekend then?'

'Mamma called me and said he'll be arriving on Friday.'

'Well?'

'Yes. If I have my ring.'

'Of course,' I said slightly sarcastically. *'Me lo immaginavo!'*

'Where did you say Caterina Bartoldi works?' asked Alex. Antonia had left and I was returning his call. I had filled him in on the day's events and although, once again, he continued to voice concerns over my involvement in the matter, he was being very constructive and supportive.

'Williams, Ricks & Stone. Why? Do you know anyone at the firm?'

'As a matter of fact, I do. Dominic works there. I'll give him a call if you like and see if I can find out anything about Caterina for you. When were you planning on contacting her?'

'After my meeting with Kettering tomorrow morning. Who's Dominic?'

'A friend of mine from Law School.'

'You seem to have friends everywhere.'

'Not really. It's just that most of my group went into the City to work for commercial firms like Williams, Ricks & Stone. Dominic specializes in commercial property litigation. I'll try and get hold of him first thing in the morning. Ring me after your meeting with Kettering. I should have some news for you by then.'

'Thanks.'

'Well, you know what they say: "forewarned is forearmed." Are you OK? You sound very flat.'

'As I said to Dorothy earlier, it's been an eventful day.'

Chapter 11

After my unproductive meeting with Gregorio Pellegrino the day before, I arrived at the offices of Smythson, Reid & Monkton with no expectations whatsoever. I had no idea what reception I would receive from Roland Kettering and, despite the comments Graham Ffoulkes had made about him, I decided to keep an open mind. I was pleased to have the opportunity to speak with him at all. As well as quizzing him in respect of the work he had carried out for the Angelino family, I was curious about his long-standing association with Mr Pellegrino. I had not had the opportunity to ask Mr Pellegrino how they came to be acquainted and that was a question I wanted to put to Mr Kettering.

The offices of Smythson, Reid & Monkton were situated in Queen Anne's Gate, within walking distance of our offices and therefore much more conveniently located for my purposes than Scarpetti, Steiglitz & Co. It was also a very different type of firm: established in the mid-nineteenth century and renowned for acting for wealthy private individuals rather than corporate bodies.

I had barely arrived and announced myself to the receptionist when Mr Kettering's middle-aged, somewhat po-faced secretary appeared and ushered me upstairs to one of the small conference rooms on the first floor. It had an oval smoked-glass table surrounded by six Barcelona-style black leather button-backed chairs. I sat down in the chair opposite the door and waited for only a few minutes before Mr Kettering himself entered the room. On seeing him I stood up. He was of medium height like Pellegrino, but exceptionally thin with regular but angular features. His skin was lined and since he was very tanned I suspected he owed his wrinkles more to too much time spent in the sun rather than his age. His grey hair was combed straight back off his face which completed the severe look.

'Miss Allen,' he said, striding forward and shaking my hand vigorously, 'I've asked Elaine to bring us some coffee. Is that all right with you?' He had a way of throwing his head back and peering down his nose when he spoke which gave him an arrogant air. His speech was also rather affected with strongly overstressed vowels.

'Yes. Thank you.'

'Now,' he said, pulling out a chair and sitting down opposite me, 'I understand that you're acting for Fabio Angelino. I must say it really is a very tragic family, first his father and now his sister. I suppose you know that I acted for his mother many years ago?' he said, with a sense of self-importance.

'Yes. That's why I'm here.'

'Oh?' I was slightly surprised by his response because I thought Fabio had made the purpose of the meeting quite clear when he originally rang for an appointment.

'I was hoping to ask you some questions about the case. I appreciate that we're talking of events which took place many years ago, but it occurred to me that you might recollect this matter because of its highly unusual circumstances.'

'I do remember it, of course, but you will appreciate that *even I* can't recall the exact details,' he said pompously.

'I wouldn't expect you to.'

'If you want the minutiae then you'd need to read the files and I very much doubt whether we still have them in storage.'

'Would you be able to check?'

'I could, but don't be too hopeful because it's the firm's policy to destroy papers after ten years.'

'I know Fabio would be grateful if you checked all the same. He's keen to reinvestigate the events surrounding his father's disappearance.'

'That's his prerogative; but is there any point? A thorough investigation was carried out at the time. I don't believe anything would be achieved by raking over the past. My advice, for what it's worth, would be to move forward. It's very negative to keep harping back on these things.'

'Yes, but Fabio doesn't accept that the conclusion reached was satisfactory, only convenient.'

'That's as maybe, but he'll never prove otherwise,' he said, with a self-satisfied look, leaning back in his chair and folding his arms in front of him.

'How can you be so certain?'

'I don't suppose you've had many dealings with Italian officials in your *limited* experience, so you wouldn't fully appreciate how difficult obtaining information on matters such as this is. When you've been practising law for as long as I have, then you might do.' I objected to him patronizing me, but I let his offensive remark pass because I saw no reason to justify myself to this priggish man. Graham's remarks about him were absolutely correct. Elaine appeared with the tray of coffee, placed it on the table and promptly left the room again.

'Do you act for many Italian clients?' I asked as he handed me my cup. I was aware that he had done so in the past from what Graham had told me, but I was curious about the present. 'Thank you,' I said as he passed me the milk jug.

'For quite a few, yes.' I poured some milk into my coffee, handed him back the jug and he did likewise.

'I presume a good proportion of your referrals come via Mr Pellegrino – like Fabio's mother, for example?' I said, picking up my cup.

'Yes. But as well as my Italian clients I do have a number of UK clients with interests in Italy. One of my specialities is advising them on all the legal formalities of buying property in Italy, including how to avoid the numerous pitfalls.' I took a sip of coffee; it was bitter and gritty and I promptly put the cup down.

'I see.' In order to ask him further questions about Mr Pellegrino I needed to find some way of steering him back to that topic of conversation. It was apparent he wished to lecture me about the advantages and disadvantages of buying property in Italy and I would have to be patient.

'I'm not sure whether you do,' he said with similar condescension as he gulped a mouthful of coffee. I was amazed he could drink it, because to me it tasted absolutely disgusting; if he offered that to his Italian clients, I am surprised he had any. 'What a lot of people don't realize is that, when it comes to buying real estate in Italy, there are a number of ways of registering ownership of the property and this makes a big difference to what happens when it is eventually disposed of. Many acrimonious family disputes could be avoided by taking proper legal advice and making sure any Will takes into account the Italian assets.'

'Then presumably you advise on the Italian law of inheritance as well?'

'Yes. I expect you're not aware how different Italian Inheritance law is from ours.' He finished his coffee.

'I am, actually,' I replied tongue-in-cheek.

'Well, I generally advise my clients to make both a British and Italian Will to ensure they're covered by the different inheritance rules of the two legal systems,' he said, ignoring my response. 'You'd be surprised how often I receive requests to help trace lost family assets in Italy which can be an unenviable task at the best of times even with all my experience.'

'Hmm… That's very interesting.' I paused for a moment. 'It must be very useful having Mr Pellegrino as a contact though,' I said, hoping to change the subject back. 'How do you know each other?'

'We met through a mutual legal acquaintance in Tuscany while I was buying property out there.' Graham had said that Mr Kettering owned property in "Chiantishire" when he was his Principal, which would be at least twenty years ago, and I supposed it was possible

Mr Pellegrino's and Mr Kettering's association began around that time.

'I didn't know Mr Pellegrino used to specialize in property law. I thought he had always been a banking law specialist,' I said innocently, hoping to draw him.

'Oh, no, you misunderstand me. The lawyer who was dealing with my affairs introduced me to him. He's a friend of his.'

'I see. So it's Mr Pellegrino's friend who's the property specialist?'

'Yes.'

'But due to the nature of your work you must have a number of dealings with him yourself?'

'As a matter of fact, I do. Anyway,' he said, glancing at his watch and cutting me short, 'I'm afraid I have an *important* meeting in five minutes. Is there anything else you would like to ask me about Emilio Angelino's case?'

'Off the record, do you think the investigation came to the right conclusion?'

'I was not instructed to give advice about the way the investigation in Sicily was conducted, Miss Allen, merely to deal with the winding up of Emilio Angelino's estate.' I felt he was being deliberately awkward.

'I appreciate that, but with respect that is not what I asked you.'

'I understood your question perfectly. I am not in a position to comment on that side of things.'

'But, you must have an opinion on the case.'

'I'm afraid I do not. Now, if you will excuse me I really do have to get to my next meeting,' he said dismissively, and standing up.

'Fabio Angelino speaks very highly of you,' I said, pretending not to have noticed his rudeness. 'He will always be grateful for the help that you gave his family. If you think of anything that could assist him please contact me. Thank you for your time today.' I offered him my hand which he accepted with indifference and then he stood aside at the door to let me pass.

'How did your meeting go?' asked Alex. As agreed, I had called him as soon as I returned to the office. I was feeling both deflated and irritated by Mr Kettering's negative responses to my questions.

'It was a disaster. I'm sure there's something going on between him and Pellegrino.'

'What makes you say that?'

'Neither of them wants to help and Kettering was very adamant about Fabio not digging up the past.'

'Perhaps he meant it kindly.' Alex had to be joking.

'I doubt that very much. More likely he doesn't want us to go looking in case we find something we're not supposed to. Oh, let's talk about this later. I can't go over it all again right now.' I was frustrated because I was hoping to make some progress for Fabio's sake.

'I take it you don't want to hear what I found out about Caterina Bartoldi then?'

'Of course I do.'

'Just checking.'

'So you managed to speak to Dominic?'

'I did.'

'And does he know her?'

'Only by sight. They've never spoken, but then she works in the commercial property department.'

'Not a banking lawyer then?'

'You mean you thought she might be because Emilio was?'

'It did cross my mind. Maybe Dominic can find out some more details about her for us.'

'I've asked him to.'

'Mind you, it might not be necessary if I manage to speak to her.'

'Let's hope she's willing to talk. When are you going to ring her?'

'No time like the present.'

'Do you want the number?'

'I have it. I looked up her firm's details on the internet after I called you last night.'

'Have you spoken to Fabio today?'

'Not yet. Wish me luck with Caterina. Are you coming over tonight?'

'Do you want me to?'

'I wouldn't be asking you if I didn't.'

'See you later then. *Ciao, bella.*'

'*Ciao.* Bye.'

I dialled the number for Williams, Ricks & Stone and asked to speak with Caterina Bartoldi. There was a time lag of about thirty seconds before the receptionist put me through to her secretary.

'Mrs Bartoldi's office. Caroline speaking. May I help you?'

'I hope so. Is Mrs Bartoldi available?'

'Whom shall I say is calling?'

'Alicia Allen.'

'Is that Miss or Mrs?'

'Miss.'

'And what is it in connection with?'

'She has been recommended to me.'

'If you'd like to hold, I'll check she's free. One moment please.' I heard a few beeps and then the secretary's voice back on the line. 'Just putting you through to Mrs Bartoldi now, Miss Allen,' she said.

'Caterina Bartoldi speaking. How can I help you Miss Allen?'

'I understand you used to work at Scarpetti Steiglitz & Co.' There was a momentary pause before she responded.

'What concern is that of yours?' she replied sharply.

'I believe you worked with Emilio Angelino.'

'And why are you interested in that?'

'Because I'm a solicitor at Crawford Ffoulkes Piper & Co. and I'm acting for his son, Fabio.' I heard her take a sharp intake of breath and then there was another pause at the end of the 'phone. For one second I thought she had hung up on me. 'Mrs Bartoldi?' I said.

'How did you find out about me?'

'I can't tell you that.' I was conscious not to say anything which might jeopardise Annette.

'What do you want?'

'Fabio is desperate to discover the truth surrounding his father's disappearance. On the basis that you worked with Emilio Angelino, we're hoping you might be able to help us.'

'You've wasted your time calling me. I really can't do anything for you.'

'Please, Mrs Bartoldi. Fabio's sister was murdered at the beginning of this week and we have reason to believe that her death could be connected to what happened to her father.'

'I'm genuinely sorry for your client's loss, Miss Allen, but as I said I cannot help you. I would rather you didn't contact me again.'

'What about Rosetta Bartlett?' There was yet another pause.

'Where did you get her name?'

'What happened to her, Mrs Bartoldi?' I replied, ignoring her question. She did not respond. 'She's dead, isn't she?' Again there was no response. I knew she was still on the line because I could hear her breathing. 'Was she murdered? Is that why you don't want to get involved?'

'I'm not prepared to talk about it. Just leave me alone,' she shouted down the 'phone and hung up.

Chapter 12

'How did you get on with Caterina Bartoldi?' Alex called out as he stepped inside the flat. I had left my front door on the latch because I was expecting him and was sitting watching a DVD of *Wait until Dark*, another Audrey Hepburn favourite of mine. 'I would have rung you, but I was stuck in a meeting all afternoon.'

'That's all right,' I replied, switching off the DVD player with the remote control, and padding out into the hall. 'There's nothing much to report anyway.'

'Why? What happened?' I watched him as he bent down to take off his shoes.

'I blew it. She wouldn't talk to me.'

'Don't be so hard on yourself,' he said, putting his arm around my shoulders and giving me a reassuring squeeze. 'It isn't anything less than we expected. I'm sure you handled the situation the best way you could. It was worth a try, and if nothing else it proves that we're on to something. I'd say that was a positive rather than a negative.'

'Hmm... You wouldn't be saying that to raise my spirits by any chance?'

'No. Don't be despondent,' he said, catching hold of my hand. 'I reckon she doesn't want to get involved because she's frightened of any potential backlash from Pellegrino and his associates. That's probably why she left Scarpetti, Steiglitz & Co in the first place – to dissociate herself from the whole Emilio scenario. How did she seem?'

'Anxious and afraid,' I replied, letting go of his hand and walking through to the living room.

'Exactly,' he said, following me in. 'And hearing from you out of the blue like that must have been a shock. I'm not surprised she reacted defensively.'

'That's as may be, Alex, but if she does know something, and won't tell us, how will we ever make any headway with this case?' Alex sat down on the sofa, but I remained standing.

'I don't imagine you were on the 'phone long enough to ferret any details out of her at all really, were you?' he asked, patting the seat cushion next to him. I took that as a hint to join him on the sofa.

'Well, long enough for me to explain why I was calling, request her help and for her to refuse!' I replied, sitting down.

'Then you didn't manage to ask her about Rosetta Bartlett?'

'Not in so many words, although she didn't deny it when I suggested that she was murdered. She hung up before I had a chance to say anything else, not that I think my further pleas for help would have made a blind bit of difference. Did Dominic get back to you with more information about her?'

'I'm meeting him for a drink after work on Monday. I realize this case is on your mind, but is everything else OK?' he said, scrutinising my face. 'Only you seem a bit withdrawn tonight.'

'Am I? I'm sorry to be such poor company. I don't mean to be.'

'How about you give me a kiss then?' he said, turning his head sideways and pointing to his cheek. 'I haven't had one yet. I'm feeling a bit neglected.' I moved forward to kiss him on the cheek but as I did so he turned his head and kissed me on the mouth. 'Gotcha!' he said. I laughed. 'It works every time. *And* I made you smile. Come here,' he said, putting his arm around me again and pulling me close to him. 'This Fabio thing is really getting to you, isn't it? How about you have an evening off from worrying about him and we go out and have some fun.'

'OK. You're on.'

'Good. It is Friday after all and I won't get to see you over the weekend because I have to work on my deal.'

'All weekend?'

'Yes. Sorry.'

'My uncle's arriving tomorrow morning. I'm meeting him at the airport and driving him down to my mother's. I was going to ask you if you wanted to join us. I didn't realize you'd be working.'

'Neither did I, but that's the way these deals are sometimes. Shall we go?'

'I'll just grab my shoes and a coat,' I said, jumping off the sofa.

'You won't need a jacket. It's baking out there tonight.'

I sprinted along to my bedroom, rummaged through the shoe boxes in the bottom of the wardrobe for the black sandals I wanted, pulled them out and was about to put them on when the 'phone rang. The cordless handset was on my bedside table and I walked around the side of the bed to answer it.

'Hello,' I said, picking up one sandal and slipping it on.

'Alicia, how are you?' It was Fabio.

'I'm all right, thanks,' I replied, trying to sound upbeat. 'How are things with you?' I asked, putting on my other sandal.

'I was just calling to hear how the meeting went with Roland Kettering and if you managed to make contact with Caterina Bartoldi?'

'Kettering was as unhelpful as Pellegrino. There's not much to choose between them. I have to say I disliked the man intensely.'

'Why? What did he say?' I summarized my conversation with him. 'I don't remember him being quite as patronizing as that, Alicia, although I always thought he was pompous. His association with Pellegrino intrigues me though. I wonder who this mutual legal acquaintance of theirs is.'

'Yes, I've been thinking about that too.' I could hear Alex tiptoeing along the hall and then he popped his head around my bedroom door. 'It's Fabio,' I mouthed, putting my hand over the mouthpiece. Alex nodded, hovered in the doorway for a second and then I heard him amble through the hall to the living room. I wanted him to listen to my conversation with Fabio and decided to join him.

'Alicia, are you still there?' asked Fabio, picking up on the momentary silence at my end of the line.

'Sorry, Fabio,' I replied, smiling at Alex who was sitting back on the sofa pulling faces and distracting me. 'I didn't find that out, unfortunately. He was more interested in trying to impress me with his knowledge of Italian property and inheritance law and I was lucky to be able to extract anything from him at all.'

'Didn't you tell him that you know all about that Italian stuff?'

'Well, I wouldn't say that I'm an expert. I'm familiar with it, but it's not an area I advise on every day.'

'Even so, he had no reason to patronize you. You should have responded to him in Italian when he spoke to you like that.'

'It wasn't worth the bother.'

'But it would have put him in his place.'

'I doubt it. His ego's far too massive.'

'So what are your thoughts about this mutual acquaintance?' he asked, reverting to the original point.

'It could be something or nothing. Kettering certainly seems to have a lot of dealings with him. I'm not quite sure what to make of the arrangement.'

'Why? Do you think that what they're involved in is underhand?'

'Possibly, but I couldn't say.' I sat down on the sofa next to Alex.

'Hmm… What about the fact that he doesn't want us to reopen the investigation? What do you think about that?'

'I'm positive he knows something about it and doesn't want us to. The problem is that all we can do at present is to speculate about what that might be. Both he and Pellegrino were only too eager to point out how difficult it would be for us to get any information and we certainly can't count on either of them for assistance in obtaining some. Having spoken to Caterina, I'm convinced that there is a connection between Scarpetti, Steiglitz & Co and what happened to your father, but I…'

'She took your call then? What did she say?' he said eagerly.

'I hate to dampen your enthusiasm, but she refused to help us. It's not what she said, but how she reacted to my questions which leads me to believe she's afraid about any involvement with the firm. I'm not quite sure what we can do about procuring proof, but I do intend to persevere with Caterina.' Although I was sitting next to Alex, I could see him raise his eyebrows out of the corner of my eye and shake his head in disbelief. He must have realized that I was not going to give up quite *that* easily.

'Maybe *I* should try and persuade her to help; after all Emilio was *my* father.'

'But you'd have to lie to get past her secretary and then she'll probably hang up if you do manage to speak to her.'

'How were you intending to talk to her again then?'

'Don't worry. I'll find a way.'

'Sorry, Alicia, what were you about to say when I interrupted you earlier?'

'Umm…I can't remember…' I paused momentarily to collect my thoughts. 'Oh, yes, it was about Kettering's part in all this. I'm pretty certain Pellegrino is involved but I believe that Kettering is too.'

'Because Kettering was the one Pellegrino recommended to deal with my father's estate?'

'Partly, since that meant he would have been kept in the loop, but more importantly Pellegrino knew he could trust Kettering. Even though I have a strong feeling they could be connected with what happened to Giulia, at present I have no idea how. I wish I had more positive news for you.'

'I can't say Will or I have made much progress here either, although there is a glimmer of hope.'

'Really? What's that?'

'I received a call from Laura this evening when I returned from

Florence. She's asked to see me alone on Sunday.'

'At least she rang you. That's a start.'

'I took your advice and it's paid off, so thank you.'

'Don't thank me just yet. Wait until you've spoken to her. You'll be staying on in Orvieto?'

'Yes, for a few days. Laura's family don't actually live in Orvieto, but up in the hills. The house is surrounded by olive groves and vineyards.'

'It sounds very picturesque.'

'Yes, it's a real picture postcard setting, but it's a bit of a hike to get there as it's well off the beaten track.'

'Let me know how it goes.'

'I will. What are you up to this weekend?'

'Uncle Vico's arriving in the morning.'

'I'll be interested to hear what he makes of all this.'

'You're not the only one. How's Will?'

'Enjoying a well-deserved glass of Orvieto abboccato, I hope. I'd better go. Speak to you later, Alicia.'

'Yes. Bye, Fabio.' I pressed the 'off' button on the 'phone and put it down on the coffee table in front of the sofa. 'Did you follow that?' I asked Alex.

'More or less. You can tell me all about it on the way to dinner. I'm absolutely starving,' he said, standing up.

'Me too.'

'You've obviously not eaten enough Pringles today,' he said, giving me a knowing sideways glance as he went out into the hall and picked up his shoes. 'Where do you want to eat?' he said, bending down and slipping them back on.

'Anywhere we don't have to sit inside. I feel like some air.'

'So how's Fabio bearing up?' asked Alex as we sat down at one of the tables outside the restaurant.

'I thought you wanted me to have a Fabio-free night out,' I replied as one of the waiter's appeared with a basket of assorted bread, placed it in the middle of the table and handed each of us a menu.

'Can I bring you drinks to start with?' he asked, standing with his hands folded behind his back and inclining himself towards Alex.

'Yes. What would you like?' said Alex, addressing me.

'Water, please.'

'Sparkling?'

'Yes.'

'Would you like the wine list, Sir?'

'Yes. Thank you.' The waiter walked away. 'In answer to your question, Alicia, I desperately want you to have a Fabio-free night, but I know you won't stop thinking about him until you've told me what's on your mind. You've been preoccupied since we left the flat,' he said, taking a small white roll covered in poppy seeds out of the basket and putting it on his side plate.

'I was considering what I've achieved so far which is precisely nothing. I'm rather anxious about where we go from here.'

'What do you mean?' he said, breaking off a piece of roll and popping it in his mouth. He then offered me the basket. 'Have some bread.' I picked out a slice of walnut bread.

'Well, I encouraged Fabio to reconsider the events surrounding his father's disappearance. Maybe we should have let it be.'

'You mean because Giulia's been murdered?' I shrugged my shoulders. 'Oh, come on, Alicia! That's nonsense and you know it. Both the incident with Fabio in Italy and Giulia's murder took place before you started asking any questions about Emilio. The only reason why you're involved at all is because you were lumbered with the Probate of Fabio's mother's estate through the association with your uncle. There's nothing you could have done to prevent those events from occurring. You've already gone out of your way to help Fabio and, contrary to what you think I believe, you are making headway.'

'I'm concerned about anyone else getting hurt or killed.'

'So am I, particularly *you*! Why do you think I'm anxious about you all the time?' he said, leaning across the table and gently squeezing my hand.

'I know.' The waiter returned with the bottle of water and poured some into each of our glasses and handed Alex the wine list.

'Are you ready to order?' he asked, looking first at Alex and then at me.

'Could you give us a couple of minutes,' I said. He nodded, smiled at me and walked away.

'What do you want to eat?' asked Alex, picking up the menu.

'Something light. I'm not that hungry.'

'I thought you said you were starving before.'

'I've lost my appetite.'

'Because of what I said?'

'No.'

'Well, something has upset you.'

'It's all this business with Fabio.'

'Let's not talk about it then. I promised you a night off, remember. I shouldn't have mentioned him.'

'There's nothing I can do about it tonight anyway.'

'Glad we agree on something!' said Alex with a smile.

Chapter 13

Although it was lovely to see Uncle Vico again and to spend more time with Nonna, the news of Antonia's engagement to Tom triggered questions about the status of my relationship with Alex which I tried hard to avoid, and I was relieved to return home on Sunday evening. I was pleased to have collected my uncle from Heathrow on Saturday morning because at least I had the opportunity to talk to him at length about Fabio on the drive down to Surrey and to sound my ideas off him. Like Alex, he was adamant that I should not reproach myself for suggesting Fabio reinvestigate the circumstances surrounding Emilio's disappearance.

He indicated that if I was able to obtain some evidence or leads in relation to the Italian side of the investigation he might be in a position to assist me. Apparently he had managed to establish links with several useful contacts in Italy over recent years and was willing to call on them. Unfortunately, he did not come up with any suggestions on how I should set about procuring evidence to confirm Pellegrino's complicity in the affair, which was disappointing.

Aware that Fabio was meeting Laura on Sunday, I repeatedly checked my mobile throughout the day hoping to hear from him. As soon as I arrived home that evening I rushed to my answerphone, but there were no messages at all, not even from Alex. I 'phoned him to find out how his work was progressing but there was no response from any of his numbers. Impatient for news of Fabio I then rang Jo to find out if Will had called, but her landline was permanently engaged and her mobile switched off.

Frustrated on all fronts, I settled down to some household chores which I had woefully neglected the previous week for one reason or another. I changed my sheets, put the dirty laundry in the washing machine, cleaned the bathroom and kitchen, and vacuumed and dusted the rest of the flat. The one remaining task – and the worst one of all – was the ironing. I was tempted to leave it, but that would only mean double the work next time around so, reluctantly, I retrieved the ironing board and my steam iron from the utility cupboard in the hall and methodically ploughed my way through it. To ease the boredom I put on the Hayley Westenra CD that Dorothy had leant me.

I then logged on to the internet to check my e-mails and, while I was online, it occurred to me that I should carry out a search to see if I could find confirmation in the records that Rosetta Bartlett was dead. I had already registered with the *Find My Past* website, so merely entered my e-mail address and password and proceeded to the Births, Marriages and Deaths section. I clicked on the relevant heading and completed the necessary details. I decided to search from around the time Emilio disappeared until a few years after in the hope of digging up an entry relating to her. I trawled through them all, but there was nothing. Undeterred, and for the sake of completeness, I scanned all the records up until 2005 although I knew the likelihood of finding something was minimal.

I was about to leave the website when I remembered that there was also the facility to search for overseas records. If Rosetta had died abroad there was a possibility that her death had been registered at one of the British Consulates and, if so, I would find it in the 'GRO Deaths Abroad Indices.' I typed in the relevant information and clicked on the search button and waited for the entries to appear. I started viewing each of the years ranging from 1990 onwards. I drew a blank until I reached 1999 and there to my amazement was the entry I was looking for. I had expected her death to be closer to the date of Emilio's disappearance and I was surprised to find the entry pertaining to her seven years after it.

Rosetta Bartlett had died in Ravello, the same place where Fabio nearly lost his life. This had to be significant. I decided to order the death certificate online and opted for the priority service as it would be the quickest way of obtaining it. If my order was processed on Monday and despatched by first class post on Tuesday, with any luck I would receive it by Wednesday.

I had given up hope of hearing from anyone that night, it was nearly midnight and I was about to climb into bed, when my 'phone finally rang. I picked up the cordless handset, sat down on the side of the bed and answered it.

'Hello,' I said, stifling a yawn.

'Alicia, it's Fabio. Sorry to ring you so late but I really need to speak to you.' He sounded much brighter, and I took this as an indication that his second meeting with Laura had been more productive than the first.

'Oh, don't worry about that. I'm glad you called. I've been thinking about you all day. How did it go with Laura?'

'She gave me quite a lot of information this time.'

'Really?'

'Yes. Did I tell you that Giulia's room was broken into on the night of her murder?'

'No, you haven't mentioned it.' I presumed that he had been so preoccupied with the murder itself that he had overlooked the fact he had not told me. Perhaps the significance of the break-in had only now become apparent, and I suspected it had something to do with the details gleaned from Laura. 'Was anything taken?'

'On the face of it, nothing seemed to be missing apart from her laptop. Although the police asked me whether anything else had been removed, I really couldn't tell. All Giulia's clothes and personal effects were still there, apart from the items she would have had on her when she was murdered, of course. The police assumed that whoever broke in was looking for something else, because the room had been searched methodically rather than ransacked, and they would not have had to search for the laptop as it was on Giulia's desk. When I saw Laura last week and asked her if she could determine whether any other items had been taken, she told me that she had already informed the police that she could not help with this. I was disappointed because, of all people, I felt Laura would be the one to know if any of Giulia's possessions was unaccounted for.'

'I suppose she must have spent more time with her than anyone else these past few months, but that doesn't necessarily mean she would be able to help with that specific request.'

'Yes, true, but when I spoke to her the first time I felt that she refused purely because she didn't want to become involved and not for any other reason. She must have had second thoughts, because she returned to Perugia on Friday and asked the police if she could look around Giulia's room.'

'Which obviously she did, hence her call to you that evening?'

'Yes.'

'And?' I assumed that she had discovered something otherwise he would not be ringing me at this time of night.

'According to Laura nothing was missing apart from the laptop which we already knew about, and one other thing; an old biscuit tin containing some papers which she says Giulia kept in the top of her wardrobe. It wasn't there and it wasn't anywhere else either.'

'How did Laura know about it?'

'Giulia showed it to her.'

'What did the papers relate to?'

'Laura said Giulia referred to them as her research material.'

'Research on what?'

'Into the family. Laura says there was a small bundle of documents in the box.'

'By the sounds of it Giulia must have been carrying out research well before you talked to me about it. I wonder why someone would want her paperwork. What use would it be to anyone else? Unless...'

'Unless what, Alicia?'

'She hit on something of relevance to your family that somebody

113

doesn't want you to discover. It's odd she didn't mention anything to you about it though.'

'It is. I don't understand why she didn't.'

'Are you sure you never saw the box?'

'Positive. The only thing I can think of is that, when we were clearing out our mother's things, she came across some of my father's papers, took them to Italy with her and used them as the basis of her research – not that I ever saw any, I have to admit.'

'What did the police say?'

'They don't know about it.'

'What do you mean?'

'Laura told them that, so far as she could tell, nothing else had been taken from Giulia's room.'

'Oh, you mean because she's too frightened to say anything to them?'

'Yes. She thinks she's being followed and doesn't trust anyone, not even the police. She's scared that if Giulia's murderer gets wind of the fact that she knows something, it won't be long before she suffers the same fate.'

'Then why tell you?'

'Because, although she doesn't want the police involved, she says she would be betraying Giulia's memory if she didn't give me information which could help in catching Giulia's murderer.'

'Hmm… Did she mention anything about the content of the box?'

'She recalls seeing a black and white photograph of a couple outside a house and Giulia referring to them as her grandparents. She also thinks that Giulia had carried out some title searches, but she doesn't have any more details than that.'

'Then presumably Giulia was trying to find out where your grandfather's family was from? To obtain those title searches she must have had an address or a name to go on. She had to get the details from somewhere.'

'There's something else.'

'What's that?'

'Laura thinks that on the night Giulia returned to Perugia she might have met someone.'

'What do you mean, "might have"?'

'Giulia called Laura when she was on the train. She said that she had been trying to track down the current owner of the property in the photograph and he had called her about making arrangements to see the house.'

'He?'

'Yes. Later that evening when she tried to ring Giulia again there was no response on her mobile, so she sent her a couple of texts. She was worried when she hadn't heard from Giulia by the next morning, and the rest you know.'

'And she hasn't communicated any of this to the police either; at least, nothing about the supposed meeting?'

'No. Because, as I told you, she thinks she's being watched. Whoever murdered Giulia is likely to have checked her mobile for contacts, recent calls and text messages. He, and I'm presuming it's a he, if it's *the* 'he' Giulia mentioned to Laura on the 'phone that evening, is probably all too aware of Laura's existence.'

'Have you tried to persuade Laura to talk to the police, Fabio?'

'She won't do that.'

'But she's withholding evidence which could help with the investigation into Giulia's murder. Her refusal to tell them also makes it very difficult for you to proceed.'

'I'm aware of that.' He sounded despondent.

'If the murderer thinks Laura knows something then she's at risk anyway. Involving the police might actually give her some form of protection and at the same time you will benefit from their input.'

'What difference do you think her evidence is really going to make? She neither knows the name of the man Giulia might have met, nor the address of the property, nor does she have any specific details of the missing documents.'

'But the murderer doesn't know that. If it is this property owner then he might think she does, in which case she's in real danger.'

'I see what you mean. I'll try and talk to her again.'

'What's Will's view on this? I presume you've discussed it with him?'

'I have. He said the same as you. I'll see if I can get hold of Laura tomorrow.'

'Are you sure she's told you everything she knows?'

'Why do you say that?' Fabio sounded perplexed.

'Because that would explain her agitation about coming forward. Maybe she does know the name of the man who called Giulia, or even where he's from.'

'Do you really believe that? Surely she'd tell me if she knew.'

'I'm not sure what to believe, Fabio. It doesn't necessarily follow that because she has spoken to you she has been completely honest with you. She could be holding something back.'

'You have a very suspicious mind.'

'No, just an open one. Experience of matters like this has taught me to question what I've been told and not to accept the information people give me unconditionally.'

'Well, all I know is that nothing is as it seems.'

'Exactly. Call me when you've spoken to Laura. In the meantime, I'll keep you posted this end. Goodnight, Fabio.' I was about to hang up but Fabio continued to speak.

'Alicia, are you still there?' There was a sense of urgency in his voice.

'Yes. What is it?'

'You've reminded me of something Laura told me.'

'What's that?'

'Before she and Giulia caught the train to Orvieto that weekend, Giulia went to the post office.'

'And?'

'She posted a jiffy bag.'

'Does Laura know what was in it or where it was going?'

'No. Giulia made Laura wait outside the post office while she went inside.'

'Maybe she posted her research papers to someone.'

'You think it could be relevant?'

'Definitely. That would explain why they couldn't be found, although it doesn't tell us to whom she sent them.'

'No, unfortunately. I'd better go. It's late, we both need to sleep and you have to get up for work tomorrow.'

'Don't remind me!' I jested.

'Speak to you later, Alicia. Goodnight.'

'Yes. Goodnight again!' I decided not to mention what I had discovered about Rosetta Bartlett to Fabio just yet. I wanted to wait until I had seen her death certificate. For all I knew she might have died from perfectly natural causes, although somehow I rather doubted that she had.

Chapter 14

Although I was physically exhausted by the time I went to bed, I slept fitfully, primarily due to the heat. It was a very humid night and the flat was hot and stuffy even with all the windows open. I had switched my fan on full blast, but the noise kept me awake and because I could not sleep my mind inevitably turned to thoughts of Fabio. I do not think I fell asleep until around three, so when I was awakened by the sound of my alarm clock ringing in my ear at six-fifteen I felt decidedly tired and grumpy.

I had taken to walking to the office during the summer months because I found it quite therapeutic, but it meant leaving home sooner than I would otherwise have done. Since Fabio had called so late the night before, I had not managed to speak to either Jo or Alex, and it was too early to ring either of them before I left for work. I met Graham on my way in and we took the lift up to the office together.

He asked me how my meeting went with Roland Kettering and was not surprised to hear that I also thought he was a pompous prig. I was glad to have the opportunity to talk with Graham because I was eager to ask him about Kettering's interests in Tuscany. I wanted to know whether he could shed any light on the legal acquaintance referred to by Kettering at the meeting.

'When we chatted about Kettering before, you mentioned he owned property in Italy.' Graham nodded. 'Did he ever talk to you about a lawyer he dealt with out there, or did you have anything to do with him?' We arrived at the third floor, the lift doors opened and

Graham stood aside to let me step out first.

'So far as I recall he had a few contacts in Italy, but I never had anything to do with them myself,' he replied, following me into reception. 'Why do you want to know?' he asked, acknowledging Susannah with a nod and catching up with me as we passed her desk. I caught her eye, she smiled at me and I smiled back.

'Because he told me he met Gregorio Pellegrino through his association with this lawyer,' I said, turning to look at him. 'I'm curious who he is. All I know is that he's a property specialist. At least, that's the only piece of information I managed to extract from Kettering.' We proceeded down the corridor towards Graham's office.

'And you think this lawyer is significant?'

'I do. I have a strong feeling Kettering is in league with Pellegrino.' We arrived at the door to Graham's office, he opened it, I hovered in the doorway and he indicated for me to come in and take a seat.

'That's a pretty serious allegation, Alicia,' he said, shutting the door behind me. He put his briefcase on the floor, took off his suit jacket, hung it on a hanger on the back of his door and sat down at his desk. 'I'm not a great fan of Roland Kettering, Alicia, as you've no doubt gathered, but accusing him is another matter altogether.'

'I'm not about to accuse either of them, Graham, I can assure you. It's just that you asked me to keep you informed, so I'm simply conveying my thoughts to you,' I replied defensively. He gave me an oblique smile.

'I'm not having a go at you, Alicia. I'm simply concerned about your position. What about evidence?'

'I have none,' I replied, shrugging my shoulders. 'That's the problem. If only Caterina Bartoldi would speak to me we might get somewhere.'

'Caterina Bartoldi? Who's she?' Graham looked confused.

'She used to work at Scarpetti, Steiglitz & Co. and left around the time Emilio disappeared. She's a property specialist too, although on the commercial side. I think she is concealing something because when I called her and asked her about Emilio and Scarpetti, Steiglitz & Co. she clammed up. I had the impression she's afraid of Pellegrino.'

'And you obtained her details from Fabio?' Although I was loath to mention Annette and the note, I did not want to lie to Graham and elected not to respond to his question. As for Rosetta Bartlett I decided to keep that completely to myself, for now anyway. 'Maybe Rachel has had dealings with her. You never know. I'll ask her.' Rachel Piper was our commercial property specialist.

'OK, but what I really want to find out is what Caterina worked on when she was at Scarpetti, Steiglitz & Co. and I doubt Rachel can help with that.'

'I understand. Well, it's clear that it wouldn't be of any benefit for you to talk to either Pellegrino or Kettering again. How's Fabio getting on in Perugia?'

'He's hoping Giulia's friend Laura will be able to help them piece together her last hours,' I said, being slightly economical with the truth – but that was all I felt able to divulge to Graham at this stage.

'Tell me if there are any developments,' he said as I stood up to leave. 'Have a read of this,' he added, picking up an issue of the *Journal of International Trust and Corporate Planning* which was sitting on his desk, and handing it to me. 'Let me know what you think of it. Personally, I think it's excellent and I'm considering subscribing to it.'

'OK,' I replied, taking it from him.

I was busy for the early part of the morning as Peter Crawford asked me to join him at a meeting with one of his family clients and advise her about a possible Inheritance Act claim. I paused at Danielle's desk on the way back to my office.

'Alex called about ten minutes ago,' she said, staring at me. 'You're looking a bit peeky. Are you OK?'

'Yes, thanks. I slept very badly last night, that's all. What did Alex say?'

'That if you can ring him within the hour he should be at his desk.'

'OK. Any other messages?'

'Yes. I've put the memos on your chair.'

'Thanks, Danielle,' I replied, walking away.

'Oh, and Alicia,' she said. I turned back. 'Elaine Weston also called.' Elaine was Roland Kettering's secretary.

'What did she want?'

'She wouldn't tell me. She gave me her direct line and asked if you could ring her,' she said, handing me a Post-it note with the number on it.

'Great,' I said, taking it.

I checked all my memos first to see if there was anything urgent and then called Elaine. I decided to 'phone her before I returned Alex's call in case I gleaned some little gem worth passing on to him. Unfortunately, I was to be disappointed in that regard. The reason why she had rung was to inform me that they no longer had Emilio Angelino's file in storage. But this was what I had anticipated being told, and at least she had had the courtesy to inform me. I rang Alex as soon as I finished my conversation with her.

'*Ciao, bella.* How was your weekend?'

'Good, thanks. I tried to ring you yesterday evening but I couldn't get hold of you.'

'I'm sorry. I had to rush off to a meeting in the City and I left my mobile behind, so I only picked up your missed call this morning.'

'Ah, then I'm not the only one who forgets my mobile?' I teased.

'No. Guilty as charged. Did you have a good time with your uncle?'

'Yes. It was great to catch up with him, and Nonna was in her element. I think she misses the family. Antonia and Tom announced their engagement too.'

'Really? I'll have to give Tom a call and congratulate him. Have they set a date yet?'

'No, but I don't expect it will be for months as Antonia is planning a big wedding.'

'Hmm... I can imagine. How's everything else?'

'Fabio rang very late last night.'

'Did he see Laura again?'

'Yes. We had an interesting conversation about her.'

'Really? What did she say?' I proceeded to relay to Alex the details of my conversation with Fabio. 'That's all very interesting,' he said, sounding slightly bemused.

'The thing is, Alex, although she gave Fabio a lot of information, there's no substance to any of it.'

'What do you mean?'

'Well, we have no details to follow up. I was hoping she might provide us with some leads.'

'I see the problem; it does seem rather bizarre. If I've understood you correctly we're looking for a missing laptop, a biscuit tin containing research papers, a man with a property that could possibly have once been the Angelino's family home, and a mystery package which Giulia posted before she left for Orvieto! I'm not surprised you're frustrated about this case. Do you really think Laura is withholding information?'

'Maybe. But, perhaps that's wishful thinking on my part because I'm desperate for someone to give us something concrete to work with.'

'What about the laptop?'

'What about it?'

'What could be the significance of its removal, Alicia?'

'Oh, that. I presume it was taken to see what Giulia had been working on. It occurred to me that she might have carried out some online searches, which is how she probably found out the details of the owner of the property Laura believes she met. The murderer must have taken it to remove the evidence.'

'It seems you have it all worked out.'

'Far from it, Alex. If that was the case I'd know who the murderer is and quite frankly I don't have a clue.'

'Hmm... Don't forget I'm meeting Dominic tonight. Let's hope he has some gen on Caterina Bartoldi for us.'

'Talking of which I have some news for you about Rosetta Bartlett.'

'What's that?'

'I searched on the internet and discovered she died in Ravello in 1999 so I've ordered her death certificate. It should arrive in the next few days.'

'That'd be good. Then we'll know what happened to her.'

'Yes. Do you want to come over after you've seen Dominic?'

'Oh yes. I should be with you about eight.'

My afternoon was remarkably uneventful and I was able to plough through my work undisturbed. I had attempted to ring Jo several times and I was concerned because it was totally out of character for her not to return my calls. On my fourth attempt she answered the telephone.

'Are you OK? I've been trying to get in touch with you all day.'

'I'm fine. It's just this awful morning sickness – this last day or two it seems to have lasted most of the day!'

'Oh, Jo, I'm sorry. I wouldn't have disturbed you if I'd known you were feeling unwell.'

'Don't be silly. I'm much better than I was first thing. I spoke to Will earlier and he's filled me in on everything. That business with Laura is a bit strange. I think you could be right about her.'

'He told you what I said to Fabio then?'

'Oh yes. How was your weekend?'

'Uncle Vico arrived; and Antonia and Tom are engaged.'

'An eventful weekend then! Does Antonia have an engagement ring yet?'

'Of course. She and Tom chose it on Saturday.'

'What is it?'

'It's a beautiful Asscher cut diamond with accent stones. It really suits her. I'm sure she'll show it to you.'

'I look forward to it. Speak to you later.'

Danielle left for the evening and, since it was very quiet, I decided to stay on for a little while because there were a couple of trust documents I needed to draft. I finished my work, logged off my computer, tidied my desk and was about to put on my jacket when Graham burst into the room.

'Oh, good,' he said. 'I'm glad I caught you.' I looked at him quizzically. 'I've been thinking about Kettering since we chatted this morning and trying to rack my brains about where it was in Tuscany that he owned property. I think it might have been Viareggio. Sorry not to be more specific, but it's such a while back I can't be sure.'

'It's better than nothing. I'm grateful for any input.'

'I also had a word with Rachel about Caterina Bartoldi. She doesn't know her.'

'Well, I didn't really expect her too. Thanks for trying.'

'No problem. See you in the morning, Alicia,' he said, shutting the door on his way out.

'I've been worried about you,' I said as Alex fell through the front door. 'You look exhausted. I thought you'd be here ages ago.' It was after nine so he was over an hour later than expected.

'I'm sorry,' he replied, bending down and kissing me. 'I hoped to be, but I had to go to Camden and then there were severe delays on the Tube on the way back.' He dropped his briefcase in the hall and then removed his shoes as usual. I took his jacket and hung it up on the coat rack.

'What did you have to go there for?'

'I met Dominic for a quick drink after work. I told you.'

'I know but Williams, Ricks & Stone is based near Liverpool Street, at least that's the address on their website.'

'It is. Give me a minute and I'll explain what happened. Hmm…something smells good,' he said, following me through to the kitchen. 'What are you cooking?'

'Another fruit cake. I'm trying a new recipe. Are you hungry? I can make you something if you are.'

'No, I'm fine. I could do with a drink though. By the looks of it you've already eaten anyway,' he said, picking up the empty tube of Pringles on the work surface next to the oven. 'Ah… I haven't had these '*Light* aromas' ones before. Red Pepper with a touch of Olive Extract. Looks like I'll have to wait to try them until another day.'

'Very funny,' I said, taking it out of his hand and throwing it in the bin. I opened the fridge door, lifted out a bottle of ice-cold Peroni beer and handed it to him. 'You were saying about Dominic.' He opened the kitchen drawer where I kept my cutlery, took out the bottle opener and removed the cap.

'Oh yes,' he said, reaching for a clean glass on the draining board. 'He did manage to find out a good deal about her actually.' I watched him as he tipped the glass and poured the contents of the bottle into it.

'And?'

'She's in her mid-forties and has worked at the firm for nearly sixteen years.' He took a big gulp of beer. We walked into the living room and sat down on the sofa. I tucked my feet under me and leaned back.

'That means she would have left Scarpetti, Steiglitz & Co not long after Emilio's disappearance,' I said, thinking out loud. 'Did Dominic say anything else?'

'Caterina's always been a commercial property specialist, but she does have an international client base and has worked in Italy as well.' He took another gulp of beer.

'That might mean something, I suppose.'

'She's also a single mother and has an only daughter who's nearly twenty.' He put his glass down on the coffee table. 'She was divorced about eighteen years ago after her husband scarpered to Italy. He left her without any financial support, she was forced to return to the law, and that's why she took the job at Scarpetti, Steiglitz & Co.'

125

'How interesting. She didn't work at the firm for as long as I thought then.'

'There's more. Apparently she had a dispute with Mr Pellegrino and he accused her of trying to steal several of the firm's clients.'

'That's a turn up for the books. How did Dominic find all this out?'

'One of the Partners told him. He said it was sour grapes because Pellegrino was aggrieved to lose her to Williams, Ricks & Stone, but I think there's more to it than that.'

'I'm sure you're right, as there's no doubt she's terrified of any involvement with Scarpetti, Steiglitz & Co. It's certainly food for thought. Does Dominic live in Camden?'

'No.'

'Then why did you meet him there?'

'I didn't. We met for a quick drink at a wine bar around the corner from the office.'

'But why did you go to Camden? I don't understand.'

'Dominic had to return to the office because he has a hefty case on at the moment and is working late tonight. He told me that Caterina invariably stays until seven and I went back with him and he pointed her out to me. As it happens she was on the verge of leaving and I decided to follow her home which means we now know where she lives and how to find her if the need arises. I've made a note of the address for you. It's in my jacket pocket, so remind me to give it to you later.' He picked up his glass of beer and proceeded to drain it.

'Thank you. You'll be dressing up in dark glasses and a raincoat next, Alex,' I teased.

'Anything to keep you happy.'

'Can I get you another?' I said, pointing to his empty glass.

'Please.' I jumped off the sofa and ambled through to the kitchen, grabbed a bottle of Peroni beer from the fridge, took off the top with the bottle opener and returned with it. 'Thanks,' he said, taking the bottle from me. 'Terrible news about Annette, isn't it?'

'What are you talking about, Alex?' I replied, re-positioning myself on the sofa. His expression was grave and I had an awful sinking feeling. 'What news?'

'It was in the *Evening Standard*. Haven't you seen it?'

'I didn't buy a copy this evening. There were none left at the newsstand near the office. What's happened to her?'

'She was attacked last night while walking her dog in Wandsworth on her way back from the Common. You can read about it yourself,' he replied, standing up. He retrieved his copy of the *Evening Standard* from his briefcase in the hall and handed it to me. 'Turn to page four. It's in the News in Brief column.' I scanned the first part of the news item. It read as follows:

Woman dies after vicious assault

A 48-year old woman has died after being attacked while out walking her dog in Wandsworth last night. The woman, who has been identified as Annette Richardson, a legal secretary, was rushed to St George's Hospital, Tooting, suffering from head injuries but was pronounced dead on arrival. Police are appealing for witnesses to the incident...

Chapter 15

'Oh, Alex, this is dreadful. You realize what it means, don't you?' I said, clutching the newspaper.

'I'm not sure I do.' He put down his beer.

'Well, she worked for Pellegrino, she gave me the note and now she's dead. It's very convenient that she should be killed like this; too convenient and too much of a coincidence for my liking.' I stood up and started to pace the floor.

'So you think Pellegrino murdered her.'

'Or had her murdered. He doesn't strike me as the sort to dirty his own hands,' I said sarcastically.

'Maybe someone saw her give you the note; in which case you could be in danger yourself.'

'Don't say that. I'm sure nobody saw us.'

'Who else knows about it?'

'You, Fabio, Will and Jo. That's all.'

'And you didn't mention it to Caterina Bartoldi?'

'No. Absolutely not. I'd hardly do that, would I?'

'OK. OK. Don't bite my head off. I'm not accusing you, Alicia. I'm simply trying to figure out what's happened here. You're going to wear that carpet out by the way.'

'What?' I snapped.

'If you keep on pacing up and down like that.'

'Sorry,' I replied, sitting down. 'I'm feeling a little pent-up.'

'I can tell. Do you think your call to Caterina Bartoldi was the trigger?'

'I don't see how. Why?' I asked, turning to him. 'You're not suggesting she had a hand in the assault on Annette, are you?'

'It was only a thought. I simply wondered whether she could have surmised from what you said that it was Annette who had put you on to her.'

'No,' I said, shaking my head. 'I very much doubt it. But even if she guessed that my source was Annette, I don't believe she's responsible for killing her.'

'You ought to be cautious nonetheless.'

'But you were the one saying that it's obvious she's terrified of Pellegrino, which explains why she doesn't want any association with Scarpetti, Steiglitz & Co. and won't help us.'

'Yes. I did say that. I just think we can't be too careful. Where's the note?'

'I have it here,' I said, getting up from the sofa, purposefully walking over to my desk, pulling open the second drawer, taking it out and holding it up.

'May I see it?'

'Of course, although it doesn't say anything other than I've already told you,' I said slightly defensively, handing it to him.

'Hmm…' he said, scanning it. 'You'll have to give this to the police now Annette's been killed.'

'I know. That will be an interesting conversation.' Alex looked puzzled. 'I'll have to provide an explanation of what it's all about which will be rather difficult since I'm not exactly sure what's going on myself. It doesn't help that the note isn't signed either. They'll probably think I'm some mad woman who is wasting police time!'

'Hardly, Alicia. One thing's for sure though.'

'What's that?'

'Caterina Bartoldi will be forced to answer some awkward questions whether she likes it or not. As for Rosetta Bartlett, I have a feeling her death certificate will make interesting reading. Then maybe Caterina will reveal what she really knows.'

'Perhaps I should try and speak to her before the police do.'

'I don't see the point.'

'You've changed your tune. You were the one who followed her home, remember.'

'Yes, but in light of Annette's assault, it's probably best we let the police take over.'

'Umm... I'll have to ring Fabio and break the news that she's probably been murdered. I don't relish making that call at all.'

'No. You wouldn't.'

'I was half-expecting to hear from him tonight actually.'

'Why?'

'Because he said he would attempt to speak to Laura again today. Maybe he didn't get the chance.'

'Have you mentioned to him what you found out about Rosetta?'

'No. I think it's best to wait until we have more details.'

'I agree. When do you intend to call the police?'

'I'll have a word with Jo before I contact them and see if she can find out who's running the enquiry into Annette's death.'

'That's a good idea.'

'Well, you know how I hate dealing with the police at the best of times,' I said, standing up again.

'I do.'

'She might be able to pre-empt some of their questions and it would make it easier for me to know who I'm dealing with.' I picked up Alex's empty glass and walked off to the kitchen.

'You just can't sit still tonight, can you?' he called out.

'I need to check on the cake. It should be cooked by now. Then I think I'll go to bed,' I said, yawning. 'I hardly slept last night.'

'Yes, you look very tired.'

'So do you. Don't go home. Stay here with me.'

As I did not want to disturb Jo too early in the morning, because I was conscious she was suffering from awful morning sickness, I waited until nearly midday before I rang her. Fortunately, she was feeling better than the previous day and I did not feel quite so guilty asking for her assistance with the police.

'I'm sorry to bother you with this, Jo,' I said.

'Don't be silly. It isn't a problem. It's not exactly very difficult for me to make a few calls.'

'I meant because you're not well.'

'Oh, Alicia, I'm fine, really I am. It'll soon pass – at least I hope it does,' she quipped. 'I'll have a word with Tina first. She's one of my best contacts at the Met.'

'What does she do?'

'She works in the Homicide unit at the Specialist Crime Directorate. She should be able to tell me who's on the Murder Investigation Team and which Detective Chief Inspector has been allotted to the case.'

'You sure you don't mind?'

'Of course not. I'll put a call into CID at Battersea as well and see what I can find out. I'll let you know how I get on. What did Fabio say about all this?'

'I haven't told him yet.'

'That fits, otherwise I'd have heard from Will!'

'Well, I only learned about Annette's death late last night, from Alex as it happens. I wanted to chat to you before speaking to Fabio. I'm worried that he'll take the news really badly. It will come as another blow.'

'Why don't you let me call him? I need to 'phone Will anyway and I can update him with developments this end at the same time.'

'Oh, OK. When were you thinking of doing that?'

'Straightaway. Why?'

'Because there's something you should ask Fabio before contacting Tina.'

'What's that?'

'It occurs to me that I never asked him for the name of the police officer he saw a couple of weeks ago when he returned from Ravello. It might be useful for you to have his name when you speak to Tina even though he was less than helpful.'

'Which is the reason you recommended Fabio get in touch with Will in the first place?'

'Exactly. It's probably still worth finding out who he was.'

'Definitely. I won't call Tina until I've spoken to Will. OK. Leave all that to me. How's everything else?' asked Jo, changing the subject. 'I bet your mother is happy about Antonia's news.'

'Yes. She's in her element.'

'Is Antonia having an engagement party?'

'She hasn't mentioned it.'

'Your mother must be excited at the prospect of having grand-children?'

'Umm... I don't think Antonia's planning on starting a family just yet. I'd better go,' I said, glimpsing at my watch. 'I need to prepare for my two o'clock meeting. I should be out by four if you need to ring me.'

'Fingers crossed I'll have some news by then. I'll keep you posted. Speak to you soon.'

'Thanks, Jo. Take care.'

'You too.'

It was inevitable that the police would contact Caterina Bartoldi, but only after they had spoken to me and seen the note. This meant I still had time to try and talk with her before they did. Although Alex doubted that anything would be achieved by this exercise and felt that I should leave Caterina to the police, I did not share his opinion. The fact that they would be questioning her might give me some leverage and encourage her to open up to me, at least that is what I hoped. The only thing which made me hesitate, was Alex's remark that Caterina might be involved in Annette's death, in which case it would not be advisable for me to ring her again. However, on balance I thought it was highly unlikely that she had any part in it and a risk I was willing to take.

I completed my preparations for my meeting and, because it was only one-thirty, I had plenty of time to spare so decided to use it to make the call to Caterina. Her personal secretary was at lunch and I was transferred to another secretary in the department.

'May I speak to Caterina Bartoldi, please,' I said.

'I'm sorry but Mrs Bartoldi is currently unavailable,' she replied, rather disinterestedly.

'Oh, I see. Is she actually in the office today?'

'Yes. She's at an external meeting, but she's due back any time. Do you want to leave a message or would you like her voicemail.' Voicemail was perfect as it gave me the opportunity to put my points across without her hanging up on me.

'Voicemail, please.'

'If you stay on the line, I'll put you through.'

'Thank you.' There was a time delay of a few seconds before I was diverted to the automated service.

'Hello. You have reached the voicemail of Caterina Bartoldi. Please leave your message after the tone. Thank you.' I waited for the beeps to finish.

'Mrs Bartoldi, this is Alicia Allen. We spoke the other day about Fabio Angelino. I don't know whether you saw the *Evening Standard* last night, but Annette Richardson has been murdered. I would not trouble you again, only it was Annette who recommended I contact you. I think you should be aware that the police will want to speak with you. I'd be grateful if you would call me at the office. Thank you very much. Goodbye.' I hung up.

I then realized that I should have given her my direct line number as she might not want to ring our switchboard, so I 'phoned back and left another message. I hoped that, by mentioning my connection to Annette, and the fact that the police might wish to interview her, I had left Caterina with just enough information to rouse her curiosity. I deliberately omitted any reference to the note and failed to explain why the police would be in touch because I wanted her to return my call and ask me herself.

Unfortunately, Danielle was still at lunch when I went into the meeting at two and I did not have a chance to explain that Caterina might ring. If she did, the call would divert to Danielle in my absence, which was not a problem. The only thing which concerned me was that if she 'phoned and I was unavailable the moment would pass, and the opportunity to speak with her would be lost.

I did not expect to hear from Jo until after four because she knew that I was engaged, but I could not help wondering what progress she was making. Typically, my meeting overran and, by the time I returned to my office, it was nearly five-thirty and Danielle was on the verge of leaving.

'You must be exhausted,' she said. 'I thought you were never going to reappear.'

'It was a bit of a long one, wasn't it? Any messages?' I asked expectantly.

'I fielded most of the calls from clients. There's nothing urgent for you to deal with tonight. I put the memos on your desk,' she said, tidying hers.

'Oh, right,' I replied, feeling rather dispirited. It was probably too much to suppose Caterina would 'phone, but I was disappointed that there was no word from Jo.

'See you tomorrow then.'

'Yes. Thanks, Danielle. Have a good night.'

'You too.'

I sat down at my desk and glanced through my memos. Danielle was quite right; none of the work was high priority but I decided to work through it nonetheless. It was around seven-thirty when my direct line rang. I thought it might be Caterina and I braced myself before answering it.

'Hello. Alicia Allen speaking,' I said.

'Alicia. It's Jo. You're sounding very formal tonight.'

'Oh dear. I'm obviously in office mode,' I replied casually. I had no intention of telling Jo that I had called Caterina because I suspected she would react the same way as Alex and berate me.

'How did you get on?'

'Fine. Tina wasn't on duty until this evening and I only managed to speak to her about half an hour ago, which is why I'm calling you much later than planned. I tried you at home first and then when you didn't answer your mobile I thought you must still be in the office.'

'I didn't hear my mobile; I only have it on vibrate when I'm at work,' I said, retrieving it from my handbag. 'You didn't leave a message,' I said, checking the display and noticing that there was a missed call from her.

'No. I wanted to talk to you.'

'Did you discover who's on the murder squad?'

'Yes. DCI Framlington is the senior investigating officer. I've never had any dealings with him; but Will has.'

'What's his view of him?'

'That Framlington's a highly competent detective and very meticulous. If he's on the case then no stone will be left unturned.'

'Hmm... That's encouraging. Let's hope he's amenable too. Did you find out who Fabio spoke to in the police?'

'Yes. It was one of the police constables at his local police station in Chiswick.'

'How did Fabio take the news about Annette?'

'He was shocked, but he's more convinced than ever that your colleague theory is spot on. He said he'd give you a ring later. There haven't been any further developments on the Laura front by the way. He hasn't managed to speak to her again and thinks she's avoiding his calls.'

'Yes. I'm convinced she knows more than she's letting on.'

'As for the investigation into Giulia's murder, that isn't progressing either. It really is frustration all round at the moment.'

'Tell me about it.'

'I'll try and make contact with DCI Framlington in the morning. I can't face it tonight. The person I used to know at Battersea CID has left so I couldn't find out anything there. I have a feeling tomorrow is going to be an eventful day, Alicia.'

'Nothing new there then!'

'Go home! I'll speak to you when I have some news.'

On Wednesday morning my post arrived before I left for work and amongst the usual bills and junk mail was the envelope containing Rosetta Bartlett's eagerly anticipated death certificate. I ripped open the envelope, and scrutinised the certificate. I could hardly believe what I was reading and immediately rang Alex to let him know what I had discovered.

'I'm sorry to call you so early but I thought you'd be interested in knowing what's on Rosetta's death certificate.'

'I am. What does it say? What's the cause of death?'

'Are you ready for this?'

'Yes.'

'Missing – presumed drowned.'

'You're joking?'

'No. That's what it says on the certificate. But it occurs to me that if she was missing, the death certificate could not have been issued for seven years which takes her death back to around the time of Emilio's disappearance. Unless her family applied to the Probate court for a declaration of death, although that's unlikely,' I said, thinking out loud.

'Who registered the death, Alicia?'

'Edward Bartlett. Her father. Do you think we should try and track him down?'

'It'd be great if we could. So now we have two missing persons presumed dead, although with no bodies how can we be really sure they're dead?'

'I suppose we can't be absolutely certain, but everything points to them having been murdered, Alex. Let's face it; if Rosetta is alive, why would Annette have directed me to ask Caterina about her?'

'Fair point.'

'I'll speak to you later. Actually, I think the police might turn up to interview me today.'

'Really?'

'Yes. I spoke to Jo just before I left work yesterday evening. She found out who's on the murder investigation team. If she makes contact with one of the investigating officers' which is what she said she'd try to do, I don't suppose it will be long before they'll want to talk to me about Annette.'

'I'm sure the police will be interested in what you have to tell them, especially with this latest twist in events.'

'Hmm… Maybe I'll be in their good books for once!'

Chapter 16

'Do you want the good news or the bad news?' Jo asked when I answered my direct line. It was only nine-thirty and I was surprised to hear from her at that time, especially since early morning starts for her these past few weeks had been blighted by morning sickness. I presumed she was calling to fill me in on her conversation with DCI Framlington.

'Give me the bad news first,' I replied.

'You'll be receiving a visit from MIT shortly.'

'I can deal with that. Any idea when?'

'Today or tomorrow.'

'OK. I'll be expecting them. What's the good news?'

'DCI Framlington wasn't available when I called and so I spoke to DS Henshaw instead. He's one of the detectives working with the DCI on the investigation into Annette's murder. I know him through Will, so that made my task much easier because I didn't have to explain who I am or to convince him to take me seriously. I've given him some basic facts and obviously I mentioned you and your connection to Annette. As you can imagine, he started to bombard me with questions about your involvement with her, which are better dealt with by you than me, and that's what I told him.'

'No problem. I was prepared for that anyway.'

'I hope it goes well.'

'Thanks. I'm really grateful to you, Jo. How are you today?'

'Not bad at all. I felt a bit queasy when I woke up but it passed very quickly so I was able to get on with making my calls!'

'You take care.'

'I will. Let me know what happens with the police.'

'Of course. I'll call Fabio when I've spoken to them.'

'Didn't he ring you?'

'No.'

'That's strange. Oh, well. Speak to you soon.'

Around mid-morning, when I was least expecting it, I received the longed for call from Caterina Bartoldi. Although I was still half hoping she would ring me I had almost resigned myself to the fact that she would not. In truth, I was amazed to hear her voice on the other end of the line, but pleased my voicemail message had delivered the desired result and she had 'phoned.

'Miss Allen. It's Caterina Bartoldi. I picked up your message when I returned to the office yesterday. So it was Annette Richardson who recommended you contact me?' I picked up the agitation in her voice. Her speech was quite staccato.

'Yes, that's right.'

'Whatever she told you about me, I can't help you.'

'Then why did you return my call? You've already made it perfectly plain that you're not prepared to assist me. You didn't need to ring me to tell me that. You could easily have ignored my message.'

'Because I want...' She stopped in mid-sentence as if she was trying to collect her thoughts.

'What do you want, Mrs Bartoldi? Tell me,' I said, pressing her.

'I want you to know I had nothing to do with Annette's death.'

'I believe you. But it's the police you'll have to convince not me.'

'I don't understand. I can't give them any information. I haven't seen Annette for years.'

'Since you left Scarpetti, Steiglitz & Co., you mean? Why won't you tell me what you know about Emilio Angelino's disappearance? What are you afraid of?'

'There's nothing to tell.'

'Well, I think there is. Are you protecting someone? Or is it that you're frightened of the repercussions if you talk about what happened? You won't avoid speaking to the police. They'll want to question you about the note.'

'Note? What note? What are you talking about?' She sounded increasingly anxious.

'The note Annette gave me.'

'And how does that concern *me?*'

'Because Mrs Bartoldi, as I explained to you when I spoke to you the other day, I am trying to carry out an investigation into the disappearance of Fabio's father. I went to meet Mr Pellegrino to seek his assistance and it was when I was leaving that Annette slipped the note into my hand. It refers to you working at Scarpetti, Steiglitz & Co. with Emilio and directs me to ask you what happened to Rosetta Bartlett, which is why I put that very question to you the other day.

'Now, I have a problem because when I produce this note to the police they are likely to ask me why I believe Annette gave it to me. I will have to provide them with the background details and explain my reasons for going to the firm in the first place. I think it's a logical assumption that they will follow up the note and wish to interview the persons mentioned in it. I know that Rosetta Bartlett is dead because I checked, so that leaves you, Mrs Bartoldi. What will you tell them when they ask you what happened to her?'

'Exactly what I've told you. I can't help you. Do you hear me? There's nothing I can do. The best thing you can do is to leave me alone!' she shrilled, and for the second time she hung up on me.

The moment I put the 'phone down, I started to analyse my conversation with her. I had intended to be forthright, but maybe I had been too forceful. On the other hand, I did not think that a more gentle approach would have resulted in Caterina volunteering any information either. I consoled myself with the fact that, at least I had used more than my best endeavours to persuade her to help us. For now there seemed little else I could do.

And then I had a rather disturbing thought. What if she vanished before the police had a chance to catch up with her? By alerting her to the fact that they would want to interview her, and in effect giving her advance warning of their impending visit, I had given her reason to disappear if she were so minded. I was probably being paranoid, but I would have to be completely frank with the police about my two exchanges with her. As it happened I did not have to wait very long before the opportunity to do that arose. About ten minutes later Danielle, looking flustered, popped her head around the door to my office.

'Sorry to disturb you, Alicia, but Susannah has rung through to tell me that there are two gentlemen waiting in reception who want to speak with you. They say they're police officers. Is everything OK?'

'Yes. I've been expecting them. Tell Susannah I will see them now. Would you mind fetching them for me?'

'All right.' She hesitated for a moment. 'You're not in any trouble, are you?' she asked, sounding anxious.

'Of course not. Whatever gave you that idea?'

'I was just concerned about you what with all this Fabio stuff.'

'Don't worry, Danielle. I'll be fine.'

A few minutes later I heard the sound of several pairs of footsteps shuffling along the corridor to my office and then Danielle opened the door and ushered the two policemen inside.

'Alicia, these are the detectives from the Metropolitan Police.'

'Thank you, Danielle,' I said, standing up. She hovered in the doorway awaiting my instructions for refreshments.

'DCI Framlington,' said the older of the two men striding forward, flashing his badge at me with one hand and then extending his other hand and smiling broadly. He was round featured, quite stocky with broad powerful shoulders and wore his dark straight brown hair very short, almost in a crew cut. He was much younger than I had anticipated, probably in his early forties, which was a welcome surprise. He seemed amiable enough – on first appearances anyway.

'Good morning,' I said, shaking first his hand and then the hand of his sergeant who also showed me his badge. The DS had curly blond hair similar to Will which flopped over his forehead. He had a willowy but athletic build, a very thin face and aquiline nose. Unlike his senior officer he seemed rather glum.

'Please take a seat,' I said, sitting down. 'Would either of you like a drink?'

'Coffee, please,' said DCI Framlington, undoing the buttons of his suit jacket and settling back in the chair opposite me. I turned to his sergeant who sat down in the chair next to him.

'The same thanks,' he said.

'Danielle, would you arrange that, please?' She nodded and disappeared.

'We understand from Mrs Brook,' said DCI Framlington, 'whom I believe is a friend of yours,' I nodded, 'that you have some infor-mation relating to the murder of Annette Richardson.'

'Well, not the murder itself, but I think that I have something which may assist you in discovering *why* she was murdered.'

'What do you mean exactly?'

'I'll explain. You'll forgive me if I repeat anything Mrs Brook told you,' I said, addressing DS Henshaw, 'but I think for the sake of completeness it's better I give DCI Framlington as full an account of my involvement as possible.' Bearing in mind the DCI was known for his assiduous attention to detail, I was sure he would not mind a little repetition of the facts if it enabled him to find Annette's murderer.

'No problem,' he said.

'Please carry on,' said DCI Framlington.

'I'm acting for a client called Fabio Angelino in relation to the Probate of his mother's estate. He was recommended to me by my uncle who's an attorney in New York and used to be a friend of Fabio's father, Emilio. A few weeks ago after returning from a trip to Italy to visit his sister, Fabio came into the office for a meeting and told me that while he was in Ravello somebody tried to run him off the road. He was convinced that it was attempted murder, but there seemed no explanation for it. He...'

'Mrs Brook indicated that he attended at Chiswick Police Station about that, but I found no record of his attendance,' said DS Henshaw, interrupting me.

'I can't comment on that. I can only tell you what I've been told. According to him he was given short shrift by the police there.'

'I see. We'll have to look into that,' said the DCI. 'Go on.'

'The thing is, his father, Emilio, disappeared about sixteen years ago in Sicily. An extensive investigation was carried out at the time and it was ultimately concluded that it was probably a Mafia job. There were a number of theories about what happened to him, but not one of them came to anything. When I discussed this with Fabio he seemed dissatisfied with that conclusion. Because of the incident in Italy, we thought that there might somehow be a connection between the two events and perhaps it was time to reinvestigate the events surrounding his father's disappearance.'

'What do you mean "we"?'

'Well, it was my suggestion that Fabio contact his father's former firm, Scarpetti Steiglitz & Co. ...'

'That's the firm Mrs Richardson worked at,' said DCI Framlington, leaning forward. I could see that he was intrigued as he was listening intently to my every word.

'Yes, it is. Anyway, I thought it would be beneficial if we spoke to some of his father's former colleagues to find out what he was working on and who with at the time he disappeared.'

'But why? They would have been interviewed as part of the UK investigation into the case.'

'We realized that, but we were not in a position to check the police files like you are. Besides, we simply wanted to talk to the people who were closest to Emilio ourselves about what they remembered.' I decided not to mention my colleague theory, well not yet anyway. 'We agreed that Fabio should arrange to meet Gregorio Pellegrino, a close colleague and friend of Emilio who worked with him at Scarpetti, Steiglitz & Co., and also Roland Kettering at Smythson, Reid & Monkton who Pellegrino recommended to Fabio's mother to carry out the Probate of Emilio's estate.'

'As you can imagine, Miss Allen, I am particularly interested in the connection with Scarpetti, Steiglitz & Co.'

'There's more than one. I presume you know Gregorio Pellegrino was Mrs Richardson's boss?'

'We haven't spoken to any of her colleagues yet.'

'Really? I presumed you already had,' I said, fishing for information. I suspected as much, but realized he would not divulge the details of his discussions with them to me.

'And did you manage to meet Mr Pellegrino and Mr Kettering?' he replied, swiftly changing the subject.

'Oh yes. Originally, the intention was for me to accompany Fabio to the meetings, but then Giulia was murdered and he had to leave for Perugia.'

'Giulia?'

'His sister.'

'How did she die?'

'She was asphyxiated. We think her murder might be linked to some family research she had been carrying out and that somebody may have killed her because of it. It is my view that her death is connected to the other incidents – it is too coincidental for it to be otherwise. And in case you were wondering, no, I do not have any evidence.' He looked bemused. I decided not to mention Laura; at least not yet.

'What's the status of the enquiry out there?'

'There's a distinct lack of progress. Will Brook's with Fabio.'

'He's in good hands then. I remember Will well,' said DCI

Framlington. Danielle returned with the tray of coffee and some assorted biscuits. I cleared a space on my desk for her to place the tray; she put it down and left the room. 'How do you take your coffee?' I asked, picking up the milk jug.

'Milk, one sugar,' said DCI Framlington.

'Just milk,' said DS Henshaw. I poured some milk into one cup and then the other.

'So what happened about the meetings with Pellegrino and Kettering,' asked DCI Framlington, reverting to the previous point.

'I went alone,' I said, handing him his coffee and then the sugar bowl. 'The first meeting was with Mr Pellegrino. He was uncooperative. It was clear he did not want us to pursue any investigation. I felt he was deliberately obstructive.' I passed DS Henshaw his cup.

'In what way?' he said as he scooped out a spoonful of sugar and stirred it into his coffee.

'He was unwilling to put me in touch with Emilio's colleagues or to do anything to help us. Biscuit?' I said, offering him the plate. He shook his head. I then offered it to DS Henshaw who took a milk chocolate Hobnob.

'And why do you think that was?'

'Maybe you should ask him yourself. You might get more out of him than I did.'

'I will, but I want to know what you think.' He took a sip of coffee and then put down his cup.

'He has something to hide.'

'Hmm… What about this Kettering character?'

'He responded in the same way to my questions; unhelpfully.'

'You said Mr Pellegrino recommended Mr Kettering to Mrs Angelino. Do you know anything about their association?'

'Yes. They met through a mutual legal acquaintance in Italy whose name I don't have. You see, one of Mr Kettering's areas of expertise is advising UK clients who wish to purchase property in Italy and he met him when he was buying a property of his own. It was the lawyer who introduced Mr Kettering to Mr Pellegrino. It's a long-standing association so I understand.'

'And do you think this has any connection with what happened to Annette Richardson?' He picked up his cup and took another sip of coffee.

'That I couldn't say. It's something I'd be keen to follow up though.'

'What is it you have which may assist us with this enquiry?'

'I was coming to that,' I said, reaching for my handbag, opening it, unzipping the back inside pocket and retrieving her note from inside. 'Take a look at this,' I said. He put down his cup and I handed it to him. I watched DCI Framlington scan the typewritten note and then pass it to DS Henshaw who did the same before giving it back to the DCI.

'Where did you get this from?' he asked, waving the piece of paper at me.

'Annette slipped it in to my hand after my meeting with Mr Pellegrino, just as I was leaving. I appreciate that you only have my word that the note is from her because it is unsigned but I am prepared to swear to it on oath if necessary.'

'Did she say anything when she gave it to you?' he asked, ignoring my last point.

'Something about knowing I'd do the right thing.'

'What do you think she meant by that?'

'Well, she was aware that the purpose of my meeting with Mr Pellegrino was to ask about the investigation into Emilio Angelino's disappearance, so I can only assume she was referring to that. She obviously wanted me to follow up on it which is why she told me to contact Caterina Bartoldi and ask her what happened to Rosetta Bartlett.'

'And have you?'

'Yes.'

'What did she tell you?'

'Nothing. She refused to answer my questions and slammed the 'phone down on me.'

'How did she sound?'

'Anxious. I think she was quite shocked to receive the call.'

'Did you explain that you obtained her details from Annette Richardson?'

'Not at that stage, no.'

'And what stage might that be?'

'When I first called her, which was last Friday morning, so not before Annette was murdered, if that's what you were thinking.' He raised his eyebrows.

'You spoke to her again?'

'Yes. I left a message on her voicemail yesterday and she rang me back shortly before you arrived.'

'This morning then?' I nodded. 'What made her change her mind about speaking to you?'

'I think she was hoping to glean some information from me.'

'I don't understand.'

'In my voicemail message I mentioned the news of Annette's murder, told her that Annette was the one who gave me her name, and that you would want to speak to her.'

'In the hope that it would prompt her to call you to find out more?' At least he was perceptive.

'Yes, but I'm concerned that my call might cause her to run.'

'Why? Do you think she has anything to do with Annette's murder?'

'No. But it's my view she knows or has a good idea what happened to Emilio Angelino, as well as Rosetta Bartlett, if Annette's note is to be believed. She's afraid of something; that much I do know. Rosetta Bartlett is dead and I have a strong feeling that both she and Emilio were murdered and that their deaths have something to do with Scarpetti, Steiglitz & Co. Caterina certainly left the firm around the time Emilio disappeared.'

'How do you know Rosetta Bartlett is dead?'

'Because I checked. I ordered her death certificate on Sunday evening and it arrived this morning.'

'Do you have it?'

'Not on me, no. But I can get it for you.'

'That's all right. What was the cause of death?'

'Missing – presumed drowned.'

'I see. How interesting. We'll track Caterina down and find out what she has to say about Annette's murder and Rosetta Bartlett's death. If you only spoke to her within the last hour and she has done a bolt she won't have gone far. I'd like you to give a statement detailing what you've told us this morning. We'll be in touch about that,' he said, standing up. 'And in the meantime if there's anything else you remember please call this number,' he said, taking out a card from the inside pocket of his jacket, picking up a biro off my desk, jotting down the number and pushing it across my desk towards me.

'Thank you,' I replied, picking it up.

'I don't suppose you get involved in many murder enquiries in your line of work, Miss Allen,' said DS Henshaw, pitching in.

'Hmm…. Well, not as many as you do, obviously, but when you deal with money and Wills there's inevitably the odd one or two!'

Chapter 17

'Is everything OK, Alicia?' asked Danielle as she opened the door to my office. I had turned my chair towards the window and was sitting mulling over my conversation with the police.

'Yes,' I replied, swivelling around to face her. 'Everything's fine.'

'I saw the two policemen leave. They were here ages. Graham wants to know what's going on.' Clearly, so did Danielle.

'I'll go and speak to him but I need to pop back home first.' I had decided to return home and pick up Rosetta's death certificate.

'What for?' she asked, picking up the tray of empty coffee cups.

'Were there any calls for me while the police were here?' I replied, avoiding her question with a question.

'Mrs Howard called about updating her Will, but she said she'd ring back later,' she replied, sounding slightly disgruntled. Danielle was sometimes too curious for her own good.

'OK. Thanks, Danielle.' She left the room.

Even though DCI Framlington did not seem overly concerned about the death certificate, I decided to give it to him and, on returning to the office, I 'phoned him to say I had it. There was no response on the mobile number he had given me so I left a message on the voicemail. I expected he and DS Henshaw were following up Annette's note and on their way to interview Caterina.

There was little point in 'phoning Alex as I knew he was unavailable, so I e-mailed him instead to update him with the latest developments. I knew he would ring me later when he had a moment. I was about to go and see Graham when he opened the door to my office.

'Nothing's happened to Fabio, has it?' he asked tentatively, stepping inside and closing the door firmly behind him.

'No.' At least, I sincerely hoped not.

'Only I understand you received a visit from two officers from the murder squad.'

'Yes. They came to see me about the murder of Mr Pellegrino's secretary.' I had not told Graham about the note which meant I would now have to explain myself.

'What?' he said, looking perplexed and taking a seat in one of the chairs on the opposite side of my desk. 'I don't follow. Why would they ask you about that? How could you possibly assist them?' He sounded completely surprised.

'More than you'd imagine,' I replied. I proceeded to give him a full account of the incident with Annette, my conversations with Caterina and my research on Rosetta. He did not say one word while I recounted the details but sat and listened intently.

'Do you really think that all this is connected with the business over Fabio's father?' he asked, folding his arms, leaning back in his chair and looking at me hard.

'Yes, I do, because Annette knew I went to see Gregorio Pellegrino to ask him questions about Emilio, so I believe the information she gave me was to assist with the investigation. What's eluding me is *how* it's all connected. One thing's for sure; all the people who have died were linked in some way to Scarpetti, Steiglitz & Co.'

'Apart from Giulia. I hate to poor cold water on your ideas, but she had nothing to do with the firm, Alicia.'

'Umm…not directly, but she was Emilio's daughter. I have another theory about her though.'

'Which is?' He unfolded his arms and sat upright.

'We've discovered from a friend of hers at the university that before she died she was carrying out some research into her family background in Italy. Unfortunately, her friend hasn't been able to give us much information, but she believes that on the night Giulia went missing she had a rendezvous with the present owner of a property which allegedly belonged to the Angelino family some time in the past. We don't have any more details than that because all the paperwork relating to it was taken from Giulia's room in Perugia.'

'But how is this significant, Alicia?' Graham seemed confused.

'You remember you told me that Kettering owned property in Tuscany?' He nodded. 'Well, he confirmed that when I met him, but also told me he advises clients about buying property in Italy and on the related aspects of Italian inheritance law.'

'You're not suggesting that he's the property owner Giulia met, are you?' Graham looked aghast.

'No. I'm not.' Even though we had not pinpointed his where-abouts that night, I doubted very much that he was anywhere near Perugia. We could obtain that information easily anyway. 'But you already know what I think about the possibility of Kettering and Pellegrino being in league together.'

'Yes, you told me the other day after your meeting with Kettering. Where is this leading to, Alicia?'

'What if their mutual legal acquaintance in Italy or someone associated with that acquaintance is the property owner Giulia met? That would give us the vital link to Scarpetti, Steiglitz & Co.'

'But why would any of them want her dead?'

'Maybe in the course of her innocent family research she revealed something they were hoping would remain hidden. Perhaps they have been carrying out shady property deals for years and Emilio uncovered what they were doing and was killed for it. They might have thought that Giulia was on to them and they had to dispose of her.'

'But what about Fabio and the incident in Ravello? How do you explain the attempt on his life?'

'Err... Alex and I discussed that before. Initially we thought that Fabio was the intended victim because Giulia wasn't in the car, but we came to the conclusion that it was probably she who was the intended victim.'

'I don't understand. Why?'

'Because at first the Alfa driver must have assumed she was in the car which is why he or she attempted to chase Fabio off the road. It was only when Fabio was forced to stop as that coach came down the hill that the driver would have had a clear view inside the car and seen that Giulia wasn't in it. I think it's significant that he or she abandoned the chase as soon as it was apparent Fabio was alone.'

'I suppose that's possible.' He did not sound at all convinced by my theory but that was hardly surprising. It seemed almost too fantastical for words. Nonetheless I felt it was a realistic explanation for what had happened. 'Have you told the police any of this?' he said slightly dubiously.

'Not yet, no. Apart from you, I haven't voiced my opinion on this particular theory to anyone. I was hoping that Caterina Bartoldi would be able to provide some much-needed evidence about the goings-on at Scarpetti, Steiglitz & Co.'

'What have you told Fabio?'

'Well, he knows all the facts but I haven't put this theory to him. We last spoke on Sunday evening. I really should ring him to tell him about my visit from the police and find out what's happening with the investigation his end.'

'OK. But keep me informed about things which potentially concern this firm,' he said, standing up and walking to the door.

'Thanks for listening, Graham.' My 'phone started to ring.

'Alicia, as your employer and while you work under my roof, I am responsible for your well-being. You'd better answer that,' he said, pointing to the telephone and left the room.

'Hello.' It was Susannah our receptionist.

'Alicia, one of the policemen who was here before is back and wants to speak with you. I saw Danielle on her way out to lunch and she said you were busy with Graham.' I presumed it was DCI Framlington who had arrived to pick up Rosetta's death certificate.

'I was, but I'm alone now. I'll come out. Give me a minute.'

There was a photocopier outside the door to my office and I wanted to make a copy of the certificate before I handed the DCI the original. Since Danielle was at lunch there was no chance of her looking over my shoulder. I returned to my office, and slipped the copy into my brief case before walking out to reception with the original certificate which I had put into a clean brown A4 envelope. To my surprise it was not DCI Framlington who was sitting waiting for me, but DS Henshaw. He stood up as soon as he saw me.

'I presume you want this,' I said, striding towards him and handing him the envelope.

'Thanks,' he said. We walked along to the lifts.

'When's Annette's inquest taking place?' I asked as I called the lift.

'I'm not sure yet. I wouldn't have thought you'd be required to attend to give evidence though.'

'Hmm... Have you managed to make contact with Caterina Bartoldi?'

'That's all in hand,' he replied. 'We'll inform you if there's anything you need to know.' I decided not to press the point, having been firmly put in my place.

'When do you want me to make my statement?' I asked as the lift arrived and he stepped inside.

'Within the next few days. I'll be in touch, but if you need to contact me in the meantime,' he said, taking a card out of his jacket pocket and handing it to me, 'call the mobile number on the back. Thanks for this,' he said curtly and waving the envelope at me as the lift doors closed.

I decided to go out for a late lunch and a stroll through St James's Park. I needed a break from the office, and some fresh air to clear my head. It was no longer stiflingly hot, and although it was still very warm, there was a cooling breeze which made it an altogether pleasant walk. I bought myself a bacon and avocado sandwich from the deli near the office and then ambled across to the Park, found myself a seat on an empty bench in a secluded corner and watched the passers-by while I ate my lunch.

By the time I returned to the office it was about two-thirty, and I was hoping for an uneventful afternoon and the opportunity to catch up on my day job. There was no point in worrying about or wondering what action the police were taking regarding Caterina particularly after what DS Henshaw had said to me. I was certain that I would find out soon enough. I needed to forget the investigation for a few hours and concentrate on matters in hand. Without any disturbances I had a relaxed but productive afternoon, at least until five-twenty when I received a call that was totally unexpected and from someone I had never spoken to previously.

'Sorry to disturb you, Alicia,' said Danielle as I answered my 'phone, 'but I have a rather agitated lady on the line. She says she must speak with you, but she won't tell me what she's ringing about.'

'OK. Did you glean her name by any chance?'

'Yes. Mrs Patricia Turnbull. Do you want to take the call?'

'Of course. Put her straight through.' I waited a moment for Danielle to connect us. 'Alicia Allen speaking,' I said. 'How may I help you?'

'Miss Allen, thank goodness you're there. I didn't know who else to turn to.' Danielle was right; she did sound extremely distressed.

'I don't mean to appear rude, Mrs Turnbull, but who are you and why are you calling me?'

'Please excuse me. I should have introduced myself. I'm Fabio's grandmother, Evelyn's mother.'

'Oh, I'm terribly sorry, Mrs Turnbull. I didn't recognise your surname. What's happened?' I asked, fearful of the worst. For one awful moment I thought she was going to tell me that some dreadful accident had befallen Fabio and that he was dead. 'Is Fabio OK?' I felt as if my heart was in my mouth.

'Yes. He is.' That was a relief.

'Then what is it?' I asked gently.

'I generally go to Chiswick every Wednesday afternoon as I have friends there. Since Fabio has been away I've been checking on the house, picking up his post and watering his plants. Well, everything was fine last week but today when I unlocked the front door I had the most terrible shock imaginable.'

'What do you mean?'

'The house has been ransacked. I've never seen so much mess in all my life.'

'Where are you now?'

'At the house.'

'Have you contacted the police?'

'No. You're the first person I've called. Fabio gave me your number in case anything happened while he was away.'

'Right. Don't worry about ringing them. I can do that for you. What about Fabio?'

'He doesn't know. He has so much on his plate. I couldn't bring myself to 'phone him.'

'OK. Let's see what we can find out first and call him later. We don't have to worry him just yet.'

'Would you mind coming over to the house?'

'Now?' I said, looking at my watch. It was twenty-five past five.

'Please.'

'All right. I'll be there as soon as I can.'

'You have the address?'

'Yes. I have all Fabio's details.'

'Oh, of course you would.'

'Provided there are no problems with the District Line I should be there in about forty minutes.'

'Thank you. I'm very grateful for your support. What a dreadful day this has turned out to be.'

'Yes,' I replied. Jo's comment the previous evening that she felt today was going to be an eventful day was no understatement. Bearing in mind there were still a few hours of the day remaining, I would reserve judgment on that for a little while longer.

155

Chapter 18

I logged out of my computer, tidied my desk, put on my jacket, picked up my briefcase and handbag and opened the door to my office. Danielle had already shut down her computer and was hovering by her desk ready to leave. We walked along the corridor to the lifts together.

'Was that a new client?' she enquired as we took the lift down to the foyer.

'No. It was Fabio's grandmother.'

'Really? Is everything OK?' It was obvious she was burning with curiosity.

'Yes.'

'Why was she calling?'

'Because she wanted to speak to me,' I replied, being deliberately evasive.

'You seem in a bit of a rush tonight,' she said as we reached the ground floor.

'I am. I have an appointment,' I said, stepping out of the lift ahead of her and sprinting off through the foyer towards the main entrance. 'See you tomorrow,' I called back before exiting through the revolving doors on to the street.

On my way to Victoria tube station I tried to call Alex to fill him in on this latest turn of events. There was no answer on his direct line and it diverted to voicemail, so I rang his mobile and left a brief message on that instead. Having assured Fabio's grandmother that I would inform the police, I proceeded to ring the number that DCI Framlington had given me. There was no response and I left a message informing him what had happened. I then called DS Henshaw on the mobile number he had given me but there was no reply so I also left him a voicemail message.

I picked up a carton of milk from the minimart at the back of the ticket hall near the entrance to the District line. I assumed that since Fabio had been away for the past nine days there would be no fresh milk in the house and I thought Mrs Turnbull might be in need of a cup of tea. I was about to walk down to the platform when my mobile rang; it was DS Henshaw returning my call. He seemed to think this was not a matter which concerned the murder squad and was rather abrupt. This irritated me because I did *not* appreciate being accused of wasting police time.

'DS Henshaw, I would not have rung you if I did not believe this break-in was *relevant* to the investigation.' I was conscious that I was standing in the middle of the ticket hall, but I had no other option but to talk with the rush hour crowd milling around me. 'All I ask is that you come to the house in Chiswick and give me the chance to explain why.' He did not respond. 'I understand that DCI Framlington is a stickler for thoroughness. I am sure he would prefer you to follow up on this rather than to leave it. Perhaps I should speak to him directly. I have left a message for him.' There was a significant pause before he spoke.

'That won't be necessary. I'll be there as soon as I can.'

'Thank you.'

'Are you going to the house now?'

'Yes, I am.'

'OK. I'm on my way. See you shortly.'

I took the tube to Chiswick Park as Fabio lived only a ten-minute walk from Chiswick High Road. I never had cause to visit his home before, but I had no difficulty finding my way. It was a Victorian end of terrace house and very well maintained. As I unlatched the gate and stepped into the front garden his grandmother opened the front door. I re-latched the gate and hurried up the path to her. She was standing waiting for me in the open doorway.

'Alicia Allen,' I said, extending my hand.

'Thank you so much for coming,' she replied, grasping my hand with both of hers. 'I saw you from the hall window.' She was a few inches taller than me so about five feet six, but rather delicate. I noticed that the skin on her hands was thin like crêpe paper. 'You made it in good time,' she said, ushering me into the house and shutting the front door. I thought she must be in her eighties, after all Fabio was in his mid-thirties, but I would never have guessed simply from looking at her face. She had a remarkably good complexion and minimal wrinkles. It was only her hands that revealed her true age.

'What a mess,' I said, dropping my briefcase in the hall and following her into the living room. 'Everything's been smashed.' The upholstery of the sofa had been slashed; the glass of the pictures broken and all Fabio's books had been taken off the bookshelves and thrown on to the floor. 'It's pure vandalism. I don't suppose you're able to tell if anything is missing, are you?'

'Well, that's the strange thing. The items you would expect people to steal like his stereo and audio equipment all seem to be here. It's as if they were looking for something in particular and when they couldn't find it decided to destroy the place. It didn't strike me as an ordinary burglary, which is why I called you first. You'll probably think me a ridiculous old woman for thinking this, but it did occur to me that perhaps the break-in is related to what happened to Giulia. What do you think?'

'I don't believe you're at all ridiculous.' In fact this was the exact thought which had crossed my mind when she 'phoned me. 'I take it Fabio has told you about Giulia's research on the family in Italy then?'

'Oh yes. He's been keeping me well-informed of events out there. Perhaps whoever it was who broke in here is the same person, or working in conjunction with whoever it was who took Giulia's laptop.'

'Thinking that Fabio had what they're looking for?'

'Yes,' she said enthusiastically.

'Which means they didn't find what they wanted when they searched Giulia's room.'

'It doesn't look like it, does it? Do you believe her friend is telling the truth, Miss Allen?'

'Please call me Alicia, Mrs Turnbull.'

'Provided you call me Patricia.'

'OK,' I said, smiling at her. 'Shall we have a cup of tea, Patricia?'

'There isn't any milk.'

'We have milk,' I said, retrieving the carton from my briefcase in the hall. 'I bought some on the way over.'

'Oh, you are thoughtful,' she said, trotting off in the direction of the kitchen with me following behind. 'There are some biscuits in the cupboard. I expect you're quite hungry.'

'I'm all right for now. So this is where they broke in,' I said, noticing the small side window which had been completely cut out of its frame. 'It looks like a professional job. You almost don't notice it as they've slotted the window back in. If you tell me where everything is, I'll make the tea,' I said, glancing around the kitchen.

'No. No. I'll do it. You sit down.' I sat at the kitchen table and watched her as she bustled about making the tea. I thought she was remarkable; an indomitable character. She reminded me of Dorothy and she was just as sharp. She was on the same wavelength as me when it came to our thoughts on this case, which was helpful. She put some plain chocolate Home Wheat biscuits on a plate. 'Just in case you're a bit peckish,' she said, offering it to me. I took one out of politeness. 'You didn't answer my question,' she said, handing me my cup of tea, putting hers on the table and sitting down opposite me.

'About Laura telling the truth?' She nodded.

'I don't think she's lying, but my gut feeling is that she knows more than she's letting on.' At that point the doorbell rang causing

Patricia to start. I was not surprised she was on edge. She had sustained quite a few shocks recently and it was stressful enough for those of us who were not emotionally involved.

'Who's that at the door?' she asked, sounding slightly uneasy.

'I expect it's the police. I rang them as I was leaving the office. I'll go and check.' I saw no point in mentioning my exchange with DS Henshaw. The main point was that he had come to the house as requested.

'Look through the spyhole before you open the door, won't you, dear?' she called out to me.

'Of course.' In fact that was unnecessary because from the hall window I had a clear view of the police car parked outside the house and then I observed DS Henshaw as he walked up the path and joined the police constable standing outside the front door. 'Thanks for coming over.' I said, opening it.

'That's all right,' he replied coldly, stepping inside, closely followed by the police constable. 'I'm a bit later than expected. Is Mrs Turnbull here?'

'She's in the kitchen. We were having a cup of tea.'

'How very civilised of you,' he said with a hint of cynicism. I sensed he was annoyed with me over our earlier conversation.

'Would you like a cup?' I said, ignoring his remark. 'How do you take it? I know you have sugar in your coffee but not how you like your tea.'

'Milk, no sugar, thanks. This place has been trashed,' he said, looking about. 'Where did they break in?'

'Through the side window in the kitchen,' I said, leading him through. The police constable remained in the hall. 'Apart from making a cup of tea we haven't moved or touched anything.'

'Excellent.' Patricia stood up as he walked into the room. 'DS Henshaw,' he said, flashing his ID at her.

'Good evening, officer,' she said. I took a mug out of the cupboard and proceeded to make his tea.

'Can you tell me what happened, Mrs Turnbull?'

'There's nothing much to tell. I arrived here this afternoon to check on the house and this is what I found. I couldn't really hazard a guess as to when the break-in took place, only that it must have been over the past week.'

'Why do you say that?'

'Because I was here last Wednesday afternoon and everything was fine.'

'I see. Well, we'll get the place dusted for prints and see what else forensics can pick up. We'll also interview the neighbours as a matter of routine.'

'Thank you,' she said, sitting down at the table. I handed him his mug of tea.

'So, Miss Allen,' he said, taking it from me, 'explain to me why you think this break-in is related to the murder investigation?' I felt frustrated because it was as if everything I had told him and DCI Framlington earlier that day had completely washed over him. I thought the connection would be obvious.

'You'll recall that when we spoke this morning I told you we believe Giulia may have been murdered as a result of some family research she had been carrying out?'

'Yes. Do I take it by 'we' that this also includes you, Mrs Turnbull?' said DS Henshaw, turning to her.

'Oh yes. And Fabio too.'

'Go on,' he said. He took a couple of gulps of tea.

'What I didn't mention was that some items went missing from Giulia's room after she died.'

'What items?'

'Her laptop and some research documents.'

'I see. And you think this is relevant?'

'Yes. That's why I'm telling you. We think that the reason she was killed, and those items were removed, is because she had inadvertently stumbled across something incriminating, possibly evidence which could lead to Emilio's murderer, and Rosetta Bartlett's, not to mention Annette Richardson's.'

'How can you say that? We have no proof they were murdered. In fact, my understanding is that we don't know what happened to Emilio, and Rosetta's death certificate refers to her drowning.' He took another gulp of tea.

'Missing, presumed drowned. In light of recent events, don't you think there's a possibility she was murdered?'

'I couldn't comment. I know nothing about the investigation into her disappearance.'

'Hmm... Well, that's as maybe, DS Henshaw,' said Patricia, coming to my defence, 'but I think you should pay attention to what Miss Allen is telling you and not dismiss it out of hand. Things are not always black and white. As a police officer you must be more aware of that than any of us?' He did not respond but he looked slightly uncomfortable. He was obviously not used to being admonished, particularly by elderly ladies.

'You can't dispute that Annette was murdered,' I said. 'And I believe that she was also killed because of something she knew. I am convinced that her murder, and Giulia's, Rosetta's death and Emilio's disappearance are all connected. They have one common link: Scarpetti, Steiglitz & Co.'

'She has a point, don't you think?' said Patricia, forcing it. 'My son-in-law disappeared in mysterious circumstances and my granddaughter has been murdered. I do not want my grandson to suffer the same fate. Please help us,' she said, momentarily grabbing his hand. 'I beseech you. He's all I have.' She was very compelling and I felt DS Henshaw slightly soften towards us.

'At the very least,' I said,' I think you should be looking a little more closely into the association between Gregorio Pellegrino and Roland Kettering and their business interests.'

'All right. I'll see what I can do about following that up,' he replied, and then addressing Patricia said, 'In the meantime, my immediate concern is securing this house. I'll arrange for someone to come around and sort out that window. Are you OK to stay here for a little while?'

'I suppose so,' she said, looking at me.

'I can stay with you,' I said reassuringly.

'Are you sure?' she asked.

'Of course.'

'I'll have to take some contact details off you, Mrs Turnbull. Where do you live?'

'Chalfont-St-Giles.'

'I didn't realize you lived so far out,' I said. 'For some reason I thought you lived in Hampstead.' I was amazed and impressed that she still managed to travel in to London once a week, although she did appear to be in remarkably good health.

'I used to, when I first returned to England.'

'You can't go back there tonight. It'll be so late by the time you get home.'

'We could arrange a car for you,' said DS Henshaw.

'Oh, that's most kind of you.'

'Or you could stay with me, if you like. I'm only in South Kensington, so not far at all.'

'That's very thoughtful of you, dear, but I'm not going to impose on you. If DS Henshaw can organize transport to take me home I'm very happy to take it.'

'That's settled then,' he said. My mobile started to vibrate in my pocket.

'Excuse me,' I said, walking out into the hall. 'Hello,' I said, answering it.

'*Ciao, bella.* What's going on?' It was Alex.

'I'm still in Chiswick and the police are here.'

'You can't talk?'

'Not really. I'll ring you when I'm home, although I don't think it will be for a while yet.'

'No problem. I'm still in the office. I won't be out of here for a few hours. Are you OK?'

'Oh yes. I'm fine. Graham was giving me a bit of a lecture today, though, about keeping him in the loop.'

'Well, at least he's concerned for your welfare and he does need to know what's going on in his firm. Don't take it personally. Listen, call me later if you can or give me a buzz in the morning.'

'OK.'

'Ciao, bella.'

'Ciao, carino. Ciao. Bye.'

I returned to the kitchen where Patricia was chatting to DS Henshaw.

'Are you all right, dear?' she asked.

'Yes. Thank you. Please don't worry about me.'

'I'll be off then,' he said, putting his empty mug on the draining board. I followed him out into the hall.

'What's happening with Caterina Bartoldi?' I asked.

'I'm afraid I can't discuss that with you.'

'Well, can you at least tell me whether you've spoken to her or not?'

'DCI Framlington had a brief chat with her this afternoon.' He walked to the front door. 'Goodnight, Miss Allen,' he said, cutting the conversation dead, and he left.

No sooner had DS Henshaw left when a couple of officers from the forensic team arrived and dusted for prints. They seemed to spend a considerable time searching for any other evidence that might assist with the investigation. Fortunately, it was not long before someone came to secure the window and check on the rest of the house. While we waited for Patricia's car home to arrive I wandered around the house. As I walked back to the kitchen through the hall I caught sight of a pile of post on the table. Seeing the post reminded me of what Laura told Fabio about Giulia making a trip to the post office on the Saturday morning before they caught the train to Orvieto.

Suddenly it dawned on me that the packet she posted could have been addressed to Fabio and that it contained those research documents. That would certainly explain why they were missing from her room, and give a reason for someone to break into Fabio's house believing that he had them. When I first heard that the papers were missing, my initial thought was that they had been taken from her room by the person, or persons, who had broken into it. That seemed a logical explanation at the time but not anymore. My gut feeling about the break-in at the apartment in Atrani was that it was not the work of a local gang despite the Italian police's confirmation of the same. Perhaps whoever was responsible for that thought Giulia had her research with her to show Fabio which was the real reason why the apartment was burgled. After all, they did not take anything.

Similarly, as Patricia had pointed out, nothing she would have expected to be stolen in the course of a normal burglary was missing from the house and it was as if whoever had broken-in was searching for something in particular. I picked up the post and started to sift through it.

'Patricia. Is this all the post that's come for Fabio?' I called out.

'What's that, dear?' she said, trotting into the hall.

'The post. Is everything here?' I asked, holding it up.

'Yes. Why?'

'Because for one glorious moment I thought we might have found the missing research documents in Fabio's post; but they're not here.'

'What do you mean?'

'Maybe Fabio forgot to tell you but, according to Laura, Giulia posted something on the Saturday before she died. I thought maybe it could have been her research and that she had sent it to Fabio. That'll teach me for being too over-enthusiastic.'

'Well, just a minute. There is something.'

'What?' She disappeared into the kitchen. 'Where are you going?'

'To fetch my handbag,' she called out.

'Why?' I said, wandering after her.

'Because,' she said, opening it, 'when I picked up the post today there was a Royal Mail "We're holding an item of mail for you" delivery card in the pile. I thought it was one of Fabio's subscriptions and I would have gone off to the local delivery office to collect it if it hadn't been for all this terrible break-in business today.'

'May I see it?'

'Of course,' she said, handing it to me. I noticed that the card was marked "packet was too big to fit through the letterbox".'

'Oh, Patricia, maybe this parcel contains those documents. It would help us so much if it did.'

'There's only one way to find out. Let's pick it up.'

'I could do that for you tomorrow, but I'll need to take proof of Fabio's identity and address. There's no point in asking them to redeliver the packet as nobody's here and we don't want them to send it back.'

'OK. There's a utility bill lying around here somewhere and he didn't take his UK driving licence with him as I saw it upstairs. We should be all right though because they keep mail for three weeks. They won't have returned it yet.'

'Not if it comes from abroad, or it's registered. I'm sure it's only one week. The card was dated two days ago so that still gives us plenty of time to collect it, but I don't think we should hang around.'

'I'm not going to sleep tonight until I know what's in that packet, Alicia.'

'Me neither! Let's hope it's not a fool's errand.'

Chapter 19

After an eventful Wednesday I wondered what Thursday would bring. Patricia and I had agreed not to contact Fabio until after I had collected the packet from the delivery office. There was no point in building up his hopes in case it was not the parcel from Giulia. That would only lead to further disappointment. I pinned all my hopes on it being from her as I was convinced her research would provide vital clues which would help us solve the mystery of all the deaths.

I saw the light on my answerphone flashing as I walked through to the living room. There was a message from my mother, and I felt guilty because I had not rung to see how Nonna and my uncle were since my return to London on Sunday evening. There was also a garbled message from Antonia in which she mentioned something about looking at designs for her wedding dress on Saturday, but there was so much background noise that she was barely audible.

It was still fairly early so I called home. I had a brief word with my mother who wanted to know if I would be down to visit at the weekend, but who had clearly not spoken with Antonia because she knew nothing about her plans for Saturday. I was pleased to hear that she, my uncle and Nonna were having a lovely time together and making the most of the fantastic summer weather we had been enjoying. I also chatted with Uncle Vico who told me he had no alternative but to return to New York the following week due to pressure of work, although he intended to come up to London for a few days before he left.

Uncle Vico was anxious to learn about the progress I was making with Fabio's investigation and was appalled to learn of Annette's murder. He had met her briefly all those years ago when he visited the offices of Scarpetti, Steiglitz & Co. He felt that the involvement of the police was a positive development, but I explained to him that I was having difficulty convincing them that the deaths were connected. I did not even mention the packet; there was no point in speculating whether it was from Giulia and what it might contain.

I then rang Antonia. I could tell from my caller display that she had rung me from her mobile and I tried that number first. When she answered the 'phone, there was an inordinate din in the background and I had to strain to pick up what she was saying.

'Hello. Hello,' she said.

'Antonia…'

'Ally, is that you?'

'Yes. Where are you? I can barely hear you.'

'What? I didn't catch that.'

'I'm returning your call.'

'What did you say?'

'Oh, this is ridiculous. Call me back later.'

'What?' There was no point in attempting to have a conversation with her so I hung up and sent her a text message. I decided to ring Alex, but there was still no answer on either his landline or mobile. I went to make myself a cup of tea and some raisin toast and sat down to watch the ten o'clock news. About five minutes later the 'phone rang. It was Antonia and this time she was loud and clear.

'You didn't have to hang up on me?' she said, sounding slightly disgruntled.

'Well, I couldn't hear you with all that racket going on around you, hence my text. Where are you?'

'I'm at a launch party. We're doing the PR for it. I've just stepped outside. Did you get my message earlier?'

'Yes. That's why I called. It wasn't very clear though.'

'I want to look at some wedding dresses. I've picked up all the magazines and I have an idea of the design I want, but I'd like to see what's out there.'

'You could always ask Dorothy to help you with that.'

'Why?'

'Because she was a seamstress at Norman Hartnell. I'm sure she'd be delighted to talk to you about designs and you could bounce ideas off each other.'

'I'll think about it. Are you free on Saturday?'

'Yes, but early morning is better for me.'

'Have you got plans then?'

'As it happens, I do.'

'I suppose they include Alex,' she said, sounding put out by the fact that I might actually have arrangements of my own.

'Give me a call on Friday evening and we'll fix up a time then. OK?' I replied, ignoring her comment.

'Oh, all right.' And she was gone.

I had just put the 'phone down when it rang again. I presumed it was Antonia ringing back, but it was Alex.

'Sorry I didn't answer when your rang before, but I was asleep.'

'Oh, Alex, I didn't mean to wake you. I thought you'd still be up,' I said, glancing at my watch. It was five past eleven and I had called him about ten minutes earlier.

'I sat down on the sofa when I came in and the next thing I remember is my mobile ringing. I must have slept through your call on the landline and the mobile. It was only the voicemail ring-back on the mobile that woke me up. It's just as well you did 'phone otherwise I'd probably have slept on the sofa all night. What's the latest on the break-in at Fabio's house?' I told Alex about my conversation with DS Henshaw and the card delivered by the Royal Mail. He agreed that it was prudent not to mention it to the police or to Fabio at this stage. 'I don't know why DS Henshaw's so hostile towards you,' he said. 'But in light of his attitude the last thing you need is to end up with egg on your face over the packet.'

'Quite.'

'Do you think he'll follow up with Pellegrino and Kettering?'

'I really don't know. He wouldn't say anything about the interview with Caterina Bartoldi, so I have no idea what's happening with that side of the investigation.'

'Well, let's hope they're carrying out a covert operation and will surprise us with their miraculous solution to the murder,' said Alex, stifling a yawn.

'Murders would be preferable. You'd better get some sleep. You sound exhausted. I'll call you when I know what's in the packet.'

'OK,' he said, yawning again. 'Speak to you tomorrow.'

On Thursday morning I was up at the crack of dawn because I was keen to collect the parcel as soon as possible and review its contents. I knew I would be late for work and since I did not want to leave a message on the office answerphone broadcasting the real reason for my absence to the whole office, I merely said that I had been up most of the night with a stomach bug but would be making it in, albeit a little later than usual.

Unfortunately, there were signal problems on the District line and it took at least an extra half an hour to reach Acton Town, the tube nearest to Fabio's local delivery office in Bollo Lane, which delayed me further. I entered the building, walked up to the counter, pressed the bell once as requested on a notice, and waited. Within a few moments a surly looking man appeared, I took the card out of my handbag, handed it to him and he disappeared out of view. Presently he returned holding an A4 sized brown jiffy bag.

'This is addressed to Fabio Angelino,' he said tersely, giving me a double take and placing it on the counter in front of him. It was then that I caught sight of the Italian stamps on the envelope; I knew that I must be right and this was the packet that Giulia had posted. I felt sick with anticipation as I was desperate to discover what was in that jiffy bag.

'That's correct,' I replied. 'I've come to collect it for him.'

'Do you have proof of his identity and address?'

'Yes,' I said, opening my handbag and taking out Fabio's driving licence and a gas bill Patricia had found for me and showing them to him.

'Fine,' he said gruffly, 'Sign here.' I did so and he handed the packet to me. I flipped it over and looked at the sender's name and address which had been written neatly in black ink on the back, presumably by Giulia. The sender's name was certainly hers, but the address was care of one in Orvieto, which I assumed must be that of Laura's parents. Obviously Giulia had not wanted the package returned to her university address in the unlikely event that it was undelivered. I unfastened the buckle of my briefcase, stuffed the envelope inside, refastened my briefcase and made my way out of the delivery office and back to the tube station.

By the time I arrived at the office it was nearly ten-thirty. As I walked into reception Susannah, who must have picked up my message, enquired after my health.

'I'm much better, thanks,' I replied without stopping to talk to her for more than a moment.

'You're looking a bit flushed,' she said as I walked off down the corridor. 'You should take it easy today.'

'Am I?' I replied, turning back fleetingly and putting my hand up to my cheek. I think 'flustered' was a more apt description of my state at that moment. I rushed passt Graham's office. Fortunately, his door was closed and he did not see me. However, I was unable to avoid Danielle who jumped up from her chair when I appeared.

'Are you OK?' she asked, scrutinising my face. I opened the door to my office and she followed me in.

'Yes,' I replied, dropping my briefcase by the side of my desk, walking around to my chair and sitting down.

'You don't look it. You're cheeks are bright red. Are you sure you're not running a high temperature?' I felt guilty because she seemed genuinely concerned about me, but I could hardly tell her that there was nothing wrong with my health without revealing the true reason for my absence that morning.

'Please don't worry, Danielle. I'm feeling better by the second.'

'Honestly?'

'Yes. Honestly.'

'Well, make sure you drink plenty of water today.' I nodded.

'See you later,' I said as she walked towards the door. I proceeded to glance through my post, but I was anxious for her to leave the room so I could open the packet. 'Oh, Alicia,' she said, hovering in the doorway. I looked up. 'Were you expecting anyone in particular to ring you this morning only your direct line has been ringing and ringing and, whenever the call diverted to me, whoever it was hung up.' I looked at her blankly.

'Maybe it was a wrong number,' I said. It did occur to me that it might be Fabio's grandmother, but then she knew I would call her as soon as I had some news. There was a remote chance that it was Caterina Bartoldi, although that was probably wishful thinking on my part.

'I suppose it might have been,' she replied, shrugging her shoulders and sounding totally unconvinced before finally leaving the room and shutting the door behind her.

The moment Danielle was gone I took the jiffy bag out of my briefcase and carefully slit open the top of the envelope with a pair of scissors from my drawer. As I pulled out the contents, which comprised a small assorted bundle of papers, an old black and white photograph of a young couple in bridal dress standing in front of an imposing villa fell onto the desk, together with a small tatty folded piece of white paper. I assumed the photograph must be of Fabio and Giulia's grandparents and the very same photograph which Laura had mentioned seeing. I picked it up, flipped it over and there on the back written in Italian were the words:

Il giorno delle nozze di Eduardo e Maria, 9 giugno 1938, Ponte a Moriano

I was almost certain that Ponte a Moriano is fairly near the town of Lucca, which tied in with what Fabio had told me about his family originating from that area of Italy, and a quick search on the internet confirmed that it is. The folded piece of paper offered more information as it was in fact a copy of Eduardo's birth certificate, *Certificato di Nascita*. The print was faded and the handwritten part of the document was indistinct, but I could just make out his name, date and place of birth: Eduardo Antonio Angelino was born on 8 December 1913 in Lucca. I could not read the other details.

As I worked my way through the bundle of papers it was apparent that Giulia had undertaken most of her research into the Angelino family background via the internet as there was print out after print out from various websites, particularly those which dealt with tracing genealogical roots in Italy and searching for family property. There was one heavily annotated page which explained how to carry out property title searches in Italy, and a good deal of information on the *Provincia di Lucca*, including a map of the area and a list of all the *comuni*. Stapled to this document was a list of all the *frazioni* into which Lucca is divided – that is, all the smaller outlying areas forming part of the *comune*, one of which is Ponte a Moriano.

I noticed that Giulia had placed an asterisk next to *Comune di Lucca* and that of *Viareggio*. *Viareggio* was, of course, the place where, according to Graham, Roland Kettering owned property. Although I was desperate to find a connection between Roland Kettering, Gregorio Pellegrino, their unknown mutual legal acquaintance in Italy and the Angelino family, Giulia's asterisk alone would take me no further and unfortunately I could find nothing in the papers to explain why she had put a marker beside it.

Of more relevance to me were the documents right at the back of the bundle as these were the property searches Giulia had completed. There was a *Visura per soggetto*, that is, a title search by name. She had obviously been able to carry this out with the details she had obtained from her grandfather's birth certificate: his name, date of birth, place of birth and the location of the villa which she had gleaned from the photograph. This search had revealed details of a property called Villa Anna.

There was also a *Visura storica per immobile* – a property title history of Villa Anna, listing the property owners names and their respective dates of birth including the present owner. The information from the first search had enabled her to carry out this subsequent search. I eagerly scanned down to the bottom of the list of owners – *Intestati* – for the name of the current owner because I knew he was a key witness/possible suspect in Giulia's murder investigation. If what Laura had told Fabio about her last conversation with Giulia on the train was to be believed, and Giulia had planned to arrange to meet him and to visit the villa, then it was crucial we tracked him down. His name was Piero Giovannini and he was born on 18 November 1970 so, in my view, a little too young to be the elusive mutual legal acquaintance of Roland Kettering and Gregorio Pellegrino. I was looking for someone whose association with Gregorio Pellegrino dated back more than twenty years. But even if Mr Giovannini was not the mutual legal acquaintance, it did not necessarily follow that he was unconnected to him or Mr Pellegrino and even Mr Kettering. Furthermore, if he had played a part in Giulia's murder, then in my mind he must be linked with them somehow, although establishing that link was another matter.

However, it was not Mr Giovannini's name which stared out at me from the page, but the name typed above it, that of Emilio Angelino born on 3 April 1947. When I saw his name on the list I could hardly believe it. From my conversations with Fabio it was evident that he knew nothing about Villa Anna, let alone his father's ownership of it. I wondered when Emilio had sold the villa to Mr Giovannini because that was not apparent from the searches. It was not that I was surprised to see his name as, after all there were also two other Angelino's on the list above him, namely a Dino Alberto Angelino born on 9 June 1912, and a Felice Angelino born on 16 March 1880, only that nobody seemed to know that Emilio had ever owned the property, least of all his two children. Clearly the next stage would be to find out when the ownership passed to Mr Giovannini.

I could find no details confirming when the property was transferred or sold to Mr Giovannini, but that was something that I could ask Uncle Vico to investigate as he had contacts in Italy who might be able to source the information for us. I did not suppose Fabio would raise any objection to that.

Evidently, this was a question to which Giulia had also sought answers because the last piece of paper in the bundle was a copy of a computer-generated letter she had written in Italian to Mr Giovannini requesting information on this very point. In her letter she had explained who she was and that she was carrying out research into her Italian background in the course of which she had discovered that Villa Anna used to be in the ownership of the Angelino family. She enquired whether Mr Giovannini had ever had any personal dealings with her father and if so, during what period. She also expressed an interest in visiting Villa Anna, tentatively suggesting a meeting between the two of them there.

The letter was dated 26 May 2008, so a few weeks before her murder and sent from her university address. There was no response to this letter in the bundle and I therefore assumed that no written response had been given, although it did not necessarily follow that the absence of such a letter from the bundle meant that there had been no written reply. Giulia had, however, listed all her contact details on the letter including her mobile number and it therefore seemed quite likely that she would have received a telephone call instead. This would certainly tie in with what Laura said about the current owner ringing Giulia to make arrangements for her to visit the villa.

Having perused all the documents, there was something that struck me as slightly odd. Normally I would have expected Giulia to include a note to Fabio explaining what she had discovered, but I had the strong impression from the rather erratic handwriting on the envelope that she had bundled the documents into the jiffy bag in haste, without having time to write one. Maybe she had intended to ring Fabio to let him know the packet was on its way to him, but never made the call because the murderer caught up with her before she had the chance. To me something was definitely amiss, even though I could not pinpoint exactly what it was.

I gathered together all the paperwork and carefully put it back into the jiffy bag which I then replaced inside my briefcase for safe-keeping. I did not want to leave any papers lying around just in case Graham or Danielle should chance to see them, particularly before I had had the opportunity of discussing them with Fabio. As a matter of courtesy I decided to telephone his grandmother first, because I was aware she was awaiting news about the contents of the packet from me and was rather anxious about the whole matter. She was relieved to hear that it was from Giulia, but slightly thrown by the discovery Giulia had made. I was doubtful whether she could shed any light on the mystery surrounding Emilio's ownership of Villa Anna but I decided to ask her nonetheless.

'Did your daughter ever mention a villa or any other assets in Italy for that matter?'

'No. I always had the impression that when Emilio's parents emigrated to New York that they left nothing behind in Italy. Certainly, throughout the course of their married life, I never heard Emilio talk about owning a villa near Lucca or anywhere else in Italy. If he still owned it at the time of his death, wouldn't Mr Kettering have turned it up when he was dealing with the Probate of his estate?'

'Hmm… Well, not necessarily if nobody knew about it.' I was becoming increasingly dubious about Mr Kettering's involvement in the whole affair, but this was another issue entirely. 'Anyway, so far as I can make out, it looks as if the property was passed over to Mr Giovannini before Emilio disappeared – if Giulia's research is accurate – which means it isn't an asset that would have formed part of his estate.'

'Then why are you concerned about it?'

'It's a bit strange, that's all.'

'At least you know who the current owner is. Are you going to inform the police about him?'

'The Italian police you mean?'

'Well, yes. The fact that Giulia wrote to him has to be significant surely?'

'Certainly, but I want to talk to Fabio before we do anything. If what happened to Emilio, Rosetta, Giulia and Annette are connected and the common link is Scarpetti Steiglitz & Co. then the police here need to know about Piero Giovannini as well. You haven't spoken to Fabio by any chance today?'

'No. I thought you wanted to wait until we found out what was in the packet. DS Henshaw didn't seem very convinced that the deaths were linked. I didn't care for his manner at all.'

'No. He's a bit brusque. Don't worry. I'll try to contact his senior officer, DCI Framlington. I found him easier to deal with. I'm going to call Fabio now so expect to hear from him later.'

'All right. Thank you so much, Alicia. I don't know what I would have done without you yesterday.'

'Please don't thank me. I really didn't do anything. You can thank me when we've brought Giulia's killer to justice.'

Chapter 20

'Alicia. Finally I get to speak to you,' said Fabio as he answered his mobile. Admittedly we had not spoken since Sunday evening and in truth I needed to talk to him about recent developments.

'I'm sorry, Fabio. Have you been trying to get hold of me?'

'I called you several times earlier this morning before I left the hotel, but I kept on getting Danielle and I really didn't want to leave any messages with her.' So it was Fabio who had been ringing my direct line; at least that was one question answered. If only everything in this case could be resolved as easily. 'The last time we spoke you said you intended to persevere with Caterina Bartoldi. Did you manage to speak to her again?'

'I did. Listen; are you in a place where you can talk to me freely, only there are things we need to discuss?'

'That sounds ominous.' I did not comment. 'If you give me ten minutes, I'll be back at the hotel.'

'Great. What's the number as I'll call you there?'

'I don't know it off-hand. I'll text it to you when I'm in my room.'

'OK,' I replied, retrieving my mobile from my handbag and placing it on the desk. 'Is Will with you?'

'He returned to Perugia yesterday. Didn't Jo tell you?'

'No. She never mentioned it. I'll call you as soon as I receive your text.'

'OK. Bye, Alicia.'

No sooner had I put down the receiver than Danielle rang through.

'Are you OK, Alicia?'

'Yes. Why?'

'I was wondering how you were feeling, that's all, and if you wanted anything?' In my excitement over retrieving the packet it had completely slipped my mind that I was supposed to be recovering from an upset stomach.

'Oh, that. I'm much better thanks.'

'Good. Alex called while you were on the 'phone.'

'OK. I'll ring him back.'

'And DS Henshaw also called.'

'Oh,' I replied, without enthusiasm. 'What did he want?'

'He wouldn't tell me. He merely asked for you to 'phone him on his mobile as soon as possible.'

'Right,' I said, looking at my watch, conscious that Fabio should be sending me that text any time soon. I did not suppose that DS Henshaw would want to speak to me for more than thirty seconds which meant that if I rang him immediately the conversation would be over before I had even received Fabio's text.

'Thanks, Danielle.'

'DS Henshaw,' I said, addressing him. 'It's Alicia Allen returning your call.'

'Yes, Miss Allen. Would it be possible for you to come in and make your statement this evening?'

'It could be. What time?'

'Six.'

'OK. I should be able to make that.' There was a slightly embarrassing pause. 'DS Henshaw, further to our conversation yesterday evening, have you decided what steps you're going to take about investigating the association between Mr Pellegrino and Mr Kettering?'

'It's in hand,' he said curtly. 'See you at six.' And he was gone. I was right; the conversation was barely thirty seconds long. Fabio's text arrived a few minutes later.

'Fabio, it's Alicia,' I said as he answered his hotel telephone.

'Thanks for calling back so quickly. What's been happening?' he asked tentatively.

'Remember I told you that I believe Rosetta Bartlett's dead?'

'Hmm… Yes. You're going to tell me she is, right?'

'Well, I did some research on the internet and the long and short of it is that Rosetta went missing off the Amalfi coast not long after your father disappeared. Her body was never found and in 1999 she was registered as missing, presumed drowned – at least that's what's on her death certificate.'

'No?' Fabio sounded incredulous. 'But that's bizarre. I mean it can't be coincidental that a close colleague of my father's also disappeared without a trace.'

'There's more.'

'More?'

'Yes. She disappeared in Ravello.'

'What?' Fabio was clearly shocked. 'But that's the very place the Alfa driver tried to ram me off the road. There has to be a connection between her disappearance and my father's.'

'On the face of it, yes.'

'You don't seem very certain, Alicia. Surely everything points to that being the case?'

'It's a question of evidence, Fabio.'

'What about Caterina Bartoldi? You said earlier that you managed to speak with her again. Presumably you asked her about this? She must know something which can help us.' Fabio again sounded desperate and I only wished I could tell him what he wanted to hear.

'After Annette was murdered I had no choice other than to disclose the note she gave me to the police. I knew that they'd want to interview Caterina, so I called her and left a message on her voicemail indicating that it was Annette who had recommended I contact her, and that the police were likely to ask her questions about Annette's murder.'

'Hoping that it would draw her?'

'Which it did, and she returned my call. She obviously put two and two together and realized that it was Annette who gave me Rosetta's name. Unfortunately, when I told her that I knew Rosetta was dead because I had checked, and asked her what she would tell the police if they questioned her over Rosetta's disappearance, she hung up on me.'

'Great.' I detected the irritation in Fabio's voice. 'Have the police interviewed her yet?'

'Two officers on the case, DCI Framlington and DS Henshaw, came to the office yesterday morning to question me about what I know. I've provided them with all the background details so they can pursue their enquiries. DCI Framlington indicated that they would be speaking to Caterina but, when I asked his DS about whether they had later in the day, he wouldn't tell me anything.'

'I was really hoping Caterina might assist. It's very disappointing.'

'I'm aware of that. Alex and I think she's terrified of the repercussions if she does.'

'What do you mean?'

'Alex has a friend who works at Williams, Ricks & Stone. He doesn't know Caterina personally, but he found out for Alex that she is a commercial property specialist and left Scarpetti, Steiglitz & Co not long after your father's and Rosetta's respective disappearances. We don't know the exact details why she left, but judging by her adverse reaction to my questions about the firm, your father, and Rosetta, I can only assume that she left to dissociate herself with the place and whatever went on there. I have no doubt that she has information which could assist us, but I have the feeling she won't divulge it for fear that it will harm her. She's definitely very afraid of any association with Scarpetti, Steiglitz & Co.'

'Let's hope the police can get her to talk.'

'I wouldn't bet on it.'

'It's typical. She's probably the only one who can help us make any progress with the murder enquiry and she won't cooperate.'

Fabio was becoming more and more frustrated by the minute.

'Well, not quite the only one,' I said softly.

'What do you mean?'

'There have been some other developments.'

'Concerning Caterina?'

'No. Your grandmother rang me yesterday afternoon and...'

'She's all right, isn't she?' he asked, interrupting me before I had the opportunity to explain why she had made the call. 'I couldn't bear it if anything has happened to her.' I detected the agitation in his voice.

'Your grandmother is fine, Fabio,' I replied gently, trying to reassure him. 'She called me because yesterday afternoon she went to your house to check on it in your absence, and I'm really sorry to have to be the one to tell you this, but there's been a break-in.'

'Oh, no.' He sighed deeply. 'This is all I need right now especially with everything else.' Unsurprisingly, he seemed despondent. 'What did they take?'

'That's the thing; nothing it would seem.'

'Really? I don't follow.'

'Your grandmother and I both think whoever broke in was looking for a specific item.'

'But what?'

'You remember you told me about a packet Giulia posted on her way to Orvieto?'

'Yes, of course I do.'

'Well, that's what we think they wanted, or rather its contents.'

'But I don't have it.'

'Giulia posted that parcel to you, Fabio.'

'What? How do you know?'

'Because I collected it from your local delivery office this morning.' There was a momentary silence at the other end of the 'phone. 'Are you still there, Fabio?' I said.

'Yes. I'm just trying to get my head around what you're telling me. Have you opened it?'

'I took the liberty of doing so, yes.'

'And?'

'It contains Giulia's research into your Italian family background.'

'Then Laura isn't lying.' I knew he must have considered the possibility that she might be. 'Did you discover anything which might lead us to Giulia's murderer?' I proceeded to tell Fabio exactly what was in the bundle of documents and what Giulia had uncovered. 'I don't know what to say, Alicia. I had no idea that the family ever owned Villa Anna in Ponte a Moriano let alone that it passed into my father's ownership. That is a mystery to me in itself.'

'I could ask Uncle Vico to check that out if you would like me to? He did mention that he has contacts in Italy so I might as well see if he can help.'

'Yes, please do.'

'Personally, I'd be interested in finding out when the ownership of the property actually passed from your father to Piero Giovannini.'

'That goes without saying, Alicia. I'd really like to see the property searches, only I wouldn't want you to fax them to me here. As for Giulia's research, I suppose it's a logical assumption that whoever is behind the break-in into Giulia's room at the university is also responsible for the break-in at my house. Now I'm convinced more than ever that the burglary at the apartment in Atrani wasn't carried out by some local gang targeting tourists as the police suggested at the time. Whoever's masterminding this clearly didn't want me to get hold of Giulia's research.' These were my sentiments exactly. 'Did you contact the police about the break-in?'

'Yes, on my way to Chiswick yesterday. I felt sure that it was relevant to the investigation into Annette's murder so I called DCI Framlington and DS Henshaw. I must say DS Henshaw was quick to arrive on the scene, made sure that the house was secure and that your grandmother was driven home.' I did not mention that DS Henshaw was actually extremely reluctant to attend at the house.

The last thing Fabio needed to hear was that yet another policeman was failing to take his case seriously. Although, after the conversation with DS Henshaw the previous evening, and in light of his response when I asked him if he was investigating the association between Pellegrino and Kettering, I felt we were starting to make some headway in bringing him around to our way of thinking.

'How did they break-in?'

'Through a side window. I'm sorry we didn't call you yesterday, but when your grandmother and I discovered the card from the Royal Mail we thought there was a chance it was the package Giulia had posted. We decided to wait until we knew whether it was or not. The last thing we wanted to do was to give you false hope.'

'And you haven't.'

'What do you intend to do about Piero Giovannini? Your grandmother thinks you should inform the Italian police of his existence. He is crucial to the investigation, after all, especially in light of Giulia's letter to him as it does connect him with her. The police here should know about him as well, bearing in mind our contention that the disappearance of your father and Rosetta, and the murders of Giulia and Annette are connected. It might give them the impetus really to pursue their enquiries on the Pellegrino and Kettering front.'

'You don't think Piero Giovannini is Pellegrino's and Kettering's mutual Italian acquaintance, do you, Alicia?'

'No. In my opinion we're looking for someone older.'

'But he could be her killer. You think he is, don't you?'

'I can't deny that it hasn't crossed my mind that he could be, Fabio. If what Laura told you is true, and he is the property owner Giulia arranged to meet the night she disappeared, then he is likely to be a prime suspect.'

'Well, if he did murder my sister, he's going to wish he'd never been born. When I think about what happened to her...if I ever get my hands on him, I'll kill him. I swear it, Alicia. If it's the last thing I do.' And from the cold, impassioned way he spoke those words I felt he really meant it.

'You're not planning on making a trip to Villa Anna, are you, Fabio?' I said, fearing that he was about to do something reckless and hoping that, if he was, I could persuade him not to. If only Will was with him he would be able to manage the situation far more easily than I was attempting to do from the other end of the 'phone. 'Don't you think you should leave it to the police? If Mr Giovannini is Giulia's killer, then he's an extremely dangerous man and the likelihood is he isn't working alone. I know you wouldn't want to take any action which would jeopardise the investigation or your own safety. And then there's your grandmother to consider…'

'Right now, I'm not quite sure what I want or what I'm going to do. Everything is such a bloody mess. I need to clear my head and have a think. I'll be better if I get out of here for a while. My head is spinning. I'll call you back.'

'Promise you won't do anything rash.'

'Don't worry, Alicia. I'm not planning to go to Villa Anna – well not yet, anyway.'

I decided to call Will but he was not answering his mobile and I rang Jo to find out if she had heard from him. She could barely believe that so much had happened in the space of a little over twenty-four hours.

'Will didn't tell me he was going back to Perugia when he rang yesterday. I thought he was still in Orvieto with Fabio. There must have been a last-minute change of plan. It's a pity he didn't stay with Fabio, but it can't be helped.'

'If Fabio does something drastic, it'll be my fault.'

'I don't see how.'

'I should have realised that when I told him about Piero Giovannini he was likely to take the news badly.'

'You had to tell him, Alicia, and let's face it there was never going to be a right time to do that. You have nothing to reproach yourself for. Fabio might be distraught, but I doubt very much that he really intends to take the law into his own hands. You said he told you he had no current plans to go to Villa Anna and I'm sure he'll call you later like he said.'

'I know I'm probably worrying unnecessarily, but I feel so responsible for him.'

'Alex is right.'

'About what?'

'You get too involved with your clients. You can't take responsibility for their actions.'

'Well, these are rather unusual circumstances, Jo!'

'I appreciate that. We simply worry about you, that's all. Do you really believe your uncle will be able to ascertain when Emilio sold or transferred Villa Anna?' she asked, swiftly changing the subject.

'Put it this way, I expect he has a contact who can. What I'd really like to know is something about Piero Giovannini's background.'

'You mean whether he's connected to Pellegrino in some way?'

'Yes.'

'Are you going to talk to the police?'

'I'll wait and see what Uncle Vico uncovers first. Fabio's grandmother and I felt that Fabio should inform the Italian police, but on reflection I think it's better if we hold off until we have more information. They won't take us seriously if we start charging in with allegations. I'll have to try and contact Fabio to caution him against contacting them just in case he is minded to after all. It would have been better if I hadn't mentioned it to him.'

'I understand your concerns, but surely it wouldn't do any harm to let them know we've found the property owner Giulia was supposed to meet?'

'Umm... Well it might, because Laura didn't tell the police anything about that, which means they aren't even aware he exists.'

'I see. I didn't realize.'

'It makes things a little more difficult, that's all. Anyway I'd better try and call my uncle. Let me know when you speak to Will.'

'Of course.'

'Thanks Jo.'

186

I wanted to have the property search documents in front of me when I spoke to Uncle Vico so I retrieved the jiffy bag from my briefcase and set them out in front of me. I was on the point of ringing him when Danielle popped her head around the door to my office causing me to start. I quickly stuffed the jiffy back into my briefcase but did not have time to squirrel away the papers.

'I didn't mean to make you jump, Alicia, only DS Henshaw called again.'

'Oh no. What could he possibly want?'

'He says he'll be in the area around six so he'll pick you up. He mentioned something about you attending at the station to give a statement.'

'Yes. That's right.'

'You must have made a good impression for him to come and collect you.'

'Somehow I think not. He probably wants to make sure I make my statement!'

'Hmm… What's that you're working on,' she said, approaching my desk.

'Nothing in particular. A friend of my mother's is looking into buying a property in Italy and wants to know the inheritance implications,' I replied, gathering together the papers to conceal them from Danielle.

'Right. Do you want me to open a new client file then?' she asked, leaning across the desk.

'Not just yet, no. Is there any post for me today?' I replied, changing the subject. I was feeling very guilty because I had done absolutely no work all morning, what with arriving late and then being continuously on the telephone, and I also wanted a reason for Danielle to leave the room.

'I'll go and find out what's happened to it.'

'Thanks.'

As soon as Danielle disappeared, I rang Uncle Vico to inform him of the latest developments and to request his urgent assistance. He expressed total amazement when I advised him about the existence of Villa Anna and confirmed that in all the years he had known Emilio he had never mentioned anything about a villa near Lucca. Fortunately, he was very positive that he could obtain the necessary information, which was an enormous relief. Apparently, since we had last spoken, he had made a few calls and lined up a contact in Italy who would be able to expedite matters for us. Since my mother had a fax machine at home the easiest option would be for me to fax the property title searches to him there, together with Giulia's letter to Mr Giovannini. I advised him that I would do that during Danielle's lunch hour when I knew she was definitely away from the office.

I pulled the jiffy bag out of my briefcase to put the papers safely away and as I did so I noticed the postmark. The parcel had not been posted in Perugia after all, but in Orvieto, and in addition to that, not until after Giulia had been murdered, which meant that she could not be the sender. I had been so obsessed with reading what was inside the packet that I had only given the outside a cursory glance. Laura must have sent it, which made sense as it was her address on the back of the parcel. I had originally thought that Giulia had used those contact details to avoid the parcel being returned to her at the university should it not be delivered. I had never seen Giulia's handwriting, or Laura's for that matter, otherwise it would have been immediately apparent to me what had happened. Now it was clear why there was no note included in the parcel.

Laura had not been completely candid with Fabio but I was perplexed why she was behaving strangely. She could easily have explained that she had sent him Giulia's research. I wondered whether Giulia asked Laura to take it or whether Laura had simply done so. Maybe Giulia gave it to her for safekeeping and, after she died, Laura was desperate to be rid of it and posted it to Fabio.

I heard Danielle's footsteps coming down the corridor to my office and slipped the jiffy bag back into my briefcase which I then moved out of sight under my desk. I needed to make a further call to Fabio, but that would have to wait until Danielle was well out of earshot.

'Sorry I've been so long,' she said, opening the door and walking into the office carrying a post tray, 'but your post went to Graham by mistake and he's not in this morning.' Had I known that he was absent from the office there would have been no need to scuttle past his door when I arrived earlier. She put down the tray on my desk.

'Thanks, Danielle,' I replied, leafing through its contents. She walked towards the door. At that moment my direct line began to ring.

'Aren't you going to answer that?' she said, turning back and hovering momentarily in the doorway. 'It might be that mysterious caller from first thing this morning!' she added slightly sarcastically, before leaving the room and shutting the door behind her.

'Hello,' I said, picking up the receiver.

'Miss Allen, it's Caterina Bartoldi.' Caterina was the last person I expected to hear from and for a split second I was lost for words. 'Miss Allen, are you still there?'

'Yes,' I replied, quickly recovering myself.

'We need to talk.'

'I'm all ears Mrs Bartoldi,' I replied. 'What is it you want to say to me *exactly?*'

Chapter 21

'I received a visit from the police. They asked me what happened to Rosetta Bartlett.' She sounded very agitated and I wondered where this conversation was heading.

'I told you they would. Annette did mention you in her note, after all.'

'Yes, that ridiculous note. She had no right to involve me, no right whatsoever.'

'I thought you were already involved Mrs Bartoldi, which is the reason why Annette told me to ask you about Rosetta.' There was a slight pause.

'Well, I told the police that I can't help them. All I know is that Rosetta died while on holiday in Italy in a tragic swimming accident out at sea. Her death has nothing to do with me.'

'I don't recall anyone ever saying it did, Mrs Bartoldi.' Again there was a pause at her end of the 'phone. 'You said we needed to talk. I thought you wanted to tell me something *illuminating.*'

'I simply wanted to make it clear to you that there's nothing I can do to help you and that I've told the police the same; there's no point in asking me any other questions. I want to be left alone.' Bearing in mind she had already made that point quite forcibly the last time we spoke it was bizarre that she should be making this call at all. I truly felt that deep down she wished to assist us with the investigation and that it was only the consequences of so doing which were holding her back.

'But if you don't know anything, why do you think Annette indicated that I should ask you about Rosetta?'

'You'd have to ask her that.'

'I would if she were still alive,' I replied sarcastically. 'I can't believe you don't care about what happened to Rosetta, Emilio and Annette. They were all murdered for a reason and I'm sure that reason has something to do with Scarpetti, Steiglitz & Co. They were your work associates. You were working with Rosetta and Emilio at the time they disappeared. What were they working on Mrs Bartoldi? It's crucial you tell me what you know, because it may have a direct bearing on their murder investigations. It may even have something to do with Giulia's.'

'Not Giulia's surely?'

'Well, she was Emilio's daughter.' I did not want to divulge to Caterina the information we had discovered from Giulia's research and the fact that we were hoping to establish a link between her murder, Gregorio Pellegrino, Roland Kettering and their mutual Italian acquaintance. I had no doubt that Caterina was withholding vital knowledge from us, and that if she did not reveal what she knew there and then, the opportunity to ask her for it again would not arise. I decided to take a slightly different approach and appeal to her maternal instincts. 'You have a daughter, don't you, Mrs Bartoldi?'

'How do you know that?' she replied defensively.

'Isn't she the reason why you took the job at Scarpetti, Steiglitz in the first place and,' I paused for a moment, 'the reason why you left?' I added, dropping my voice. Of course, I did not know this for sure, and it was pure conjecture on my part based upon the details Alex had obtained from Dominic, but I was hoping it would encourage Caterina to open up to me. While she was still on the line there was always a chance that she might.

'I'm sure I don't know what you mean. I took the job at Scarpetti,

Steiglitz & Co. after my husband returned to Italy. Olivia was only a baby; he left us without any financial support and debts to pay off and I desperately needed the job.'

'And what about your dealings at the firm?'

'I don't follow. What dealings?'

'Did you work with Rosetta and Emilio?'

'Rosetta was a property specialist like me, but unlike me she was a Partner and I was an Assistant solicitor. I only worked on files she allocated to me and as such had limited knowledge of her caseload. There are many cases I simply did not work on at all.'

'What about Emilio?'

'I never worked with him.'

'Did Rosetta?'

'Well, no, that is, not usually.'

'Then she worked with him occasionally?' I continued, pressing her.

'Umm...'

'Mrs Bartoldi?'

'All I know about is one time, shortly before he disappeared, when she was working closely on something with him.'

'Do you know what that was?'

'I believe Rosetta was helping Emilio with some research.'

'What kind of research?'

'He was assisting a client who was trying to trace lost assets in Italy and needed her property expertise.'

'I see.' I recalled Roland Kettering mentioning *en passant* that he often received requests about tracing lost family assets in Italy, and in the back of my mind I could not help thinking that maybe he was in some way linked with the research Rosetta and Emilio undertook on behalf of Emilio's client. 'You said you believe that's what she was helping him with. Why?'

'Because I happened to overhear a conversation they were having about the client.'

'Right. Who was the client, Mrs Bartoldi?'

'I can't tell you anything else.'

'You mean, you won't?' It was patently obvious that Caterina felt she had overstepped the boundaries in divulging to me even the most meagre of details, which meant that extracting any more information from her would be a challenge.

'I didn't say that.'

'Why did you leave Scarpetti, Steiglitz & Co.?'

'I was offered the job here.'

'But you left very soon after Rosetta went missing.'

'It just turned out that way. The timing was merely coincidental.'

'And you parted on good terms with Scarpetti, Steiglitz & Co?'

'Yes.'

'That's not what I heard. I understand that you had a dispute with Mr Pellegrino and he accused you of trying to steal several of the firm's clients.'

'How do you know that?'

'So it's true?'

'Yes, but there was no truth in it.'

'Then why did he make those allegations?'

'To put pressure on me.'

'Not to talk about Rosetta and Emilio?'

'He didn't quite put it like that.'

'How *did* he put it?'

'Please understand. I had no choice. My daughter is all I have. I would have done anything to ensure her safety.' She was becoming increasingly agitated.

'Are you saying he threatened you, Mrs Bartoldi?' She did not respond. 'Did Mr Pellegrino threaten to harm Olivia?' I asked again, pressing her for a response. 'Is that what happened?' Still she did not answer. 'Mrs Bartoldi?'

'All right,' she said, slightly reluctantly, 'but I really don't feel comfortable talking to you about this while I'm in the office. It's not very private here.' She paused for a moment and I could hear her take a few deep breaths before proceeding to speak. 'Would you be able to come to my house this evening?'

'I have an appointment at six which should take an hour or so but could be with you after that if convenient?' I was certainly not about to turn down the opportunity of meeting with her.

'Yes. You'd better have the address and my telephone number.' Of course I already knew that she lived in Camden because Alex had followed her home, but she was not aware of that and I duly took the details from her. In any event it was useful to have her home telephone number. 'Oh, and Miss Allen, I will agree to help you but there are conditions.' I should have realized that there would be some stipulation.

'What are they?'

'You must give me your word that you'll leave me out of it and that you won't tell the police or anyone else that you're coming to my house tonight or that you have been here. I don't want to be linked in any way with Scarpetti, Steiglitz & Co.'

'I can't guarantee that, Mrs Bartoldi. This is a murder investigation after all.'

'Those are my terms. They're not negotiable.'

'All right,' I replied, slightly hesitantly. 'You have my word.' I was surprised that my assurance was all she requested from me. She must have been certain that I would honour our agreement.

'Thank you. What time do you think you'll be over?'

'Around eight.' I did not know how long I would be kept at the station but hopefully I would be able to make my way to her house by eight.

'I'll expect you then. Goodbye, Miss Allen.'

'Goodbye.'

No sooner had I put the telephone down from Caterina than Danielle popped her head around my office door. I thought she would ask me who had rung but she did not.

'I'm off to lunch now.' I glanced at my watch; it was nearly one o'clock and I had still not done any work since my late arrival that morning. 'There have been a few calls for you,' she said, pushing open the door and walking towards my desk. She handed me some memos.

'Thanks, Danielle,' I replied as I glanced through them.

'Will you make it out for lunch or do you want me to bring you something back to eat?'

'I'm all right actually, Danielle. I don't think I could stomach anything, but I might go out for a short walk.'

'I don't suppose you're feeling up to eating but you should probably try to have something light. At the very least make sure you hop out for some fresh air.'

'I will. I promise.' I felt guilty because I was perfectly well and I did not want Danielle to worry about me. 'Go and enjoy your lunch break.'

'OK. Don't forget to call Alex. He rang back while you were on the 'phone.'

'Oh, right. Thank you.'

Although I was eager to speak with Alex I wanted to fax through the paperwork Uncle Vico required first. Some of the documents were faint and on the wrong sized paper so I decided to photocopy them onto A4 paper and changed the setting on the photocopier to make the copy quality darker before sending them. Fortunately, nobody was around and I was able to accomplish both tasks undisturbed and well before Danielle's expected return.

Alex was actually at his desk when I rang him and I told him everything that had occurred since we had spoken the night before, except for my conversation with Caterina and my planned meeting with her that evening. Even though it was against my better judgment not to confide in him, I felt I owed it to Caterina to keep my word to her. I hoped that once we spoke face-to-face I might be able to persuade her to cooperate fully with the police investigation and then there would no longer be any requirement for secrecy.

Consequently, I deliberately steered clear of any conversation about her, and even refrained from commenting when Alex remarked that it was a shame she had been very unhelpful with the investigation. Instead I concentrated on Giulia's research, the discovery of Villa Anna and Piero Giovannini, Giulia's letter and the fact that I had asked Uncle Vico to use his Italian contacts to make some enquiries about both the house and Mr Giovannini.

'I hope he manages to turn something up for you. I think you're quite right in holding off telling either the Italian police or the police here about Piero Giovannini until you have more details, as you wouldn't want to go blundering in. You'd look pretty ridiculous if you started accusing Mr Giovannini and it turned out that he's not actually involved at all although, by the sounds of it, there is a strong possibility that he is.'

'I'm going to give Fabio a ring when we've finished and find out how he is.'

'I thought you said he would call you later. Anyway, isn't Will with him?'

'No. He's gone back to Perugia. Fabio's in a very vulnerable state and I'm worried about him.'

'Hmm… That's understandable. Just remember there is only so much you can do or be expected to do to help.'

'I know that.'

'How long do you think you'll be with DS Henshaw this evening?'

'Why?' I said slightly defensively. I suspected Alex was about to ask me what plans I had for the rest of the evening, and of course I had already arranged to meet Caterina.

'Because I thought that you could do with a bit of fun. I expect you'll need it after dealing with DS Henshaw.'

'Oh, Alex, I think I'm going to go straight home. I wouldn't be very good company tonight. I'm really tired,' I replied casually, trying to put him off.

'Do you want me to come over instead? I could give you some well-deserved TLC.'

'Umm... No. Not tonight, Alex. I think I need an early night.'

'I could always come round and tuck you in,' he quipped.

'Not tonight,' I repeated, slightly more insistently.

'Is everything OK, Alicia? You would tell me if something was wrong, wouldn't you?'

'Nothing's wrong. I'm just tired. I'd better go. I haven't done any work since I came in this morning and I'm really behind,' I replied, deliberately pushing him off the telephone.

'Oh, OK. I'll let you go then,' he said, sounding slightly bewildered.

'Bye, Alex,' I said, hanging up.

I felt dreadful for lying to Alex and also because I did not want him to think that I was avoiding him, which could not be further from the truth, but any explanation would simply have to be deferred until after my meeting with Caterina. Fabio was not answering his mobile, so I left a message on his voice mail explaining that if he was minded to contact the Italian police it was more prudent to wait for positive news from Uncle Vico. I also sent him a text asking him to ring me as soon as possible. My concern was that he might have already contacted the police, in which case my messages would be too late, but I was powerless to do anything else.

I could not justify leaving the office for longer than it took to buy myself a chicken sandwich as I had a backlog of work which had been steadily increasing over recent days and which I needed to clear before I left the office that evening. Of particular urgency was a set of Trust and Estate Accounts which had to be finalized, and a Discretionary Trust which I should have drafted earlier in the week. In fact, one of the calls Danielle had received was from the client on whose behalf the trust was being prepared. I decided to return all the calls from clients first and then place my 'phone on DND (do not disturb) so that any others would be routed through to Danielle for the rest of the day.

Danielle herself did not disturb me when she arrived back from lunch and fortunately I was able to concentrate on my work without interruption for the whole afternoon. Just before five-thirty Danielle knocked on my door.

'Are you off home now?' I asked, looking up at her as she stepped into the office.

'In about five minutes. You've had a few messages,' she said, walking up to my desk and handing the memos to me. 'And Fabio's grandmother, Patricia Turnbull, also rang.'

'Oh, right. When was that?'

'About an hour ago. She was hoping for a quick word with you but she said it wasn't urgent and she didn't want me to disturb you. She asked if you could possibly call her before you left the office today.'

'Of course. I'll give her a ring now. I don't suppose DS Henshaw will be late and he won't want to be kept waiting I'm sure.'

'Would do him good, I'd imagine,' said Danielle, winking at me. 'You seem much brighter. Are you feeling better?'

'I'm fine now, thanks. I'll see you in the morning. Have a good evening.'

'You too. I hope everything is OK with Fabio's grandmother and that your statement doesn't take too long.'

'I sincerely hope not. Goodnight, Danielle.'

'Goodnight, Alicia.'

I telephoned Patricia immediately as I presumed the reason for her call was because she had news of Fabio.

'Patricia, it's Alicia. How is everything?' I asked tentatively.

'Fabio rang. He said that he received both your messages and not to worry because he hasn't contacted the Italian police.'

'That's good. How was he, because he was in a terrible state when I spoke to him?'

'He seemed quite calm when he called. He was on his way back to Perugia to meet up with Will Brook.'

'Oh, that's a relief. I was very concerned about him.'

'Yes, I know, dear, which is why I wanted to let you know that he's all right.'

'You mean as much as he can be in the circumstances.'

'Well, quite.'

'I'm very glad Fabio's been in touch with you, Patricia. And what about you? How are you feeling? Are you OK?'

'Oh, I'm bearing up. You have to, don't you? What other choice is there? The last thing Fabio needs right now is for me to fall to pieces. Anyway, I don't want to keep you. I'm sure you have many other things to attend to.'

'You're not keeping me. I appreciated your call.'

'And I appreciate your support and kindness to my family.'

'You're very welcome.'

'Bye for now, Alicia.'

'Bye, Patricia.'

It was about ten minutes to six when I received a call from Susannah.

'I've been trying to ring you. DS Henshaw's in reception. He said you're expecting him.'

'Yes. Tell him I'll be right out,' I replied, logging off my computer. I was pleased that DS Henshaw was early as I was anxious about making my appointment with Caterina on time.

DS Henshaw was remarkably affable to me as we drove to the station, which took me somewhat by surprise. I wondered what I could possibly have done for him to be so uncharacteristically pleasant to me. Unfortunately, I was still unable to elicit a definitive response from him when I questioned him about Mr Kettering and Mr Pellegrino. Although he confirmed that enquiries were being made, he did not elaborate or provide any details of what those enquiries entailed which was frustrating. For my part I did not mention Caterina, nor did I comment when he confirmed what I already knew, which was that she had received a visit from the police but that they had gleaned very little from her.

Typically, my statement took far longer than I could have anticipated and it was nearly seven-thirty by the time I had finished
running through all the details with DS Henshaw. He told me he
was driving into the West End and offered me a lift home. I
explained that I had arranged to meet a friend in Leicester Square as
I knew I could catch the Northern Line up to Camden from there,
and he agreed to drop me at the tube station. By the time I arrived
at Leicester Square tube it was nearly eight and I was becoming
increasingly anxious that Caterina would cancel our arrangement. I
had programmed her telephone number into my mobile after we
had spoken and rang her. The 'phone must have rung at least eight
times before she answered it; in fact I had almost given up hope of
her doing so, when she did. She sounded strained.

'I'm really sorry,' I said, 'but I was unavoidably detained. I'm at
Leicester Square tube station. Would it still be convenient for me to
come over tonight or would you rather we made it another evening,
tomorrow perhaps?'

'Not tomorrow, no. Olivia's home from university for the
weekend. Tonight's the only night I can possibly see you.'

'All right. I'll be there as quickly as I can.'

When I arrived at Camden Town tube station about twenty minutes
later I rang Caterina again to let her know that I would be with her
shortly, but this time her landline was engaged. I was not familiar
with the area and wanted to double check Caterina's address so I
stood for a few moments in the tube station perusing my pocket
London A to Z. Her house was actually very close and no more than
a brief walk away. I came out of the tube station, crossed Camden
High Street and turned into Inverness Street which leads straight
into Gloucester Crescent which was where Caterina lived. As I
walked along Inverness Street I noticed a midnight blue Audi with
blacked-out windows double-parked on the right hand side of the
street and facing in the direction of Camden High Street. I could
not see who was sitting in the car, but the engine was running and

I had the impression the driver was waiting for someone.

I crossed onto the opposite side of the road and continued into Gloucester Crescent. I did not know on which part of the crescent Caterina's house stood and walked slowly, searching for the right number. It was still daylight but there was not a soul about and the crescent was eerily quiet, save for the faint hum of traffic in the distance. I had barely turned into the crescent when I heard what sounded like a heavy door being slammed shut and then I saw a man running along the street towards me. I assumed he must have come out of one of the houses much further down the street but which one I simply did not know, and besides he seemed to have appeared from nowhere.

He was tall and well-built, and from his physique I estimated him to be in his late twenties or early thirties, although I could not really tell as I could not see his face clearly because he was wearing a baseball cap with the peak pulled down over his eyes. I noticed he was wearing a dark grey tracksuit and trainers and was carrying a small duffle bag. I had to step out of the way to allow him to pass otherwise he would have knocked me over. I turned around and watched him as he raced off up Inverness Street and then, to my utter amazement, I saw the front passenger door of the Audi open, he scrambled inside and the Audi sped away in the direction of Camden High Street. I was not quite sure what to make of the whole incident, but instinctively I knew there was something suspicious about it.

I proceeded on down the street in the direction this man had sprung from until I arrived at Caterina's house. Like other houses in the crescent hers was a magnificent five storey Victorian period house with floor-to-ceiling windows on the first floor and traditionally brick-built with white stucco-fronted raised and lower ground floors. If this house was anything to go by, she had certainly managed to turn her life around financially since her husband left her almost twenty years before, which was nothing less than commendable. It was certainly a most impressive house and beautifully maintained and looked as if the outside had been recently decorated because the paintwork was absolutely pristine.

The black painted wooden front gate was wide open and I stepped inside the front garden. I shut the gate behind me and then walked up to the front door which was actually at the side of the house and set back from the front of the building. I rang the doorbell; there was no response, but I waited a few minutes before ringing again because I thought perhaps Caterina was upstairs and that if she was at the top of the house it would take her at least that long to make her way downstairs. After ringing a second, and then a third time there was still no reply and I was now feeling rather anxious as to her whereabouts. I dialled her landline again but the number was engaged. I knew that it was the right number because I had called her when I was at Leicester Square tube station. If Caterina was on the telephone I could not believe that she had not heard me ringing the front doorbell and would not have answered the door especially as she was awaiting my imminent arrival. I waited a further five minutes, there was still no sign of her and I was becoming ever more fearful for her welfare by the second. Something had to be wrong; maybe she had had an accident, had tried to reach for the 'phone and dropped it.

It was still light and I walked around to the front of the house and peered through the raised ground floor windows into the double reception room. The curtains were not drawn, so I had a clear view through to the back of the house, but I saw nothing which raised cause for concern. Nevertheless I was concerned because Caterina was expecting me, I had spoken to her barely thirty minutes earlier and now she appeared to have vanished.

I looked through one of the lower ground floor windows; I could see a dining room and beyond that a kitchen which led out on to the garden and, unless my eyes deceived me, the French doors leading from the kitchen into the garden were open. I walked down the front steps and around the side of the house. I assumed there must be access to the back garden from there because I had noticed a high wooden gate when I entered the front garden. Although the gate appeared to be closed, when I approached it I could see that it was actually ajar, so I pushed it wide open and walked purposefully along the side of the house and into the main part of the back garden. It was simply designed but meticulously maintained with a small central lawn and patio area nearer the house which was arranged with decorative tubs and pots containing a variety of evergreen shrubs and box. It was clear that Caterina was keen to preserve her privacy as there was an exceptionally high trellis covered in climbers at the back of the garden.

As I approached the open kitchen doors I called out Caterina's name. There was no reply, and I took the liberty of stepping inside the kitchen which was designed in a contemporary style with light coloured units and dark granite worktops. The kitchen was very tidy and nothing seemed to be out of place except that the telephone on the wall-mounted telephone unit was hanging down – which explained the engaged tone I had been receiving. I was feeling agitated about Caterina and I was not exactly at ease in the house either, but I felt compelled to find out where she was. I glanced through into the dining room, but that offered me no clues as to her whereabouts. I left my briefcase in the kitchen, stepped out into the hallway and called out her name for a second time, but again there was no response. I started to walk up the stairs to the raised ground floor and had almost reached the top stair when I heard a whirring noise that sounded like a washing machine coming from down the corridor. With my heart pounding in my chest I walked back down the stairs and through the hallway towards the closed door of what I assumed was the utility room. I turned the handle slowly to open the door and, as I did so, the washing machine started its spinning cycle, which made me start and step backwards. I took a few deep breaths and then gingerly pushed open the door and stepped inside. There was no natural light so I was unable to see clearly and, as I fumbled for the light switch, I stumbled and knocked over a basket of laundry which had been left on the floor.

I bent down to pick up the contents of the basket and to my horror saw Caterina – at least I believed it must be Caterina because I had never seen her before – slumped on the floor on the far side of the room. As the room was poorly lit, and her head was on her chest, I could not see her face properly. I felt myself coming out in a cold sweat and my heart was beating so fast that I could hear it pounding in my head. As I drew nearer I noticed a bluish tinge to the skin on her face and a blue discolouration to her lips. I bent down on my knees to her; she was not breathing and I could not find a pulse, and then I noticed deeply defined brownish-red marks on her neck which seemed to continue around its circumference. I could not be sure, but to me it looked as if Caterina had been strangled with some form of wire or cord.

All I knew was that I was too late, there was nothing I could do, and that Caterina Bartoldi was dead.

Chapter 22

I scrambled for my mobile to ring the emergency services but my hand was shaking and I could barely hold the 'phone steady, let alone dial the number. When finally I managed to make the call I was in such a state of nervous agitation that I found myself stumbling over my words. I was amazed the operator at the other end of the line was able to make sense of the garbled details I relayed to her. She was very reassuring, informed me that an ambulance would be at the house within the next ten minutes and the police were also on their way. Since I knew that DS Henshaw was on duty, I decided to ring him directly to ensure that he was on the scene as soon as possible, which at least would spare me the ordeal of having to answer the questions of another investigating officer.

'Caterina Bartoldi's dead. I think she's been strangled. You've got to get over here now,' I blurted out to him all in one breath.

'What are you talking about? Get over where?' He seemed rather taken aback by my outburst.

'Caterina's house in Camden.'

'What are you doing *there*?'

'I arranged to meet her this evening.'

'I thought you said you were meeting a friend at Leicester Square,' he said, sounding perplexed. I did not respond. Explanations could wait until he arrived at the house. 'Are you sure she's dead? I mean have you called for an ambulance?'

'I'm sure, but yes, I did call for an ambulance.'

'OK. I'll be there as quickly as I can. Don't touch anything.'

I staggered through the kitchen, and then out into the garden. I could not remain inside the house a moment longer as I felt sick and faint and in need of fresh air. I sat on the garden wall with my head in my hands and waited for the paramedics and police to arrive. First on the scene were two male paramedics who, having examined Caterina, did their best to assure me that there was nothing I could have done to save her. They asked me if I was feeling all right, and I told them that although I had felt faint earlier, I was better now I was sitting outside. Then DCI Framlington arrived with some other police officers I had not seen before. I was actually relieved that it was he rather than DS Henshaw who was accompanying them.

'DS Henshaw is on his way,' he said, looking at me as he walked towards the open kitchen doors. 'I'll come back and talk to you in a minute. I just want a word with the paramedics.' I observed him as he stepped inside the kitchen and spoke to the one who was standing nearest to the doorway. The paramedic shook his head and then DCI Framlington and he disappeared out of view. I presumed that he had gone to survey the murder scene. He had the advantage on me because he had met Caterina, so at least he would be able to confirm that it was indeed her body lying there, not that I doubted it for one second. Presently he returned and perched on the wall next to me.

'Are you OK?' he asked quietly, placing his hand momentarily on my back.

'I'm cold,' I replied, and shivered.

'It's the shock,' he said. 'I'll get you a blanket.' He strolled across to the other paramedic who was now standing outside talking to a police constable, said something to him which I was unable to hear, the paramedic disappeared inside the house and then returned with a blanket which he handed to DCI Framlington. DCI Framlington walked back to me and put it around my shoulders.

'Thank you,' I replied, glancing up at him.

'You should probably go to hospital to be checked over,' he said.

'That's really not necessary. I'm not hurt in any way. I'm just shocked, as you say.' The last thing I wanted was to be stranded at some hospital on the other side of London too far from home for hours on end.

'Well, shock can do strange things to people.' He paused for a second and looked at me hard. 'I hate to press you but I really need to know what happened here tonight. Are you up to answering some questions?'

'Yes. I think so.'

'Good, because it's always better to go over the details while they're fresh in your mind.'

'I don't think I'm ever going to forget what I saw, Chief Inspector.'

'No.' He took a deep breath. 'I realize you probably don't feel comfortable about going back inside, but it's chilly out here now. I think we should go and sit in the reception room upstairs.'

'Well, it would be warmer I suppose,' I said, wrapping the blanket around me. I followed him into the house through the kitchen, out into the hallway, up the stairs to the raised ground floor and into the front reception room. It was a very elegant room with many original features including cornices and an exquisitely carved ceiling rose. The curtains were royal blue, of a textured fabric and draped to the floor with matching tie-backs. There was a magnificent rectangular Pier glass mirror with a decorative gold frame above the fireplace and a delicately coloured Persian rug in the centre which picked up the gold and blue décor of the room. There were a couple of two-seater Regency style sofas upholstered in a cream-coloured silky fabric on either side of the room. DCI Framlington indicated for me to sit down on the one behind the door facing the window, then closed the door and seated himself on the one opposite me. While the sofa was comfortable I did not feel at all at ease and found myself perching on the edge of it.

'Why did you come here, Miss Allen?'

'To see Mrs Bartoldi.'

'Yes, I gather that, but I understand from DS Henshaw that you told him you were meeting a friend in Leicester Square tonight.' DS

Henshaw must have called him immediately after I had spoken to him.

'That's right.'

'Then I don't follow. Was it a last-minute arrangement?' he said, sitting forward.

'No. I'll explain. As you know I've been trying to get Caterina to open up to me about her time at Scarpetti, Steiglitz & Co. and her association with both Rosetta Bartlett and Emilio Angelino.' He nodded. 'Well, she called me this morning and although she was reluctant to give me any information at first, when I pressed her on the subject she told me that before Emilio's disappearance Rosetta assisted him with some research on a case where the client was trying to trace lost assets in Italy.'

'I see. And did she give you the name of the client?'

'No.'

'But you asked her for it?'

'Of course I did, but she didn't want to talk about it in the office and invited me to come here this evening.'

'Why did you lie to DS Henshaw about where you were going?'

'Caterina's offer to give me information was conditional upon me not telling anyone that I had been to her house. She didn't want any involvement in the murder investigation. I only agreed to her wishes because I thought that when I met her I would be able to persuade her to go to the police. Unfortunately, I'll never find out now about the client Emilio Angelino was helping.'

'If Caterina had valuable evidence why, in your opinion, did she never come forward with it?'

'For the very same reason she initially refused to help me with the current investigation – fear for her safety and that of her daughter.'

'Her daughter?'

'Yes. Olivia. She's a student. Caterina didn't mention her to you when you interviewed her then?' I scanned his face.

'No. Does she have any other relatives you know of?'

'She didn't speak of any, but there was no reason why she should.

She has an ex-husband, but I don't think she's had anything to do with him since he scarpered back to Italy when Olivia was a baby.'

'I see. Well, we'll have to inform her daughter.'

'She's due back from university tomorrow night, if that's any help.'

'How do you know that?'

'Because I arranged to meet Caterina at eight this evening and, because I was running late, I called her to ask if she would prefer me to come over tomorrow. She told me that would be inconvenient because her daughter was returning home for the weekend.'

'Right. Can I just take you back to what you were saying before?'

'About Caterina being afraid, you mean?'

'Yes. Exactly. Would you care to elaborate?'

'Caterina took the job at Scarpetti, Steiglitz & Co. after her husband ran off, leaving her with Olivia to support, but with substantial debts. She left the firm soon after Rosetta disappeared, although not on good terms. Mr Pellegrino accused her of trying to steal the firm's clients, but according to her it wasn't true.'

'Then why did he do that?'

'I believe it was to pressurize her not to divulge what she knew about Rosetta and Emilio. I think he threatened to harm her daughter if she talked.'

'Is that what she told you?'

'Not in so many words, but when I put it to her that this is what happened she didn't deny it. That's when she asked me to come over here. I'm sure she intended to tell me everything she knew, but she was stopped before she had a chance. I knew she was terrified for her safety; clearly her concerns were not unfounded. But what I don't understand is why she's been killed now. It's nearly sixteen years since she left Scarpetti, Steiglitz & Co. and she could have talked at any time. If somebody wanted to ensure that she never divulged what she knew, you would have thought that he or she would have silenced her long ago. How could anyone possibly have known that she was even considering revealing certain pertinent facts to me?'

'Someone must have.'

'Hmm... I realize that. I suppose if we knew, then we would be a good way to finding her killer. She *was* strangled, wasn't she, only the paramedics didn't tell me anything?'

'There'll have to be a post mortem but, yes, we believe she was.'

'Well, at least establishing a time of death won't be a problem as it has to be between eight and eight-thirty.' He looked at me quizzically. 'She was alive at eight because I spoke to her, as you know. I arrived at Camden tube station at eight-twenty and rang her again but this time the line was engaged. I presumed she was on the phone and didn't think anything was amiss.'

'A logical assumption.'

'I arrived at the house at about eight-thirty. I rang the doorbell three times and when she didn't answer I tried calling her landline and, as it was still engaged, that's when I went around to the back of the house. I didn't realize at that stage, of course, that the 'phone must have been taken off the hook deliberately which is why I was getting an engaged tone. I suppose it must have been about eight forty-five when I found her. To be honest the last thing I was thinking about was the time. But you'll know that from the record of my call to the emergency services.' He nodded.

'Why did you go around the back?'

'I could see through the lower ground floor windows that the kitchen doors were open. I'm not certain what went through my mind, but I just knew that something was wrong.'

'I see. Did you notice anything strange on your way to the house this evening?'

'I'm not sure whether you'll categorize what I'm about to tell you as strange, but as I was walking down Inverness Street I noticed a dark blue Audi with blacked out windows double-parked so that it was facing up the street in the direction of Camden High Street. The engine was running and I thought the driver was waiting for someone. As it happened he was.'

'How is this significant?'

'As I turned into Gloucester Crescent I was suddenly aware of a man running towards me. Unfortunately I didn't see where he sprang from, but he seemed to come from nowhere. Anyway, he belted off up Inverness Street and jumped into the parked Audi which then sped off towards Camden High Street. I haven't really had time to think about this, but I suppose there's a possibility he could be connected with Caterina's murder.'

'Can you describe him?'

'He had an athletic build and I'd say he was well over six feet. I couldn't see his face though because he was wearing a baseball cap and it was pulled forward.'

'What about the rest of his clothing?'

'Trainers and a dark grey tracksuit.'

At this point DS Henshaw burst into the room.

'Sorry to interrupt, Sir,' he said, glancing at me, 'But the pathologist's here and he wants a word.'

'No problem. I think Miss Allen's answered enough questions for this evening,' he said, standing up.

'Do you think somebody could give me a lift home?' I asked, remaining seated. 'I wouldn't ask but I…'

'Of course,' replied DCI Framlington nodding his head. 'DS Henshaw will drive you,' he said, directing him. 'Is there anyone who could come and stay with you tonight? I'd rather you weren't alone.'

'Oh, please don't worry about me. I'm perfectly fine honestly.'

'Nevertheless, I think that someone should be with you.'

'OK,' I said reluctantly. 'I'll ring Alex and see if he can scooter over.'

'Who's Alex?' asked DS Henshaw.

'A friend,' I replied, wishing to reveal as little detail about my personal life as possible. I only hoped that Alex was still speaking to me after I had given him the brush-off that afternoon. My explanation for my earlier behaviour would now have to be provided a little sooner than I had anticipated.

'What's his number?' said DS Henshaw, taking out his mobile.

'Oh, it's all right. I can call him.'

'Give DS Henshaw the number,' said DCI Framlington gently.

'You don't trust me to call him, do you?' I said, charging him, but I did give DS Henshaw Alex's contact details, and actually I was relieved that I would not have to try and give an account of the evening's events to him over the telephone. At least it would be easier for me once I was home.

'Good, that's settled then,' said DCI Framlington. 'I'll give you a ring in the morning,' he said, walking to the door. 'DS Henshaw will stay with you until your friend arrives.'

'I need to get my briefcase,' I said, standing up. That was something I did not want to leave behind, not with Giulia's package inside it.

'Where is it?' asked DCI Framlington.

'In the kitchen. I dropped it there when I came into the house.'

'DS Henshaw will fetch if for you.'

Ten minutes later I was on my way home, my briefcase safely retrieved.

'Are you sure you've no other rendezvous lined up that you'd like to tell me about?' said DS Henshaw slightly sarcastically as we pulled away from Caterina's house. He seemed irritated with me and perhaps it was because DCI Framlington had asked him to drive me home. Certainly his mood had changed since earlier that evening when he had been remarkably affable.

'No. But perhaps it's worth noting that if I hadn't come here this evening Caterina's murder wouldn't have been discovered until tomorrow, when either her colleagues became concerned that she hadn't turned up for work or her daughter returned home. I think it's fortuitous that I did arrange to meet her, because at least now her daughter will be spared from finding her body.' I paused and turned to look at him. 'I'm sure even you would agree with that.'

'OK. Point taken. Any other points you'd like to make while you're about it?'

'Yes. I'd rather we didn't discuss this anymore tonight. I've already been through everything with DCI Framlington. I'm very tired and simply want to go home and sleep.' Normally I would not have let DS Henshaw's asides bother me but, I was in a frame of mind where I found them upsetting. Even so I was determined not to let my feelings show.

'You'll be there soon enough.'

'What did Alex say?' I asked, steering the subject away from Caterina.

'He's on his way. He said he'll be at your flat as soon as he can. He seems like a good friend,' he added, casting me a sideways glance. I ignored his remark.

'I appreciate the lift home, but you really don't have to stay with me until Alex arrives.' I sincerely hoped Alex had set off immediately as I did not relish the idea of spending longer with DS Henshaw than was absolutely necessary.

The rest of the car journey passed in silence and, as we turned into my road and pulled up in front of the house, to my great relief I saw Alex's black Scarabeo Aprilia scooter parked outside. Alex was nowhere in sight though, but Dorothy's front curtains were not drawn, the lights were still on in her flat and it occurred to me that he might be waiting with her. No sooner had I opened the car door than Alex appeared. He ran down the front steps towards me, and although he smiled it was a strained smile and I could tell he was trying to conceal his anxiety from me.

'Are you OK?' he said, taking me gently by the shoulders and scanning my face. 'I was really worried when the police called me.'

'I'm fine,' I replied, trying to sound as upbeat as possible and trying to allay his concerns. 'I'm very pleased you're here though,' I added, giving him a momentary squeeze. I was bursting to talk to Alex about the night's events but I was conscious that DS Henshaw had stepped out of the car and was hovering in the background. It was clear he had no intention of leaving before speaking to Alex. Fortunately Alex was quick to pick up the signals, although I had the feeling that he was as curious to meet DS Henshaw as the latter was to meet him.

'Alexander Waterford,' he said, removing his hands from my shoulders and extending his right hand to DS Henshaw.

'So I presumed,' said DS Henshaw, taking it. 'You made it here in good time then?' he said, glancing at Alex's scooter. I stood back and observed DS Henshaw observing Alex. DS Henshaw was scrutinizing Alex's face.

'Remarkably. Thank you for driving Alicia home,' he said, putting his arm around me. 'She's really tired and I need to get her to bed.'

'Well, I'm sure you can manage that quite admirably all by yourself,' he said with a sneer, and turned on his heel and walked back to the car.

'Goodnight then,' called out Alex, ignoring his remark. DS Henshaw lifted his arm in acknowledgement before settling back into his car. 'What a rude man,' said Alex as we turned away and walked up the front steps to the main door.

'I told you. He doesn't like me.'

'I expect it's more to do with the fact that you're constantly questioning him about the investigation and he doesn't like that. He comes across as arrogant and I expect he's used to dismissing people out of hand. I'm sure it's not you; he's probably like it with everybody.'

'Hmm… The odd thing is he was actually quite pleasant to me earlier. Is Dorothy all right?' I asked, noticing that her curtains were now closed as I fumbled in my handbag for my keys.

'Yes. She's in good form this evening. I arrived about five minutes before you returned and she saw me loitering on the pavement and beckoned for me to come and sit with her until you appeared. I never realized what a great view she has of the street from her window.'

'She sees everything that goes on. She doesn't miss a thing, as you know. Here we go,' I said, opening the door and stepping inside. Alex bent down and picked up his small backpack. He must have dropped it in the hall before rushing out to greet me. We started to walk up the stairs to my flat. 'Did you tell Dorothy the reason why you're here?' I said, turning back to him.

'Do I need a reason to spend the night with my girlfriend? She probably thinks it's good old-fashioned lust.' He winked at me. We reached the door of my flat.

'You're incorrigible,' I said, putting down my briefcase and swivelling around to face him. I put my arms around his neck and kissed him on the mouth.

'Only when it comes to you,' he replied, breathlessly pulling me towards him. 'Don't worry. I didn't tell her anything about Caterina. I simply told her that you'd gone to make your statement this evening and you'd been taken ill and so I was coming over to look after you. I knew you wouldn't want to alarm Dorothy.' He paused for a moment. 'Are you ever going to open that door?'

'Give me a chance,' I said.

'I'll do it,' he said, taking the keys off me and gently moving me out the way. 'You're all fingers and thumbs tonight. But I'm not surprised after the evening you've had. Here we go,' he said, opening my front door. 'Home Sweet Home.' He stepped inside and placed my house keys on the hall table.

'Thank goodness,' I said, picking up my briefcase and following him in. I slipped off my shoes and jacket and dropped my handbag and briefcase in the hall. I traipsed through to the living room and flopped down on the sofa. 'I feel exhausted,' I said as Alex walked into the room. 'And my legs feel like lead.' I moved them so that Alex could sit down and then promptly put them on his lap. 'I also feel very guilty.'

'Whatever for?' he said, stroking my right leg. 'Unless you're about to tell me you murdered Caterina?' he said, leaning forward and making a ghoulish face.

'Hardly,' I said. 'I meant for lying to you this afternoon.'

'Forget it. You had your reasons, I'm sure. I'm not going to berate you, Alicia, but is it any wonder I concern myself with your welfare? What if the murderer had still been in the house when you went in there?'

'I thought you said you weren't going to berate me?'

'I'm sorry. It's probably best we don't talk about it.'

'Oh, but I need to tell you what happened.'

'All right, but shall we get something to eat first? I'm starving as I haven't had any dinner and I don't suppose you've had anything to eat either.' I shook my head.

'I'm not really hungry.'

'You need to eat. How about you have a soak in the tub and I'll rustle something up for us, if you don't mind me raiding your larder, that is?'

'No, not at all. You can cook anything you like – provided you promise not to burn it.'

'Very funny.'

'What have you prepared?' I said, popping my head around the kitchen door about twenty minutes later and noticing a large covered saucepan steaming on the hob.

'It's a surprise. Cute pyjamas by the way.'

'It looks like mushroom risotto to me,' I said, lifting the lid.

'It's not ready yet. I've made some tea. Do you want a cup?'

'Yes. I would thanks. It's very good of you to cook for me,' I said, stifling a yawn and pulling myself up onto the kitchen stool. 'Especially at this time of night,' I added glancing at the clock. It was now after eleven. 'I do appreciate you being here, even though I don't understand why DCI Framlington was so insistent about someone staying with me overnight. It's not as if I'm injured or anything.'

'Well, I don't need much of an excuse to come over, as you well know. But I expect DCI Framlington's probably heard the rumours,' said Alex as he poured my tea.

'What rumours? What are you talking about?' I said, yawning again.

'About your secret Pringle eating,' said Alex teasingly as he handed me my tea. 'He knew that if nobody was here to keep you in check that's all you'd end up having for dinner.'

'No I wouldn't.' I took a sip of tea.

'I'll believe you.'

'It's true. But only because I don't have any!'

'And who was it that said I'm incorrigible?' I laughed. 'It's good to hear you still have a sense of humour,' he said.

'On a serious note, do you mind if we talk about Caterina now?'

'Of course I don't. I'm interested in hearing what happened tonight.'

'Do you think Gregorio Pellegrino's behind Caterina's murder, Alicia?' said Alex, flopping onto the sofa next to me after we had finished dinner.

'I wouldn't be surprised, but if he wanted to silence her to prevent her talking about Rosetta and Emilio I'm sure he'd have disposed of her before this evening.'

'Not necessarily. Let's face it, it's only since Giulia started all her research, and questions have been asked about the investigation into Emilio's disappearance, that Giulia, Annette and now Caterina have been murdered. I reckon that letter of hers triggered the whole sequence of events.'

'If that's the case, then Piero Giovannini must be connected in some way to Scarpetti, Steiglitz & Co. or at least to Gregorio Pellegrino.'

'Hmm... I don't suppose your uncle has any news on Villa Anna and Piero Giovannini yet?'

'No, but I only faxed him the details at lunchtime today so I should think the earliest we can expect to hear anything is tomorrow. Going back to Caterina, I did wonder whether it's possible that Pellegrino found out she planned to talk to me.'

'I don't see how. Judging by how wary she was about divulging details to you, I think it's highly unlikely she would have confided in anyone even remotely connected to him.'

'Well, if it was him, he must have been alerted somehow.'

'Did the police ask you who you think might be behind her murder?'

'No. I had the feeling DCI Framlington was more concerned with getting a full account of the night's events from me while they were fresh in my mind.'

'What did he say about the man you saw running away from her house?'

'That's just it. I can't swear he was running away from her house because I didn't witness him doing that. What I saw was a man running up the street from the direction of her house. I did not see him leave her house. The fact that I believe he could well be the one to have murdered her is not proof that he did.'

'Yes. Of course. He needs to be tracked down to eliminate him if nothing else.'

'Exactly. All I know is that Caterina was alive at eight because I spoke to her and dead by eight-thirty when I arrived at the house, so we know she was murdered during that half-hour period. I'm hoping that one of her neighbours saw something and will come forward with some evidence. Mind you, when I walked down her street this evening there was nobody about.'

'Presumably she knew her attacker, because from what you've told me it sounds as if there was no sign of a break-in?'

'Well, to be honest with you I didn't think to look, but I'm sure I would have noticed. The back gate was unlocked, but the lock itself certainly hadn't been forced and the French windows leading on to the kitchen were open which is how I managed to enter the house in the first place.'

'You don't suppose she opened the front door thinking it was you arriving early?'

'No, because I called her and told her I was running late.'

'Hmm… Then on the facts it's likely she let her killer in by the front door and it's the killer who went out the back way. It seems logical that he would escape via the garden bearing in mind she was killed in the utility room which is on the lower ground floor level, rather than running up the stairs and letting himself out through the front door.'

'Yes, and it would be less conspicuous for him too. Oh well, that's for the police to work out. The person I feel most sorry for right now is her daughter, Olivia. Can you imagine what a terrible shock Caterina's murder is going to be for her? And I don't know how I'm going to break the news to Fabio. I'll have to ring him in the morning. After the way he was today I wouldn't like to predict his reaction. I wish I had some positive news to give him.'

'I know this is cold comfort, Alicia, but you have to console yourself with the fact that you are making headway with this case. Caterina confirmed that Rosetta was helping Emilio with some research for a client who was trying to trace assets in Italy. Both Emilio and Rosetta were probably murdered as a result of this research and the common thread in all this is Gregorio Pellegrino. He happens to be a friend of Roland Kettering who told you that he has experience in tracing lost assets for his Italian clients. This adds greater weight to your theory that Pellegrino and Kettering may have been involved in underhand property dealings with their mutual Italian acquaintance, and Emilio and Rosetta got wind of what they were doing which is why they were murdered.'

'If only Caterina had told me the name of the client. I can't see what we can do to progress the case without it.'

'Something will turn up, I'm sure. It's not like you to be so down-hearted. Everything will seem clearer in the morning when you've had some sleep.'

'Except, Alex, Caterina will still be dead.'

Chapter 23

'Why didn't you wake me?' I said, all in a panic as I staggered out into the kitchen where I found Alex, who was already showered and dressed, preparing breakfast. 'I'm going to be very late for work now.' It was already after nine.

'Well, it won't matter this once, sweetheart. And besides I thought you needed a lie-in. Don't worry; I've already called Susannah and told her you'll be in a bit later.'

'Great. Now the whole office will know my business.'

'Alicia. You hardly think I told her about Caterina's murder, do you? I merely said you were still off colour after your sick bug yesterday.'

'I'm sorry, Alex. Thank you for doing that. I just feel guilty.'

'What for this time?' he said, rolling his eyes upwards.

'Well, I was late arriving at the office yesterday because I went to pick up Giulia's package, I hate saying I'm ill when I'm not, and I don't like lying. I'm not exactly feeling very good about it.'

'You have too much of a moral conscience. I don't know anyone more conscientious than you nor more solicitous to her clients, which is, after all, why you're in this current predicament. Why don't you have a chat to Graham today? I think you'll find he'll be very supportive about what's happened, especially if you keep him informed. Now, how about you eat some breakfast? You hardly touched your dinner last night.'

I arrived at work about ten-thirty. I wanted to speak to Graham immediately but unfortunately he was engaged with a client. Danielle seemed very concerned to see me there at all.

'You really don't look well,' she said, following me into my office. 'You're so pale. You shouldn't have come in today. I half didn't expect you.'

'I'm all right, Danielle. Thank you for your concern though,' I replied, sitting down at my desk. 'Have there been any calls?'

'Yes. Alex rang. He wanted to know whether you were in yet and if you were OK. You see, I'm not the only one who's worried about you.' I smiled.

'Has anybody else called?'

'Are you expecting anyone in particular, Alicia?'

'Clients, Danielle!'

'Oh, right. No. It's been very quiet. There's a lot of post for you though. I'll fetch it.' She turned and walked towards the door.

'Thanks, oh and Danielle, did those Trust and Estate Accounts go out?'

'Yes,' she replied, turning back. 'I'll only be a tick.' I turned on my computer and waited for it to boot up. Danielle returned with my post. 'How did it go with DS Henshaw last night, if you don't mind me asking?'

'No, of course not. My statement took forever. I thought it would never end.'

'No wonder you're off colour. I'll leave you to it. Shout if you need anything.'

'Could you let me know when Graham's free? Only, I want a word with him.'

'No problem.'

'Thanks, Danielle.'

'Are there any files you want from the filing cabinet while I'm standing here?'

'No. It's all right. I'll get them.

I checked my e-mails and there was one from Antonia which she had also forwarded to my personal e-mail, but I had not seen it because I had not logged on to my computer when I returned home the previous night. She had attached some links to websites for wedding dress designers for me to peruse prior to our shopping trip on Saturday, which was of course tomorrow. I clicked on a couple of the links, scanned through the websites and made a note of any of the designs I thought might suit her. I then sent her a reply confirming that I would see her at eleven the next morning.

Danielle was right; there was rather a lot of post, but most of it was general Probate paperwork which was straightforward enough. I retrieved the relevant files from the cabinet and set about ploughing my way through it. By the time I had dealt with my post, and a number of client calls in between, it was nearly lunchtime and I thought that Graham must surely now be free. I left my office to take my dictation tapes to Danielle, but she was not at her desk and I presumed she had decided to take an early lunch. I wandered down to Graham's office and the door was ajar so I pushed the door open. Graham was sitting at his desk dictating notes from his meeting but put down his Dictaphone as soon as he saw me.

'Do you have a minute?' I asked.

'Of course,' he said with a broad smile. 'Shut the door and pull up a chair.'

'Thanks,' I said, closing the door. I sat down in the chair in front of his desk.

'I'm sorry, Alicia. Danielle left a message that you wanted to speak to me but I haven't had a moment this morning. My meeting took much longer than anticipated. How are you feeling today?'

'Well, that's what I wanted to talk to you about. I need to explain the reason for my recent absences from the office.'

'What's wrong? Is there a serious medical issue I need to know about?' he asked, looking concerned and leaning forward.

'Oh, no, Graham there's nothing wrong with my health,' I said, reassuring him. 'Let me explain.'

'Go ahead.' Graham sat back and listened in absolute silence while I relayed to him the events of the last forty-eight hours. He seemed totally amazed by what had occurred.

'So the upshot is I expect the police will want to ask me further questions about Caterina's murder. They may come into the office again so I thought you should know.'

'Have you told Fabio about Caterina's murder?'

'Not yet. I feel I ought to call him before he hears it from another source.'

'Yes. You must. He has to be told. Feel free to call him from the office.'

'Thank you.' I paused for a moment. 'I wish you knew who Roland Kettering's mutual acquaintance was, Graham. Are you sure you don't remember him mentioning anyone when you worked with him?'

'It's funny you should mention it again, as I've been racking my brains over that one since you asked me. And the more I think about it, the more I'm sure Kettering had a contact based in Viareggio.'

'What makes you say that? Is it because Kettering bought property there?' It had been of course Graham who had told me that he thought Kettering owned property in Viareggio when we previously spoke on the subject.

'Yes, but I have the strongest feeling that the Italian contact is the reason why he acquired property there.'

'Hmm... It's possible I suppose. When I was going through Giulia's papers I noticed that she made a mark beside Viareggio, but there's nothing else among those papers to explain why she did that. Only, now you tell me this, it occurs to me,' I said, thinking out loud, 'that we've been approaching the case from the wrong angle.'

'What do you mean?' Graham looked bemused.

'Well, we've been assuming that the person who responded to Giulia's letter about the ownership of Villa Anna was Mr Giovannini himself. What if this elusive mutual legal acquaintance happens to be both Kettering's contact in Viareggio and Mr Giovannini's lawyer and he's the one who called her? After all, it's perfectly logical that in response to such an enquiry Mr Giovannini would have passed the letter on to his lawyer who then dealt with the matter on his behalf.'

'By murdering Giulia?'

'Or having her murdered.'

'Hoping to put an end to the matter once and for all, you mean?'

'Something like that.'

'But I thought you said Giulia was planning to meet the owner.'

'That's what Laura told us and I have no doubt Giulia believed she was about to meet him, except it probably wasn't him. Don't forget Giulia had never met the owner before, so how would she know whether it was him or not? The fact that she wrote a letter to the owner doesn't necessarily mean the call she received in response to it was from him, but in her innocence she presumed that it was.'

'This is all very tenuous, Alicia.'

'Maybe, but it makes sense.'

'It's a pity you don't have anything to substantiate your arguments.'

'Let's see what Uncle Vico can turn up about Villa Anna. He's very resourceful. If the mutual acquaintance is Giulia's murderer then we have established a connection between Pellegrino and Kettering.'

'So what you're now saying is that the current owner of Villa Anna, Piero Giovannini, is innocent of Giulia's murder?'

'Well, put it this way, I no longer believe he was the one actually to kill her, although that doesn't mean he's not in on the murder. Remember I said to you before that I thought the mutual legal acquaintance might be associated with the owner of Villa Anna.' Graham nodded. 'I still think it's quite possible that he is. That's why I asked Uncle Vico to help me find out about Mr Giovannini's background as well as the circumstances surrounding the transfer of the ownership of Villa Anna from Emilio to him.'

'Let's hope your uncle turns something up. Well, all right,' he said, leaning back, 'thank you for keeping me in the picture and please tell me if there's anything I can do to help.'

'Thanks, Graham,' I said, standing up. 'I will.'

'What did you think of that issue of the *Journal of International Trust & Corporate Planning* I gave you to look at?' he asked as I walked to the door. 'I presume you've had a chance to flick through it?' I nodded.

'I think it's worth subscribing to.'

'Good. I'll speak to you later,' he said, picking up his Dictaphone.

I decided to go for a walk and brace myself before calling Fabio. I hated to be the bearer of bad tidings yet again, but as Graham had said he had to be told about Caterina's murder. I tried to call Alex but his line was engaged as usual, so I called Uncle Vico instead and explained what had happened the previous evening.

'Oh, my God! Someone else has been murdered every time I speak with you.'

'Not quite, Uncle Vico, but it's starting to seem that way. Do you have any news yet?'

'No. Maybe later. Don't worry.'

'Oh, but I *am* worried.'

'Do you want me to give Fabio a call? That would take the pressure off you.'

'I should call him myself. Thanks for offering though. Let me know as soon as you have any news from your contact in Italy.'

'Of course. *Ciao*, bye.'

'Bye.'

I was on my way back to the office when Alex rang my mobile.

'I picked up your message and I've been trying to 'phone you back because I have to go into a meeting in a few minutes time and won't be free until after five.'

'Sorry, Alex. I just gave Uncle Vico a quick ring to find out if he has any news for us.'

'I see. Does he?'

'No, unfortunately. Thanks for your call earlier by the way. Danielle said you rang.'

'I wanted to make sure you were OK. How's your day going? Have you managed to speak to Graham?'

'Yes. He was very supportive like you said.'

'Good. And what about Fabio?'

'I'm intending to call him as soon as I get back to the office. I'm psyching myself up for it.'

'I'm glad you haven't talked to him yet.'

'Why? What makes you say that?'

'Because I have some news which might help soften the blow of hearing that Caterina's been murdered.' I could not possibly think what that might be and I was slightly perplexed.

'What news, Alex?'

'I've tracked down Rosetta Bartlett's father and he's agreed to see us tomorrow.'

'Really?' This was a totally unexpected, but welcome, piece of news. 'How did you find him?'

'I did one of those electoral register searches online after you obtained her death certificate last week and found an address for him. There was no telephone number though and directory enquiries didn't seem to have one for that address, so I wrote to him. I didn't mention it to you in case nothing came of it. Anyway, to my surprise he called me this morning explaining that he moved about a year ago, but is still having his mail forwarded and only received my letter today. He said he's happy to talk to us about Rosetta's disappearance. I gave him some background details so he has a good idea of the information we're after. Actually, I had the impression that he's quite lonely and doesn't get many visitors.'

'Oh, that's awful. Maybe he doesn't have any other relatives. Where does he live?'

'Only in Richmond, which is really easy for us to get to.'

'What time is he expecting us, because I'm going on a wedding dress hunt with Antonia tomorrow. Remember?'

'Around six. That's OK, isn't it? You and Antonia should be finished by then surely?'

'Clearly you don't know my sister,' I replied, laughing. 'But, yes, that's fine. Where do you want to meet?'

'I'll come and pick you up about five-thirtyish.'

'OK.'

'All right, sweetheart. I hope the call to Fabio isn't too difficult.'

'Thanks.'

'Any news from the police today?'

'No. I've been expecting to hear from them all day. I'll keep you posted.'

'I'll chat to you later then.'

'Yes. *Ciao, carino mio.*'

'*Ciao, bella.*'

Fabio took the news about Caterina remarkably well and he seemed much calmer than when we spoke the day before. As Alex had anticipated, the knowledge that we had managed to track down Edward Bartlett appeared to lift his spirits somewhat and he was enthusiastic about our forthcoming meeting with him. I also felt that Will's steadying influence was a major contributory factor to his more composed state and I was therefore relieved that he had rejoined Will in Perugia.

We discussed my earlier conversation with Graham and my view that Mr Giovannini might not be Giulia's murderer at all. Fabio was keen to hear whether Uncle Vico had discovered any information on him which might corroborate my theory, and was a little disappointed that I had no positive news for him in that regard. I promised that I would ring him as soon as I heard from Uncle Vico, but in any event after Alex and I had visited Edward Bartlett. I then asked him if he had had any further communication with Laura and he told me that she had failed to return any of his calls. This was very frustrating, especially as I was convinced she was withholding vital evidence from us, but short of travelling out to Italy to attempt to extract it from her myself, for the present there was nothing I could do about that.

Around four o'clock Danielle opened the door to my office.

'Alicia. I hate to tell you this, but those two policemen are back and want to speak to you. Shall I fetch them for you?'

'Yes, please,' I replied, tidying the papers on my desk.

'What could they possibly want?' she continued. 'I thought you'd already answered all their questions and you've given them a statement.' Danielle, of course, did not know anything about Caterina Bartoldi and now was not the time for explanations. Besides I did not wish to involve Danielle in any of this for her own protection, if nothing else, which is partly the reason why I had told her as little as possible about the police investigation in the first place.

'Oh, you know what policemen are like Danielle. I'm sure they've found something else to ask me,' I replied airily.

'Hello again, Miss Allen,' said DCI Framlington as he and DS Henshaw walked into my office. 'How are you feeling today?'

'I'm fine, thank you.' I indicated for them both to sit down. 'I appreciated the lift home,' I said, directing the words at DS Henshaw.

'No problem,' he said matter-of-factly, leaning back in his chair and folding his arms.

'How can I help you?' I asked, looking at DCI Framlington. 'I'm not sure I can really tell you any more than I told you last night. Has Danielle offered you a drink by the way?'

'Yes, she has. We're fine thanks,' he said. 'We had one about half an hour ago. You told me that Caterina rang you yesterday from the office,' DCI Framlington continued.

'Yes. That's right.'

'What time was that? Can you remember?'

'Umm... About ten to one I'd say. Is the time relevant?'

'According to Caroline, her secretary, Caterina received a call yesterday afternoon from a man claiming to be a former client of hers. He said his name was Christopher King. Caroline has told us that Caterina was very distressed after speaking to him and left the office soon thereafter. The reason why I asked what time she rang you was because I was curious whether the 'phone call from this man triggered her call to you, but clearly it didn't.'

'Right. I take it Christopher King isn't this man's real name?' I asked, scanning both their faces.

'As it happens Caterina did have a client called Christopher King many years ago. We understand that he was one of a number of clients who followed her to Williams, Ricks & Stone from Scarpetti Steiglitz & Co. when she joined the firm. However, the man who called her yesterday couldn't have been the Christopher King for whom she acted because he is dead. We spoke to his widow this morning who confirmed he died eight years ago.'

'I see. Did Caroline make any comment about the sound of his voice?'

'Only that he was well-spoken with the trace of a foreign accent, although she says she could not really hazard a guess as to where he was from as she's not very good at recognising accents.'

'That's a shame. I take it that you think that the man assuming Mr King's identity has something to do with her murder?' I said, addressing DCI Framlington.

'I do.'

'And do you not also think it rather interesting that the firm of Scarpetti, Steiglitz & Co. has cropped up yet again? Everyone who has died has had some connection with that firm. I think it is ironic that the person who rang Caterina chose to assume the identity of one of the clients she took from that firm.'

'Why do you say that?'

'Because, as I told you last night, it is my belief that when Caterina left Scarpetti, Steiglitz & Co. Mr Pellegrino accused her of trying to steal the firm's clients so as to pressurize her into not divulging what she knew about Emilio and Rosetta. I bet that when this man called her yesterday he threatened her. He may even have threatened to harm her daughter, and I know from what she told me that she would do anything to protect her.' I suspected that the call might have been from Pellegrino himself. When I met him I had picked up only a trace of an Italian accent and had even detected a slight American one and so it would hardly be surprising if Caroline had been unable to recognize where he was from. I could not be certain and, rather than accuse him outright, I hoped that the police would come to the same conclusion, but there was no harm in pressing the issue. 'I know that you must have interviewed Mr Pellegrino after Annette Richardson was murdered, although you were evasive with me on that point, but have you interviewed him since then, bearing in mind what has happened?'

'We called in on the offices of Scarpetti, Steiglitz & Co. this morning after checking out who Mr King was,' said DS Henshaw, sitting forward.

'And?'

'Mr Pellegrino wasn't there,' said DCI Framlington.

'So where is he?'

'Italy. He left on the first flight out to Pisa this morning.'

Chapter 24

'Did the police say anything else?' asked Alex after I had relayed my conversation with DCI Framlington and DS Henshaw to him. It was only five-thirty, but I was no longer in the office because Graham had sent me home soon after DCI Framlington and DS Henshaw had left. I felt extremely guilty for leaving early, and had taken some paperwork home for the weekend despite Graham insisting that I do no such thing. Fortunately, I had taken Giulia's jiffy bag out of my briefcase the night before and I had room to stash a couple of files in there without him noticing.

'All I managed to extract from DCI Framlington is that Pellegrino has flown to Pisa, which is where I presumed he'd go anyway bearing in mind it's basically equidistant between Lucca and Viareggio. He wouldn't tell me whether the police were going to do anything about him – at least I couldn't pin him down on that particular point.'

'You're working yourself up into a frenzy, Alicia. You have to leave it to them. They'll only act on the evidence they have. You know that, as well as I do. You've done all you can.'

'Maybe from this end.'

'What do you mean?' Alex sounded worried about what action I was planning to take.

'Perhaps it's time to go out to Italy. As you said yourself Giulia's research into the Angelino family background in Lucca seems to have been the catalyst for recent catastrophic events. Italy's where we should be looking.'

'But you already are. You have your uncle on the case trying to source legal information about the ownership of Villa Anna and personal details on Piero Giovannini. I thought that you were waiting on that hoping to obtain confirmation of the association between Pellegrino, Kettering, their legal acquaintance and Giovannini before approaching the police either here or in Italy with those facts.'

'I am, but it's very frustrating. We don't seem to be moving forward.'

'I appreciate that, but I don't see what you hope to achieve by flying out to Italy. Where's Fabio right now?'

'With Will in Perugia.'

'What about Laura?'

'I don't know. I think the university term is coming to an end or has already ended, so she may have returned home to Orvieto. I wish I could talk to her.'

'Do you think she'd open up to you?'

'I couldn't say, but I'd do my best to persuade her.'

'I imagine you would. You can be most persuasive when you put your mind to it.'

'It might be worth going out to Italy just for that. Anyway, I'm sure Fabio could do with some support.'

'He has Will.'

'Hmm... Well, let's hope Edward Bartlett talks tomorrow.'

'I have no doubt he will. It's whether he has anything to say which can help us with the case that's the issue. I'd better run; I have another meeting to go to. I didn't realize what time it was.'

'You'll be working late again tonight then?'

'Yes. I won't be able to come over. You don't mind, do you?'

'Hardly. You can't help it if you have deals to complete.'

'I'm free on Sunday though. I thought that you could come and stay with me tomorrow night after we've seen Edward Bartlett, as I'm always over at your place and then maybe we could spend a lazy Sunday together.'

'I'd like that.'

'Good. Have a think about whether there's anything in particular that you'd like to do on Sunday.'

'OK. I'll see you at five-thirty tomorrow then.'

'I'll give you a ring in the morning before you go out with Antonia. In the meantime, try and go to bed early. You didn't get much sleep last night.'

'Neither did you.'

'But I'm used to being up all night with my deals. And I can have a lie-in tomorrow as it's a Saturday. Have a good evening.'

'You too. Hope you don't have to work too late.'

'Me neither!'

I changed into some casual clothes, made myself a cup of tea and settled down at my desk to work on the files I had brought home. It was too early for dinner and I was not particularly hungry anyway. I had been sitting there for only half an hour when I was disturbed by someone pressing the video Entryphone buzzer to my flat. I was not expecting any visitors and I thought that the buzzer had probably been pressed in error, but I went to check nonetheless. I could hardly believe my eyes; to my amazement Uncle Vico was standing on my front door step. He had not mentioned that he had any intention of coming up to London when we spoke earlier.

'*Ciao. Buona sera.* What are you doing here?' I said, picking up the handset and pressing the door release button to let him into the building. He was the last person I was expecting to call on me.

'*Ciao carina.* I have news for you which will not wait.' That could only mean that his contact had found out something significant about Villa Anna, Piero Giovannini or both. I opened my front door, put it on the latch and eagerly waited for him at the top of the stairs. I noticed he was carrying a small leather holdall and presumed he was intending to stay the night. 'Hello, my darling,' he said as he turned the stairwell and walked up the last few steps towards me. 'You're looking tired,' he said, bending forward and kissing me on both cheeks. I ushered him inside the flat and closed the door.

'If I'd known you were coming into London I'd have made us some dinner. Why didn't you get Mamma to call me? I feel awful now. The bed's not even made up in the spare room.'

'No need. After we spoke I had a call from a former New York business associate of mine who moved over to London a few years ago. He and his wife invited me to dinner so I'm staying with them tonight,' he said, placing his bag on the floor and seating himself on the sofa. 'But I thought that since I was going to be in town I might as well come and see you and tell you what I've discovered.'

'Well, it's always a pleasure to see you, uncle. I'm sorry you're not staying for dinner, but how about a drink? You must be thirsty after your journey?'

'An ice-cold beer wouldn't go amiss. It's awfully humid this evening,' he said, taking off his jacket, folding it inside out and laying it on the seat next to him.

'I thought you'd be used to the stifling humidity having lived in New York after all these years,' I said, walking through to the kitchen, opening the fridge door and taking out a bottle of Peroni beer.

'Actually, that's something I've never quite got used to.'

'Well now, tell me what you've discovered,' I called out as I took out a glass from the cupboard and the bottle opener from the kitchen drawer.

'Let's wait until you're sitting down.' I opened the bottle, poured the contents into the glass and returned to the living room.

'Go on then,' I said, handing him his beer. 'What have you found out?' I sat down on the edge of my armchair opposite him.

'Intrigue, corruption and murder – enough to make an excellent film plot.'

'I thought we had that already,' I said slightly tongue-in-cheek.

'I know you specifically requested that I look into Piero Giovannini's ownership of Villa Anna and when and how the property was transferred from Emilio to him,' he said, sipping his beer, 'and I will come back to what I found out about that, but I've also had enquiries made re the transfer of ownership from Dino Angelino to Emilio.' Dino was the name immediately above Emilio's on the property title document for Villa Anna which I had found among Giulia's papers. 'When you told me that Emilio was listed as one of the owners I was perplexed, but what intrigued me more was his relationship to Dino because that is not a name I ever recall Emilio mentioning to me.'

'He didn't tell you much about his family either then?'

'Well, I knew his father Eduardo and I remember Emilio referring to a grandfather called Felice because he and Evelyn considered naming Fabio after him and talked about it when they asked me to be his Godfather.'

'I see. So who was Dino and how did he come to own the property?'

'Emilio's uncle.'

'Which means he was Eduardo's brother. But how did he become the sole owner of Villa Anna on their father's death? Surely he and Eduardo became equally entitled to the property? I don't understand.'

'According to the records at the *Comune*, Felice died a widower in 1958. My contact enquired about a Will because, as you know, in Italy Wills are recorded in a public register after the testator's death at the Succession Office of the Court House which has jurisdiction for the particular area in which the testator lived. As I'm sure you're also very aware, unlike English law, under Italian law a testator does not have the freedom to leave his assets to whomsoever he chooses, it is not possible to disinherit certain family members and at least a fixed percentage of the estate has to be left to them. In a scenario such as this, where there is no spouse and two children, two-thirds of the estate would pass to them and the testator is only free to leave one-third of his estate to whoever else he wants to bequeath it.'

'But that's not what happened here, so presumably there was no Will,' I said, scanning his face.

'Correct. My contact couldn't find one and it would seem that Felice died intestate.'

'But if Felice died intestate, a widower with two living children, under the strict Italian rules of intestacy, shouldn't the estate have been shared equally between his two sons? At least, that's my understanding of how it would be distributed.'

'Yes. That's right.'

'Then what happened?'

'My contact has uncovered documents which stipulate that Dino was the only surviving child and that Eduardo had no children. Accordingly Dino inherited the whole estate.'

'False documents?'

'It would seem so, yes.'

'Are you saying Dino falsified them and stitched up his own brother?'

'The evidence points to it.'

'But how did he get away with it? Surely he would have had to prove that Eduardo was dead?'

'We haven't found out all the details yet. Believe me, it's hard enough obtaining the information as it is.'

'Yes, it normally takes weeks to get records. A couple of years ago I remember writing off to the *Stato Civile* for some marriage records for a client and then I had to follow up my letter with another one and several calls. This acquaintance of yours must have contacts in all the right places, that's all I can say. Who is he, Uncle? I didn't like to ask you before, but this information has been obtained legally, hasn't it?' Again I scanned his face.

'Of course it has. My contact is a high-ranking official and has his sources. To obtain information like this quickly, Alicia, it is sometimes necessary to bypass the ordinary channels. These are exceptional circumstances after all. We are fortunate that he is willing to assist us because, as you will recall, when Emilio originally went missing I tried to investigate the case, but with no resources available to me and no contacts to call on, all my efforts came to nothing.'

'I'm not complaining. And I really appreciate your input,' I said, backtracking slightly.

'Just remember this is a murder investigation and we don't have time to waste, hence my slightly unorthodox, but not illegal, methods. You do want to catch the murderer or murderers, don't you?'

'Yes. I'm sorry if I sounded ungrateful.'

'There's no need to apologise, Alicia. I understand your concerns, but you mustn't worry.'

'How did Emilio end up owning Villa Anna?' I continued, returning to the main issue.

'It was left to him by Will. Dino died in 1993 and the property was transferred then.'

'But that raises three points. First, why after denying his brother his rightful inheritance, would Dino then leave the property to his nephew – unless perhaps he had a sudden tinge of conscience? Second, how did he get around the fact that he had a nephew when he had sworn a legal document confirming that his brother had no children? And third, how could the transfer take place in 1993 when Emilio disappeared in 1992? Or are we to assume that he resurfaced in Italy the year after his mysterious disappearance? Are you quite sure those details are correct?'

'The full details of the transfer of title for Villa Anna are in *La Conservatoria* in the Province of Lucca, Alicia, and that's what the records say. As for the Will don't forget as a bachelor with no children or surviving parents in accordance with Italian law there were no family members to whom Dino was obligated to leave a fixed percentage of his estate. He was entitled to leave the whole of his estate to whomsoever he chose – which happened to be Emilio. No reference is made in the Will to Emilio being his nephew.'

'Of course. I see how it could be done. When was Dino's Will made?'

'A few months before he died.'

'Which does support the argument that he was trying to make

recompense for denying his brother his legal share of the estate. And when did the ownership pass from Emilio to Piero Giovannini?'

'In 1994.'

'But that's even more bizarre and would mean Emilio was still alive in 1994. Unless,' I said, thinking out loud, 'someone who knew he was already dead and was aware of his entitlement under the Will, passed himself off as Emilio and then legitimately sold the property on to Mr Giovannini. I know it seems too fantastical to be true, but what do you think?' I said, hoping for a positive reaction.

'Well, as they say, fact is stranger than fiction.'

'Yes, but could it be possible?'

'Who would know about both Dino's Will and Emilio's affairs?'

'Someone associated with them both.'

'Yes. I realize that, Alicia. But who? I don't mean to dampen your enthusiasm, but why don't we concentrate on what we do know for now rather than stabbing around in the dark. If you're looking for something concrete to work with we've discovered a connection between Dino and Piero Giovannini.'

'Really? What is it?'

'The firm which made Dino's Will also happens to be the firm which handled the transfer of ownership of Villa Anna into both Emilio's and Mr Giovannini's name.'

'That must surely be significant. What's the name of the firm?'

'Studio Legale Marchese. The main branch is based in Lucca, but there's a branch office in Viareggio.' I could hardly believe what I was hearing.

'Did you say Viareggio?'

'Yes.'

'But that's where Graham said he thought Mr Kettering's contact was based. This can't be coincidental, Uncle.'

'I presume you're referring to the mutual legal acquaintance of Kettering and Pellegrino?'

'Exactly.'

'What do you know about him?'

'Only that he's a property lawyer and his association with Pellegrino and Kettering goes back at least twenty years. Graham said to me today that he was fairly sure that the reason why Kettering bought property in Viareggio was because his contact was there. This has to be a line of investigation worth pursuing. What we need is to find out details of the lawyers who work at Studio Legale Marchese and whether any of them have a connection with Pellegrino or Kettering. I'm sure your trusted source can make some discreet enquiries about that, and obtaining details of the lawyers in the firm should be easy enough. I could do that.'

'No need. I'll look into that for you. I'm keen to find out a little more about this firm myself.'

'You know, Uncle,' I said, sitting back, 'if one of the lawyers at Studio Legale Marchese is both the elusive legal acquaintance and Mr Giovannini's lawyer, then I can't help thinking that my theory about him being the one to respond to Giulia's letter must be correct. There has to be dirty work at the crossroads. With Emilio dead, that estate should have passed to the children. Somebody somewhere must have been falsifying papers. I reckon that whoever is, or are, responsible for Giulia's murder thought she was on the verge of revealing the truth, which meant she had to be killed before she discovered it and exposed him/her or them. Villa Anna must be some property, that's all I can say, if people are prepared to forge documents and murder for it. I'd really like to see it for myself.'

'The estate doesn't only comprise the villa you know. There's the land that goes with it, including farming land and an olive grove. It's all listed at *La Conservatoria*.'

'In which case I find it hard to believe that Fabio's grandfather didn't pursue such an inheritance or tell his son about it. He must have realized he was entitled to a share of his father's estate. There's something odd about that too.'

'It is quite bizarre, yes.'

'Oh, well, I suppose I had better call Fabio and give him the news.'

'Why don't you ring him now while I'm still here and then we can discuss our plan of action together?'

'OK. Good idea. But I can't imagine what Fabio's going to make of these latest revelations.'

Chapter 25

'I can hardly take in what you're telling me, Alicia,' said Alex. It was the following morning and he had called as promised. 'Your uncle's certainly something else. How did Fabio take the news?'

'I think he's reeling. He wants me to go out to Italy to help with the investigation. I know you don't think I should but...'

'It's not that. It's simply that I can't see what assistance you could give him and to be perfectly honest I'm concerned about you endangering yourself unnecessarily.'

'Well, unless Graham allows me to take the time off work I won't be able to leave, so it's all hypothetical at the moment anyway.'

'What did you tell Fabio?'

'That I'd have to talk to Graham about it. Don't worry, I didn't promise that I'd go or anything.'

'Oh, but I do worry, Alicia. Where are you meeting Antonia?'

'She's coming here.'

'Are you still OK for five-thirty?'

'Yes. I'm looking forward to meeting Edward Bartlett. Maybe he can shed some light on the mystery surrounding Rosetta's disappearance.'

'Well, let's hope our conversation with him is as enlightening as the one you had with your uncle last night. I'll see you later then. Enjoy your shopping with Antonia.'

'I'll do my best. *Ciao, bello.*'

'What time did you say Alex was picking you up?' asked Antonia, glancing at her watch. We were sitting out on the balcony after returning from our shopping trip discussing her wedding plans.

'In about two minutes. Have you decided on the style of dress you want? I've lost count of the number of dresses we looked at today. I still think that Sassi Holford dress you saw was perfect. It was so elegant and you could carry it off as you have the height. Why don't you have a think about having a dress designed by her?'

'I will. Oh, look. There's Alex,' she said, pointing down to the street below. Alex had pulled up outside the house. 'So where are you two off to then?'

'To meet a friend of Alex's in Richmond,' I replied, standing up and stepping back inside the flat. Antonia picked up her wedding brochures and followed me in. 'Who's that then?' she asked as I locked the French windows.

'I don't know him,' I replied nonchalantly, ambling through to the hall and picking up my handbag and keys from the hall table. 'What are you up to tonight?' I asked, changing the subject.

'Tom and I are going out to dinner with a couple of his colleagues. Actually I'd better dash as I need to get home, shower and change,' she said, slipping on her denim jacket and following me to the door. At that moment there was a knock on it and I presumed it must be Alex as I certainly was not expecting anyone else.

'The downstairs door was open so I thought I'd come up and surprise you,' he said, planting a kiss on my cheek. 'Better not hang around for long though as I had to double-park and I caught sight of a traffic warden as I was driving up the road.'

'We saw you arrive,' said Antonia, brushing past Alex in the open doorway. She started to walk down the stairs.

'Alicia told me about your engagement,' he called after her. 'I'm very happy for you.'

'Thanks,' she said, pausing halfway down the stairs, turning back and waving her left hand at him to show off her ring. 'Tom said you called to congratulate him.'

'Yes. I suggested that the four of us should go out to celebrate soon.'

'That'd be good. I must run. Have a good evening. Bye, Ally,' she said, blowing me a kiss. 'Hope you don't get a ticket, Alex,' she added, and then rushed off down the stairs.

'I'm never quite sure what to make of your sister,' said Alex, standing back while I double locked the front door.

'Well, that makes two of us then,' I said, putting my keys into my handbag, and swivelling around to face him.

'Did your day go well?'

'It did actually and it's not over yet,' I said, winking at him. 'I'm hoping this evening will prove to be even better.'

'I presume you're referring to *after* our meeting with Edward Bartlett.'

'Well, that depends on how things go with him, doesn't it?' I said, catching hold of his hand, pulling him towards me and kissing him. 'Come on. We'd better go if there's a warden lurking around the corner. You can give me the details of what you've told him about the investigation on the way.'

Edward Bartlett's apartment block was located on the slopes of Richmond Hill and within easy access of Richmond town centre. It was a purpose-built but prestigious mansion block of flats; it had porterage, and was well-maintained, with very attractively arranged communal gardens. Mr Bartlett only lived on the first floor so Alex and I took the stairs rather than the lift. We arrived at his flat, rang the doorbell and waited for several minutes before he came to the door. We could hear him slotting the security chain into the fitting on the front door before opening it, albeit only the few inches which the security chain permitted.

'Mr Bartlett, it's Alex Waterford. We spoke on the 'phone yesterday morning,' said Alex, speaking through the gap in the door.

'Oh yes,' he said. 'Just a minute.' He pushed the door shut, unhooked the chain and opened the door fully. 'How do you do?'

he said warmly, extending his bony right hand to Alex. I noticed that he was slightly unsteady on his feet and his hand was trembling a little.

'How do you do?' Alex replied, and then turning to me said, 'This is Alicia Allen, the one doing all the research, as I explained.'

'Oh yes. How do you do?' he said, taking my hand and smiling at me. He had a very kindly expression, bright blue eyes and cherubic cheeks. I calculated that he must be in his late seventies or even early eighties, but he certainly seemed much younger. His hair was silvery grey and from what I could tell he still had all his own teeth. 'Please come in,' he said, standing back to allow us to enter the flat. I was immediately struck by how light it was, and certainly the entrance hall was remarkably spacious. 'The reception room's the second door on your right,' he said, closing the front door. 'You go on ahead and make yourself at home,' he added, seeing that Alex and I were hovering in the hallway waiting for him. 'You're a bit faster on your feet than I am these days,' he said.

He was clearly somewhat of an art connoisseur because every inch of wall space was covered in paintings. He was obviously also a lover of classical music as there was a cabinet in the hallway crammed full of classical CDs. As we walked down the corridor to the reception room I glanced left into what I presumed was one of the bedrooms and noticed that it was shelved from floor to ceiling with books. Clearly he was a bibliophile as well. Directly opposite the door to the reception room was a large antique wooden bookcase which was crammed full of art books and, as in the hallway, paintings filled the walls. It was quite remarkable, and made me feel is if my own walls at home were positively bare.

'You have an impressive art collection,' said Alex as Mr Bartlett entered the room. 'I was just admiring it,' he added.

'Thank you very much.' He indicated for us to take a seat on the cream, navy and burgundy striped sofa at the far end of the room, but remained standing. 'Now, before I sit down would either of you like a drink?'

'I'm all right at the moment,' I replied.

'Alex?' he said, looking at him.

'I'm fine, thanks.'

'In which case I'll take the weight off my feet,' he said, and settled himself into his armchair opposite us.

'You must have been accumulating these treasures for a good many years,' I said.

'Longer than I can remember. I studied Art History and then I worked as a dealer for over forty years and I have to admit I made some good finds along the way. My wife was also a great art and music lover. She was Italian. I understand from Alex that your mother is Italian too.' I nodded. 'Rosetta was our only child you know. Her death was a terrible blow to us and my wife never got over it.'

'When did your wife die?' asked Alex.

'Five years ago; from pancreatic cancer. She always hoped Rosetta would be restored to us. After she went missing we did everything we could to persuade the Italian authorities to keep the investigation open, but all the evidence pointed to the fact that she must have drowned and so the case was closed.'

'I see. I understand from Alex,' I said, glancing at him, 'that he has explained to you that we're actually investigating the disappearance of a colleague of Rosetta's called Emilio Angelino. They worked together at Scarpetti, Steiglitz & Co. and he vanished a few months before she did in equally mysterious circumstances.'

'Yes. I know. Rosetta left the firm soon after he disappeared.'

'Do you know whether her decision to leave was prompted by what happened to him?' I asked.

'I remember her being very distressed about the whole affair and she was certainly desperate to leave the firm as soon as possible after that.'

'Right. We've discovered she was working on some research with Emilio before his disappearance, but I don't suppose you would know anything about that.'

'No. The person you should be speaking to is the young solicitor she worked with. Let me think now who that was,' he said, sitting back and closing his eyes momentarily. 'Her name's on the tip of my tongue. She was devastated when Rosetta went missing. She tried to assist with the investigation and she even came to her memorial service. Unfortunately, we lost touch with her soon after. Oh, what's her name? It's so frustrating.'

'You don't mean Caterina Bartoldi, by any chance, do you?' Caterina had told me that she was Rosetta's assistant so there was a strong possibility that she was the young solicitor to whom Mr Bartlett was referring.

'Yes. That's her name. You know her then?'

'I was given her contact details and told that I should ask her about your daughter.' I was, of course, referring to the note which Annette Richardson had handed to me.

'And presumably you did?'

'Well, yes, but she said that the only thing she could tell us was that Rosetta drowned in a tragic swimming accident while on holiday in Italy.'

'Didn't she mention that she was the one on holiday with Rosetta in Ravello? They were good friends and remained so after Rosetta left the firm.'

'No.' I looked at Alex who shrugged his shoulders.

'But she was the one who raised the alarm. If anybody knows what Rosetta and Emilio were working on it would be her. My advice would be to speak to her again.'

'That's not possible unfortunately.'

'Why not?'

'Because she's dead, Mr Bartlett.'

'What? When did she die?' He seemed genuinely stunned by the news. 'What happened to her?'

'Caterina Bartoldi was murdered on Thursday evening,' said Alex, cutting in. Mr Bartlett took a sharp intake of breath.

'But why would somebody want to kill her? I don't understand.'

'You said just now that if anybody had knowledge of what Rosetta and Emilio were working on it would be her. We feel sure that's the reason why Caterina was murdered – because she *did* know. I spoke to her on Thursday morning and she invited me to her house that evening, I presume to tell me what happened all those years ago. Unfortunately, our meeting never took place because she was already dead by the time I arrived.'

'But if Caterina was murdered to prevent her revealing what she knew, which I presume was the reason she was killed, then that means that whatever Rosetta and Emilio were working on must have been something worth murdering for.'

'So we believe, yes.'

'Do you think there's a possibility that my daughter was murdered too, Alicia?' he said, focusing his blue eyes steadily on me. 'At the time foul play was ruled out, but I've always had my doubts. Unbeknown to my wife, I hired a private investigator to see if he could discover anything for me, but he was unable to do so.'

'Well, we're pretty certain your daughter was murdered.'

'And Emilio Angelino?'

'Yes.'

'Do you mind if I use the loo?' asked Alex, interrupting the conversation.

'No. Of course not. The bathroom's at the far end of the corridor.'

'Thanks,' said Alex, standing up. He left the room.

'Who do you think is responsible for my daughter's murder, Miss Allen?'

'Probably the same person who arranged for Caterina to be murdered.'

'And do you know who that is, or aren't you permitted to tell me?'

'All I can say is that the people who have been murdered have a common link and that link is Scarpetti, Steiglitz & Co.'

'I understand,' he said, nodding. 'I'm sorry that I can't help you with your investigation. Believe me, if I knew anything which could assist you I would have told you, because if Rosetta was murdered there is nothing I would want more than to be the one to bring the perpetrator to justice. You will keep in touch with me, won't you, if you make any progress with your enquiries?'

'Of course,' I said reassuringly. It was then that I espied a silver framed photograph of a little girl in a white dress which I presumed to be Rosetta on the table behind his armchair. 'Is that Rosetta?' I asked.

'Yes. That was taken at her First Communion.'

'What a lovely little girl she was,' I said, studying it.

'Yes. She was.'

'Are you finished?' asked Alex, returning to the room and signalling with his eyes for me to make a move. He seemed decidedly anxious to leave for some reason. I could not understand quite why, but I sensed there was something he wanted to say to me which would not wait.

'I think we are,' I said, smiling at Mr Bartlett and standing up. 'Oh, please don't get up,' I said as he started to haul himself out of the chair. 'We can show ourselves out.'

'The exercise will do me good,' he said. 'I'll walk you to the door.'

'When you studied Art History,' said Alex as we ambled out into the hallway, 'did you specialize in any particular period?'

'French seventeenth century. Nicolas Poussin is one of my favourite artists. Are you interested in art?'

'Alex is passionate about Canaletto,' I said.

'Then we have something else in common – so was my wife. Perhaps you and I can have a chat about Canaletto some time soon.'

'Yes, I'd like that,' said Alex as we reached the front door.

'Thank you so much for agreeing to see us this evening,' I said. 'Alex and I really appreciate your time and for talking to us,' I added taking his hand.

'I'm sorry I couldn't really help you,' he replied, squeezing mine.

'You have,' said Alex. I was slightly perplexed by Alex's remark. I was sure that I would have noticed if Mr Bartlett had given us some little gem of information which would assist us.

'Well, goodbye,' he said. 'Hope to hear from you,' he added, turning to me and then he shut the door.

'He seemed like a nice old man,' I said as we traipsed down the stairs. 'Pity he wasn't able to tell us anything to help progress the investigation, but then I didn't really expect that he could.'

'Well, he told us that Caterina and Rosetta were close friends which confirms why Rosetta would have confided in Caterina about what she and Emilio had discovered.'

'Unfortunately, it doesn't take us any nearer to finding out who the client was for whom Emilio and Rosetta were carrying out their research.'

'Hmm…'

'You seem preoccupied,' I said as we walked out to the car. 'Why did you say he had helped us and why were you so keen to leave?'

'Do you think Mr Bartlett is telling us the truth, Alicia?' he replied, ignoring my questions.

'What makes you say that?'

'Because if he hasn't seen Caterina for years and couldn't remember her name, how is it that her details are in his address book and I found a postcard from her in the kitchen?'

'What? I thought you were gone a long time. Were your rummaging around the apartment?'

'The kitchen door was open and I caught sight of a picture postcard on top of the work unit inside the door. I was curious and picked it up. You can't imagine my surprise when I flipped it over to see that it was a scene of the Amalfi coast and from Caterina. It was dated last month so she was definitely in touch with him then. His address book was on the hall table next to the 'phone so I had a peek inside and all her contact details are in there.'

'But why would he lie to us? He seemed truly shocked by her murder. I don't believe he knew about it.'

'Oh, I have no doubt that his reaction to news of her death was real enough, but as to why he lied my guess would be for the same reason that Caterina initially refused to assist you – fear of what might happen to him if he divulges what he knows. I'd bet on it that Caterina confided in him about what happened to Emilio and Rosetta.'

'So do you think he saw us purely to find out what we know?'

'I wouldn't be surprised.'

'And, if he is fearful for his safety, now that Caterina has been murdered, the chances of him opening up to us are even more remote.'

'Exactly, and especially if he thinks Caterina was murdered because she was about to reveal the truth.'

'Unless we can persuade him otherwise.'

'What did you have in mind?'

'Well, if he does believe his daughter was murdered and wants to avenge her death, he must be aware that telling us the truth might actually bring about the result he desires.'

'So what are you going to do?'

'I'll see how things go and, subject to that, I'll contact him again. He asked me to keep in touch and let him know how the investigation is progressing. I'll find some way of getting him to talk to me. How many more murders do there have to be before somebody tells us the truth?'

'Just remember that whoever is carrying out these murders is remorseless and won't think twice about removing anyone who could expose them – and that includes you, Alicia.'

'Yes. I'm aware of that, Alex, but it's a risk I'm prepared to take.'

250

Chapter 26

It was a few minutes after nine on Sunday night when Alex dropped me off at home. He decided not to stay but to drive straight back to his flat as he had a few chores of his own which required attention. Barely seconds after unlocking my front door and stepping into the hallway the video Entryphone buzzer sounded. I presumed that Alex had changed his mind and I picked up the handset with one hand while the index finger of my other hand hovered over the door release button ready to let him into the building.

'Hello,' I said. I could not see anyone standing by the door, and I waited for a few moments but when nobody appeared I replaced the handset and wandered through to the bedroom. I slipped off my shoes and blue linen jacket and was in the process of hanging my jacket in the cupboard when the video Entryphone buzzer sounded again and I ran back into the hall to answer it. This time I could see a young woman hunched in front of the doorway. I could barely make out her features from the grainy black and white screen but I had certainly never seen her before.

'Hello,' I said, slightly warily picking up the handset.

'Is that Alicia Allen?' she asked hesitantly, but in a very clear English voice.

'Yes, but who are you?' I replied.

'Olivia. Caterina Bartoldi's daughter. I understand you discovered my mother's body. I'd like to speak to you if I may.'

'Of course,' I said, pressing the door release button. 'Come up. I'm on the first floor.'

I opened my front door and waited for her at the top of the stairs. I could hear her shut the outside door, shuffle across the hall and start to walk up the stairs. Every step she took seemed to be with a heavy heart.

'Hello again,' I said as the gangly teenager rounded the stairwell and slowly climbed the remaining few stairs to my flat. She was wearing fitted black denim jeans and a cropped black denim jacket which drew attention to her long thin legs, and slung across her body was a small red handbag. As she reached the top stair she looked up at me and smiled weakly. She was very pale and drawn and hollow-eyed, which was hardly surprising in the circumstances, but I was immediately drawn to her rather doe-like eyes which reminded me of Audrey Hepburn. She wore her dark brown hair in a loose pony-tail. 'Do come in,' I said, standing back against the open door and inviting her into the hall. 'Go straight through,' I added, looking up at her and pointing her in the direction of the living room. I closed the front door and followed her in. She was standing awkwardly in the centre of the room. 'Please take a seat,' I said. She perched nervously on the edge of the sofa and folded her arms in front of her, slightly ill at ease. I sat down in my armchair opposite. For a moment there was an awkward silence and I wondered when she would speak.

'I'm sorry to descend on you unexpectedly like this. I came around earlier but you weren't in.'

'No. I've been out of London today. You haven't been waiting for me all day, have you?'

'Only since early this evening.'

'I'm sorry you had to wait at all. Where did you go?'

'To one of the cafés around the corner. I kept hopping back hoping you'd be here.'

'How did you know where to find me?'

'DS Henshaw told me where you lived. He mentioned driving you home the other night.'

'Yes, that's right.'

'The police told me everything.'

'I'm truly sorry about what happened to your mother, Olivia. I really don't know what words of comfort I can give you. I...'

'There aren't any,' she said, interrupting me, 'and I didn't come here for your sympathy, appreciated though it is. I came here because I want you to help me track down my mother's killer.' She focused her soft brown eyes on me. I could detect the emotion in her voice – but it was controlled.

'Me?' I said, putting my hand up to my chest.

'Yes. You,' she said gently. 'The police told me why you contacted my mother.'

'I expect they did.'

'My mother has always tried to protect me from the past, but I've known for some time that she was concealing some terrible secret and that it was connected with Rosetta Bartlett's disappearance and Scarpetti, Steiglitz & Co.'

'Would you like to elaborate on that?' I said, leaning forward.

'I suppose you're aware that my father walked out on us when I was a baby?' I nodded. 'Well, my mother needed a job and the reason why she went to work for Scarpetti, Steiglitz & Co. was because Rosetta Bartlett worked there. You see they were friends and it was she who recommended her to Gregorio Pellegrino.'

'But I thought that your mother only met Rosetta after she joined the firm.'

'No. Rosetta's mother gave private music lessons. She used to teach my mother the piano, so the two families had known each other for some years.' Edward Bartlett had certainly never mentioned that.

'Then they were very close?'

'Oh yes. The best of friends. Rosetta was my Godmother.'

'Then it's likely that Rosetta would have confided in your mother about any concerns she might have had on both a personal and professional basis?'

'Most probably.'

'Which means your mother must have known all about Rosetta's reasons for leaving Scarpetti, Steiglitz & Co.'

'You have to remember that I was only three when she disappeared and over time my mother was very sparing with the details and so I only knew what I had been told. I wasn't even in Ravello, because I was staying with friends of ours in London. When Rosetta went missing the only thing my mother said was that one night Rosetta went out for a late night swim and never returned. It was only later that she told me that Rosetta had had a disagreement with Gregorio Pellegrino which was the reason why she left the firm.'

'Did your mother ever mention the cause of her falling out with him?'

'She was always very reluctant to discuss Mr Pellegrino at all, but reading between the lines I know she suspected him of playing a part in Rosetta's disappearance. As I'm sure you're already aware, my mother left Scarpetti, Steiglitz & Co. soon after Rosetta disappeared, but it was all very unpleasant because he accused her of stealing several of the firm's clients and pursued a legal case against her.'

'Yes. I did know that.'

'To make matters worse our house was actually broken into on two separate occasions around that time and completely ransacked, but nothing was taken and the police never caught whoever it was. I think my mother suspected that Pellegrino was behind it, but she never said as such to the police.'

'For the same reason that she declined to become involved when I initially spoke to her, I suppose – fear of any repercussions. Was he looking for something or was it merely to frighten her into submission and silence, do you think?'

'As I said to you, I was only a little girl then and merely picked up how distressed my mother was, and I had no idea what the burglaries were about. I didn't know the full facts and why my mother was so terrified of any involvement with Mr Pellegrino. A couple of years ago when we were going through a box of old photographs we came across some of Rosetta and I asked her about what happened. She told me that some things were better left in the past and refused to talk about it. When I pressed her on the subject she became very distressed and so I felt that it was better to leave it.'

'But weren't you curious?'

'Yes, but I decided that if that's what my mother wanted I would honour her wishes. But then a few days ago she rang me and we had the most bizarre conversation in which she said that she had been thinking about the past and she started talking about Rosetta. She told me that she had made a new Will and was insistent that if anything should happen to her I must go to her office immediately to collect it. She said it was being stored in the deeds room there. I never imagined that she would be murdered. It's almost as if she knew that something terrible was going to occur. I now know, of course, that her call to me was prompted by your calls to her. The police explained that you had contacted her and asked her about Rosetta Bartlett.'

'I tried to persuade your mother to open up to me on several occasions but she wouldn't tell me anything. In fact she hung up on me twice. It was only when I spoke to her on Thursday morning that she agreed to meet with me. The reason why I contacted her is because I'm acting for somebody called Fabio Angelino whose father Emilio Angelino disappeared in Sicily a few months before Rosetta disappeared in Ravello. I'm trying to help Fabio find out what really happened to his father. In the course of my investigations I discovered that Emilio was working with Rosetta on some research and I believe that this research is the key to both his and her disappearance. I learned that you mother worked with Rosetta at Scarpetti, Steiglitz & Co. and I hoped she could shed light on the mystery.'

'The police told me all this. Now I understand why my mother behaved the way she did and never came forward with any information.'

'She was trying to protect you. She made it very clear to me when I spoke to her that your protection was her first priority.'

255

'Yes, but I just wish she had told me the truth.'

'I think she was on the point of telling you. I believe she knew the name of the client for whom Emilio and Rosetta were acting and that she intended to tell me who that client was on Thursday evening.'

'I know,' she said, in a definite tone.

'What do you mean?' I asked, perplexed by her response. 'What do you know?'

'The name of the client,' she said lifting her handbag over her head, unzipping the central pocket, taking out a C5 sized brown envelope, standing up, striding purposefully over to me and handing it to me. 'Look inside,' she said, thrusting the envelope into my hand. 'When I went to my mother's office yesterday to collect her Will this letter was with it.' I glanced at the envelope and noted that it was addressed to Olivia. The envelope had already been slit open at the top so I pulled out the contents which comprised a hand-written letter to Olivia, written in black ink, on three sheets of paper and signed by Caterina and dated the beginning of the week.

'But this letter is personal. I can't read it,' I said, handing it back to her.

'Oh, but you must read the last two paragraphs of the letter. It's relevant to the investigation,' she said, holding out the last page. 'It isn't much to go on, but it's a start. Remember just now you asked me whether I thought when the burglaries took place that whoever was responsible was looking for something?'

'Yes.'

'Well, read those paragraphs and you'll have your answer.'

'All right,' I replied, taking the sheet of paper from her. She sat back down on the sofa and placed her handbag on the floor. As requested I scanned the two paragraphs. They read as follows:

Please contact a solicitor called Alicia Allen. She works at Crawford Ffoulkes & Piper in Belgravia. Tell her to ask Roland Kettering about Ellen Petronelli. She is the client for whom Emilio Angelino (Alicia will know who that is) and Rosetta were carrying out their research before they both disappeared. They were tracing family assets for her in Italy and Rosetta was working on the property side. There is no paperwork to give her because I destroyed it. I had no choice. Rosetta gave me the file for safekeeping but after we were burgled the first time I shredded the papers. I have no doubt that Gregorio Pellegrino suspected that I had it and I am convinced that the house was burgled on those two occasions for that very reason.

Emilio and Rosetta suspected that Gregorio Pellegrino and Roland Kettering were working with a contact in Italy supposedly helping Italians abroad trace their assets in Italy, but what they were doing was helping themselves to a slice of the family inheritance. When Emilio disappeared in Sicily, Rosetta's suspicions were confirmed and, after challenging Gregorio Pellegrino, she left the firm, but before she did she gave me Ellen Petronelli's file. When Rosetta disappeared I was convinced she had been murdered and I also believe that Emilio was murdered and so I left the firm. I never doubted for one moment that Roland Kettering and Gregorio Pellegrino were behind their murders but I remained silent about this because I did not want to jeopardise your safety. I know that if you are reading this letter it is because I am no longer with you. It is up to you to decide what to do with the information I have given you, but I believe that Alicia Allen is trustworthy, I feel she will follow this up, and I suggest you do not contact the police until you have spoken to her.

'Does that help you at all?' she asked, scanning my face.

'Hmm… Well, yes, I think it might. We have the name of the client which is definitely something,' I said, trying to sound positive. 'I fully understand why your mother destroyed the file, but it's a pity we don't have it because, from an evidential point of view, proving a link to Roland Kettering and Gregorio Pellegrino is going to be rather difficult. Also we don't have any details of the case.'

'You think it's a non-starter then?'

'Not at all,' I said, standing up, walking over to the sofa and sitting down next to her. 'I don't give up that easily. We'll just have to bluff it.'

'What do you mean? Let Mr Kettering think that we have the file in our possession?'

'Exactly.'

'Can we pull it off?'

'It's worth a shot. It might flush him out. On the face of it, the contents of that file would appear to be the cause of at least three deaths and it is looking more likely by the second that Mr Kettering has something to do with all three. I appreciate that your mother didn't want police involvement but are you intending to show the letter to them?'

'No. Unless you feel we ought to, but I'd rather we went to see Mr Kettering first. I picked up the letter late on Friday afternoon. I did try to call you around five-fifteen but your secretary said you had already left the office for the day.'

'Yes. I went home a bit earlier than usual.' I paused for a second. 'I realize that you don't want to go to the police yet and I agree that we must be careful not to take any action which might alert Mr Kettering for fear that he absconds. What I suggest is that we pay him a visit at his office together first thing tomorrow morning and contact the police immediately afterwards.'

'OK.'

'I hope you don't mind me asking you this, but how well do you know Edward Bartlett, Rosetta's father?'

'What makes you ask?'

'Because I went to see him yesterday and he told me that he lost contact with your mother not soon after Rosetta went missing and I know that is simply untrue.'

'I don't understand why he should say that. I haven't seen him for years I have to admit, but I'm fairly certain my mother was in regular contact with him. Maybe they had a pact not to talk about what happened. I know his daughter was murdered, but I guess he's old and he's frightened of the consequences of becoming involved in any investigation.'

'And what about you?'

'I want to be involved. My mother was murdered and I need to find out who is responsible for her death. I can't think about anything else right now. Anyway, if she hadn't wanted me to take any action then she wouldn't have written that letter and asked me to contact you.'

'Point taken.' I admired Olivia; I thought she was a very courageous nineteen-year-old and I was impressed by how calm and collected she was considering her mother had been murdered only forty-eight hours earlier.

'Do you think Mr Pellegrino is responsible for my mother's murder?'

'I can't prove it yet, but I believe he is involved, yes. Did the police tell you about the call your mother received on Thursday afternoon from a man who pretended to be a former client of hers from Scarpetti, Steiglitz & Co?'

'Yes. They did. They asked me if I had any idea who it could have been, but I couldn't tell them anything.'

'Well, I think there's a strong possibility that it was Mr Pellegrino himself who made that call.'

'Did you tell the police that?'

'No. Not directly, but I hinted as much.'

'I suppose I should be making tracks,' said Olivia, standing up to leave.

'Why don't you stay here tonight?' I said. 'There's no point in your traipsing home now only to have to come all the way back in the morning.'

'I don't want to impose.'

'You're not.'

'I'm not at the house actually. I didn't want to go back there. I've been staying in a hotel these past two nights.'

'Whereabouts?'

'Oh, in Camden. I can't bear it in that house now. I'm never going to live there again. I'll sell it as soon as I'm able to.'

'I can understand that. I'll go and make up your bed,' I said, walking to the door. 'Would you like anything to eat? You must be hungry. There's chicken salad in the fridge but I can rustle up some pasta for you if you'd prefer.'

'I'll have the salad, please.'

'Well, help yourself,' I said, hovering in the doorway.

'Thank you. You're very kind.'

'And you are very welcome.'

'How did you sleep?' I asked when Olivia surfaced from her bed the next morning. I was already up and dressed, but had left her to sleep as I felt she needed the rest, if nothing else.

'A bit fitfully.'

'Are you sure you're up to coming with me to see Roland Kettering? I really don't mind going alone.'

'I want to meet him. I'll be all right after a few cups of coffee. Do you mind if I take a shower? It might help clear my head. We have time, don't we?'

'Plenty of time. There's no point in arriving at his office before nine-thirty and it's not even eight o'clock yet. It won't take very long to get there. We only have to take the tube to St James's Park station.'

'Do you think he'll see us?'

'I think there's a strong possibility he will if we tell the receptionist that we've come to talk to him about Ellen Petronelli.'

'Are you OK about being late for work?'

'Don't worry about that. I'll give my boss a call and let him know what's happening.'

We arrived at the offices of Smythson, Reid & Monkton at twenty-five to ten. I walked straight up to the reception desk but Olivia loitered momentarily in the lobby before joining me at the desk.

'Good morning,' I said to the rather disinterested-looking receptionist who was slouching over her desk. Clearly Monday mornings did not suit her. 'My name is Alicia Allen and this is Olivia Bartoldi,' I said, standing to one side so that the receptionist could see Olivia. 'We've come to see Roland Kettering.'

'I see,' she said, sitting bolt upright. 'Do you have an appointment?'

'No. But I met with him a week or so ago and I believe that if you tell him we've come to discuss Ellen Petronelli then he'll find time to talk to us.' I cast Olivia a sideways glance.

'I'm afraid that won't be possible,' she said firmly.

'Couldn't you at least put a call through to his secretary and ask if it is.'

'You don't understand.' She shifted uncomfortably in her seat.

'No. I'm afraid I don't,' I replied, beginning to feel rather irritated. 'Is there a problem, because if there is, perhaps you'd care to explain what it is?'

'Mr Kettering isn't here.'

'Is he still on holiday?'

'No.' The receptionist seemed to be becoming increasingly uncomfortable with my questions.

'Is he expected in today?'

'No.'

'Well, where is he?'

'Mr Kettering is dead, Miss Allen,' she blurted out.

'What?' I exclaimed. I was totally shocked.

'What happened to him?' asked Olivia.

'He's been murdered. I'm sorry, but that's all I can tell you.'

Chapter 27

'I think I'm going to be sick,' said Olivia as we staggered out of the building onto the street.

'You need some air,' I said. I was feeling slightly shaken myself as news that Roland Kettering had been murdered was the last thing I expected to hear that morning. 'We can walk back to the office through the park. Let's go and sit for a while, watch the ducks and take stock.' We wandered slowly from Queen Anne's Gate into St James's Park. It was early morning so there were plenty of free benches from which to choose.

'I thought Mr Kettering was a key suspect in the murder investigation. It's bizarre that he himself should be murdered, don't you think?' said Olivia as we took a seat on one of the benches near the lake.

'Maybe somebody has caught up with him from *his* past. If the details of your mother's letter are correct, then there are a lot of people out there who must have a grievance against him.'

'How are we going to find out about Ellen Petronelli now Mr Kettering is dead?'

'You never know. Some new fact may turn up,' I replied, determined to remain positive for her sake if nothing else. 'We should call the police anyway and show them your mother's note. Maybe we can glean some details from them about Roland Kettering's murder at the same time.'

'Yes. Shall we go back to your office then and call DCI Framlington?'

'There's no rush. We can sit here until you're ready.'

'Is Graham free?' I asked Susannah as I whisked Olivia through reception to avoid any awkward questions.

'Yes. I believe so,' she said, calling after us as we sped off down the corridor towards his office. I tapped on the door and then opened it. Graham was sitting at his desk and looked up from his work as we walked in. On seeing Olivia he immediately stood up and rushed around to our side of his desk.

'I'm Graham Ffoulkes,' he said, taking her hand briefly. 'I'm dreadfully sorry to hear about your mother,' he said gently and with compassion in his voice. 'Is there anything we can do to help you?'

'Alicia has already been very kind,' she said, glancing at me, 'but if you mean from a legal point of view I'm definitely going to need some assistance with that side of things. There's so much to do. I need to attend to my mother's funeral arrangements and then there's the police investigation to think about as well. It's overwhelming and I don't think I've really taken in the enormity of what has happened yet.' Her eyes welled up with tears.

'Please don't worry,' he said reassuringly. We can assist you with all the formalities.'

'Thanks for calling me this morning, Alicia, and filling me in on everything,' he said, turning to me before walking around to his side of the desk and settling back into his leather executive chair. He indicated for us to sit down which we did. 'How was your meeting with Roland Kettering?'

'There was no meeting,' said Olivia, sounding despondent.

'Why? What happened?' he said, looking perplexed.

'Roland Kettering has been murdered,' I said.

'What? When?' He sounded incredulous, leaned forward across his desk and looked at me in disbelief.

'We don't have any details. That's all we were told. Olivia and I need to speak to the police anyway and I'm hoping we'll be able to find out the facts when we do.'

'I really don't know what to say,' said Graham. 'Stunned is the word,' he added, sitting back. Olivia and I stood up to leave and at that moment Graham's telephone rang.

'Hello,' he said, answering it, 'Yes, she's right here,' he continued, indicating for me to stay. 'Just a second.' He put his hand over the mouthpiece. 'Alicia, your uncle's on the line. The call has diverted to Danielle. Do you want to take it in your office?'

'Yes. I will. Thanks.'

'OK, Danielle,' I heard him say as Olivia and I left the room. 'Alicia's on her way back to her office now.'

'Hello, Uncle,' I said, rushing to my desk and picking up the 'phone. I sat down in my swivel chair and Olivia took a seat in the chair opposite my desk.

'Are you OK?'

'Yes. I was talking to one of the Partners and had to sprint back to answer the 'phone. How are things? Have you managed to obtain any more information?'

'Yes. You'll be pleased to hear that I've established a connection between a lawyer at Studio Legale Marchese and Gregorio Pellegrino and I'm one hundred percent certain he's Pellegrino's and Kettering's mystery Italian contact.'

'Who is he?' I said, with baited breath.

'His name is Enrico Tomasino. He was the senior lawyer there and now works primarily on a consultancy basis at their branch office in Viareggio. He's the same age as Pellegrino; they went to the University of Siena together, graduated at the same time and worked together when they first qualified before going their separate ways. He's a property specialist which also fits in with what your Mr Ffoulkes told us and even with what Mr Kettering himself said.'

'It sounds as if he could be our man.'

'Yes. Definitely. Enrico Tomasino owns a villa down the coast at Torre del Lago, but he also has a yacht. As you know there's a yachting community in Viareggio and so he's obviously part of that wealthy set. I wouldn't be surprised if that's where Pellegrino's hiding out right now since he seems to have gone to ground. I'm planning to get that checked for you.'

'If you could that would be fantastic. Have you managed to glean anything about Piero Giovannini?'

'I was just coming to that. He's Tomasino's nephew. Piero's mother is Tomasino's elder sister.'

'Which explains where he fits in, doesn't it?'

'Yes. But it gets better. Listen to this. His father Aldo Giovannini is one of Tomasino's colleagues.'

'Very neat. Talk about keeping it in the family.'

'And there's something else too.'

'Tell me.'

'Aldo Giovannini was born in Ravello. His other son, Matteo, is living there currently.'

'He doesn't happen to own a blue Alfa Romeo with blacked out windows does he?' I was of course referring to the Alfa which Fabio alleged had tried to ram him off the road between Atrani and Ravello.

'That I don't know, but we can find out. All the missing links seem to be fitting together though, Alicia. Now tell me your news. Have there been any developments your end?'

'Oh, yes. I have some rather astonishing news for you.' I paused for a moment. 'Caterina Bartoldi's daughter, Olivia, is with me by the way.'

'Which means you can't talk freely?' My uncle was quick to pick up on my situation without me having to stress it.

'Only on that particular issue, but we can discuss everything else.'

'I follow. So what's happened?' I told my uncle about the trip to see Edward Bartlett on Saturday evening, Caterina's letter and the purpose of our visit to Mr Kettering's office that morning. As for the news that Roland Kettering had been murdered, he seemed completely flabbergasted. 'Well, that's thrown a spanner in the works, hasn't it?' he said. 'How was he murdered?'

'I don't know yet. Somebody didn't like him very much, that's for sure. I don't know how we can find out about Ellen Petronelli, bearing in mind we don't have anything much to go on. Are you sure Emilio never mentioned her name to you?'

'Absolutely. Believe me I'd remember if he had.'

'It's very frustrating.'

'Have you spoken to Fabio?'

'Not since we called him on Friday evening.'

'Then you will have a lot to tell him. Have you thought further about flying out to Italy?'

'I haven't discussed taking time off work with Graham yet. I know that Fabio wants me to join him and Will out there, but it may well be that I'm unable to. I'd better let you go, Uncle, as I know you have things to do and Olivia and I need to call the police, but I'll give you a ring later and let you know what's been decided on the Italy front. I can't tell you how grateful I am for all the assistance and support you have given me with this case.'

'It's a pleasure.'

'How much longer are you able to stay with Mamma? Will you have to return to New York this week?'

'It's looking that way, unfortunately.'

'I'm sorry we haven't exactly had the chance to spend much time together since you've been here.'

'I know, but you'll just have to come out to New York for a holiday. Speak to you later then. *Ciao, carina.*'

'If you're thinking of travelling to Italy, I'd like to come with you,' said Olivia when I put down the 'phone.

'You would?'

'Yes. I want to help with the investigation. I have a vested interest in tracking down these murderers, don't forget. When are you likely to leave?'

'As you heard me say to my uncle, I must speak to Graham about taking time off first, so nothing is definite yet.'

'OK.'

'Let's call DCI Framlington.' She nodded. I dialled his number and put my 'phone on loudspeaker so Olivia could hear what I said to him. His mobile rang about four or five times before he answered it. There was a good deal of background noise and it sounded as if he was walking along a busy street.

'DCI Framlington, it's Alicia Allen. I have Olivia Bartoldi with me and we'd like to talk to you about Caterina if you have a moment.'

'Where are you?' he asked.

'At my office in Belgravia,' I replied.

'Can it wait until this afternoon?' he said. 'I could make it to you around three?' I glanced at Olivia. She nodded.

'Three o'clock is fine,' I said.

'Good. I'll see you then.'

'Thanks. Bye.' I pressed the loudspeaker button to terminate the call.

'I'm going to nip over to Camden,' said Olivia. 'I left my bag at the hotel and I need to change. I didn't think I would be staying with you so I have nothing else to wear.'

'Why don't you bring your bag with you? You might as well stay at my flat, at least until things settle down.'

'Are you sure?'

'Of course. I wouldn't be asking you if I wasn't. Will you be back here by three?'

'Definitely. I don't want to miss speaking to DCI Framlington. Let's hope that he comes alone.'

'You're not keen on DS Henshaw then?'

'No. I think he's very rude.'

After Olivia left, I called Alex and explained what had taken place after he had dropped me off at home the night before.

'I can't leave you alone for a few hours these days without somebody else being murdered,' he quipped. 'It's unbelievable; barely twenty-four hours since I've seen you and you've had Caterina Bartoldi's daughter turning up on your doorstep giving you a letter from her dead mother naming the client for whom Rosetta and Emilio were acting, and you've gone to see Mr Kettering to question him about her only to be told that he's been murdered! What have you found out about his murder?'

'What I've told you.'

'At least you're making progress with the Italian side of the investigation.'

'True. Thanks to Uncle Vico and his sources we have more information to put before the Italian authorities.'

'So I suppose you're intending to leave for Italy now? What have you decided about that?' Alex sounded anxious to hear my plans.

'Nothing yet, although I'm still keen to go as you know. I haven't rung Fabio because I'm waiting until Olivia and I have spoken to DCI Framlington. I'm hoping he'll tell us how Roland Kettering was murdered.'

'Do you really think you can achieve anything by going to Italy?'

'I'm desperate to talk with Laura.'

'You really believe she's withholding vital evidence necessary to progress the investigation out there, don't you?'

'Yes, I do. I'd bet on it that it was Enrico Tomasino who responded to Giulia's letter and I believe Laura is in a position to confirm whether it was him or not. If she were able to do that then we would have established the crucial link between him and Giulia's murder, although I'm fully aware that persuading her to confide in me and then the police won't be easy.'

'Bearing in mind her reluctance to discuss the matter with Fabio to date, I can imagine it will be an uphill struggle. You said that you thought the man Giulia met was Piero Giovannini's lawyer and, by the sound of it, that's Enrico Tomasino, so I have to concede that it's definitely worth pursuing this with Laura. I'd better run. Let me know how it goes with DCI Framlington and what you decide about the trip to Italy.'

'Of course I will.'

'Where's Olivia now?'

'She went to collect her belongings from the hotel in Camden. I invited her to stay with me for a while.'

'That's very good of you in the circumstances. Please don't take this the wrong way, Alicia, but you can't take on her problems as well. You have rather a lot to contend with already.'

'I'm conscious of that, Alex, and I appreciate what you're saying. I'm simply trying to help her through a very difficult time. She's only nineteen, for goodness sake, her mother has just been murdered and she doesn't have any other family here.'

'I know. But you can't let her become too dependent on you, that's all I'm saying.'

'Don't worry. I think you'll find there's no danger of that. I'll ring you later.'

'All right. I'll wait for your call.'

'Oh, good. You're off the 'phone,' said Danielle, stepping into my office. 'Is everything OK?'

'I'm sorry, Danielle. So much has happened these past few days. I can't begin to tell you how much, but you must be wondering what's going on?'

'Well, I didn't like to ask. I have been concerned about you though as you've been looking rather wan. Who's the young woman who was in the office this morning?'

'Her name's Olivia Bartoldi. Her mother Caterina used to work with Fabio's father and another lawyer called Rosetta Bartlett who disappeared shortly after he did. I contacted Caterina because I thought she might be able to shed light on the mystery surrounding Emilio's and Rosetta's disappearance.'

'I see. And has she?'

'Well, that's what I was hoping. The thing is Caterina's been murdered, and…'

'Oh,' she said, holding her hands up to her face in dismay and sounding suitably appalled. 'Her poor daughter. She's so young. Was she the one to find her?'

'No. I was.'

'What? How? I mean when?'

'I arranged to meet Caterina at her house last Thursday evening but she was already dead when I arrived. She had been strangled.'

'Oh, Alicia. I can only imagine what a terrible shock that must have been for you. Now I understand why you looked so strained on Friday morning. I wish you had told me. I know I shouldn't say this what with Caterina having been murdered, as it probably sounds a bit callous, but what's happening with the investigation? What I mean is that if you didn't have the chance to meet her to talk about what she knew how can you hope to take things forward?'

'Well, we do have something to go on fortunately.'

'What's that?'

'She wrote Olivia a letter a few days before her murder asserting that it was her belief Rosetta and Emilio were murdered and that Roland Kettering and Gregorio Pellegrino were complicit in those murders.'

'Right. Can the police go after them on the basis of her letter?'

'From an evidential point of view it's very tenuous. She destroyed the client file that Rosetta and Emilio were working on and she's not even here to give evidence. Mr Pellegrino has done a runner to Italy and I have no doubt we could catch up with him, but it's a question of having something to pin on him. As for Roland Kettering it's too late to do anything about him, I'm afraid.'

'Why not?'

'Because, Danielle, he too has been murdered.'

'You're joking? I mean, I know you're not, but I can hardly take in what you're saying. I think I need to sit down,' she said, pulling up the chair in front of my desk.

'I know. It's incredible. I can hardly believe it myself.'

'Was he murdered at his villa in Italy then?'

'What makes you say that?' I had never discussed anything about him owning property in Italy with Danielle, only with Graham, and I wondered how she knew about it.

'You'll remember that Fabio wanted me to liaise with both Mr Pellegrino's and Mr Kettering's secretaries to set up your meeting with each of them?'

'Yes.'

'Well, when I spoke to Mr Kettering's secretary she was very affable and we had quite a pleasant conversation actually. You know how I like to chat.' I did not comment, but gave her a Mona Lisa smile.

'Go on.'

'As you'll recall we had difficulty fixing up the appointment because he was going on holiday to Italy the following week. I asked her whereabouts in Italy and she told me that he owned a villa in Torre del Lago. She mentioned something about him being a great Puccini fan, which is partly the reason why he bought his villa there.'

'Yes, Puccini had a villa in Torre del Lago and the Puccini opera festival is held at the open-air lakeside theatre every year. Oh, Danielle, that's fantastic. You don't realize the importance of the information you've just given me.'

'What do you mean? I don't understand.'

'It's complicated. I'll tell you about it later.'

'OK,' she said, looking bewildered.

'I must speak to Graham,' I said, leaping from my chair. I dashed out of the room and along the corridor to his office, leaving a somewhat dazed Danielle sitting by my desk.

Chapter 28

'Sorry to disturb you,' I said, pushing open Graham's door and stepping inside his office.

'You're not,' he replied, looking up and putting down his pen. 'Take a seat.' I sat down in the executive chair opposite him. 'How can I help?'

'There are a couple of things I'd like to discuss with you.'

'Fire away. I'm listening.'

'It's Torre del Lago,' I said enthusiastically.

'You've lost me. What is?'

'Where Kettering bought a villa.'

'How do you know?'

'Danielle told me.'

'Danielle?'

'Yes. Kettering's secretary mentioned he had a villa there.'

'When?'

'The day she made the appointment for me to meet with him.'

'It's very encouraging that you've discovered where Kettering purchased property, but you still need to find out the name of the contact in Italy and establish a link between him, Kettering and Pellegrino.'

'That's what I've come to tell you. My uncle called earlier, as you know.' Graham nodded. 'He's discovered that the senior lawyer at Studio Legale Marchese is called Enrico Tomasino and not only did he attend Siena University with Gregorio Pellegrino and subsequently work with him, but he's also a property specialist and owns a villa at Torre del Lago just like Roland Kettering. Coincidence is one thing, Graham, but don't you think that is one coincidence too many? You yourself said you thought Kettering's contact was in Viareggio. Well, the branch office of Enrico Tomasino's firm is certainly based there, and Torre del Lago is only a stone's throw away. My uncle even suspects that Pellegrino is hiding out there right now.'

'OK. From what you tell me I agree that it's likely Enrico Tomasino is the Italian contact, but what about Villa Anna? How do you hope to make the connection between Mr Tomasino and the Angelino family?'

'Dino Angelino's Will, and the transfer of the property into both Emilio's and Piero Giovannini's name were all carried out by Mr Tomasino's firm. It turns out that Piero Giovannini is also his nephew. I haven't pieced it all together yet, and I don't quite know how they managed it, but somehow Villa Anna was transferred into Emilio's name despite the fact that he was already dead, and then legitimately sold on to Piero Giovannini. If Tomasino is corrupt and has been working with Pellegrino and Kettering, and their speciality is hiving off other people's inheritance, as Caterina put it in her letter, then that property would have been ready for the taking.'

'I don't dispute what you're saying, but how did they become aware of Villa Anna's existence in the first place? It's not as if Emilio knew about a potential inheritance and talked of it to Pellegrino or Kettering.'

'That's something which is puzzling me too, and I have no answer to that right now.'

'Well, there has to be a logical explanation somewhere. I suppose it's necessary to keep digging in Italy. I'm sure that's where you'll find your answer.'

'Yes, I agree and that's something else I wanted to run by you.'

'What's that?'

'Fabio has been asking me to join him and Will out in Italy, but obviously I can't take the time off work without your permission.'

'When were you thinking of going?'

'Tomorrow. I am keen to be there with them, but I realize it's very short notice for you.'

'It is a bit, but I appreciate that these are rather exceptional circumstances, Alicia. How long do you think you'll need to be away?'

'Only a few days at the most.' I presumed that would be sufficient time to make some progress with the case, at least that is what I hoped. He sat and pondered for a moment.

'All right. I think we can cover for you. What have you said to Fabio about joining him?'

'Nothing. There was no point until I had spoken to you. If I promised to fly out there, and then you said I couldn't, it would only lead to disappointment all round. Alex doesn't want me to go at all. He's very dubious about it.'

'That doesn't surprise me. I myself wouldn't be at all happy if you were out there alone in the circumstances, but it's reassuring that you have Will and Fabio with you.'

'I appreciate your concern, but I am aware of the dangers.' Graham raised his eyebrows. 'Olivia wants to accompany me too.'

'Hmm... I'm not sure that's a good idea.'

'She seems quite determined to join me.'

'Perhaps you can use your powers of persuasion to make her change her mind.'

'I think it should be her decision.'

'Nevertheless,' he said, looking at me hard, 'try to dissuade her. When are you going to speak to Fabio?'

'I'll ring him later after I've seen DCI Framlington. He's coming to the office at three.'

'Now do you accept that there is a connection between Scarpetti, Steiglitz & Co. and the murders of Emilio, Rosetta, Giulia, Annette and Caterina?' I said, stressing the point as DCI Framlington finished reading Caterina's letter.

'I don't recall denying that there was,' he said, taking off his reading glasses, folding them and placing them in the breast pocket of his jacket and looking up at me. 'But there are procedures, Miss Allen.'

'I accept that, but let us not lose sight of the fact that people are being murdered and our first priority must surely be to catch the perpetrator or perpetrators of these terrible crimes.'

'You are not the one whose mother has been murdered, Chief Inspector,' said Olivia cutting in. 'What action are you taking to find her murderer?'

'We're doing everything we can.'

'It doesn't seem like it,' said Olivia.

'Don't you think it's time you linked up with the Italian police? Mr Pellegrino has fled to Italy after all,' I said. 'Even if there is insufficient evidence to charge him with anything, now that Mr Kettering has been murdered it's more crucial than ever that we catch up with him.'

'You heard about his murder then?'

'Yes. Olivia and I went to his offices this morning to ask him about Ellen Petronelli. That's how we found out.'

'So what steps are you taking to deal with Mr Pellegrino?' said Olivia, interrupting me before I had the opportunity to quiz DCI Framlington about Roland Kettering's murder. 'Although I was only a little child when all the events my mother refers to in her letter were unfolding, and I was not privy to what went on at Scarpetti, Steiglitz & Co., it is clear from her letter that she believed Mr Pellegrino and Mr Kettering were responsible for the murder of both Emilio Angelino and of Rosetta Bartlett. Mr Pellegrino may well be behind my mother's murder, and I think you owe it to her to track him down.'

'We have no details of the contact your mother mentions,' he said, addressing Olivia and ignoring my point.

'Oh, but we do,' I said. 'As it happens we know a great deal about him. I think you will agree that there is definitely a case to answer when I tell you what we have discovered.'

'Then tell me.' I detected the irritation in his voice but I decided not to react to it because we needed his assistance. He listened very intently while I recounted all the information I had obtained from Uncle Vico about Enrico Tomasino and his connection to the Angelino family. He seemed genuinely impressed and suddenly more positive which was a relief. 'Your uncle has been very thorough with his investigations. I agree that it seems perfectly possible that the contact to whom Caterina refers in her letter might well be Enrico Tomasino.'

'Then you would also agree that some action must now be taken to pursue the matter out there?'

'Has Fabio informed the Italian police about all this?' Again he did not answer my point and I suspected that the British police might already be working in conjunction with the Italian police, not that he would tell me if that were the case. I therefore felt it was necessary to explain what my own views were regarding the involvement of the Italian authorities.

'My uncle and I spoke to Fabio on Friday evening, but Fabio doesn't know about the details my uncle gave me this morning. As you will appreciate, when I found out about the owner of Villa Anna, and I informed Fabio, I was concerned that he would take matters into his own hands because that would endanger him and jeopardise the whole investigation. I wanted to obtain some evidence to substantiate my theories before involving the Italian police, particularly as I was keen to avoid taking any action which would alert Pellegrino's Italian associates. Too many people have already been murdered and I don't want Fabio or anyone else for that matter to suffer the same fate at the hands of these evil people. I am intending to leave for Italy very shortly, but if your murder team here could intervene with the Italian police then that would greatly speed matters along,' I added.

'When are you planning on leaving?'

'Tomorrow hopefully.'

'All right. I'll see what I can do.'

'Thank you.'

'OK. Is that everything?'

'No. DCI Framlington, I would like to talk to you about Roland Kettering's murder.'

'I thought you might.'

'Yes. I hope you don't mind me asking you this, but how was he murdered?'

'Roland Kettering was found by his housekeeper last night with a meat cleaver stuck in the back of his skull.'

'Oh, my God!' said Olivia, raising her hands to her face in horror.

'I see,' I said, swallowing hard.

'No you don't. Well, not quite.'

'What do you mean?'

'A rather strange note was found next to his body. Do you read Latin, Miss Allen?' I was slightly perplexed by the question.

'I studied it at school. But I'm a bit rusty now. Why?'

'Because the note was written in Latin,' he said, reaching into the inside pocket of his jacket and taking out a folded piece of paper. 'This is a copy of it,' he said, handing it to me. 'I don't want you to tell me what it means. I already know that. What I'd like is for you to tell me what you make of it.'

'OK. I'll do my best.' I scanned the piece of paper. It read as follows:

NEMO DAT QUOD NON HABET
NEMO IUR AD ALIUM TRANSFERRE POTEST QUAM IPSE HABET

As soon as I read the note I realized the significance of these words.

'May I look,' said Olivia. I passed her the piece of paper. 'You might know what it means,' she said, addressing DCI Framlington, 'but I do not. Please explain these phrases to me.'

'Literally: *nemo dat quod non habet* translates as *he who hath not cannot give* and *nemo iur ad alium transferre potest quam ipse habet* translates as *no-one can transfer to another a right that he does not possess.'*

'Why would anyone leave a note like that next to his body?' asked Olivia.

'Well, I think I'm right in saying that these two phrases are to do with the Roman law of property ownership,' I said.

'What has Roman law got to do with Mr Kettering?' said DCI Framlington, looking puzzled.

'Nothing. It's what these phrases denote which is important. You have to put it into context. Caterina told us in her letter that when Kettering and Pellegrino assisted their clients trace family assets in Italy they were helping themselves to a slice of these clients' inheritance, so quite clearly they have been stealing property from the rightful owners. Those Latin phrases give us the reason why Kettering was murdered. He stole property which didn't belong to him and then passed it off as his own and sold it on. In my view, the person who wrote this note is telling us exactly why he or she murdered Kettering – payback time for stealing what wasn't his.'

'Why not just try and reclaim the property instead of killing him?' said Olivia.

'I'm not an expert in Italian property law, you'd have to ask Enrico Tomasino that,' I said slightly tongue-in-cheek, 'as it would appear that he is rather adept at it, but my understanding is that under Italian law an owner can lose his or her rights to property if he or she doesn't reclaim it within certain time limits. I'm not sure what those time limits are and there must be certain conditions and caveats.'

'Hmm… That's very interesting,' said DCI Framlington. 'Perhaps you'd like to turn your head to another aspect of this murder which has been perplexing us,' he said. 'I'm interested in hearing your thoughts on it.'

'OK. I'll do my best.'

'Roland Kettering's right hand was completely severed. It was found placed upon the note a foot or so away from his body. Now it was apparent why DCI Framlington had not produced the original note to show us; it must have been soaked in blood. 'What do you make of that, Miss Allen?'

Chapter 29

'I can't believe I allowed you to persuade me to let you come to Italy with me, Alex,' I said as we walked into Perugia's Piazza IV Novembre where we had arranged to meet Fabio and Will. We had checked into our hotel in Piazza d'Italia and had walked the length of Corso Vannucci which runs from Piazza d'Italia to Piazza IV Novembre.

'Well, somebody has to keep an eye on you, and anyway I didn't want to miss all these wonderful Italian sights,' he said, looking all around him.

'Hmm… Don't be flippant. We're not here on a sightseeing trip! Maybe I shouldn't have dissuaded Olivia from accompanying me after all, since you don't seem very interested in solving this case.'

'That's not true and you know it, but there's no harm in appreciating the fantastic Italian evening summer sunshine and the beauty of our surroundings. Here we are in Perugia's main square and over there,' he said, reading from his guidebook, 'we have the magnificent Fontana Maggiore, one of the most beautiful fountains of the medieval period, with reliefs by Nicola and Giovanni Pisano. On the west side of the square,' he said, pointing to it, 'we have the Archbishop's Palace with the Museum of Natural History, and beyond that…'

'All right, you've made your point,' I said laughing. 'I'm sorry. I'm just a bit preoccupied that's all and I'm anxious to catch up with Fabio and Will.'

'What time did you arrange to meet them?'

'Six-thirty.'

'Oh, good,' said Alex looking at his watch. 'Nearly time then. I could do with an ice-cold beer. Has Fabio heard from Laura?'

'No. She's still not responding to his calls.'

'So how can you expect to make any progress with her? If she isn't prepared to speak to him, why would she talk to you?'

'I'm hoping to persuade her that it's in her best interests to help us.'

'Hmm... Have you had any more thoughts on Kettering's severed right hand?'

'I have actually, but you're going to think me pretty ridiculous.'

'No. I'm not. Tell me what's going through your mind.'

'If I'm right some of the credit should go to Dorothy for helping me solve this one.'

'What do you mean?'

'Dorothy leant me a Hayley Westenra CD a couple of weeks back. I played it while I was doing some household chores and didn't think anything more about it. Then last night while I was packing, Olivia and I were chatting, and she said she'd like to listen to it. It was when I heard Lauretta's aria *'O mio babbino caro'* from Puccini's opera *Gianni Schicchi* that it suddenly dawned on me why Roland Kettering's arm may have been severed. Dorothy went to Glyndebourne a few weeks ago and she told me that one of the opera's she had seen was *Gianni Schicchi*. I remember saying to her that it was one of my favourite operas, which is why I think she lent me the CD because it has *'O mio babbino caro'* on it, and that should've been uppermost in my mind. It occurred to me that Kettering's murder might be some sort of ritualistic killing.'

'What are you talking about?'

'Are you familiar with the plot of *Gianni Schicchi*?'

'What makes you ask?'

'Because I think there are parallels between the plot and Kettering's murder.'

'Well, I've only seen the opera once, a few years ago, but so far as

I recall it's set in Dante's Florence and starts off with an old man having died and his relatives gathering around his bedside hoping to get a share from his Will only to discover that he has left all his money and property to the local monastery. One of the relatives asks Gianni Schicchi to help them because he's known to be cunning and resourceful, but because they've been nasty about his background and origins he's reluctant to assist them. I think I'm right in saying that his daughter Lauretta begs him to help because she's in love with one of the members of the dead man's family and that's when she sings 'O mio babbino caro'. Gianni Schicchi impersonates the dead man so that they can rewrite the Will, only he double crosses them and leaves all the money and property to himself.'

'That's the gist of it, but you've missed out the really important part.' Alex looked at me blankly. 'When the relatives try to persuade him to have the Will re-written in their favour, Gianni Schicchi warns them of the penalty for falsifying a Will – the loss of the right hand for the malefactor and his accomplices.'

'Oh, of course. Now I understand the parallels between the plot and Kettering's murder. Roland Kettering was falsifying Wills and stealing his clients' inheritance, and that's why his murderer hacked off his right hand – as if he, or she, was exacting the penalty against him.'

'That's what his murderer seems to be telling us. Whoever it was must know that Kettering was a fervent Puccini fan. It's as if the murder was tailored especially for him.'

'Hmm… What about pretending to be somebody else to avail himself of the inheritance? Do you think that Kettering impersonated Emilio Angelino to get hold of Villa Anna?'

'Personally, I don't think it was him, although I still believe that is how the house was obtained.'

'Have you told DCI Framlington any of this?'

'No. You're the first person I've spoken to about it. What do you think? Could I be on the right lines or am I just reading too much into all of this?'

'I'd say there's a strong possibility that you're on the mark. Isn't that Will?' said Alex, stopping in mid-flow and pointing to one of the figures walking towards us. 'And that must be Fabio with him.'

'Yes,' I replied, increasing my stride, 'It's them.'

'Alicia,' exclaimed Fabio, kissing me on both cheeks. 'I'm so glad you could make it out here.' Although he sounded cheerful he looked strained.

'How are you?' I said, scanning his face.

'I'm OK. Will has been a great support,' he said, glancing sideways at him, 'and I'm better for seeing you,' he said, smiling at me.

'Hello, Will,' I said, giving him a hug. He hugged me back.

'I've just been speaking to Jo. She sends her love.'

'Is she OK? I haven't had a chance to speak to her these past few days.'

'She says the morning sickness is easing up a bit which is a relief.'

'Yes. She's been quite poorly with that this last couple of weeks.'

'Good to see you again,' he said, shaking Alex's hand.

'I don't think you two have met, well not officially anyway,' I said, addressing Alex and Fabio.

'I'm Alexander Waterford,' said Alex, extending his hand to Fabio. 'I saw you sitting in the reception of CFP & Co. a few weeks ago and I've heard all about you.'

'Yes. I thought I'd seen you somewhere before,' Fabio replied. 'Alicia has mentioned you to me. What would you like to do? I thought it would be quite pleasant to wander down Corso Vannucci and grab something to eat there. It has a good atmosphere at night.'

'We've just come from there,' said Alex, sounding slightly unenthusiastic. 'I thought it was fairly quiet.'

'But it really comes alive in the evening,' I replied. 'We can watch the gorgeous people of Perugia enjoy the nightly *passeggiata*.'

'What are you talking about?' said Alex.

'It's a custom we Italians have. We like to take a leisurely stroll

283

along the street, savour the atmosphere, window shop, eat an ice cream, and chat to other passers-by. It's the thing to do here. Everybody does it!'

'What do you want to drink?' said Alex, pulling up a seat for me outside one of the bars along Corso Vannucci.

'I'll have an iced coffee,' I replied. The waiter appeared, I ordered my coffee and Fabio, Alex and Will each ordered a bottle of beer. While we sat drinking our refreshments we discussed recent events and our plan of action.

'You're not the only ones who've had an eventful few days,' said Fabio.

'What do you mean?'

'Well, I've been feeling increasingly frustrated over these past weeks what with the distinct lack of progress over Giulia's murder investigation and insufficient evidence to connect Pellegrino and Scarpetti, Steiglitz & Co. with her murder, not to mention my father's disappearance. So after we spoke on Friday evening I decided it was time I became more proactive.'

'In relation to what *exactly*?' I asked tentatively. Both Alex and Will were listening very intently; neither said a word.

'You remember we talked about a client of my father's called Luigi Fagiolini who committed suicide after he lost all his money on some speculative property deal?'

'Yes. Of course I do. Your father was helping him raise finance for it and, according to Pellegrino, when it all went pear-shaped Luigi's brother Angelo blamed your father for the suicide and threatened to kill him. After Emilio disappeared Angelo became a murder suspect and was arrested but there was insufficient evidence to pin Emilio's murder on him and he was released. But why are you asking me this, Fabio?'

'Because before Giulia died you suggested that you thought someone had tried to frame Angelo to divert the investigators attention away from him and suggested that it was probably one of my father's colleagues who was responsible.'

'That's correct. I thought it was highly possible because a colleague would be well-placed to know your father's work commitments and client deals and therefore it would be easier to manipulate the facts to his own advantage. I was even more suspicious when you explained that Angelo was picked up by the police on the evidence of the independent witnesses whose identity remains hidden. Oh,' I said, pausing momentarily, 'I think I know where this is heading. You think Pellegrino stitched up Angelo and that somehow this is part of some revenge campaign against him?'

'Yes. I can't believe it hasn't crossed your mind?'

'To be honest, no, it hasn't. I have no doubt that Pellegrino was one of the independent witnesses, but as for Angelo murdering Kettering, there's no evidence that he's involved. Anyway, why would he want to murder Kettering when his grudge is against Pellegrino?'

'I suppose so.'

'You said a few minutes ago that you decided to become proactive. In what way?'

'Will and I went down to Rome on Saturday to visit Luigi's widow, Anna.'

'But how did you know where to find her?'

'As you're already aware, Anna contacted my mother after my father's disappearance and it occurred to me that my mother might have a record of her contact details somewhere. I was sure that they had exchanged letters and my mother was such a hoarder that I knew she would have kept any correspondence she had received from Anna. I called my grandmother and asked her if she could sift through my mother's papers, which she did, duly finding one letter from Anna. We discovered she was still living at the same address so I persuaded Will that it was worth taking a trip to Rome on the off-chance that she might see us.'

'Which I presume she did?'

'Oh yes,' said Will.

'Everything my mother told me about Anna not holding my father to blame for her husband's suicide is true. It isn't that I doubted my mother, but after all that has happened I needed to hear Anna say that it wasn't his fault. Can you understand that?' he said, looking at me intently. I nodded. 'Anna said it came as a terrible shock when Angelo was accused of conspiring to murder my father because he had had a long-standing working relationship with Luigi and had come to be regarded as a trusted family friend. The vile allegations against Angelo seemed to spring from nowhere and were totally without substance and justification. It was very traumatic for the family and at one stage Angelo himself tried to commit suicide.'

'Oh, that's terrible. To be falsely accused and then driven to attempt suicide as a result. Where's Angelo now?'

'Anna says that after the case against him was dropped he left Rome and moved to Milan, but they lost touch after he was married.'

'That's a bit odd, don't you think?' said Will. 'Do you think she's telling the truth?'

'Why would she lie?' said Fabio.

'She might want to protect him. Maybe she thinks he's been through enough. But I expect we could track him down relatively easily if we needed to,' I said.

'On a different subject,' said Will, 'we thought it would be a good idea to set off for Lucca first thing tomorrow morning. Is that all right with you?' he asked, looking first at Alex and then at me.

'I'm keen to go to Ponte a Moriano as I really want to see Villa Anna,' said Fabio. 'I have to say I still don't understand how my father could be entitled to such a magnificent property and not know about it.'

'According to Uncle Vico this happens quite frequently,' I replied. 'Sometimes members of the family leave Italy and decide not to return there and a few generations down the line their descendents often don't even know about the family assets, let alone that they are entitled to claim them.'

'Is there any way we can reclaim the house?' said Fabio.

'I'm not sure of all the legal formalities,' I replied, carefully choosing my words and not wishing to build up Fabio's hopes. 'I suppose you might still have a claim to it under the Italian Civil Code. We'd need to look into what rights you have, if any.'

'I find the whole Italian law of inheritance and property law quite baffling to be perfectly honest.'

'Which is no doubt how Pellegrino, Kettering and Tomasino have managed to swindle a good many people out of their rightful inheritance and property,' said Will.

'They must have thought Giulia was close to discovering the truth to murder her,' said Fabio.

'Well, now that Kettering has been murdered,' said Alex, 'Pellegrino and Tomasino and whoever else they have within their employ, must be wondering how many others know about their shady dealings. Let's face it, news of his murder was a shock to all of us and must have been the last thing they anticipated. Alicia has a theory all of her own about that, don't you?' he added, turning to me.

'What's that?' asked Fabio. I explained that I felt the murder had parallels with the plot of *Gianni Schicci*. 'Well, it does fit,' he said.

'I feel that it's significant,' I said. 'I brought you a copy of the papers Giulia sent you by the way. I'll dig them out of my suitcase so you can look at them on the drive to Lucca tomorrow.'

'Yes. I'd like to see them. You should have checked into our hotel,' said Fabio. 'You're on the other side of the city from us.'

'We tried,' I said, 'but at such short notice it was fully booked. It's the tourist season after all. In an ideal world we would have liked to have caught a direct flight to Perugia rather than having to change in Milan, but the only flight with Ryanair was full. We chose to stay in Piazza Italia as it was convenient.' I paused for a second. 'There is one thing I would like to do before we leave Perugia.'

'What's that?' said Will.

'Make contact with Laura. Is she still here?'

'Yes,' replied Fabio. 'I saw her friend Emma yesterday and she said Laura isn't intending to return to Orvieto until the weekend.'

'Then we must try to talk to her again while we still have the chance. If you give me her number I'll ring her now.'

'Now?'

'Yes. There's no time like the present.' He called up her number from the contacts list on his mobile, I programmed the number into my own mobile and pressed the talk button.

'*Pronto*,' she said, answering the 'phone.

'Laura?'

'*Sì. Con chi parlo?*'

'*Mi chiamo Alicia Allen. Conosci un amico mio.*'

'*Un amico tuo?*'

'*Sì. Fabio Angelino.*' There was a pause at the end of the line. '*Sono qui in Perugia stasera e vorrei parlare con te.*'

'You can speak to me in English,' she said in a thick Italian accent. 'I do understand. I lived in London for two years.'

'All right. As you wish. Will you meet me?'

'There's no point. I can't help you.'

'I'm not expecting you to. I'd simply value the opportunity to talk to you about Giulia. You see she was my friend too,' I said, stretching the truth, 'and I miss her. It would help me to speak with you. I'd be very grateful.'

'Oh, OK,' she said half-heartedly. 'Where are you staying?

'Piazza Italia.'

'If you send me a text message with details of your hotel I'll meet you there.'

'All right. What time?'

'In about half an hour.'

'I'm going to have to pass on dinner,' I said, closing my mobile and placing it in my handbag.

'Why? What has happened?' said Fabio, looking concerned.

'Laura has agreed to meet me back at the hotel.'

'But that's fantastic news,' he said.

'Don't get too excited yet. Let's wait to see what she has to say first.'

'If anything,' said Alex.

'There's no need to be negative.' I cast Alex a disparaging look.

'What time are you meeting her?' asked Fabio.

'In about twenty-eight minutes,' I replied, glancing at my watch.

'I'll walk you back,' said Alex with more enthusiasm. 'Depending on how long she's with you, I see no reason why we can't all have dinner together later. It's still very early so there's plenty of time.'

'OK. I'll text her the hotel address from my 'phone,' I said, retrieving my mobile from my handbag and then sending her the text message. 'I'm arranging to meet her in the hotel lounge.'

'Well, let's hope your meeting is a productive one,' said Alex.

'At this moment, Alex, I'm just praying she turns up!'

Chapter 30

'Laura, what are you afraid of?' I asked as we sat down amid the splendour of the richly decorated and elegant hotel lounge with its large stone sixteenth-century fireplace, original wooden floor and high-coffered ceiling. I could tell how nervous she was from her body language because she was holding herself rather awkwardly and seemed altogether very ill at ease.

'I don't know what you mean,' she replied, avoiding my direct gaze as she pushed back a wayward strand of her curly shoulder length mid-brown hair from her face. I was observing her closely and when she picked up the glass of red wine she had ordered and took a sip, her hand was visibly shaking.

'I think you do. You cared for Giulia, didn't you?'

'Yes. Of course,' she said, looking up at me fleetingly and catching my eye. She had very blue eyes and because her face was tanned it seemed to intensify their colour. Judging by the grooves under her eyes she had not slept well for some time. She pushed the wavy strand of hair behind her ear.

'I believe you did, which is why I can't understand why you won't tell us *everything* you know.'

'I have.' Again she averted my gaze.

'I saw the postmark on Giulia's parcel, Laura. Why didn't you explain to Fabio that it was you who posted it, not her?' She did not respond. 'Please tell me what you're afraid of. I believe you know the name of the man who called Giulia. I think you also know where he comes from,' I said, leaning forward.

'I don't understand what you mean. I've already told Fabio that it was the owner of the property who rang her. That's what Giulia told me,' she replied defensively. I watched her shift awkwardly in her seat.

'Yes, but it's apparent to both of us that the only reason why Giulia told you that is because she assumed the call was from Mr Giovannini, the owner, on the basis that he was the one to whom she had written the letter. But that isn't correct is it, Laura?'

'I don't follow.'

'I think you do. The person Giulia met rang you the morning after she was murdered, didn't he? He wanted to find out what Giulia had told you and whether you knew where her research was. Isn't that what happened, and why you posted her research to Fabio, to get rid of it, and the reason you decided not to reveal any of this to the police? You were frightened that if you told them the truth and they started making enquiries that it would not be long before Giulia's murderer realized that the source of their information was you, that you had had her research and were aware of what was in it.'

'I explained to Fabio why I wouldn't speak to the police. I gave him the facts.'

'Yes, but not the full facts.'

'I can't help you. I'm sorry,' she said, standing up to leave.

'For goodness sake, Laura,' I implored, catching hold of her arm and fixing my gaze on her, 'how many more people have to be murdered before you're prepared to help us? Please, Laura, I'm begging you. We can still catch the people who murdered Giulia and stop them from murdering anybody else. If you *truly* cared for her and want to avenge her death you must tell me everything you know.' I let go of her arm. She stood for a moment and stared at me without saying a word and then much to my relief she sat down again.

'All right. I'll help you. But it didn't quite happen the way you think.'

'Then tell me how it did.'

'I told Fabio that Giulia posted the parcel before we caught the train to Orvieto, but that was a lie.'

'I assumed that it was.'

'The fact is Giulia didn't intend to post Fabio anything at all. She simply brought the papers with her because she wanted to do some further research over the weekend. As you know we were due to return to Perugia together on the Sunday evening, but I wasn't well and I had no choice but to stay in Orvieto. Giulia was in a hurry to catch the train and must have forgotten to pick up the bag containing her research which was in my bedroom. When she called me from the train she told me she had received a call from the owner of Villa Anna and had arranged to meet him later that night. She was agitated because she couldn't find her papers and said that she must have left them at my house. It was only at that point that I discovered she had left them there and I promised I'd keep them safe for her and bring them back with me when I returned to Perugia. I was really concerned about her meeting this man alone and I begged her not to, but she said she'd be fine, I was not to worry and she would ring me after she had seen him.'

'Did she tell you where she was going to meet him?'

'In Perugia. She didn't give me an exact location. I presumed it would be in the city centre. When there was no call from her later that night I became very anxious about her. I rang her mobile a couple of times and sent her some text messages but obviously there was no response.'

'Then what happened?'

'Well, the next morning we had the news that she was missing and then later that day the police rang and said her body had been discovered at Lake Trasimeno. I didn't hear from him until that evening when he called me on my mobile. I suppose *he* must have obtained my contact details off Giulia's mobile and realized I was aware that she had arranged a meeting with him because of the content of my text messages.'

'When you say 'he' who do you mean?'

'I presumed it was the owner. He didn't give me his name.'

'I don't expect he did. What did he say to you?'

'He made it very clear that if I spoke to the police about Giulia's plans the night before, he'd make sure I'd never say anything to anyone ever again.'

'He threatened you?'

'Yes.'

'Did he say anything else?'

'He asked me if I knew where Giulia's research material was.'

'And what did you tell him?'

'That I had no idea what he was talking about, but it was obvious he didn't believe me. I realized that her research must be very important if she was murdered for it, so I decided the best thing to do would be to post it to Fabio in London. I've stayed with Giulia there a few times and I have the address. When Giulia's room was broken into I was certain that he must be behind it, but I was terrified of telling the police.'

'Because of the potential consequences for you?'

'Yes. Please don't think badly of me.'

'I don't.'

'I've been so afraid.'

'With good cause. The people who murdered Giulia will stop at nothing to prevent anyone from revealing the truth. None of us is immune.'

'But how can we hope to bring them to justice?'

'I appreciate you've never met the man who contacted you but would you recognize his voice if you heard it again?'

'I think so. Why? What do you want me to do?'

'I'll explain. We have reason to believe that the man who contacted you is not the owner of Villa Anna, but a lawyer called Enrico Tomasino whose practice is based in Viareggio and who also happens to be the uncle of the current owner of Villa Anna, Piero Giovannini. We all assumed that it was the owner who contacted

Giulia because she addressed her letter to him.'

'I understand. How did you find out about Enrico Tomasino?' I explained the connection between Emilio Angelino, Gregorio Pellegrino, Roland Kettering and Enrico Tomasino and how we had made that connection.

'So how can I help you?'

'I'll tell you. I'm planning on setting up a meeting with him at his office in Viareggio and…'

'You want me to accompany you?'

'No. That would be far too dangerous. I remember Fabio saying that you thought you were being watched, in which case Tomasino might have a description of you. If he recognized you it would be totally disastrous. Quite simply all you have to do is listen at the other end of the 'phone when I ring him to arrange the appointment and tell me if he's the man who called you.'

'But what if you don't manage to speak to him on the 'phone? You may not get past his secretary. Why don't I simply come with you? If I'm going to assist you I might as well do it properly.'

'Nobody will ever recognize you now,' I said as Laura peered at herself in the full-length mirror of my hotel bedroom in Viareggio. 'By wearing that dark wig and those glasses you've completely altered your appearance.'

'It is a dramatic change, isn't it? Provided Enrico Tomasino doesn't speak to me I should be able to carry it off.'

'Well, there's no guarantee he won't,' said Alex. 'You're running a huge risk.'

'I'll do all the talking,' I said. 'If Laura doesn't say a word there's no danger of him recognizing her voice.'

'Even so, Alicia, I'd really advise against Laura being there at all.'

'Yes. You're right.' I paused for a moment. 'I don't think you should come to the meeting Laura,' I said, turning to her. 'You already confirmed after you listened in on my conversation with him earlier today that he is the same man who called you.'

'But I need to see him. I can't explain it really; it's something I must do.'

'OK,' I said reluctantly. 'Then what I suggest is that as soon as we're about to go into our meeting with Tomasino, I'll call Alex so he's on stand by, then I'll introduce you as my junior colleague and after a few minutes Alex will ring me on my mobile and I'll make some excuse for you to leave. You could meet Laura and bring her back here, Alex.'

'Fine, but what about you?'

'I'll call you as soon as I'm on my way.'

'I hope this scheme of yours works, Alicia,' he said dubiously. 'It's disturbing enough allowing the two of you to step foot in Tomasino's office at all, but as for you remaining alone there with him…well, put it this way, I'd really rather you didn't. I think you're putting yourself unnecessarily in danger.'

'How else will we ever get to the bottom of this case?'

'You should leave it to the police rather than jeopardise your own safety. What time's your appointment anyway?'

'At four.'

'It's a nuisance that Fabio and Will are staying at a different hotel from the three of us. Don't get me wrong; I understand why you insisted they must and why it was necessary for us to check in separately. I think we did well to smuggle you into the hotel, Laura, without registering you.' She nodded.

'I know it's inconvenient, but I felt it was the right thing to do. I thought it would be safer for Fabio not to be seen with us and I could hardly let Laura check in just in case Tomasino knows somebody here at the hotel. The last thing we want is for him to get wind of Laura's presence hence the purchase of the wig for her in Perugia.'

'I'm aware of that. What did you say to Tomasino to persuade him to see you?'

'Alicia simply told him that she needed an Italian property lawyer with expertise in tracing and reclaiming family property and that he came highly recommended by Roland Kettering,' said Laura.

'Yes. I felt that would be enough to rouse his curiosity and that he would agree to meet with me. I made out that my Italian is very limited as I want him to speak to me in English, and because he'll be more relaxed about talking to any of his colleagues in my presence and may let something slip. I never conversed with Pellegrino in Italian and he's not aware I'm bilingual.'

'You're playing a dangerous game, Alicia. Did your uncle find out whether Pellegrino is hiding out in Viareggio?'

'He didn't come back to me on it, no.'

'Well, one thing's for sure; if Pellegrino is out here, which is highly likely, it won't be long before Tomasino realizes who you are.'

'Oh, but I want him to know who I am. That's the whole point of the exercise, Alex. With any luck once I make it clear that we are aware of his dealings it will prompt him to take some action. I intend to ask him about Ellen Petronelli.'

'I don't like the sound of this at all. It's the action he might take which concerns me. Talk about playing with fire.'

'You have to fight fire with fire.'

'But Alicia…'

'We'd better start making a move,' I said, addressing Laura and cutting Alex short.

'What time are Fabio and Will due back?' he asked. Fabio and Will had left for Lucca that morning and planned to go on to Ponte a Moriano as Fabio was keen to take a look at Villa Anna.

'I'm not sure what their plans are after they've been to the police headquarters in Lucca. They may be staying there tonight.'

'You didn't mention anything about that. When did they decide to go there?'

'Fabio received a call from Commissario Marco Galliano of the Questura di Lucca last night. According to Fabio he didn't say too much over the 'phone, but reading between the lines it would seem that there is some ongoing investigation regarding Enrico Tomasino's affairs and he wants to talk to Fabio.'

'I'd have thought he'd be better off speaking to you because you're the one who tracked Tomasino down.'

'I think you're confusing me with Uncle Vico's contact, Alex.'

'You know what I mean. At the very least, don't you think the Commissario should know about your meeting with Tomasino?'

'I asked Alicia not to involve the police yet,' said Laura, stepping in. 'You're not the one who was threatened,' she said sharply. 'I've promised Alicia that I'll go to the police after the meeting and tell them what I know. No police is the condition upon which I agreed to help her.'

'All right,' said Alex, raising his hands. 'I'll wait for your signal.' He waved his mobile at me as he walked towards the door. 'I won't be far away.'

Laura and I arrived at the Viareggio offices of Studio Legale Marchese with five minutes to spare before our appointment. The offices were within walking distance of our seafront hotel in Piazza D'Azeglio so we went there on foot. It was a blisteringly hot day and understandably Laura was finding wearing the wig very uncomfortable. As we sat waiting in the marble reception area she began fidgeting with it.

'For goodness sake, Laura,' I whispered so that the receptionist could not hear me, 'do you want to draw attention to yourself?'

'Of course not,' she replied, glaring at me from behind the thin wire-framed glasses we had also provided for her.

'Then leave your hair alone,' I said.

'Miss Allen,' said the receptionist in the prettiest of Italian accents, 'Mr Tomasino will see you now. 'Please follow the stairs around. His office is the second door on the right.' I rang Alex to give him the signal to call me back and Laura and I made our way up the magnificent marble staircase with its wrought iron balustrade to the first floor.

'This place gives me the creeps,' she whispered, looking all about her.

'Association of ideas,' I replied. 'There's nothing wrong with the building, only some of the people who work in it.' We arrived at the top of the staircase and I was about to knock on the second door to the right as instructed when it was opened to us and we found ourselves face to face with Enrico Tomasino, a short fat swarthy-looking man with heavy features and a receding hairline.

'Ah, you must be Alicia Allen,' he said, studying my face, 'and who's this?' he quizzed glancing at Laura. 'My understanding is that you would be coming here alone.' He had a deep gruff voice and an unmistakably strong Italian accent.

'My colleague Katie,' I replied, answering on her behalf. She looked at him fleetingly and then averted her gaze.

'*Piacere,*' he said, shaking first my hand then Laura's with his rather fleshy hand before leading us into his office. He indicated for us to sit down in the two chairs in front of his desk and shut the door. Laura opened the notebook she had brought with her, and sat with her pen poised ready to take notes.

'Do you mind if I close the window?' he said, walking over to it and slamming it before we had a chance to respond. 'That's better,' he said, turning around and smirking at us. 'Now we can hear ourselves think.'

There was something about his sycophantic manner and the way he seemed to be analysing my face with his dark beady brown eyes that I found unnerving. Although he was smiling his eyes were cold. He took off his cream linen jacket, sat down behind his desk and leant back. He was wearing an open-necked blue cotton shirt and had rolled up the sleeves and I could see that he was positively hirsute. Although he had a distinct lack of hair on the top of his head he certainly made up for it with the copious amounts elsewhere on his body. 'Now, how can I help you?' he drawled, staring hard at me. At that moment my mobile rang.

'Oh, I'm terribly sorry,' I said, in my most apologetic tone of voice, 'but I must take this call.'

'Go ahead,' he said.

'Yes…right…OK,' I replied and then hung up. Turning to Laura I said, 'There's a problem with one of your cases back in London and the client needs to speak with you. It's urgent so you'll need to call straightaway.'

'She can always use our 'phone,' said Mr Tomasino pretending to be accommodating.

'That's very kind of you to offer, but it's not necessary. You'd better go, Katie,' I said, directing Laura to leave which she did without the need to be prompted further.

'Now, how can I help you,' said Mr Tomasino as Laura left the room.

'Well, as I told you on the 'phone, Roland Kettering recommended me to you. I believe that you and he had a long-standing professional relationship spanning many years and that he was actually introduced to you through your mutual friend Gregorio Pellegrino.' This was of course what I had surmised, but he did not dispute it so I presumed I was correct in my assumption.

'And what can I help you with *exactly?*' he said, leaning forward and resting his elbows on the table.

'I'm acting for someone called Fabio Angelino. His father Emilio was a colleague of Mr Pellegrino's but vanished in Sicily sixteen years ago.'

'Yes. It was a terrible tragedy,' he said, looking at me steadily.

'You know what happened then?' I asked, observing him. His countenance was inscrutable but it was clear he understood my meaning.

'Nobody does,' he replied, sitting back.

'Well, the thing is, Mr Tomasino, we are certain he was murdered.'

'But why on earth would you think that?' he said with supposed incredulity.

'Because we believe that in the course of his work he discovered that an underground organisation of crooked lawyers was defrauding clients out of their rightful inheritance and he was murdered to prevent him from exposing them.'

'*Mamma mia!* But this is fantasy,' he said, throwing his hands up in the air in a dramatic gesture. 'These are things that happen *only* in the movies, not in everyday life. What evidence do you have to substantiate this?' His eyes narrowed as he scrutinised my expression for clues. It was obvious he was keen to ascertain how far my beliefs were based upon fact.

'Roland Kettering's murder is a reality, Mr Tomasino,' I replied, challenging his point without answering his question. 'He was brutally murdered. You knew him better than most. Why would anyone want him dead?'

'Lawyers aren't the most popular people, Miss Allen, as I'm sure you're aware,' he replied evasively. 'You're not suggesting that his murder has any connection with Emilio's disappearance?'

'You tell me.'

'Tell you what?' I detected the irritation in his voice. 'I thought you wanted me to help you with some property matter.'

'I do. Does the name Ellen Petronelli mean anything to you?'

'No,' he said flatly.

'Before he disappeared Emilio Angelino was trying to help her trace her Italian family inheritance.'

'What does that have to do with *me*?'

'I want you to help me find what happened to it.'

'But that's impossible,' he said, raising his arms up in the air once again in a grand gesture. 'I'm very flattered by your confidence in me, but I do need some information to go on.'

'But I can provide you with the data you require,' I said lying. Of course I had no details relating to the case whatsoever, but even if he suspected me of not telling him the truth he could not be certain.

'What is it?' he asked, sounding slightly more enthusiastic. Clearly I had engaged his interest.

'A file.'

'And what's in it?'

'A portfolio of names and details of property transactions. It doesn't mean much to me, but I think it would to you.' I hesitated for a second. 'Would you be prepared to look at it?'

'Where's the file?'

'I don't have it with me but I...'

'Have you shown it to anyone else?' he asked, interrupting me.

'You mean the police?' He nodded.

'No. I wanted you to look at it first.'

'You did the right thing. Don't be anxious,' he said in a smarmy voice, pretending to sound reassuring. 'I must attend an urgent meeting now, but we'll speak later,' he said, standing up. 'I have all your contact details.' I raised myself to my feet. 'Please wait there a moment,' he continued, indicating for me to sit down again. 'I need a word with one of my colleagues.'

He left his office and crossed the hall to the office opposite. I jumped up from my chair and walked to the door which he had left ajar. He probably did not feel the need to close it as he thought it unlikely I would be able to overhear him and besides he was under the misconception that I barely understood Italian. I had neither a view of the person to whom he was speaking, nor could I hear what that other person was saying although I was listening intently. All I was able to ascertain was that it was a male voice – I thought perhaps it might be Gregorio Pellegrino, but I was unable to tell for certain. However, I only needed to pick up a fraction of Mr Tomasino's side of the conversation to discover that their intentions towards me were malevolent.

Despite this, I felt I was relatively free from danger at this point because Mr Tomasino was under the false impression that I had that portfolio and he wanted it. Until he had it in his possession, or at least knew of its whereabouts, his sinister plans for me would not be put into operation. Nonetheless I had no desire to remain at the offices of Studio Legale Marchese any longer and decided to make a hasty exit. I had run halfway down the marble staircase when Mr Tomasino called after me from the top of the stairs.

'Is anything wrong?' he said, still smiling at me.

'No,' I replied, turning back momentarily.

'Then why the rush?'

'I have an urgent call to make,' I replied, trying to remain composed while feeling myself coming out in a cold sweat. I continued running to the bottom of the stairs.

'We'll talk later,' he said. 'Don't worry, Miss Allen. You're safe in my hands!'

Chapter 31

'Did anybody follow you on your way to the hotel, Laura?' I gasped, closing the door of our hotel suite and standing flat against it catching my breath. I had literally sprinted back to the hotel from Studio Legale Marchese and was feeling particularly on edge after overhearing Mr Tomasino's remarks. 'Only, as I turned into Via Niccolò Machiavelli I had the distinct impression that I was being trailed. Maybe I'm becoming paranoid, but you know how you suddenly feel conscious that somebody is watching you?' I said, running my hands through my hair.

'I don't think you're at all paranoid, Alicia,' she said. 'In light of recent events it wouldn't surprise me if you were followed today. Did you actually get a good look at whoever it was?'

'I glanced around a couple of times and noticed a dark-haired man wearing black sunglasses – but there are a lot of men fitting that description, especially around here!'

'It's likely to be one of Tomasino's mob though, don't you think?'

'Most probably.'

'Hmm… What happened with him after I left?'

'I'll tell you. Just give me a minute,' I said, moving away from the door, slipping off my suit jacket and trudging through to the bedroom with it. I hung up my jacket in the fitted wardrobe, took off my shoes and dropped them on the floor next to the bed. 'Where's Alex?' I called out as I walked through to the bathroom, washed my hands and doused my face with cold water. 'I thought he'd be here,' I said, picking up a towel and patting my face dry and then drying my hands. 'He did come and meet you, I hope?'

'Oh yes. He hasn't been out long. He was expecting you to ring so he won't be far. How was the meeting? I felt sick leaving you there alone with him and I can't begin to tell you how pleased I am to see you – in one piece,' she said. I traipsed back through to the bedroom, picked up a large bottle of mineral water and two glasses from the bedside table and wandered out into the sitting room.

'Do you want some water?' She shook her head. I poured myself a glass and flopped down in one of the elegant but functional armchairs. 'My throat's so dry. It's baking out.' Laura was standing by the window gazing out onto the promenade but she came and seated herself in the armchair opposite mine. 'Enrico Tomasino's an odious man,' I said, swallowing a large mouthful of water. 'It's apparent that he and Pellegrino have no moral conscience and are prepared to mow down anyone who steps in their path.'

'Hearing his voice again sent shivers down my spine. I can't begin to explain how it felt sitting in front of the man who probably gave the order for Giulia to be murdered.'

'Hmm… I appreciate it isn't much comfort, but your evidence will put him right in the frame. I do realize how traumatic it has been for you since her murder, but there's one last thing I need to ask of you.'

'What's that?'

'Talk to the police.'

'I promised you I would do that.'

'Thank you. I'm sorry I snapped at you while we were waiting in reception. Only you were fidgeting so much and I didn't want you drawing attention to yourself. I see you've taken off the wig.'

'Oh, yes,' she said tousling her hair. 'I removed it as soon as I could. Tell me what you said to Tomasino?'

'I told him…' At that moment Alex burst through the door cutting short my conversation.

'Thank goodness you've returned safely,' he said, sounding relieved. 'I've been on tenterhooks ever since you left,' he continued, perching on the arm of Laura's chair. 'Why didn't you call me?'

'I'm sorry. I didn't mean to worry you.'

'I don't care provided you're all right. You're looking very flustered. What happened back there?'

'I was about to tell Laura when you came in, that Mr Tomasino is hopefully now under the misapprehension that I have a file containing details of clients and property transactions which somehow relate to the research Emilio was carrying out on Ellen Petronelli before he disappeared.'

'Are you sure he believed you?' said Alex, sounding sceptical.

'I think he may suspect that I'm lying but on the other hand he has too much to lose if he chooses not to take me seriously and it turns out that I am telling the truth. And, if nothing else, his reaction to me when I mentioned Ellen Petronelli and the file, confirms that Emilio was removed because he had uncovered various irregularities which Kettering, Pellegrino and Tomasino preferred nobody knew about.'

'He didn't threaten you, did he?' asked Alex, scanning my face.

'Not directly, but I overheard him talking to one of his colleagues about tidying up loose ends and I believe he was referring to me.'

'Well, that's it then,' said Alex, jumping up off the arm of the chair. 'Start packing. We're not staying here a moment longer.'

'I think Laura ought to leave,' I replied, turning to her. 'There really isn't any further need for you to put yourself at risk,' I said.

'And what about your security, Alicia?' said Alex. 'We must go to the local police and inform them about his intentions.'

'That's the last thing we should do. Besides we don't know who to trust and there's the possibility that Tomasino may have contacts within the police who might alert him to our actions, and that could have dire consequences for everyone concerned.'

'Corrupt policemen, you mean?' asked Laura.

'Possibly. If Laura catches the train to Lucca, Fabio and Will can meet her at the station and accompany her to the police headquarters there. At least then we'll have the reassurance of knowing that

Laura is out of harm's way and she'll be able take the police through her evidence. I'll call Fabio and brief him so he knows what to tell them.'

'Is that all right with you?' asked Alex, concerned, and then turning to Laura.

'Perfectly.'

'You'll need to put your wig back on though. You don't mind walking Laura to the station do you, Alex?' He shook his head. 'I know it's only a stone's throw away from the hotel, but I want to make sure she's put safely on the train.'

'And what about you?'

'I'm planning to remain in Viareggio until Tomasino contacts me.'

'You can't meet him alone, Alicia!'

'I'm not intending to. I shall wait for police backup and I'll delay seeing him until I know that it's available.'

'Hmm… Well, if you insist on remaining here then I'm staying with you.'

After Alex and Laura left for the railway station I telephoned Fabio to apprise him of the latest developments and to advise him when to expect Laura in Lucca. He was pleased that she had agreed to cooperate and provide the police with a statement, but like Alex he was uneasy and rather apprehensive about the situation with Tomasino.

'On no account must you agree to meet him without police backup,' he urged.

'I won't, Fabio.'

'Promise me!'

'All right, I promise.'

'When do you think he'll contact you?'

'I have no idea, but I think it will be sooner rather than later.'

'Then you'll definitely need that backup in place. I spoke at length with Commissario Galliano earlier and mentioned you – but he already knows who you are.'

'DCI Framlington must have contacted him then. He did say he would speak to the Italian police.'

'Yes, DCI Framlington has been in touch. The Commissario is certainly very well-informed about the UK side of the investigation. I thought you would have heard from him by now because he told me he would be calling you. I'll give you his details so you can ring him directly, if you suddenly find you're in a situation where you need to make urgent contact. Do you have a pen handy?'

'Yes,' I said, picking up the pencil and the pad from the bedside table. 'What's his number?' Fabio read it out and I scribbled it down.

'I'll text you when Laura arrives otherwise you'll be worrying. I intend to take her straight to the police.'

'Make sure she goes through with it, you mean.'

'Something like that.'

'Somehow I don't feel you have to concern yourself about that. What's happening with the police in Perugia?'

'My understanding is that the Questura in Lucca is now liaising with the Questura in Perugia because that's where Giulia was murdered. Is Alex with you?'

'No. He's taken Laura to the station. He'll be back soon.'

'Keep safe, Alicia, and in touch.'

'I will. Thanks, Fabio.'

'Bye, Alicia.'

'We can't stay cooped up in here all night,' said Alex later that evening. 'We should go out, at least for dinner anyway.'

'I can't understand why Tomasino hasn't rung me,' I replied, pacing the floor. It was after nine o'clock and there had been no word from him. 'Maybe he didn't buy my story after all. I don't understand what's going on.'

'Personally, I don't feel you will hear from him tonight. It's probably part of his tactics – to make you sweat. He knows you're anxiously waiting for his call and he doesn't want you to think he's desperate for that file. There's no point in sitting here waiting for the 'phone to ring.'

'I'm not so sure. I'm glad we made Laura leave though. I feel happier knowing that she arrived safely in Lucca and is with Fabio and Will.'

'Have you had any further news from Fabio?'

'Not since he sent me the text to confirm that he'd picked up Laura from the station.'

'I thought Commissario Galliano would have contacted you by now. What about the backup he's supposed to be providing for you?'

'Umm... Well, that's why I need to speak to him.'

'What do you mean?'

'To find out what he intends to do about providing backup.'

'So it's not guaranteed? Great. Call him now.' I had programmed the number Fabio had given me into my mobile, so I retrieved it from my contacts list and pressed the 'phone key to dial it. There was no answer and the call diverted to his voice mail.

'He's not answering,' I said, holding the 'phone away from my ear.

'Leave a message,' said Alex emphatically.

'Pronto. Buona sera, Commissario Galliano. Mi chiamo Alicia Allen. Fabio Angelino mi ha dato il suo numero di telefono. Credo che Fabio le abbia detto tutto, ma ho bisogno di parlarle prima di prendere un appuntamento con il Signor Tomasino. È una questione della massima urgenza. Aspetto la sua chiamata. Mille grazie. Arrivederci.'

'At least you've made contact with him,' said Alex. 'Let's hope he checks his 'phone. Shall we go out then?'

'I thought you were concerned about the lack of police protection.'

'We'll just have to take the risk.'

'But this afternoon you didn't want me to meet with Mr Tomasino because you felt it wasn't safe.'

'That was different. Anyway nothing will happen to you while you're with me. Any preferences for dinner?'

'No, provided we find somewhere crowded. I'll feel more secure if there are a lot of people around.'

'Let's eat at one of the local fish restaurants at the southern end of the promenade. I was there earlier and it seems a really vibrant and busy area with all the local shops, designer boutiques, cafés and bars. If you want to surround yourself with people I can't imagine a better place. At this time of night there must be a real throng down there.'

'OK.' Alex and I walked from our seafront hotel along the glitzy promenade. We sat down at a fish restaurant with outside seating along the marble crazy-paved promenade and Alex ordered a fillet of fresh sole and I seafood risotto.

'The architecture here's really great, isn't it?' he said. I did not respond. I was focussing on the man at the table about six feet away from us. I had the uncanny feeling that he was observing our every move. 'There's quite an eclectic mix of architectural styles here,' Alex continued. 'I rather like the Art Deco buildings. In different circumstances I expect Fabio with his professional background would love this place. Don't you agree?' Alex paused for a moment. 'Alicia have you listened to one word I've been saying?' he said, waving his hand in front of my face.

'You were talking about architecture,' I replied, without taking my eyes off the man.

'What are you looking at?' said Alex, sounding slightly annoyed because I was not giving him my full attention. I turned to face him.

'There's a man sitting at the table in the far corner and I think he's watching us.'

'What man?' said Alex, swivelling around to see who I was talking about, but he had disappeared.

'I don't understand,' I said, perplexed. 'He was there a second ago.'

'Well, he certainly isn't now.' The waiter brought Alex's fillet of sole and my risotto.

'You don't believe me, do you?' I said indignantly, handing Alex the pepper mill and then picking up the pot of Parmesan cheese and in my irritation vigorously sprinkling a couple of teaspoons over my risotto.

'I didn't say that,' he replied in a slightly scolding tone.

'It's just that I'm sure we're being followed,' I said, leaning across the table and lowering my voice to almost a whisper. 'I can't be absolutely certain but I think the man who was sitting at that table was the same one who was trailing me this afternoon.'

'What man? Why on earth didn't you mention this earlier?'

'I thought I might have been mistaken.'

'So presumably you didn't say anything in your voicemail message to Commissario Galliano either?'

'No.'

'Oh, Alicia!'

'Your fish is getting cold,' I replied, ignoring his remark and swallowing a forkful of risotto.

'Let's go to Torre del Lago when we've finished up here,' he said, changing the subject.

'What tonight? Are you sure it's safe, especially after everything you've said about my security? You're the one who wanted me to leave here, remember.'

'We'll just have to be careful then.'

'But how are we going to get there? We don't have a car and I'm not walking four or five kilometres or whatever it is in the dark, Alex, particularly if we are being followed. We can't catch a bus either because there's no bus route from here to there.'

'We'll go on the scooter.'

'What scooter?'

'The one I hired this afternoon while you were at your meeting with Tomasino. I thought it might come in handy in case we needed to travel about.'

'Oh, that's where you were!'

'Put your arms more tightly around my waist,' said Alex as we left Viareggio and rode off towards Torre del Lago on the Scarabeo Aprile he had hired. 'The last thing I need is for you to fall off and injure yourself.' He had already checked that I had put my crash helmet on correctly, not once, but twice.

'It'd be one less accident for Tomasino to arrange, wouldn't it? You'd better check that no-one's following us.'

'Stop it!' We rode into Viale dei Tigli, a beautiful avenue of lime trees and the primary route to Torre del Lago. It cuts through a lush pine-forest which covers most of the surrounding area. 'Isn't this fantastic scenery?' shouted Alex. He needed to raise his voice as otherwise I could not hear him, what with the sound of the scooter's engine and the wind drag. We continued to ride down the avenue. 'Does this forest have a name?'

'I think it's called Pineta di Levante.'

'It's idyllic here.'

'Yes, if Tomasino didn't exist, it'd be perfect.'

A few kilometres later and we arrived at the quiet seaside town of Torre del Lago. Alex slowed down to look at the road signs before we headed into the town.

'This place really is a Puccini lover's paradise, isn't it?' he said. As we rode through the town centre we noticed that bars and restaurants are named after characters in his operas. 'Did you see that street called Via Bohème?'

'Yes. I've also seen a Via Tosca and a Via Butterfly.'

'Shall we head towards the marina?' he asked.

'If you want to take a look at the open air theatre and Villa Mausoleum where Puccini lived and worked we need to make for Lake Massaciuccoli.'

'The Opera festival's not on yet, is it?'

'No. I believe it starts next month.'

'Good. Then we'll have the place all to ourselves.'

311

We followed the signs to 'Festival Pucciniano', finally arriving at the massive open air-theatre in Piazzale Belvedere which is situated in a dramatic setting right on the shores of Lake Massaciuccoli with the Apuan Alps in the background.

'Shall we stop and have a look around?' he said. 'I know it's night time but there's still plenty to see and there's something rather special about the atmosphere at night, don't you think?'

'Eerie, you mean?'

'No. Tranquil. Let's park the bike down here,' he said, pointing to some parking spaces along the road near the lake.

'It's certainly deathly quiet,' I said, climbing off the back of the scooter and unfastening my crash helmet. I lifted it off my head and ran my fingers through my hair which had been flattened by the helmet.

'The air smells good though,' said Alex, taking my crash helmet from me, jumping off the bike and loosening his own helmet. 'It must be the combination of the sea and all this natural habitat,' he continued, taking a deep breath and inhaling the cool night air. He removed his crash helmet, put it into the storage compartment and locked the bike.

'Well, the lake is a unique bird reserve and part of the nature park of Migliarino-San Rossore,' I replied, walking off towards the theatre. 'Now that we're here, what do you want to do? Shall we stroll down to the jetty or up to Puccini's Villa and take a look at the outside?' Alex did not reply and I turned around to see where he was but he was nowhere in sight. 'Alex? Alex where are you?' I called. I stood for a moment and waited for him to respond but he did not. I was beginning to feel very agitated. 'Come on, Alex. This isn't the time to start playing games.' Then I heard a dull thudding sound which seemed to have come from the dense bushes behind me. For a second I could not move as my legs were frozen to the spot.

With my heart pounding in my chest I took a few tentative steps towards the area to investigate further. 'Alex?' I called out again more nervously this time as I glanced all around me. My legs were shaking, but although I was terrified I felt compelled to move closer and took another couple of steps nearer to the bushes. I had almost reached them when out of the darkness somebody grabbed me from behind and with one arm pressed tightly around my body and with a hand placed firmly over my mouth to prevent me from screaming, spun me around and dragged me backwards. I struggled to free myself and writhed about trying to kick whoever it was – but it was hopeless. Suddenly I was conscious of somebody else's presence and then I felt something cold and metallic pressing into the side of my head.

Chapter 32

I closed my eyes and waited for the trigger to be pulled, but nothing happened although the gun remained firmly pressed against the side of my head for several minutes. Presently I half opened one eye and then the other, and there standing in front of me was none other than Gregorio Pellegrino. I was unable to speak because his henchman's hand was still covering my mouth and in any event I could barely breathe as his arm was placed firmly across my chest in a vice-like grip. Nonetheless, I was shaking uncontrollably.

'*Buona sera*, Alicia Allen,' he smirked, pointing the gun in my face. 'If you promise not to scream I won't shoot you.' I tried to nod in agreement but I could hardly move my head. His henchman removed his hand from my mouth and repositioned his arms so that he was now pinning down both of mine with his. I was desperate to discover what he had done with Alex, but at the same time I was terrified to ask in case Alex was still alive and my words might prompt Pellegrino to kill him if he had not already done so.

'If...if...you're going to shoot me why don't you do...do it?' I stammered. I was scarcely able to talk as I had begun hyperventilating and was short of breath.

'It's too messy,' he replied. 'We're going on a little boat trip instead.'

'You...you mean you're going to make my death appear like an accident. Make it look like I...I drowned. Is that how you killed Rosetta Bartlett?' I said, my voice trembling.

'I didn't kill her.'

314

'Well, not you personally but you and…and Kettering and Tomasino were all in on her…her murder,' I said, continuing to stumble over my words.

'Her accident was genuine enough, but I'm not sorry she's dead. The stupid interfering bitch had it coming to her and I *would* have killed her had she not drowned. You see, she and Emilio were too clever for their own good and interfered in matters which were of no concern to them – just like you. It really doesn't pay to do that,' he said, grabbing my chin with his hand and pushing it upwards.

'Tell me about Ellen…Ellen Petronelli,' I said, forcing out the words.

'You really want to know, don't you? Well, I shan't tell you,' he taunted, letting go of my chin and standing back.

'You arranged for Emilio to go to Sicily,' I said, catching my breath. 'You wanted it to look like a…a Mafia killing. Then you framed Angelo Fagiolini for his murder and it was you…you and Tomasino who gave evidence against him. What I don't understand is how…how you found out about Villa Anna.'

'Are you afraid to die?' he asked sadistically, thrusting the gun in my face. 'I know you are. I can hear the fear and trepidation in your voice and I can see it in those big eyes of yours. Why don't you beg me not to kill you? Go on,' he said, shouting at me, 'I want you to whimper like a dog. On your knees, bitch,' he shouted. His henchman pressed me down and twisted my arms behind my back causing me to wince with pain. 'Now what were you asking me? Ah, yes, Villa Anna. We didn't know about it until after we'd dispensed with Emilio and only came upon the details by chance. Emilio's poor grieving widow Evelyn handed Roland Kettering a box of papers and in the box,' he said, leaning forward so that he was within inches of my face, 'there was a letter which referred to a villa in Ponte a Moriano, so we decided to investigate it. Dino Angelino was old, infirm and partially sighted and had never seen Emilio. Imagine how delighted he was when his supposed long lost nephew unexpectedly turned up on his doorstep. It wasn't difficult to persuade him to make a Will in his favour and then to forge the paperwork and the necessary documents which enabled us subsequently to inherit the property.'

'And you impersonated Emilio?' I said, trying not to let my voice tremble and drawing on all my inner strength not to cry.

'No. Hardly,' he said dismissively.

'Who then? Tomasino?'

'Of course not. Don't be ridiculous. He's a lawyer. He couldn't possibly risk being recognised. He has standing in this community and a reputation to maintain.'

'Where's he now?' I said quietly.

'On his yacht. He's having a party and we're going there shortly. Well, you're not. We'll be dropping you off on the way,' he said, sneering at me.

'I suppose you thought nobody would ever discover your secret, and then Giulia started her research into the Angelino background.'

'Yes. That was very unfortunate.'

'It was the trigger for her murder, wasn't it?' He did not respond. 'Who was driving the Alfa when Fabio was nearly rammed off the road in Ravello? Was it Marco Giovannini?' Uncle Vico had of course discovered that Marco was the brother of Piero, the current owner of Villa Anna, and that their father Aldo Giovannini was not only a colleague of Eduardo Tomasino but also his brother-in-law. We already knew that Marco lived in Ravello, but not whether he was the driver of the Alfa, although we had surmised that it in all probability it was him.

'You ask too many questions. That's why you're here now, for sticking your nose in where it's not wanted,' he said, grabbing my nose and squeezing it so hard that it made my eyes water with pain. '*Ficcanaso! Ficcanaso!* he mocked. 'I don't feel like talking anymore,' he said, letting go of my nose. At that point my mobile, which was in my trouser pocket, started to ring. 'Who's that?' he said, shouting at me. I thought it might be Commissario Galliano but I was not likely to share that information with Mr Pellegrino. 'Get up!' His henchman hauled me up onto my feet. 'Where's the 'phone?'

'In my left trouser pocket.' He reached into it and removed my mobile, dropped it on to the ground and stamped on it with his shoe, then crushed it into the ground with his heel.

'Now we won't be disturbed. Anyway, you won't need this where you're going, talking of which, it's time we started making a move.' His henchman let loose his hold on me and forcibly pushed me to the ground again, but this time he twisted me around and my right ankle in the process. He strode off in the direction of the parking area down by the lake. 'Don't even think of trying to run away,' said Pellegrino, standing over me and pointing the gun straight at my face yet again.

'But if you're going to kill me you might at least tell me the truth,' I replied, looking up at him and wincing because my ankle was throbbing.

'Yes. All right,' he snarled, bending down and pulling my head back by my hair causing me to scream with the pain. 'We wanted Giulia dead. Marco thought she was in the car.' This is exactly what Alex and I had presumed all along.

'Then there's Annette Richardson. Why did you have her murdered?' I said, forcing back the tears.

'I discovered she was in touch with Caterina Bartoldi and when I caught her trawling through archived files I knew what she was up to. It was then that I decided it was also time to remove Caterina, but I had to wait for the right moment.' As he let go of my hair he forced my head forward. He started to pace up and down in front of me.

'What do you mean?' I said sniffing.

'I've been following her every move for years. You've spoken to her secretary Caroline, haven't you?' I nodded. 'Well, she's one of mine,' he said triumphantly, standing still. 'She informed me when you called Caterina, and listened in on at least one of your conversations with her. And there was you thinking you were so clever – little Miss Detective.'

'Was it you who rang her and pretended to be her former client Christopher King?' I asked, trying to compose myself.

'Of course.'

'And what about her murder? There was no sign of a break-in at her house so her assailant must have been known to her because she opened the door to whoever it was.'

'Oh yes,' he said laughing. 'That was so easy. She left the office in such a rush that she forgot to take some papers with her. Caroline rang her and explained she would arrange for them to be couriered to her at home. Of course the person who arrived at her house wasn't a courier at all!' I had wondered what the man running along Caterina's street was carrying in the duffle bag I saw him holding and now I knew.

'Stand up,' he growled. 'Time is running short,' he added, glancing at his watch.

'I can't. I think my ankle's sprained.'

'I said get up!' he shrieked, grabbing my arm.

'It's no good,' I replied, trying to raise myself onto my feet but falling back onto my knees. 'You may kill me, but you'll never get away with it. I'm not the only one who knows about your dealings. Whoever it was who murdered Kettering is on to you and it won't be long before you're the next victim yourself. Then there's Laura. She'll tell the police that it was Tomasino who met Giulia the night she was murdered, and don't forget the file I have in my possession.' I managed to stand but could not put any weight on my right ankle.

'Laura will be dealt with. She's only a minor irritant – like you. We *will* remove anyone who stands in our way and as for the file, it doesn't exist,' he sneered.

'How can you be so sure?'

'Because, my dear Miss Allen,' he sneered, 'I destroyed the original and you have no evidence.' · I was confused because according to Caterina's letter Rosetta had taken the file and then given it to her for safekeeping and it was Caterina who destroyed it. And if Mr Pellegrino was telling the truth what was the purpose of breaking-in to Caterina's house on the two separate occasions she had mentioned in her letter. I refrained from referring to the letter for fear that it might have repercussions for Olivia. 'Come on,' he said, tugging me by my arm and pulling me along the ground on my knees.

He could only have dragged me a couple of feet when he was stopped short by the sound of a gunshot close by and then a further gunshot seconds later. 'What the hell was that?' he said, looking all around him as he continued to pull me down towards the parking area. When we approached what I presumed was Pellegrino's large black saloon car, which may have been an Alfa, I caught sight of his henchman lying on the ground motionless. As we drew nearer I noticed a pool of blood; it was coming from the back of his head, or at least what was left of it. I let out an involuntary scream and started to sob uncontrollably.

'Shut up,' Pellegrino bawled, slapping me violently across the face. He stepped callously over his dead henchman and then opened the rear passenger side door. 'Get in,' he yelled, frantically trying to push me into the back of the car. I sensed that he was now petrified for his own safety and was desperate to leave the scene before he suffered the same fate as his henchman. He forced me across the seat but somehow I managed to find the strength to kick him in the face with my left foot, catching the corner of his right eye and the top of his right cheek with the heel of my shoe and wounding him. There was blood trickling down the side of his face and for a moment he seemed disorientated. I took my opportunity and scrambled to open the other rear passenger door in an attempt to crawl out, but impeded by my right ankle I could not make it quickly enough. I was only halfway out of the car when he grabbed my already weakened ankle and hauled me back. The pain in my ankle was excruciating.

'You can't get away from me,' he mocked, leaning into the car and pointing the gun straight at me. 'Just one little flick of my finger and it's all over, Alicia.'

I screwed my eyes shut; three gunshots were fired and for a split second I could not quite take in what had happened – but I was still alive. I slowly opened my eyes and there, slumped between the open car door and the car seat and within inches of my feet, was the limp body of Gregorio Pellegrino, with three bullet holes in his back. His gun was nowhere to be seen and I assumed he must have dropped it when he was shot. There was blood splattered everywhere including over me and I screamed. Impeded by my ankle, with some difficulty I slowly edged out of the passenger door and, as I did so, somebody touched me lightly on the shoulder and I screamed yet again. I must have fainted because the next thing I remember was hearing a female voice. I opened my eyes and looked up at the woman standing in front of me.

'Don't be afraid,' she said gently. 'I'm here to help you.' She was around her mid-forties and dressed up like a cat burglar. 'We don't have much time,' she said in a perfect English voice as she bent down to my level. I noticed a smoking Beretta pistol in her gloved right hand. It was evident she had fired the shots which had killed Pellegrino. 'Are you hurt?'

'My right ankle's badly sprained.'

'Can you walk if I help you?' I nodded. She put her arm around me and helped me out of the car and, with her assistance, I limped to a secluded spot near the bushes where I presumed she thought we would not be noticed. She helped me to sit down and then sat on the ground next to me.

'He is dead, isn't he?' I asked, stretching out my right leg in front of me. The fabric of my trousers was torn at the knees which were quite severely grazed and bleeding.

'Yes.'

'Where's his gun?'

'I have it,' she said. 'We don't want to leave a loaded gun lying around just in case any of Mr Pellegrino's associates are in the vicinity.'

'You saved my life. But *who* are you and *what* are you doing here?'

'Haven't you guessed?' I looked at her blankly.

'I have no idea who you are.'

'These days I'm called Maria Bianchi, but sixteen years ago I was known by the name of Rosetta Bartlett.'

Chapter 33

'But you're supposed to be dead,' I exclaimed, staring at her in disbelief. 'I don't understand.'

'It's lucky for you that I'm not.'

'But not for Alex. They killed him,' I said, choking back the tears. 'We've got to find him. Please help me,' I said, clutching hold of her arm in my appeal to her for assistance. I finally broke down and wept on her shoulder.

'It's all right,' she said softly, putting her arm around me. 'He's alive. He's had a nasty blow to his head, but he'll be OK.'

'What?' I said, wiping the tears off my cheeks with both hands. Where is he?'

'Right there,' she said, pointing behind her. 'I spun around and saw Alex staggering towards me. He was very unsteady on his feet and leaning heavily on his companion whom I assumed must be associated with Rosetta in some way. Alex was holding what seemed to be a piece of rag to his head and it was soaked with blood. As they drew nearer and I was able to see the man's face more clearly, I noticed that he bore an uncanny resemblance to the person I had observed on two separate occasions earlier that day – the man I had suspected of following me.

'Oh, Alex!' I said, hauling myself up off the ground, hobbling towards him, flinging my arms around his neck and hugging him tightly. 'You're alive. I thought you were dead and that I'd never see you again. Thank God! Oh, your poor head,' I said, examining his forehead. 'Are you seriously hurt?'

'I'll be fine. I know it looks bad but it's only a superficial cut. Head wounds always bleed profusely. I'll probably end up with a black eye, but I can cope with that. I must have caught it on a stone or something as I fell because I was actually hit on the back of my head judging by the lump here,' he said, letting go of his companion and touching the area with his hand. 'I must have been out cold for about ten minutes. When I came round, Marcus,' he said, smiling at the mystery man standing next to him, 'was attending to me. I'm probably concussed as I feel very woozy, but clearly I fared better than you. Your cheekbone is bruised, you've got marks all over your arms, your knees are grazed and by the looks of it you've sprained your ankle. You're also splattered with blood. It's even in your hair.'

'It doesn't matter. The main thing is we're still alive. I thought they'd killed you.'

'Where are they now?' said Alex.

'They're dead,' said Rosetta. 'I shot them. Pellegrino would have killed Alicia had I not shot him first.'

'Who are *you?*' asked Alex.

'Rosetta Bartlett.'

'What?' Alex sounded flabbergasted. 'I appreciate I've just had a blow to the head, but did I hear correctly? I thought you were dead.'

'And that's exactly what I wanted everyone to believe,' she said.

'This is really weird,' said Alex, addressing me. 'Remember how we talked about the possibility of Rosetta being alive because her body was never found.'

'Emilio, too, as I recall.'

'Well, sadly Emilio *is* dead,' said Rosetta.

'And *who* are you?' I asked, turning to the young man.

'Ellen Petronelli's grandson.'

'But I thought you were one of Tomasino's heavies. It was you following me earlier today.'

'We've been tailing you since you arrived in Viareggio,' he replied, in perfect English and with no accent. 'All for your own protection, you understand.'

'Will you please explain what's going on,' said Alex, sounding really frustrated.

'Let's sit you down first,' said Rosetta. We sat down in the shadows and waited for her to speak. 'When Emilio Angelino was a young lawyer in New York, he acted for an Italian client called Antonio Petronelli. They became good friends and remained so until Antonio's death in the mid 1980's. Ellen, his wife, was twenty-five years his junior and was only in her fifties when he died. They'd been married for twenty years but had no children and under his Will, administered in accordance with Italian law, he left her everything.'

'I'm sorry, but I must have misunderstood something,' I said. 'I thought you just told us that there were no children of the marriage.'

'That's correct.'

'Then how can Marcus be Ellen's grandson?'

'Good point. I'll explain.'

'Ellen was actually English, and with no family in Italy decided to return home. She met up with Emilio when he relocated to England and confided in him about her past.'

'But surely he knew about that?' quizzed Alex.

'Not quite. When she was sixteen, and long before she married Antonio, she had a daughter whom she gave up for adoption. She felt incredibly guilty about what she'd done and after Antonio died took measures to discover her daughter's whereabouts so that she could follow her progress. She explained to Emilio that she wanted her daughter to inherit her money but not to know the source of her new-found wealth.'

'Oh, I think I see where this is heading,' I said. 'Emilio consulted Pellegrino who put him on to Kettering so that he could prepare a Will for her.'

'Yes. Kettering suggested they make a fully secret trust, that Emilio be the secret trustee because Ellen trusted him to carry out her wishes, and Emilio agreed to take on the role.'

'I always forget how secret trusts work. It's been years since I studied trust law. Can you remind me?' said Alex, looking at me.

'Well, it's quite straightforward really. In simple terms the testator makes a Will leaving property to the secret trustee, having agreed with the trustee that the property is actually intended for a third party whose name must be kept secret and to whom the secret trustee will pass the property after the testator's death. On the face of the Will it looks as if he is the beneficiary, whereas in fact he is secretly holding the property on trust for the third party.'

'But what if the secret trustee dies?'

'Well, if he dies before the testator then the trust fails.'

'Is that what happened here?' asked Alex, turning to Rosetta.

'No,' she replied. 'There's more to it than that.'

'Now why doesn't that surprise me?' he said.

'I was unfortunate to have to work with Gregorio Pellegrino on a number of his cases. I noticed that he referred a high percentage of clients to Roland Kettering and I became curious as to what the deal was with him and I started digging around. Through my research I ascertained that Pellegrino, Kettering and their Italian contacts were siphoning off assets in Italy rightfully belonging to their clients. I approached Emilio whom I knew to be trustworthy and informed him of their illegal actions.'

'How did you know you could trust him?' asked Alex.

'I just did. Call it instinct.'

'What did he do?' said Alex.

'Unfortunately, he made a grave error of judgment.'

'He challenged them, didn't he?' I said.

'Yes. I think he threatened to blow the whistle on them if they didn't agree to cease their operations immediately. He never told them that I was his source, although I knew Pellegrino suspected me.'

'But Caterina said that Emilio and you were working on some research for an Italian client.'

'That's what I led her to believe. I never told her the full facts because I felt that it was safer for her to remain ignorant of them.'

'Did you give her Ellen Petronelli's file?' This was a point which had been perplexing me since Mr Pellegrino announced he had destroyed the original.

'I'm coming to that.' She paused for a moment. 'Did you hear a noise?' she said, glancing about her.

'No.' I looked at Alex. He shook his head, as did Marcus.

'What happened next?' I asked. She did not respond for a moment but continued to sit and listen for any further sound. 'Go on, Rosetta,' I said, pressing her for a response.

'Well, while Emilio was in Rome on business, Ellen was killed in a car crash.'

'Do you think Pellegrino was behind it?'

'In this instance, no, but I believe he took advantage of the situation to remove Emilio who was then sent to Sicily on some bogus business trip. I think he was probably killed by one of Tomasino's hit men out there, in the hope that everyone would conclude that it was a Mafia killing. Then of course they tried to pin the blame on Angelo Fagiolini.'

'Yes, I know. The poor man nearly committed suicide as a result.' She did not comment, but looked at me very hard.

'Pellegrino and Kettering decided to re-write the Will and leave the money to some fictitious person they had created to enable them to steal the inheritance. After Emilio disappeared I was convinced they had murdered him and I copied the whole of Ellen Petronelli's file as an insurance policy because I realized that before long all her details would be permanently erased from our database and the hard copy records destroyed.' Now what Mr Pellegrino told me made sense – Rosetta had not taken the original file as I was led to believe, but only made a copy of it. 'I knew that Pellegrino was becoming increasingly suspicious of me and that he had realised that it was I who had informed Emilio about his underhand dealings. For my part I became increasingly uneasy about working at the firm and decided to leave. Then on my last day, as I was clearing my desk, he stormed into my office and threatened me in no uncertain terms that if I ever disclosed any details I had gleaned while working at the firm I would regret it. I understood his meaning exactly, particularly when the next day I was nearly run over while crossing the road.'

'Why didn't you go to the police?' said Alex.

'I was frightened of the repercussions for my family. I gave Caterina the copy of Ellen's file for safekeeping. I decided that the only way I would ever be free of him would be to feign my own death. I knew that for my family to be absolutely safe I wouldn't be able to contact them again.' She swallowed hard and I detected the emotion in her voice. 'That was the hardest decision I've ever had to make.'

'Then your father genuinely believes you're dead?'

'Yes. He does. I planned it all down to the last detail, even taking the identity of someone who had died so that I could create a new life for myself. It was far easier to reinvent yourself in those days than it would be now.'

'Was Caterina party to all this?'

'No. I asked her to accompany me to Italy because I wanted her to be a witness. She never knew the truth.'

'Surely you didn't mastermind your disappearance completely by yourself? Somebody must have assisted you.'

'You're very perceptive. There was only one person I could confide in, and who had himself suffered at the hands of Pellegrino and Tomasino. He was only too aware how easy it was to become innocently embroiled with them and agreed to help me. He arranged it all. He had a boat, picked me up and whisked me away before anyone was any the wiser as to what really happened the night of my disappearance.'

'Who was it?' said Alex.

'Angelo Fagiolini.'

'But Fabio went to see Angelo's sister-in-law in Rome. She told him Angelo lives in Milan now, with his wife, but that she lost touch with him,' he said. 'She...'

'You're his wife, aren't you?' I asked, interrupting Alex. She nodded. 'Is he here with you?'

'Currently he's in Viareggio.'

'Watching Tomasino?'

'You could say that.'

'With my brother, Paul,' said Marcus.

'Did you murder Kettering, Rosetta?'

'No. News of his murder was as much a surprise to me as I'm sure it was to you, but I don't suppose he was exactly short of enemies.'

'Did you have a hand in it?' I said, addressing Marcus.

'That's a pretty apt way of putting it considering the circumstances of his murder,' muttered Alex.

'No. But after what he did to my family and countless others he deserved it.'

'But if you didn't murder him who did? Was it Angelo?' asked Alex, sounding totally perplexed.

'Absolutely not. We have no idea who's guilty, but we're very grateful to whoever it was,' he said coldly.

'But how did you track down Marcus and his brother, Rosetta?'

'You forget, I've had over sixteen years to do my research, Alicia, and I always was very thorough,' said Rosetta. 'Sixteen years awaiting my revenge and I've waited a long time for this moment. As they say here in Italy, *"Revenge is a dish best eaten cold"."*

'What happens now?' I asked. 'Pellegrino and Kettering are dead, but what about Tomasino and anyone else he may have working with him?'

'In precisely three minutes time neither Enrico Tomasino nor any of his cohorts will be bothering us ever again,' she said, glimpsing at her watch.

'Why? What have you done?' I glanced at Alex.

'He's having a party on his yacht.'

'So Pellegrino told me.'

'With any luck it will be his last.'

'You mean it's been rigged?' She did not respond, but simply smiled at Marcus. 'What do you intend to do? Disappear again?'

'I don't suppose anybody is going to be interested in a dead woman who was declared dead nearly eight years ago unless you tell them about me...'

'Can you hear voices?' said Marcus, addressing Rosetta.

'It must be the police.'

'They took their time,' said Alex sarcastically.

'We have to go,' said Rosetta, rising to her feet.

'Make sure you both seek some medical attention,' said Marcus, standing up.

'Buon coraggio!' she said, turning back.

As she and Marcus disappeared into the darkness, Alex and I heard a huge roaring sound in the distance. It seemed to reverberate all around us like thunder causing me to jump out of my skin.

'Tomasino's yacht!' I exclaimed, turning to Alex. 'Oh, my God!'

'It sounds like his party went with a bang,' he said with a straight face.

'Oh, Alex! This isn't the time to be cracking jokes.'

'What's the matter, Alicia? You can't be sorry if they're all dead. I very much doubt they would have had much of a conscience about dumping you at the bottom of the ocean.'

'It's not that, Alex. Actually, I was thinking about all the people they've murdered.'

'Hmm... What are you going to tell the police about Rosetta?'

'Nothing.'

'But how are you going to explain who shot Pellegrino and his aide?'

'I won't need to. I simply didn't see who it was. You understand me.' I paused for a moment. 'And let's face it the name of Rosetta Bartlett is hardly going to be at the top of their list of suspects. If it wasn't for her, I'd be dead. Besides, I think enough people have suffered in this case.'

'She must trust you.'

'And you.'

'Maybe she'll be reunited with her father now.'

'Who can say?'

'But what about Tomasino and his yacht?'

'He had a number of enemies. I'm sure the police will conclude that his past finally caught up with him – just like Kettering.'

'So you believe Rosetta and Marcus didn't murder him then?'

'Let's leave it to the police to work it out. It's time they took over the investigation.'

'That's the first sensible thing I've heard you say for a long while,' said Alex, putting his free arm around me. He was still holding the bloody rag to his forehead with his other hand. 'And if I'm not mistaken, there are the police,' he said, commenting on the three policemen striding toward us. 'I wonder if the Commissario is among them and what he has to say for himself.'

'It's highly unlikely the Commissario is here, Alex, unless he's a mind-reader, bearing in mind I never actually spoke to him and told him we were coming to Torre del Lago, but with this case nothing would surprise me!'

Chapter 34

Two days later and Alex and I were in Lucca helping Commissario Marco Galliano with his enquiries, as well as recovering from our ordeal at Torre del Lago. We had been reunited with Fabio, but Laura had left for Orvieto and Will had flown home from Pisa as understandably he did not want to delay returning to Jo a moment longer. We discovered that it was Commissario Galliano who had 'phoned me on my mobile while I was with Pellegrino. Apparently he had received a tip-off from an anonymous caller who had confirmed that Alex and I were at Torre del Lago. I could only assume that this caller was made by one of Rosetta's companions.

According to the Commissario, Eduardo Tomasino and some of his colleagues at Studio Legale Marchese including Aldo Giovannini, his brother-in-law, had been under police surveillance for some time on suspicion of a number of criminal activities. As for discovering who had shot Mr Pellegrino and rigged Mr Tomasino's yacht, despite an intensive investigation, the police made little progress in solving the mystery. The Commissario rapidly arrived at the conclusion that the perpetrators must indeed be one or more of their numerous enemies.

During our stay in Lucca Alex had insisted on visiting some of its marvellous sights. Since cars are not allowed in the centre of the city, Fabio and Alex would have hired bicycles and cycled around, but since Alex had been concussed that was not an option. In any event I would have been unable to join them as my sprained ankle and heavily lacerated knees prevented me from riding a bicycle.

Nonetheless, Alex and Fabio managed to take a whirlwind tour of the major attractions, including Puccini's house, the Roman Amphitheatre, the Basilica of San Frediano, the Church of San Michele, the Cathedral of San Martino and the fifteenth century Guinigi Tower, unique for the oaks that grow from it (and down into the room below) and from where they had a marvellous view of the landscape that surrounds Lucca.

On the third day Commissario Galliano arranged for Fabio, Alex and I to visit Villa Anna. I had spoken to my uncle the night before, now home in New York, who told me he was making enquiries about the ownership of the villa and Fabio's entitlement to the estate. I mentioned nothing to Fabio having no desire to build his hopes too high. We left Lucca and made the short car journey to Ponte a Moriano.

'How far is the Villa from here?' I asked Fabio as we drove into the village.

'The house is over there,' he said, pointing to a charmingly restored eighteenth century villa set in the magnificent gentle rolling Tuscan landscape amidst tall and stately black cypress trees and surrounded by meticulously tended olive groves and vineyards. As we drove up the gravel and rather bumpy road to the villa we noticed a silver Ferrari parked in front of it. 'Who on earth can that be?' said Fabio as he pulled up in our hired Fiat Croma next to the Ferrari. 'I wasn't expecting anyone to be here.'

'Fabulous car,' said Alex. 'It must be worth a fortune. What model is it? Is it a Spider?'

'No. It's a Scaglietti,' said Fabio.

'Of course, I should've guessed you'd know,' said Alex, with a hint of sarcasm. As we stepped out of the car the driver of the Ferrari opened the door of his and I noticed that the interior of the Ferrari was red leather.

'You must be Fabio Angelino?' he said in a very thick Italian accent, addressing Fabio as he scrambled out of his car to greet us. He was wearing a fine wool navy suit and smart loafer shoes, his hair was dark, straight and slicked back and his look was completed by his black Gucci sunglasses which added to his mystique. He was incredibly tall and it was amazing to me how he fitted into his two-door coupé with such long legs. He simply towered over me and must have been a good few inches taller than Alex and Fabio who were both well over six feet.

'I am, but *who* are you and *what* are you doing here?' answered Fabio warily.

'My name is Gianni Mancini,' he replied inclining his head towards him. 'I'm a friend of Ludovico Magnani. I've been expecting you.' Fabio looked perplexed.

'Oh, I know who you are,' I said interrupting. 'You're my uncle's contact and the one who has been helping us, aren't you?' He did not respond but simply smiled. 'I don't know what we'd have done without your assistance,' I continued. 'We're all very grateful, and I for one can't thank you enough. I always felt that there was a connection between Gregorio Pellegrino and the murder of Fabio's father, but establishing it seemed nigh on impossible, let alone linking him with all the other murders. The information you obtained for us was invaluable to the investigation.' I sensed he was not prepared to answer questions about his ability to access information for us.

'You're very welcome, Alicia,' he replied. 'I'm very pleased to make your acquaintance having heard so much about you from your uncle and Commissario Marco Galliano.'

'The Commissario?'

'Yes. He was very complimentary and has nothing but praise for the way you handled the situation with Enrico Tomasino and Gregorio Pellegrino. I think you underestimate your own contribution to the murder investigation.'

'Yes,' said Fabio. 'If it weren't for your determination, and persistence then I doubt whether we would have resolved the mystery surrounding my father's disappearance and discovered why Giulia was murdered.'

'You flatter me too much, but thank you. So, what can you tell us about Fabio's inheritance?' I said, looking up at Villa Anna. 'I presume that's why you're here.'

'You're very perceptive.'

'Not really. It seemed a logical assumption to make.'

'Let's walk,' he said, 'if you can manage it,' he added, glancing at my bandaged knees and ankle. 'There's something I want to show you, Fabio.' We followed him as he wandered off through the meadow to the olive grove behind the villa. 'As you know Lucca is famous for its olive oil production,' he continued. 'It would seem that you are the proud owner of this one,' he added.

'How? Does that mean I own Villa Anna, after all?'

'What do you understand by the term 'adverse possession', Fabio?' he said.

'Isn't it acquiring the right to something by virtue of having had possession of it for a given period of time?' replied Fabio, glancing sideways at me for confirmation.

'The significant question for us is: what is the time frame in which you could lose your inheritance by adverse possession under Italian property law?'

'I really don't know the answer to that one,' said Fabio. Alex looked blank.

'There are various time frames depending on the circumstances and the types of property concerned, aren't there?' I said.

'Yes,' said Mr Mancini. 'The time frames are ten, twenty and even thirty years when it comes to agricultural property. Now in your case, the ownership of Villa Anna was transferred to Piero Giovannini in 1994 so over ten years ago. This means that in the usual course of events the ownership would have passed to him after that ten year period and you would not be able to challenge the validity of his deed of ownership.'

'I don't follow,' said Fabio. 'So you're saying is that I've lost my right to Villa Anna.'

'Not at all. You see, even where a deed of ownership is in

existence, after the ten year time frame has passed, the potential owner will still not acquire legal ownership of the property unless other conditions are met. These are that he must have continuously occupied the property for the whole of that period, paid all his taxes throughout the years and have acted in good faith, genuinely believing that he was the real owner of the property. It's the last condition which is of relevance to you because, if we can prove that Piero Giovannini was aware of your existence and show that he was not acting in good faith, then there is a strong possibility that you will be able to reclaim your family property.'

'But that's unbelievable news,' said Fabio. 'What will I have to do?'

'We'll need to file a Declaration of Succession, the official document in which you declare your existence and set out your claim to Villa Anna. At the same time as we file the Declaration, we'll need to lodge a title search to the property showing the ownership status. We should do that as quickly as possible.'

'I can't believe it,' said Fabio, taking hold of me and hugging me. 'Villa Anna could be mine after all.'

'Well, if there's any justice in the world, Fabio, this beautiful Villa will be yours.'

'I wonder how Fabio is really,' I said to Alex as we left Uncle Vico's house on East 71st Street at the corner of Park Avenue. It was now September and Alex and I had taken up Uncle Vico's offer to visit him in New York. Since my last trip to New York a few years before he had moved home and so this was the first time I had seen his 1920's mansion-style house on East 71st Street. Alex and I wanted to catch a bus downtown so we needed to walk two blocks west to Fifth Avenue and cross over onto the other side of the road and pick up a limited bus from the stop near the Frick Collection. I was glad we had decided to wait until September before making the trip as it was much cooler than it had been, although today was a little humid.

'According to your uncle, he seems to be coping well and has thrown himself into refurbishing Villa Anna. The project has been keeping him busy these past few months.'

'Hmm... I think it's been hard for him which is why I'm very pleased he's kept in touch with Laura. Did I tell you that he introduced her to Olivia and they've become firm friends?' Alex shook his head.

'Sisters in distress, I suppose,' he said. 'Are you planning to keep in touch with them all?'

'Well, Fabio's Uncle Vico's Godson, and what with everything that's happened he's almost part of the family anyway. As for Olivia and Laura, they feel like younger sisters to me now. I can't believe how close my Uncle's house is to the apartment on 169 East 71st Street where Audrey Hepburn's character, Holly Golightly, lives in *Breakfast at Tiffany's*,' I said, digressing for a moment. 'It was fun to go there again. It's a shame the Plaza Hotel featured in the film no longer exists as a hotel, but least we went to look at it. Thanks for tagging along with me. I'm also very pleased we saw Cesare yesterday. It was good to catch up with him after so long.'

'Hmm... Whatever makes you happy,' said Alex, taking hold of my hand as we crossed onto the other side of the road to the bus stop.

'I'm very happy to be here with you,' I said, giving him a kiss.

'I'd thought it'd be a bit of a tame trip for you with no murderers to pursue,' he said, digging me in the ribs.

'I've had enough murder investigations to last me a lifetime, thank you very much. I've no intention of becoming involved in another one.'

'Do you want to give me that in writing?'

'Very funny, Alex, but I hardly think that's necessary.'

'With your track record, I'm not sure I'd agree.' The bus arrived; we climbed on, put the exact change for our fare into the little box on board and sat down. There was a good deal of traffic as it was the middle of the afternoon so our journey was slow.

'DCI Framlington called me last week,' I said.

'You didn't mention it. What did he have to say for himself?'

'He told me that the police had caught up with Pellegrino's associates in London. He said they've been running a covert operation these past few months. Apparently the men they believe responsible for both Annette Richardson's and Caterina Bartoldi's murder are among them. He asked me if I'd be willing to identify the man who is alleged to have murdered Caterina. The police are positive he's the one who passed me in the street the fateful night of her murder and judging what Pellegrino said to me I think it has to be him.'

'But I thought you said you couldn't see his face clearly. How can you hope to identify him?'

'I'll do what I can to help the police, Alex.'

'And there you were assuring me just now that you've no intention of becoming involved in any other murder investigations.'

'I'm not. This is the same one, remember.'

'All right,' he said, rolling his eyes up in despair. 'Come on, this is our stop,' he said, grabbing my hand and pulling me off the bus at the corner of Fifth Avenue and 56th Street. He walked me across the Avenue bustling with pedestrians to the corner of 57th Street where the massive grey marble building of Tiffany's stands.

'I don't know why you wanted to come here, Alex,' I said, slightly disgruntled for being dragged off the bus. 'I thought we were supposed to be shopping for a wedding present for Antonia and a souvenir for Dorothy.'

'Well, it's the last stop of the *Breakfast at Tiffany's* tour, isn't it?' he replied.

'But it's not as if either of us hasn't been here before.'

'I understand that they're holding a workshop here today.'

'Workshop? I didn't come to New York to attend a workshop, Alex.'

'That's a shame. I was hoping you'd be interested in this one,' he said, shrugging his shoulders.

'Why?'

'I thought it was about time we made our relationship permanent. I was thinking of buying you something and thought you might like to attend the workshop on how to choose the perfect engagement ring, but if you're not interested I do understand, although somebody has to keep you in check and I'd be very happy if it could be me,' he said, all in one breath.

'What do you mean keep me in check?' I snapped, and then the realization of what he had said hit me. 'Did you say engagement ring, Alex?' I asked, looking up at him.

'I did.'

'Oh, Alex, I don't know what to say.'

'I was rather hoping you'd take me up on my offer.'

'Well, what are we waiting for?' I replied, catching hold of his arm and dragging him toward the door of Tiffany's.

'I'll take that as a "yes" then,' he said. 'I'm glad that we actually agree on something for once.'

'What do you mean 'for once'? We agree on many things.'

'Including not involving yourself in any more murder investigations?' he said winking at me.

'Yes, Alex, I quite agree.'

THE END

Read the first part of the trilogy…

ALICIA ALLEN INVESTIGATES 1

A MODEL MURDER

By Celia Conrad

Alicia Allen is a London solicitor about to discover she has
an unusual flair for solving crime. When her Australian
neighbour, Tamsin Brown, a model, is brutally raped and
beaten to death, her flatmate Kimberley Davies begs for
Alicia's help and she cannot easily refuse. After her
inquisitive elderly neighbour Dorothy Hammond is
savagely attacked, Alicia knows there's no turning back and
she soon becomes embroiled in the hunt for Tamsin's killer
and the sleazy world of hostess clubs. Meanwhile, having
accepted a new job at the firm of Wilson, Weil & Co.,
where Kimberley works as a secretary, she discovers that
nothing there is as it seems and that nobody can be trusted,
not even a Junior Partner called Alexander Waterford to
whom she is attracted. Alicia's tenacious investigations,
however, have life-threatening consequences for those drawn
into the evil web created by Tamsin's killer, who believes
there is such a thing as a model murder…

ISBN 978 09546233 26 (0 9546233 2 0)
PUBLISHED BY BARCHAM BOOKS
£10.99
ORDER YOUR COPY NOW

Read the second part of the trilogy…

ALICIA ALLEN INVESTIGATES 2

WILFUL MURDER

By Celia Conrad

Soon after starting at a new law firm, Alicia Allen, a young
London solicitor, acquires a new client, Isabelle Parker, who
has lived in Australia most of her life. Unhappy with
Holmwood & Hitchins, the firm dealing with her English
grandfather's multi-million pound estate, Isabelle instructs
Alicia to draw up a Will in contemplation of her marriage.
Isabelle tells Alicia that she believes her brother and grandfather were murdered. On a journey to Brisbane, Alicia
meets a Partner from Holmwood & Hitchins who is travelling on to Melbourne, and when she changes planes in
Singapore learns that Isabelle's fiancé has been killed in an
explosion in London. Subsequently she hears that the
partner at Holmwood & Hitchins has been discovered with
multiple stab wounds. Isabelle implores Alicia to investigate,
and as devastating revelations about Isabelle's family history
come to light, Alicia realizes she is looking for a psycho-
pathic killer guilty of premeditated and wilful murder...

ISBN 978 09546233 3 3 (0 9546233 3 9)
PUBLISHED BY BARCHAM BOOKS
£10.99
ORDER YOUR COPY NOW

Celia Conrad was educated at King's College at the
University of London and now lives and writes in London.